# HER OWN WAR

*Château de Verzat Series*
*Book Three*

## DEBRA BORCHERT

LE VIN PRESS

Cover design by Lynn Andreozzi
Book designed and typeset by Bookery

Published by Le Vin Press
Year of Publication 2024

ISBN: 979-8-9899931-0-9 (Ebook)
ISBN: 979-8-9899931-1-6 (Trade paperback)

First Edition

OR BERRY

THANK YOU FOR MAKING ME LAUGH

AND SERENADING ME EVERY EVENING.

I LOVE YOU.

# CAST OF CHARACTERS

| | |
|---|---|
| ABBÉ NODIER | Royalist spymaster |
| AGIERS | Older soldier and navigator serves Colonel Louis LaGarde |
| ANNE (MUSHROOM WOMAN) | Catholic Royalist who grows mushrooms and is a courier |
| AUGUSTE FOUQUIER-TINVILLE | Half-brother of Geneviève |
| AURÉLIA VERZAT | Formerly enslaved African, wife to Henri de Verzat, mother to Charles and Briella; mute due to the trauma of enslavement |
| BRIELLA | Daughter of Aurélia and Henri Verzat |
| BONAPARTE | Général Napoleon Bonaparte, husband to Joséphine |
| CAPITAINE | Former slave trader who captured and sold Aurélia |
| CAPTAIN WILLIAM SYDNEY SMITH | Captain of the Royal Navy and *HMS Tigre* |
| CATHERINE | British spy |
| CHARLES VERZAT | Son of Aurélia and Henri Verzat |
| CHOUAN | Royalist spy who protects and seeks shelter from Château de Verzat estate |
| CHOUANS | Royalist insurgents who fought against the government; Chouan literally means screech owl, the signal used in warfare |

| | |
|---|---|
| COLONEL ANTOINE DE PHÉLIPPEAUX | French émigré Royalist serving in the Royal Navy |
| EMANUEL | Resident of the Verzat estate; his kitten dies in hailstorm |
| EMILIE | Resident of the Verzat estate, becomes Simon's wife |
| ÉTIENNE CHASTAIN | Marries Madame Françoise Amoulin, becomes Simon's stepfather |
| ETTY | Wife of Antoine Quentin Fouquier-Tinville, stepmother to Geneviève, mother of Auguste |
| FLEURY | Young soldier serves Colonel Louis LaGarde |
| FORTUNÉ | African boy of about eight years who is enslaved as the doorman at Madam Brissault's bordel |
| GENDARME | Police officer |
| GENEVIÈVE, TANTE GEN | Wife of Louis LaGarde. Dressed as a man, her false papers list her as Jean Detré, dressed as a woman she is listed on Louis's false papers as Magdeleine Corrié. Stepmother of Louisa, mother of Nicolas (Tante means aunt) |
| GUILLAUME PRICAUD | Son of Joliette (Guillaume Henri Verzat Pricaud) |
| HENRI, LIEUTENANT VERZAT | Henri Detré learned he was of noble blood and his title was: Comte Henri Charles Lenogue Saulnier de Verzat, Lieutenant Verzat serves Colonel Louis LaGarde |

| JOLIETTE, MADAME PRICAUD | Former Comtesse de Verzat, widow of Baron Guillaume Pricaud |
| JOSEPH | Joseph former vigneron and vintner of the Verzat vineyard |
| JOSÉPHINE BONAPARTE | Formerly Vicomtesse Rose de Beauharnais, wife to Napoleon Bonaparte, former lover of Barras |
| LOUIS LAGARDE, COLONEL LAGARDE | Husband of Geneviève, formerly Comte Louis de LaGarde, carries false papers of Louis Corrié, Colonel in Bonaparte's army |
| LOUISA | Daughter of Louis LaGarde and Magdeleine Corrié, stepdaughter of Geneviève whom she calls Tante Gen |
| LOUIS XVIII (FUTURE KING OF FRANCE) | Brother of Louis XVI, Count of Provence, future king of France (Louis XVII, son of XVI, died before taking the throne) |
| MADAME BRISSAULT | Madam of her eponymous Parisian bordel |
| MADAME DETRÉ | Henri's milk-mother, Aurélia's mother-in-law |
| MADAME FRANÇOISE | Mother of Simon, wife of Étienne |
| MADAME ORNAY | Oldest woman on the Verzat estate |
| MAGALI | Former sister at Abbaye de Penthemont |
| MONSIEUR COMBON | Resident of the Verzat estate |
| MONSIEUR GUYETTE | Resident of the Verzat estate |

| MONSIEUR JACOB | Resident of the Verzat estate |
| MURAT | Commandant Joachim Murat serves in Bonaparte's army |
| NICOLAS PHILIPE LAGARDE | Son of Geneviève and Louis LaGarde |
| ONCLE | Uncle |
| PAUL BARRAS | Director in the Directoire, ex-lover of Joséphine Bonaparte |
| RIBOU | Youngest soldier serves Colonel Louis LaGarde |
| SIMON, BRIGADIER AMOULIN | Husband of Emilie, son of Françoise Amoulin, stepson of Étienne Chastain, serves Colonel Louis LaGarde |
| SOPHIE | Louis's camel |
| SUZANNE | Former prostitute, resident of Louis's Orphanage |
| TANTE | Aunt |
| TANTE NICOLE | Former courtier, Marquise Nicole de Bourran (Tante means aunt) |
| THÈRÉSE (MUSHROOM WOMAN) | Catholic Royalist grows mushrooms and is a midwife |
| TOUPIN | Soldier serves Colonel Louis LaGarde |

HER

OWN

WAR

# 1

# *Geneviève*

*Loire Valley, France*
*August* 1797

Across the still Loire River dark clouds mushroomed above workers reaping hay. A rainstorm could harm the harvest; hail would ruin it.

Weeks of hot weather had ripened a bountiful grape crop, and all four hundred families who lived on the estate were in the vineyard furiously picking. I reached beneath the leaves, clipped grape clusters, and placed them in a large basket. Removing my straw bonnet, I wiped sweat from my brow and rubbed my lower back. Could this ache be a sign I was with child? There was no time to revel in the thread of hope running through me. Every harvested grape went toward paying taxes the estate owed.

A few feet away, Aurélia clipped a bunch of grapes and smiled at me, her round black eyes offering sympathy. Tall and slim, she moved with the grace of a poplar bending with a breeze. She pulled a fan from her hanging pocket and offered it.

"Thank you." I waved it, savoring the stirring air. A finely hand-painted scene on delicate silk depicted the Seine. "This is Paris. I hope when we are not at war, we can visit the city together." I closed it and held it out, but she put up her palm.

Wearing a simple blue day gown and long white apron, she had the regal bearing of a queen. She mouthed, *You need it more than I.*

I understood Aurélia, without her voice, although I hoped she'd regain her ability to speak. I tucked the fan into my belt and smiled at my past foolishness—I had feared I could never be friends with my former-lover's wife. Aurélia was more than a friend; she was the sister I had always wanted. "Were you able to speak before you were captured and enslaved?"

She grinned and brought her fingers to her thumb, repeatedly, indicating she never stopped talking.

"Do you miss your voice?"

She pretended to hold a baby in her arms and mouthed, *I miss singing.*

Down the hill, a distant spot of color caught my eye. Two officers on horseback trotted along the river road, their red frock coats flaring against the gray clouds.

The last officers conscripted four of our fine men, and they all died on the battlefield. I wiped my sticky hands on my apron. "I'll not let them take any more of our men to waste in their war." I searched the vineyard and spied my husband. "Louis!"

He stopped the team of horses pulling a wagon laden with grapes.

I pointed at the two soldiers.

He handed the reins to a worker and ran, shouting through the fields. Young men darted around vines. The officers would die of starvation before they found them in the network of Verzat caves.

The sky darkened. "Aurélia, a storm is coming. Best take the children to the château."

She mouthed, *Rain will be cooling.*

"But it might hail."

She shook her head. *We will be fine.*

I hoped she was right. My four-year-old stepdaughter sat on the dry, cracked earth holding a basket nearly as big as she was and waving her hand. "Tante Gen, why are there so many wasps?"

"They like the sweet juice." I swiped at a lock of hair stuck to my cheek. Louis and I had been married a year and still Louisa called me *aunt*. I feared I was not a good maman, but I didn't know how to be a better one.

Aurélia's three-year-old son sat on the ground next to Louisa, holding another basket. As she clipped clusters, Aurélia gently toyed with the vines, making the leaves tickle Charles. He threw back his head and laughed.

A low rumble stopped my picking. The advancing clouds darkened to the color of charcoal. "I pray the clouds empty themselves before they cross the river." The officers turned their horses and headed east, toward Tours. My shoulders relaxed as I resumed clipping. But a stirring in my stomach nagged me. Should I order everyone to seek shelter now in case of hail?

The workers were so loyal, I doubted they would leave their work, but I could at least send the elderly and children inside.

Louisa screeched at a wasp. "I want to go home, now."

Lightning flickered over the distant hayfield. A louder rumble followed. Everyone continued their work. I dared not leave. I waved my apron over her. "I won't let them hurt you."

Charles reached out. "Take my hand, Louisa. I'm not afraid."

"You are very brave, Charles," I said.

Louisa grabbed his hand. "I'm brave, too."

Cold air dropped over us like a curtain. Lightning brightened the sky. Gooseflesh ran up my arms. A sharp odor, like scorched metal, sliced the air. Had lightning struck a wagon? Workers in the hayfield flung their scythes away and threw themselves flat upon the ground, covering their heads with their arms.

"Everyone!" I shouted, "Take shelter!"

The sound of a roaring river charged toward us.

Louisa screamed and covered her ears. I swept her up and brought her to my chest.

Lightning lashed across the sky like a whip. A deafening crash followed.

Torrents of rain poured down like we were standing under a waterfall. I bent over, protecting Louisa, and the force of water pushed the breath from me.

We dared not run for cover. Lightning sought the highest target, and that would be us, should we run.

The rain lessened. Pinging and clacking sounds seized my breath. "Hail," I shouted. "Aurélia. Cover Charles with your basket."

Pebbles of ice the size of pearls popped and bounced on the crusty earth.

"Papa!" Louisa cried. "I want Papa."

I grabbed her basket and dumped the grapes on the ground. Falling to my knees, I pushed Louisa down.

Aurélia slapped the ground under the vines.

"Good idea." I pulled Louisa under the vines for shelter. "Curl up on your side, like a puppy." She whined and fought me as I wrangled her under the basket. "Hush, you will be safe."

Aurélia brought Charles next to Louisa and put her basket over him. Louisa's fingers crept out from under the wicker and searched for Charles. His hand gripped hers.

Thunder boomed so loudly my teeth chattered. Hail needled my arms and face.

I screamed at the workers, "Cover your heads!"

With the children between us, Aurélia and I joined arms and pressed ourselves over the baskets. "Keep your head down and your bonnet covering your face."

Hail broke off chunks of my straw hat. Leaves and vines whirled past. Hailstones floated atop sheets of rainwater that slicked the impenetrable ground, pushing the pellets against the vine roots and piling up the hail like snowbanks. A shard of ice stung my cheek. I wiped the burn, and blood stained my fingers.

Louisa screeched and kicked the basket, knocking it off her. I lunged, pulled it atop her.

"I want Papa!" She kicked a hole in the basket, thrusting out her foot. I pushed it back.

Charles shouted, "Don't cry, Louisa. I'm here."

Ice chunks, now as large as plums, crashed over us like a rockslide.

Punishing hailstones pounded my back. A strange clacking noise surrounded us. Hailstones clattered atop piles of icy pellets. Blood dripped onto my skirts.

I prayed Louis and the pickers had taken cover under the wagon. Please, don't let it get worse. Please, let no one be injured. Please, don't destroy everything.

Lightning cracked. I counted to three before thunder boomed again. The storm was moving east of us—away from the vineyard, not deeper into it. I prayed the northern slope was spared. My grip on the basket eased. Please let everyone be safe.

The rumbling and crashing stopped as suddenly as it began. The wind calmed. Rain pattered. Ceased. Hailstones bobbed in rainwater, mixed with the dust, and sluiced around us in chalky streams. A bank of ice surrounded my legs, making me shiver.

Strong sunlight beat upon my back. I straightened, squinting in the brilliant light. Where was Louis?

Broken shoots dangled from vines. Splintered canes stabbed the earth. Battered leaves and smashed grape clusters littered the vineyard. A blackbird lay squawking, fluttering its crippled wing.

We were ruined.

# 2

# Geneviève

*Château de Verzat Vineyard*
*August* 1797

MY ARMS TREMBLING, I lifted the baskets from the children. "Are you hurt?"

Louisa shivered. Charles grinned, one hand gripping Louisa's, the other holding a handful of hail. "Snow!"

I picked up Louisa and examined her shaking body. She clutched me and sucked her thumb, something she had not done in two years. "I want Papa."

"I'll find him." Rubbing her back and arms, I scanned the vineyard. A few people struggled up the debris-strewn hill. I hoped all the workers had taken shelter. "I must see if anyone is hurt. Can you take the children to the château, Aurélia?"

*You are bleeding.* She pressed her handkerchief along my cheek and handed me the stained cloth.

The scratch wasn't bleeding too much, but my cheek felt bruised. "I'll send your papa to the château as soon as I find him, Louisa, and your papa, Charles."

Aurélia took the children's hands and led them up the hill.

The alarm bell rang. A young boy pulled the rope so hard, his feet swung over the ground, and he had to grab the post to steady himself before pulling it again.

I shoved the handkerchief in my hanging pocket and raced for the tasting room—where everyone on the estate knew to meet in emergencies.

The elderly and children would be severely injured if they hadn't taken shelter, and we'd have to take them to the surgeon in Tours. The image of the helpless bird flashed in my mind. We might have lost goats, sheep, chickens, pets.

Murmuring hushed when I entered the tasting room. Pressure built in my chest as I scanned the room until I spotted Louis unloading boxes of grapes at the entrance to the crushing room. He rushed to me. "You are hurt."

I captured his hand as he caressed my cheek. "Are you injured? Where's Henri?"

He kissed my fingers and pointed. Henri was dumping grapes into the crusher.

"Send him to Aurélia?"

"After you address this crowd." He smiled, his eyes telling me he knew I hated exactly that. But I had no choice.

Grim-faced men and women in battered straw hats, torn tunics, and dripping aprons made a path through the crowd for me to reach Joseph, the old vigneron.

Joseph's tattered tunic and lack of hat told me he must have worked in the hail to save the grapes overflowing from the baskets behind him. I smiled. "Merci." He nodded and placed his hand on his chest.

His loyalty pinched my heart, and I looked away so that I did not cry. I had to appear the strong leader, even though I felt beaten. I wiped a bit of blood from my cheek, turned, and faced my neighbors, searching for faces that might have the experience we desperately needed.

A young man, his tunic muddied and shredded, placed a wooden crate upside down and offered his hand to help me stand upon it.

My heart beat rapidly. I removed my hat, my grip squeezing water from it. "Has everyone been accounted for? Is anyone seriously hurt? Is everyone's neighbor here?"

Heads turned. Monsieur Jeoffrey brought his finger up, pointing, mouthing numbers. I had trouble keeping track of Louisa. How did he track his ten children? Please let them all be safe. A little boy, Emmanuel, sniffled in his maman's arms. He held a very still, too still kitten. I pressed my lips together and blinked. At least Emmanuel appeared to be unharmed. "No one missing?"

"Seems we're very fortunate, Tante Gen," Monsieur Jeoffrey whispered.

I exhaled in relief, but the room darkened as if water were rising above my head. I cleared my throat, hoping my voice would not betray my lack of confidence. "You all know that the Republicans would like nothing more than for us not to be able to pay their ever-increasing taxes. They want us to fail so they can seize this property—just as they have stolen the surrounding vineyards."

Murmurs tinged with hot anger moved through the crowd.

"I know you all want to overcome this setback. Have any of you harvested during a hailstorm before today?"

Madame Ornay, withered by seventy years of toil in the vineyards, raised her walking stick, whittled from root stock that, she'd once proudly told me, was older than she was.

I motioned her toward me. "Anyone else?"

A wiry man with ruddy cheeks and dark eyes approached.

My shoulders relaxed as I positioned them in front of me. "These people are our experts, our guides. We've not much time and those who choose to work throughout the nights with me, I thank you now."

I leaned toward the old lady. "You knew Madame de Verzat?"

She nodded shyly.

I got down and helped her step onto the box. "What should we do first, Madame Ornay?"

She jerked in surprise. "How do you know my name?" Her eyes, blue as the sky, sparked.

"Did you not dance with me and my husband on our wedding day?"

Everyone laughed as she blushed like a young girl.

I wanted to kiss her. "Tell us what we must do first."

With a voice bigger than I thought possible of her, she shouted, "We pick up all the fruit, remove the damaged berries, and crush the remaining grapes immediately." She pounded her walking stick on the box. "We follow Madame de Verzat's rules. Even if we have fewer grapes, any that are bruised, moldy, or rotting are thrown to the pigs." She pounded the stick again. "Selecting each grape by hand is what makes Verzat wine the finest in the world."

Laughter came from a group of boys on the cusp of

manhood, pushing one another, probably relieved to have avoided the conscription officers.

Glaring at the boys, she waggled her stick. "If you miss a wounded berry, it can cause all the others to rot. Be hawk-eyed and thorough in your examinations."

All five of the boys stilled and nodded, their faces infused with respect.

I hugged her and turned to the old man. "Monsieur Guyette, what do we do after collecting the grapes?"

He stood proud. "We collect all the broken shoots, examine them for damage." He pulled some greenery from his apron and ran his fingers over a vine. "And immediately graft the unwounded shoots to vines with undamaged bark."

He passed one of the vines to a woman in the crowd. "The younger shoots, like this one, will have suffered more, so we must graft the healthy shoots to older undamaged ones." He passed some greenery to another woman. "Look at the vines I am passing around. This one is healthy." He wiped his hands and dug into his hat for some leaves. "We must also remove all damaged leaves and shoots, like these. If we do not, they may develop mildew that will spread to healthy vines and destroy next year's grapes."

I pressed my hands together. These people deserved a medal of honor, but I suspected they would refuse any reward for they were proud of their equal ownership of and devotion to the estate. I hoped to be the leader they expected of me. I inhaled deeply and gazed at all the eyes watching me. "I will work with you all—day and night—until the vineyard of Château de Verzat is restored to its glory. I will not disappoint you."

A cheer went up, along with Madame Ornay's stick.

"And we will not allow the Republicans to take this land!"

Their cheer grew deafening.

My eyes burned. I feared speaking, for doing so would break the dam that held back tears, but I pushed myself. "I feel the spirit of Madame de Verzat in this room, and I believe she would be proud and grateful to each and every one of you, as I am." I wiped my eyes. "I thank you for her. Now, divide up into three groups." I motioned people. "This group collect healthy, undamaged shoots and vines." I pointed to another. "All of you, remove damaged leaves, vines, and fruit." I turned to the remaining crowd. "You examine the vines. When you find healthy stock, shout for a healthy vine and graft it." I clapped. "Let us get back to work!"

The workers ran out, hollering and shouting instructions.

I dabbed Aurélia's handkerchief at my cheek. We would salvage what we could. We'd plant root vegetables and sell them in the market. Children would fish and catch eels and frogs in the Loire for suppers, but we would pay the taxes. The Republic would not seize this property. Not while I was vigneron.

Hands clasped my shoulders, and I turned. Tiny lines curled up from the corners of Louis's green eyes.

"Louisa is waiting for you in the château."

"I will quickly kiss Louisa and return." He ran a finger over my cheek. "Does it hurt?"

I shook my head.

He kissed my nose. "I know you *hate* asking for help. But you gave these people an opportunity to feel needed and important. And humbly asking for help has made these people loyal to you."

"I had no choice."

He caressed my cheek. "You could have pretended you knew."

I laughed. "Would *I* do such a thing?"

His laughter followed him out into sunshine.

Before I joined everyone, I had to visit the stables. The boys who worked there would know where I could find a kitten already weaned for Emmanuel.

I walked out into the heat and breathed in the scent of honey-sweet grapes. A rainbow arced over the Loire. With everyone working day and night, we might be able to return the vineyard to its glory.

All I really had to worry about were Bonaparte's soldiers seizing our men, crops, wine, animals, stored food.

A worker called out, "I need a healthy vine!"

A woman ran, clutching vines above her head. "I have two!"

At least I wouldn't be working or worrying alone.

# 3

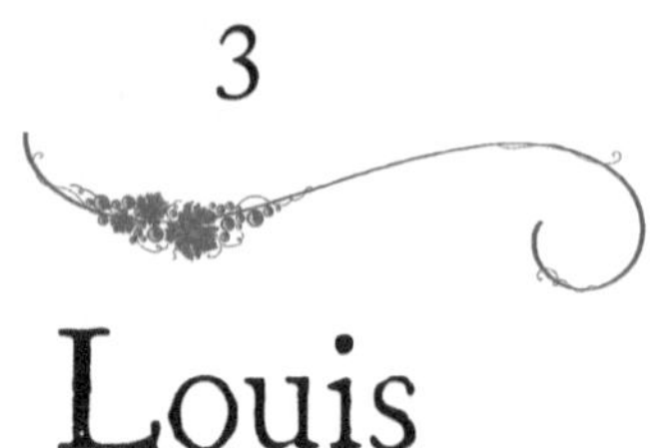

# Louis

*Loire Valley, France*
*September 1797*

AFTER WORKING DAY and night for a week, Louis longed to get back to the goal of enlarging their family. He had to get Geneviève away from the estate, so he proposed a morning at the Tours market. He tucked Geneviève's hand around his elbow and led her around Place Plumereau.

"Would you like to picnic along the Loire?"

She tipped her bonnet coquettishly. "If our lunch doesn't include grapes."

His appetite for her bloomed as they strolled past half-timbered houses. Ahead, people crowded before a wall where a worker was posting notices. Some raised fists. Voices rumbled.

He slowed. Whatever the news was, no one liked it. "The Directoire must have made another *popular* announcement."

His sarcasm tasted bitter. "Hopefully, not another wine tax."

They wove through the people and read:

# 18 FRUCTIDORE V

*Due to the Coup of 18 Fructidore,*
*The New Directoire Decrees:*

*The Law of 1793 shall be enforced. All noble*
*émigrés are ordered to leave France within fifteen*
*days. If they do not, they will be judged by a mili-*
*tary commission and, upon proof of identity, will*
*be executed within twenty-four hours.*

"Henri, Aurélia, and Charles returned less than a year ago, and now they must depart?" Geneviève's face reddened. "Aurélia has become a sister to me."

Louis worked his jaw from side to side. He, like Henri, was also a noble, but fortunately, Louis had never left France.

"Where will they go?" she whispered.

"We will talk on the way home." He purchased broadsheets and a pamphlet of ship sailing dates. Injustice clouded his mind as they returned to the stables.

When they were alone in the wagon, Geneviève's voice wavered. "We're at war with England. They won't be able to go there, and I doubt Aurélia would want to return to America—

she'd be considered a slave there."

Louis's grip on the reigns tightened. "The Royalists were gaining power, and that warmongering General Bonaparte wants them out of his way—it is clear he wishes to be the next king of France." His tone was thick with disgust. "That is the true reason nobles are being forced out of the country."

"We could drive them beyond the border to Brussels or Germany or Austria." She moved closer to him. "They would have the protection of the Royalist army in Koblenz, but that might mean Henri would have to join them."

Louis weighed the options—none of which was pleasant. The man and his family had every right to remain, but the Directoire had once again deemed noble émigrés traitorous criminals. Louis was grateful his own identity papers were false.

He led the horses under the porte cochère at the front of the château and helped his wife down. "Aurélia is not a noble, and although Henri's son was born in America, where there are no titles, in France, Charles is a Noble of the Sword."

"That means they all must leave." She knotted her shawl at her waist.

"They may choose to stay." He stopped her hands. "Whatever Henri's decision, you must honor it."

She pulled away. "I should think escaping the guillotine a second time would be more than anyone could bear."

Louis placed his hand on the door, blocking her. "It is his decision to make, and we must support his choice."

She rearranged her skirts, avoiding his eyes. "The only choice he must make is where to take his family."

Louis would assist Henri whatever his choice, even if that displeased Geneviève.

# 4

# *Geneviève*

*Château de Verzat*
*September 1797*

"THE DIRECTOIRE DEMANDS all noble émigrés depart or face execution." My words rushed like the wind. I stood at the salon entrance, twisting the pamphlet.

Henri sat at the desk, his hands raking his hair. He was learning how to keep the winery's accounts—my task before he had returned—and I imagined his frustration.

The room of pale green silk brocade walls and silk drapes and gilt-edged mirrors seemed a calm oasis. Aurélia sat on the couch, her long fingers caressing the silk ribbon at her waist. Louisa and Charles played with wooden toy soldiers and horses at her feet.

Louisa jumped up. "Papa!" Louis scooped her up, kissed her. She giggled and waved at me. "Bonjour, Tante Gen."

"Bonjour." I smoothed her hair.

"We are playing war, Tante Gen." Louisa would be broken-hearted if Charles left. He was like a brother to her.

Louis put Louisa down, nodded to Henri, and walked to a table topped with a carafe of brandy and a few glasses.

I charged toward Henri, holding out the broadsheet. "You can read it yourself, but all noble émigrés must depart—again." The paper trembled. "You all must leave."

Charles rushed to his father, and Henri picked him up, walked to the couch, and sat next to his wife. He patted Aurélia's shaking hands. "Do not worry."

Louis held out two glasses of brandy. Aurélia shook her head. Henri drained his and took the other.

I rolled up the paper and tapped it against my thigh. "If you remain, you will be executed within a fortnight."

Henri grimaced, grabbed the broadsheet, and read. Aurélia cocked her head and caressed his arm.

Why weren't they packing? "There is money in the account for passage." I slapped the shipping times against my skirts. "You can take a neutral Dutch ship."

"Geneviève—" Louis's tone cautioned me.

"It leaves in two days." I glared at Louis.

"In America I could write an article against this decision and not lose my head. That is democracy." Henri's shoulders rounded as he sighed. "I cannot ask Aurélia to board another ship."

"You can if she wants you to live," I huffed.

Louis cleared his throat.

"Many nobles are in England, Germany, Austria, Italy." I couldn't stop myself.

Henri caressed Aurélia's cheek, his smile radiating love for her. She nuzzled his hand, and his eyes shone with adoration. "Aurélia is with child. Neither of them would survive a voyage."

I pressed my lips. He couldn't leave her. I was such an idiot. "Félicitations," I whispered.

"That is wonderful news." Louis brought up his glass. "Félicitations."

"Louis and I could drive you all in the carriage to Switzerland or Germany where other nobles have found refuge." My voice was high. "You all would be safe."

"Whatever you both decide," Louis stood, "Geneviève and I will help you."

"You cannot stay." I flung out my arms. "If you are found here, everyone on the estate will face the guillotine for harboring émigrés!"

A small laugh escaped Henri. "Aurélia and Charles are Americans, not émigrés."

Charles held out a toy soldier to Louis. "I am an American, Oncle Louis!"

Louis accepted the toy. "You are a proud American." Louis beamed at the boy. "And you are also a Noble of the Sword."

Louisa sprang up. "I am a Noble of the Sword, too!"

"What is Noble of the Sword, Papa?" Charles asked.

I was losing patience with the game, charming though it was, we had to make plans. "It means you must leave France."

Louis gripped my hand. "France welcomes Americans. You are safe here, Charles."

"And Maman, too?"

Louis nodded. "And your maman, too." His grip on my hand tightened. I knew I was upsetting them, but Henri's life was in danger. And Aurélia's happiness was at stake. They could not live without each other. She was about to have a baby. She needed him. Why was it not clear to them they all had to leave?

Aurélia reached out and touched Henri's heart, then held up three fingers.

"I nearly forgot." Henri jerked his head to Louis. "Joliette's ship arrives in three weeks."

My shoulders fell. How could I forget his sister? I wrote her daily reports on the vineyard. When she arrived, she would also be a noble émigrée. "She has no idea of the danger awaiting her."

Henri began pacing. "I wrote her when I thought it was safe to return with her son."

Aurélia rocked herself. I sat next to her and rubbed her back. Her eyes filled with tears.

"Are you afraid for Joliette?"

She nodded and pressed her heart. *She is my sister, like you.* I hugged her.

Louis returned his glass to the table. "Let us know what you decide, Henri. Geneviève and I must return to the vineyard." He pulled me toward the door.

"Thank you, both. We all thank you," Henri called.

"You need to leave in two days." My voice was sharp, and I regretted it. Aurélia was expecting and needed calm. "We can drive Joliette to join you wherever you go."

Louis gripped my shoulders and walked me out of the salon.

I took three steps and turned. "Germany is a seven-day drive from here."

"It is not your decision. Henri must make his own choice, just as you would wish to make your own."

The devil. He was right.

He put his arm around me and guided me out into the falling dusk. "You know Henri will not put anyone on this estate at risk."

Workers still moved among the vines as a few drops of rain splattered in the dirt.

Losing Aurélia snagged my heart in the same way I felt the loss of my mother and Louisa's maman. But I would rather Aurélia stay alive, even if I missed her.

Joliette would not be happy about returning only to abandon her family's beloved vineyard. I had to convince Henri to travel with his family or be prepared to hide them. But what place would be safe for an African woman with child? How would I protect them and all the people on the estate?

5

# *Geneviève*

*Château de Verzat Vineyard*
*September 1797*

THE NEXT DAY, I stood in the vineyard examining the roots and heard Henri's voice. Please, God, let him have the wisdom to take his family to Austria.

He and Louis walked down the hill. Louis's face was calm. Yet his eyes warned me, and I heard his words in my head: *It is Henri's choice to make.*

I gripped the cold secateurs and pruned a vine, bracing myself. I knew he would never endanger the lives of those living on the estate, but none of us would be happy about his departure.

Louis put his arm around my waist. I itched under the heat of him.

Henri removed his hat and dragged his forearm across his forehead. "I will petition the Directoire to return, but in the meantime, I'll take the Dutch ship myself." He toed the chalky earth. "I have a favor to ask of you both."

Heat and humidity closed around me, reminding me of the day Henri left me in Paris five years earlier. We had stood in the trampled Tuileries Garden abuzz with flies, swarming the spilled blood of the Swiss Guards. He'd asked me to accompany him to America, and I'd refused because he hadn't professed his love. "Anything, Henri."

"Will you protect and care for Aurélia, Charles, and our unborn child until my petition for return is granted?"

I grabbed his hand. "We promise. Caring for them both, and your child to come, is an honor to us."

"Thank you. I know I can trust you both." He squeezed my hand. "Simon will ride with me to Le Havre.

"Please, allow Louis and me to drive you. We could bring Aurélia and Charles in the carriage. They would have more time with you."

"I must do this my way. We leave within the hour." He put on his hat and walked up the hill to the château.

I called after him, "I will arrange passage for Joliette and her son to join you."

He waved a hand. His gait was slow. My sigh of relief caught. Aurélia must be heartbroken. I had to be strong and support her. I would be the sister to her that I would want for myself. I would also petition for his and Joliette's return.

Louis gripped my hand. "I do not envy him. I would never

wish to leave you." He kissed the special place on my neck, sending a thrill down my spine.

I leaned into him. "Nor I you, Louis." I pressed my hand to his chest, feeling the steady beating of his heart. A sense of foreboding pulled at me like a strong current.

# 6

# Geneviève

*Nantes, France*
*October* 1797

**A** STIFF ATLANTIC WIND buffeted ships anchored in the harbor and whipped my skirts about. My dread of giving Joliette the news sat in my stomach like sour wine. I hoped she would voluntarily follow Henri, if not, I had to convince her.

I tucked my cold hands around Louis's elbow as we watched the passengers disembark. The last time I traveled to Nantes I was awaiting the return of Henri, when I was in love with him. When he arrived with a bride and son, I thought my life had ended.

I leaned my face into Louis's frock coat and inhaled his scent of a newly mown hayfield. I was so happy as Louis's wife, and I owed my happiness to Henri. If he had not abandoned me, I would not have realized Louis loved me, or that I loved him.

I recognized Joliette from the portrait that hung in the château. Her cheeks had thinned, making her dark eyes more prominent. Wearing a deep green velvet cloak and holding her son's hand, she stood on the wharf, waiting for an officer to stamp her papers.

I had communicated with her over the past two years, reporting on the vineyard and implementing her instructions. I was anxious to meet the astute businesswoman. Through all my correspondence with her, she was decisive and pragmatic. She couldn't possibly choose to stay.

Louis opened the carriage door. Aurélia and Charles climbed down. Charles rolled up on the balls of his feet and pointed. "Look, Maman. Guillaume."

Aurélia stood behind him, her arms crossed over his chest.

The officer waved Joliette and her son toward the dock. Joliette grabbed Guillaume's hand, and they ran toward Aurélia. Both boys broke from their mothers' grasps. Their laughter rang out over the water as they grabbed each other and spun around, whooping and hollering.

Tears streaked Aurélia's cheeks as she embraced Joliette. They wrapped their arms around one another and wept. The wind swirled their skirts about them. When they broke apart, Aurélia's smile was bright as a child's.

I rubbed at the grape stains around my knuckles. Their love for one another made me miss my half-brother. A hollow opened in my chest as I remembered Auguste's joy over sailing the paper boats I folded for him. My stepmother had threatened to report me to the Committee of Public Safety and probably had. I would not be able to be with Auguste until he left her care.

Louis hooked my hand around his elbow. "Shall we greet them?"

Distracted by my memories, I stumbled a bit.

Sorrow laced Joliette's smile. "I remember you from Versailles, Comte de LaGarde."

Louis brought his finger to his lips. "Please call me Louis." He nodded instead of the bow he would have delivered in a time long gone. "May I present my wife, and vigneron of your estate, Geneviève."

Her brown eyes lit up. She took my hands in hers, kissed both my cheeks, and stood back. "Henri and I are indebted to you for eternity, for preserving the Verzat legacy, Geneviève. It is my greatest pleasure to finally meet you." She held my hands, rough and stained, not soft and pale like hers.

Would she be this happy when I told her she had to leave tomorrow? "It is my pleasure to meet you, Joliette." Her warm hands let go. I shoved mine under my shawl.

"Guillaume, come meet your Tante Geneviève and Oncle Louis."

I smiled at her calling me her child's aunt. I hoped I would retain the privilege.

Four-year-old Guillaume was tall for being just six months older than Louisa. He stood before me, his green eyes sparkling, his golden curls shining. He bowed to me and Louis. "I am pleased to meet you, Tante Geneviève and Oncle Louis."

I laughed. "You are already a gentleman."

Louis rested his hand on Guillaume's shoulder and crouched down to the child's level. "I knew your father when he was a Garde du Corps for our Queen. He was a very brave and loyal man. He would be most proud of you."

Guillaume smiled shyly. "Merci, Oncle."

Louis looked up at me and winked. I wanted so much to give Louis a son.

Joliette wiped away a tear. "Is Henri so busy with the estate he could not greet us?"

"Madame Pricaud!" A male voice called. We all turned.

Behind Aurélia stood a lanky man, dressed in tight brown velvet breeches, a brown-and-white striped satin frock coat with deep cuffs and ridiculously wide lapels of shiny pink silk. His graying hair hung in curls over which he wore the now fashionable hat, a bicorne. I had read in the pamphlets about the Incroyables, foppish dandies who dressed to mock the former aristocracy, but I had never seen one.

"You have returned to your homeland."

Joliette pursed her lips and grabbed Aurélia's hand, pulling her close.

He pointed an ornate walking stick, topped by a miniature silver ship at Aurélia. "And, you've returned with your slave!"

My hand reached for the pistol in my hanging pocket.

Joliette stiffened as her gaze drilled into the Incroyable.

Aurélia wrapped her arms around Charles, hiding him in her skirts. Her eyes took on the look of a wary cat.

Louis tensed, and he brought his hand to his sword hilt.

"Do you not recognize your Capitaine?" The Incroyable smiled an oily smile.

Trembling, Aurélia shrank around her son, who stared open-mouthed at the man.

He must have been the ship capitaine who had enslaved Aurélia. Henri's description of the horrors of the voyage flashed in my mind as his voice whined, *Do you know they brand them?*

*Like cattle? Every man on the ship had intended to use Aurélia before Joliette bought her freedom.*

I wanted to hold Aurélia, comfort her, tell her the Capitaine could no longer harm her. Realizing why she did not join Henri in England chilled me like a cold wave. Men like the Capitaine recaptured former slaves and sold them again. But she was safe in France where slavery had been abolished.

Joliette stood taller. She held a tiny pearl-handled pistolet. "Your costume indicates you are no longer a capitaine, Monsieur."

"No need for weaponry, Madame." The Capitaine circled his stick at Aurélia. "Tell me, what price did you get for your dark beauty?"

Joliette cocked the hammer of the gun and brought her hand up, aiming at him.

Louis drew his sword. "You becloud this beautiful day." He took two steps toward the man, blocking Joliette's aim. "Move along, Monsieur."

The dandy skittered like a scared rabbit. "I see she is no longer pure." He laughed like a mad man. "You must have gotten a very good price for her!" He lifted his bicorne, bowed mockingly, and strode away.

I took in every detail of the man, his height, his gait, his mannerisms, his greasy scent.

Joliette released the hammer and shoved the pistolet in her reticule. She pulled Aurélia to her, holding her tightly. "He will never hurt you again. Never."

I also wrapped my arm around Aurélia. "You are safe." She trembled so I thought she might shake apart.

"After the ship, did you ever see him in America, again?" Louis sheathed his sword.

"Every time his ship arrived, he looked for her. One time he knocked on our door. We moved often." Joliette rubbed Aurélia's back. "We kept her hidden whenever a ship was sighted."

"Could he have followed Henri or you?"

"He was not on our ship." She looked at Aurélia, who shook her head.

Charles pulled his mother's skirts. "I will not let him hurt you, Maman."

"You are a true Noble of the Sword, Charles," Louis said.

"Where is Henri?" Joliette asked.

Aurélia began to write in the little book that hung from a ribbon around her wrist, but I touched her hand lightly.

"I will tell her."

Aurélia's eyes clouded with worry.

"Just after Henri wrote, telling you it was safe to return, the Directoire issued a proclamation, ordering all noble émigrés to leave within a fortnight or face execution."

Joliette's eyes searched mine. "Is he safe?"

"Yes, but he had no other choice but to sail to England, where he awaits you."

A little cry escaped her. Aurélia pulled her close.

"A Dutch ship sails to England from Le Havre in three days." I waited for her agreement.

She closed her eyes, wrapped her arms around herself, and shook her head.

"Do you wish to sit down?" Louis asked.

Joliette pressed her hands to her face. A thin gold band on her ring finger glinted in the light, reminding me her husband had been guillotined five years earlier. "I cannot run again."

"You have trusted me with the vineyard and the estate for five years. Trust me now," I pleaded.

She shook her head.

"Are you known on the émigrés list as Comtesse de Verzat?" I asked.

She stood tall, anger etching her face. "No. I am Madame Pricaud."

I regretted asking but probed. "Was your husband of noble blood?"

She straightened. "He was a baron."

My shoulders dropped. "If they trace the name, you will be taken to the guillotine."

"I evaded them the first time. Now they will have to find me." She swept up her cloak and climbed into the carriage. "Let us go home, now."

"But military commissions are roaming the country, on the lookout for returning nobles." I did not want to say it, but I could not help myself. "Think of your son."

She lifted her chin. "My son is an American citizen."

"Who will be an orphan if you do not join Henri in England."

"Merci for your concern, Geneviève. I would like to go home now."

Louis helped Aurélia and the children up into the carriage. "We will make haste."

I stepped up to the door, but he closed it after them. "Ride on the bench with me."

I chastised myself. He had warned me, and I hadn't listened. Once again, I spoke without thinking. I had just spoiled Joliette's homecoming and upset Aurélia.

Nonetheless, I would get Joliette on that ship if I had to truss her up like a lamb for shearing.

7

# *Geneviève*

*Château de Verzat*
*October* 1797

RELIEVED TO RETURN to our cottage on the estate, Louis and I cuddled before the fire, sipping wine.

"Had I not been imprisoned, I, too, would be a noble émigré." The firelight made the gold flecks in his eyes sparkle.

I pressed myself closer to his warmth. "Where would you have gone?"

"I would have honored my brother and joined the Royalist army." He pushed out his lower lip. "Probably Koblenz."

"Do you wish for the monarchy to return?"

"There was never such senseless bloodshed under any King of France. This new Republic is a mere cloak for indiscriminate slaughter, and I no longer support it." He drained his glass.

"What do you support?"

He chewed the inside of his lip. "A democracy, like the Americans have created. Our Rights of Man were based on their constitution, but the Revolutionaries were powerless for so long, the Directoire created a Republic, which is reluctant to share power."

"Would it be better to return to a monarchy?"

"It would be better to return to bed and make more French citizens." He grinned.

A battering on our cottage door awakened me. Louis jumped from the bed. The door crashed open.

Carrying a lantern, Magali rushed in. "Aurélia is gone!"

"What do you mean?" I grabbed my dressing gown. "Where is Charles?"

"With Joliette. His cries woke her." The ruffle of Magali's nightcap trembled. "When Joliette entered Aurélia's chamber, she found Charles in the bed, but Aurélia was nowhere to be found. We have looked everywhere."

Louis grabbed his cloak from the peg. "I will meet you in her chamber." He ran.

I bent over Louisa's bed and began to wake her, but Magali's hands stilled mine. "I will bring her. You go."

I slammed my feet into my boots, grabbed my shawl, and ran. Did Aurélia go after Henri? She would never abandon her son. If someone made her leave, she'd be blind with worry for Charles. But who would take her? Everyone on the estate loved her gentle and kind nature. A dull weight pulled in my belly. I closed my eyes against the image of the Capitaine and headed for the château's kitchen door.

Joliette paced before the fireplace. She grabbed my hand, and we climbed the grand steps. Candles, nearly burned out, sputtered in the sconces.

"Was Aurélia's door locked?"

She shook her head.

I searched for scuff marks on the wall, a bit of gravel on the rug, scratches on the balustrade. "She would never leave Charles." I scanned the hall for a scrap of paper from her tiny book, steadying my breathing, trying to calm myself.

Louis was studying the room when we entered. "Do not disturb anything."

Joliette stood hugging herself, her eyes flicking from the bed to the floor to the windows.

The pink light of dawn seeped into the room, but it did not dispel the shadows. I had thought Aurélia was safe here. I inhaled the faint smell of Aurélia's jasmine perfume…and something else. "Do you smell something odd?"

Louis sniffed. "What do you think you smell?"

I inhaled deeply, sensing a faint earthy scent. "Mud?"

He began examining the parquet floor and toed something. "A few dried chunks of mud. But did Aurélia or Charles bring them in?"

"If they had, Aurélia would have cleaned it up." I walked to the tall glass-paned doors leading to a balcony. "The lock has been broken." I pointed at the scarred brass fitting. "He must have used a knife to get in through here."

Louis pushed open the door, stepped out, and stood at the iron railing, looking down at the front of the château. "He climbed atop the porte cochère, crossed the roof, and up over this railing." He leaned over, examining the drive. "He must have stood atop his horse. See the hoofprints? There are many, close together, like the horse was trying to find his footing."

I pointed at a smear of mud on the balcony rail. "Look."

He rubbed his fingers along the railing, flaking specks of dried mud.

A queasiness rolled in my belly. "The Capitaine?" I whispered.

"No doubt."

Joliette stifled a cry. "God help her."

I longed to reassure her, but there wasn't time. "Aurélia is smart. She must have left something for us to discover, like a message to help find her." I strode to the bed. The duvet and sheets were in disarray; she had struggled, but I was relieved not to find blood. The pillow was indented where her head had rested.

I crossed to the other side, where I imagined Charles had slept as the bedclothes were not as rumpled. A patch of the pillowcase reflected the early light, and I ran my fingers over the shiny spot. Candlewax? But the candlestick was on the table on the other side of the bed.

"There is a puddle of candle drippings on the pillow."

Joliette peered at the stain. "That is observant of you, but what does it mean?"

"I imagine the Capitaine held a dripping candle near Charles, with his knife at the sleeping child's throat, all the while he commanded Aurélia to dress for travel."

"He took great pleasure in threatening her." Joliette ran her trembling hands over the pillow. "Why would he not take Charles, too?"

"He can get a very high price for Aurélia, and he wanted to get away with her first." My mouth grew sour. "Aurélia would have fought him like a tigress. He could not fight her and take Charles."

"This is where I found Charles, crying for his maman."

"How long ago?" Louis asked.

"A few minutes before I sent Magali to get you."

Louis rubbed his jaw. "Charles could have awakened long after Aurélia was taken."

"The mud on the railing is dry. How long would that take?" I asked.

Louis sighed and shook his head. "Minutes? Hours?"

I opened the armoire. Aurélia's blue day gown, boots, and cloak were missing. I turned to her dressing table. The blue ribbons she used to fasten her bonnet hung from a brass ring alongside the mirror. The brush, combs, bottles, everything was as tidy as it always was.

But her fan was open. "Joliette, don't ladies close their fans when they store them?

"Certainly. Fans are far too delicate to leave open. Why?"

"Louis?" I pointed. The fan lay fully open, revealing the painting of Paris.

"Aurélia lent her fan to me the day of the hailstorm. I admired the painting of Paris and told her that she would enjoy seeing it one day." I picked it up and examined its back. "Do you think she left this as a clue?"

Louis drummed his fingers on the table. "Yes."

"Please do not keep anything from me." Joliette wiped her tears.

"Madam Brissault runs the most expensive bordel in Paris." He cleared his throat. "She specializes in exotic women."

Joliette grabbed hold of the bed and sat.

I closed my eyes, fighting tears.

"Charles is also in danger. The Capitaine will return to sell the boy into slavery as soon as he has gotten a good price for Aurélia." Louis's tone was flat.

"We can ride after him. He can't have gotten far with two on one horse." I would kill the bastard.

"I will go. I know where he might try to sell her." Louis grabbed my arm. "Take Joliette, Guillaume, and Charles to the orphanage. He must not find Charles here, should he return."

"Henri never left France." Joliette's voice was high, her tone desperate.

A chill swept across my back. "Where did he go?"

She pressed her hands to her ribs. "Aurélia told me Simon would hide him in the caves, and he would never be far from the château. He pretended to leave France to protect everyone on the estate. If they do not know he is here, they cannot be arrested for harboring him."

"Ignorance is no proof of innocence to the purveyors of the guillotine." I slapped my hands against my legs. "He's risked everyone on the estate—especially Simon. Have you—"

"Yes, I sent for Simon."

I wiped sweat from my face. "When you find her, Louis, you can't rescue her alone. I'll go with you."

He nodded. "I shall go to Paris, then meet you and Henri at the orphanage in three days. I hope I will have located her by then." He kissed me and looked at Joliette. "Tell Henri I will find her." His footsteps thundered down the stairway.

"I'll get the carriage and meet you all out front." I ran down the steps and out the grand doors. Kneeling, I examined the patterns the horse had left while the Capitaine stood on its back. Then I walked down the drive. The prints were deeper in the mud, due to the weight of another rider. The edges of mud were dry.

How could we have protected Aurélia from something we could not imagine? I ran to the stables. We would get Aurélia back, no matter what it took.

8

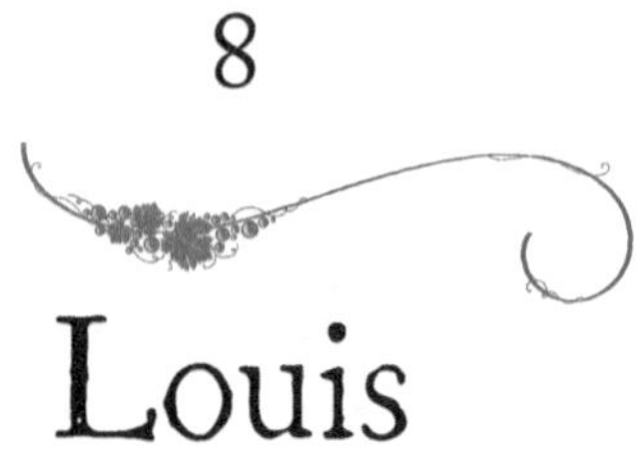

# Louis

*Château de LaGarde Orphanage*
*October* 1797

Louis stood amongst frock coats and matching breeches hanging from pegs in the anteroom of his bedchamber, a bitter taste like walnut skins drying his mouth. He had not dressed as a courtier in more than five years. His clothing was far from stylish—more subdued colors and less lace were in fashion. The Madam and her ladies had to find him convincing—Aurélia's life depended upon it.

Although he had turned twenty of the thirty bedrooms in his château into dormitories for the orphanage, he had kept his family's private quarters and his former courtier wardrobe locked away. Stacks of lace-edged jabots and embroidered waistcoats sat on upper shelves and a troop of red-heeled, silver-buckled shoes stood at attention across lower shelves. Had he once thought this frippery attractive? He selected the plainest frock coat.

Scenes of his days as a courtier of Versailles flashed in his mind, of his doomed affair with the Comtesse, who had humiliated him when he had professed his love. *Sex is not love, mon amour.* She had laughed so hard she began gasping and her maid rushed into the chamber as he stood there naked and embarrassed. He finally stood to his full height, looked down his nose, and said, "At your age, you've not much time for either." That had stopped her laughter.

Louis had taken comfort at more than one bordel, until he met Magdeleine, and it was she who taught him to love by challenging him with: *You are a man, but you have less courage than a little boy.* He ran his fingers back and forth over the blue velvet frock coat. She had been so kind, understanding, loving. He pressed his hand to his heart. He was madly in love with Geneviève, but he would be forever grateful to Magdeleine for teaching him to love and giving birth to his daughter. And he was forever grateful to Geneviève for rescuing Louisa and protecting her until he was able to care for her.

Tying the jabot at his throat, he laughed. "Geneviève would find this adornment far too much!" He removed his wedding ring and secreted it in his waistcoat.

Slipping his pistol into his pocket, he practiced tilting his head and looking down his nose. Were the newly rich as arrogant as courtiers were?

A soft knocking at the door stilled him. He plucked up his cloak and wrapped it around himself, covering the splendor.

To make Magdeleine happy, he had agreed to welcome her friends: prostitutes and their illegitimate children. He had presented himself as their equal, and he did not wish to be discovered dressed as a noble. Most of the women were hard workers and cheerful. Except for the leader, a catty woman who appointed herself lady of the château. Out of pity, Louis allowed Suzanne her fantasy.

He stood, sweating, before the gilded door. "Yes?"

"Louis, I must speak to you privately."

He swallowed a groan. Suzanne. There was nothing to do but face the firebrand. He slipped out of his chamber and locked the door behind him. "I have not much time."

Her dark eyes glittered and her hair, red as harvest grape leaves, shone. She inhaled, making her breasts bulge. "You are so handsome, Louis. Must you leave so soon?" She reached.

He stepped back. "What is it you wish?"

"You. Always you." Her laugh was deep and throaty.

Louis gently brushed her hand aside. "Excuse me. I must reach Paris within the hour." He hurried down the steps to the great hall.

"I'll be waiting up for you." Her cackle followed him out into the night.

Her open desire was becoming tiresome. Should she learn he was married, her jealousy might make her a hindrance rather than a help at running the orphanage. He could not banish her—he had promised Magdeleine that her best friend, Suzanne, and her son would always have a home here.

As he saddled his horse, he worried about being recognized as the former Comte de LaGarde. For if a Madam or prostitute recognized him and informed on him to the gendarmes, he was certain the Directoire would realize he had been sentenced to the guillotine and might sentence him again—for the mere crime of being born a noble.

9

# *Geneviève*

*Château de LaGarde Orphanage*
*October* 1797

**I**T TOOK THREE days to travel from the estate to the orphanage, and we were all on edge. Henri paced the length of the chamber like a caged animal. Joliette plunged her needle into her embroidery, yanking the thread and plunging the needle again and again.

I stared out of the window, envisioning rescuing Aurélia. If Louis learned she was at a bordel, I could dress as a prostitute, but I doubted I'd be convincing. I had not the bosom nor the allure. I wiped my hand across the back of my neck and felt grit. Dust covered my breeches and frock coat. I regretted forgetting to pack clothing for myself. I'd been too busy packing Louisa's warm clothing and poupette and reassuring her Louis would meet us.

Henri slammed a log into the fireplace. Sparks flew onto the hearth.

I stepped on the glowing embers. "Would you like some brandy?"

"Yes, please," Joliette's voice was high. "A very good idea."

"Had I seen the Capitaine, I'd have killed him." Henri slapped his palm against the wall. "I never should have left her."

"Louis will find her." I handed him a glass. "And if he hasn't already rescued her, we will."

"It's my fault. I brought Aurélia to France because I thought she would be in less danger here than America." He swallowed the brandy and paced.

I looked to Joliette, carefully examining her brother. "I would like one too, please."

I poured another. Henri had escaped a lynching mob by diving into the Seine and traveled the Paris tunnels to save not only his but also Joliette's life. He had discovered his father—murdered—and had to flee his country, leave his mother, and escape the guillotine aboard a slave ship. I had no doubt he could rescue his wife, but he seemed lost without her. He was not in a strong position to save Aurélia. His love for her would cloud his sense of reason. But he would insist upon rescuing her. Louis and I would have to plan a role for Henri to play that would not endanger anyone. I handed the glass to Joliette.

The chamber door opened. Louis strode in and quietly locked the door behind him.

I rushed into his arms, breathing in his scent, but instead of a fresh hayfield he smelled of something exotic, sandalwood? I began to pull back, but he pressed me to him, wrapping his arms about me. My cheek slid against the satin trim of his frock coat. What were these silly, decorative things he was wearing? And why did he smell so odd? I had thought prostitutes smelled of lilies.

He released me but held my hand. "I have found where the Capitaine took Aurélia—"

"Where is she?" Henri's dark blues eyes reddened with fury.

"In a Parisian bordel." Louis put his hand on Henri's shoulder. "She is guarded day and night by two armed men the size of oxen."

"I don't care. I'm going to get her." Henri slammed the glass on the table.

"We must have a plan, otherwise we could endanger her further."

Henri's shoulders stiffened.

"Trust Louis," I whispered. "We escaped the Conciergerie."

"Where exactly is Aurélia?" Joliette sat stiffly.

Louis cleared his throat. "I believe a bordel madam has bought her."

Henri moaned, collapsed onto the sofa, and raked his hair. "I never should have left her."

I lurched as it dawned on me that Aurélia had been sold and would be forced to have sex—with many men. A vinegary taste filled my mouth. As a woman, I could get closer to her than Henri or Louis. "I can dress as a prostitute and find her in the bordel."

"The other ladies would not welcome the competition." Louis arched at eyebrow at me and poured a glass of brandy. "No one could have foreseen the diabolical actions of the Capitaine."

"May I have another brandy?" Joliette abandoned her embroidery to the table.

Louis poured three more glasses and handed one to each of us. He sat with his back to the fire, staring at the amber liquid. "Forgive me, but I must speak frankly."

Joliette sat next to Henri, her fingertips lightly resting on his hand. She nodded.

"Aurélia is being held captive in the most expensive and ornate bordel in the city."

Henri pressed his shaking hands to his face.

Louis stood and watched the fire. "Madam Brissault specializes in offering exotic women who satisfy the most prurient desires. Many women are not there by choice. She sells virginity as well." He put a hand on the mantel and kicked at the hearth. "I expect Madam bought Aurélia because she can charge a very high price for Aurélia's beauty."

Nausea and rage swirled in me. "Bastard." Aurélia would fight like a wild cat, but she might not survive. If she harmed one of Madam's customers, he might kill Aurélia, or worse, the Madam might summon the Capitaine to tame her.

"The man brands human beings like cattle." Henri shouted. "Joliette bought Aurélia's freedom to prevent all the men on the ship from using her!" He drained his glass.

I pressed my hand against my stomach. I feared I might vomit.

"How do we get her back?" Joliette, ever calm, asked.

"We go in and take her, that's how." I grabbed the brandy carafe and poured everyone another measure.

"Your passion is one of the reasons I love you, but we must be calm and try to foresee problems." Louis caressed my back.

Heat washed over my face. His eyes sparked. Why did I

not think first? "I apologize, Louis. I want to go and get her right now."

Louis examined Henri. "I was told Aurélia put up quite a fight."

"You've been in the place where she is kept?" Henri wiped his face.

A wave of revulsion swept over me, but I kept my mouth shut. How did Henri bear this? I jumped to my feet. "We will kidnap her back."

Louis put up his palm. "She is held in an attic room, outside of which two armed men stand guard. We need a plan that will not endanger anyone."

It was then that I really saw Louis's attire. I stifled a laugh. He looked more like a woman than I did. An image of him at Université flashed in my mind. He'd been wearing pink silk embroidered with silver. He had dressed like that when he'd been a courtier at Versailles, and he must have kept the clothing. "You and Henri will disguise yourselves as customers?" I asked.

Louis nodded. "We need another man, one who desires Aurélia and can afford her."

I cleared my throat. "Surely, dressed in such male finery, I could be that man."

Louis shook his head. Henri shook his head. Joliette's lips formed a little smile.

A small thrill moved through me. Joliette thought like I did. "Why not? I fooled both of you when we were students."

"You *were* very convincing." Henri sipped more brandy. "You certainly surprised Louis."

"You were dressed and acted as a commoner, not a noble." Louis's voice was a growl.

I wondered if he was remembering how I had embarrassed him at Université. But he'd had the last laugh when he sliced his rapier through my waistcoat, exposing my breasts. "There are many commoners, newly rich, who don't know how to act as courtiers, and I suspect many of them frequent that bordel."

Joliette's eyes brightened. "I should have you negotiate some wine contracts. You are most convincing."

I stood a bit taller.

Louis rolled the empty glass in his hands. "I hesitate to subject you to the debauchery you are guaranteed to witness."

Had my husband seen debauchery that evening? That would explain his strange scent. What else had he done to learn of Aurélia? I shut my eyes against my imagination conjuring Louis in another woman's embrace. "I would not be shocked."

Henri stood and wavered. "I agree with Louis. We cannot endanger you."

"I want to rescue Aurélia, and I will do anything that requires." They dared not stop me. "Aurélia is my sister, my dearest friend, and I will never abandon her."

Joliette stood. "Perhaps I, too, should join you."

"No." Both Louis and Henri spoke at the same time.

Louis drained his glass. "We will need someone to get us out of prison, should we be caught, and you, Joliette, excel at negotiations."

"Let us think on how we will rescue Aurélia this evening and finalize a plan in the morning." Louis set down his glass. "A plan that will bring everyone home safely."

I drained my glass. "Whatever the plan, I will be a part of it."

# 10

# Geneviève



*Château de LaGarde Orphanage*
*October 1797*

Louis locked his chamber door.

"Did you learn anything about Aurélia you could not tell Henri?" I asked.

"My informant told me the captured woman put up quite a fight, and she wondered why the woman did not scream. I am certain she means Aurélia." He lighted a candle and brought it to a clutch of them in a silver candelabrum.

"What else?"

"She said all the women fled as soon as the Capitaine arrived. They all know he cannot complete the sexual act without beating a woman."

A queasiness moved through my belly—disgust and rage battling.

His eyes sparked. "The Madam would not buy damaged *property*, so I am certain he did not take Aurélia before or after he sold her."

"That is one thing to be thankful for. How will we get her out of there?"

He handed the candelabrum to me, removed a key from his waistcoat, and opened a locked door. "Bring the light, please."

Curiosity skittered through me.

He stood in a room the size of our cottage at the estate. Holding the candelabrum high, I circled the room, feeling like I had walked into a garden. Hanging from pegs on every wall were matching frock coats and breeches in a rainbow of colors. Embroidered silk waistcoats lay on tilted shelves, their silver and gold threads glinting in the candlelight. Tricorns trimmed in fur, pearls, and jeweled braid sat on shelves above.

"Whew. Are those pearls and gems real?"

"Yes."

I set the candelabrum on the table in the center of the room. "All these…are yours?"

He stared at the floor, a blush rising. "I had intended to give these to the women here, to remake them into gowns. But should we ever need the money, we could sell the jewels and clothes." He shrugged off his frock coat and hung it on a peg in the blue section.

I grabbed a decanter sitting on the table, poured a glass, and drank.

"Pour one for me?" Louis unbuttoned his silver-thread encrusted waistcoat. "Since we will need such costumes for the bordel, I am glad I did not. Although they are no longer in fashion."

I jerked the decanter, spilling a bit of brandy. "That means I will accompany you?"

"We must plan, think of all the possibilities. I do not want to endanger you."

At least he was thinking of including me. "She is my sister. I want to go."

He caressed my cheek. "I want your word you will not reveal yourself—no matter what may happen."

I placed my hand on his chest. "You have it."

"Geneviève?" His eyes grew serious. "Say, 'you have my word, I will not reveal myself no matter the circumstance.'"

I wanted to sigh at his insistence at such a trifling matter, but I put my hand over my heart. "You have my word. I will not reveal myself no matter the circumstance."

"Remember, your word defines your honor upon which our trust is built."

"Our trust. I understand." He took his Noble-of-the-Sword honor so seriously. One's word could not always be kept when saving another's life. But I would not argue since he had agreed to allow me to join him.

He folded the waistcoat and returned it to its place.

I ran my hand over a fine gold-embroidered frock coat. "I hope Joliette can alter something to fit me. I cannot sew well."

He tilted his head, took the key, and beckoned me to another door.

"There's more?" My voice squeaked. I picked up the candelabrum.

He opened the door to a matching room, just as opulent and brimming with luxurious clothing as the first. Dust sat thick on the table, but the clothing looked fresh, like someone had brushed it. Adrien, Louis's devoted butler, must have pre-served the clothing.

"This was my brother's dressing room."

I lowered the candelabrum onto the table, remembering Louis in the prison cell, distraught with grief. "He was killed during the attack on the Tuileries?"

He gulped the brandy. "As a Noble of the Sword, he devoted his life to being a courtier."

"I am so sorry, Louis. Were you close?"

"Inseparable." He snorted a laugh. "We were hellions. Terri-fied both our parents." He sipped again. "But after the market women attacked Versailles, he realized how vulnerable the monarchy was and became a Garde du Corps. He was mur-dered while protecting the King from his subjects."

I placed my hand on his back as he stared into the distance. "You loved him very much."

He stretched his neck, bringing his face up as if to look at the ceiling. "He was smaller than I." He strode to a corner where clothing was folded and stacked according to size. "And Maman kept all his clothing from when he was a child—she doted on him." He patted a yellow frock coat embroidered with gold. "Something in this section should fit you." He returned to his dressing room.

A pale-blue ribbon with an *L* embroidered on it was stitched inside the collar of the frock coat, waistcoat, and the waistband of the breeches. A tailor's mark identifying LaGarde clothing. I picked up the candelabrum and followed Louis. My arms were heavy, useless, but I sensed he did not wish to be questioned. I cared not a fig for the clothing. I wanted to comfort him. All this time we'd known each other, he had never spoken of his family—every one of them lost in the Revolution within weeks of each other. And then Magdeleine, my friend, too, but she was Louisa's maman.

Untying his jabot, he yanked the cloth from his neck and tossed it on the table.

A smear of red caught my eye. "What's this?"

He shook his head. "Lip rouge, I expect."

"You expect?" I knew he had gone to a bordel, but I hadn't let myself imagine him in it. "Did you go *inside* the bordel?"

He let out a puff. "How else would I look for Aurélia?" He unbuttoned his breeches and stepped out of his buckled shoes.

"I…thought maybe you watched from outside."

He tilted his head.

"Whose lip rouge is it?

He dropped his breeches on the floor. "Désirée's."

I took a swallow of brandy. "What an appropriate name." I hated the sourness in my voice. It made me appear lacking in confidence, and I was. Bordel whores were beautiful, and I was no beauty. The glass grew slippery in my hand.

He hung his breeches on a peg and pulled a nightshirt over his head. "Désirée gave me information and kissed my cheek in thanks for the money I gave her." He sat on the bed.

Swirling the liquid, I inhaled its vapor to clear the scent of sandalwood clinging to my nostrils. "Did you give her anything besides money?"

"Such as?"

"You stink of her perfume." I opened a window, letting in a chill wind.

"All bordels reek of perfume."

"Oh, you've visited more than one." I crossed my arms.

"You know I met Magdeleine in one." His voice was soft.

"Yes, I remember." I hated my own suspicions. I was reacting to the memory of Henri's betrayal—asking me to join him in America and then his returning to France with Aurélia—and his son.

Yet, this was different. I felt…threatened—by the beauty of a woman named Désirée. A woman I had never seen. Did I dress as a man because I was not beautiful? I had felt pretty in the gown I'd worn the night I fell in love with Louis. But I didn't feel confident in women's clothing, not that night, not ever. "Did you know Désirée before this evening?" What a stupid thing to say. I truly did not want to know that. Stupid, stupid, stupid.

The disappointment in his eyes cut me deeper than any answer. "I'm sorry." I waved the question away. "Forget I asked."

Louis rose from the bed. "I have never hidden my past from you."

"I know." I stared at my wide hands, short fingers, ragged nails.

He stepped closer to me. "What is it you truly wish to ask?"

The memory of Henri breaking my heart made my face burn. I did not think I could bear it if Louis had betrayed me—well, maybe—if his infidelity was necessary to save Aurélia.

"Geneviève?"

I turned away and closed the window, my breath collecting on the cold glass.

"Do you remember our marriage vows?" His voice was gentle.

My God. My heart curled around itself. I was being ridiculous. This was Louis, not Henri. But fear swarmed me, and I could not hear clearly.

Louis wrapped his arms around me. "Did we not promise to be faithful?"

My heartbeat pounded so loudly I barely heard him.

He turned me toward him and caressed the edge of my cheek, right below my eye, where I knew wrinkles deepened when I was fighting tears. "You must never worry. I have always been…and will always be…faithful to you."

The charging fear drained from me, and I slumped against him. "I am sorry. I trust you… but…" I was such a fool. Shivering took hold of me. "You must have been tempted. There must have been many beautiful women there." My words burst like an accusation.

"There were."

I pulled back to see the golden flecks in his green eyes sparkling in the candlelight. He *had* been tempted. A bit of fear niggled its way back. "Being faithful to me must have been difficult." I turned away pretending to playfully challenge him.

"Not difficult at all. I thought of you the entire time." He kissed the special spot on my neck he knew made me surrender to him.

He had banished my fear with just a few words. I pressed myself against him, aching for him, running my hands over his muscular shoulders.

"As a result, I have worked up quite an appetite." His voice was matter-of-fact.

"I don't care where you get your appetite…as long as it is me you devour."

He growled and bit my neck. I let out a little cry, releasing all the fear that had rushed through me.

He picked me up and laid me on the bed. After yanking off my boots he crouched over me.

"What is it like at a bordel?" I ran my fingers through his hair, so much more enticing than the silly wig.

He unbuttoned my breeches—one, by, one. "The mansion is ornately decorated." He pulled off my breeches.

"I mean the women…and men."

He puffed out his lower lip, like he always did when he was discounting something. "Everyone is scantily dressed."

"Even the men?"

He peeled off my stocking. "Mmm hmm."

"I might not mind seeing that."

His eyebrows jumped.

I felt like a naughty child, and a little trill of excitement ran through me. "What were they doing?" I whispered.

He tossed my stocking over his head. "Women ran plumes over naked areas of some soldier's bodies."

"That might feel lovely. Did the men…" I was breathing fast.

"Become aroused?"

I nodded, like I had no brain, like I was a marionette.

"I did not notice." He peeled off my other stocking.

I jumped up. "I'll be right back." I ran to the dressing room, plucked up a tricorne and ripped its feather from the crown. I stood by his side, and he lay back on the bed. I skimmed the plume along his leg. "Like this?"

He groaned and plucked up the feather. "Let me show you." He pulled me onto my back in one smooth motion. The feather danced along my inner thigh.

I breathed down to my toes. "Tell me more."

"Another woman wore a sheer gown, leaving little to the imagination, and sat on the lap of a toad-of-a-man to whom she fed oysters and champagne."

I laughed. "Who could eat at a time like that?"

He let out a belly laugh and tugged the tunic over my head. His descriptions, the feather, his ardor had aroused me, and I felt myself blush.

"I tell you these things so that if you go to the bordel you will not be shocked." His hand covered my breast.

"Ah…so we should practice?" My breathing quickened.

He teased my nipple. "You find the imagery a bit arousing?"

"No…" I groaned and wrapped my legs around him.

He grinned, caressing me with the feather. "Maybe just a little bit?"

Panting, I lifted my hips and pressed against him. "Forgive me." I reached for him. "I must be convincing so the Madam will find me a believable libertine."

"I will help you in every possible way, my love."

# 11

# *Geneviève*

*Château de LaGarde Orphanage*
*October* 1797

**A**FTER MY FATHER'S execution, I knew my stepmother was penniless and had no place to go. Louis offered to write to her, explaining her husband had arranged for her and her son, Auguste, to live at the LaGarde Orphanage forever. Thankfully, she believed Louis. Whenever we went to the orphanage, I dressed as a man and secretly visited my half-brother. If we were caught rescuing Aurélia, I'd be executed, and Auguste would never know what happened to me. I left a letter for him in Louis's chamber in the event I did not return, but I'd not seen Auguste in months, and I longed to visit with him. We weren't leaving until dusk, so I sought him out.

Auguste sat on the pond's shore alone, staring across the

water while three boys fished from a wooden pier jutting into the pond.

I longed to scoop him up in my arms, but he was eleven— far too big for lifting and cuddling. Keeping my hat brim shadowing my face, I called out to him. He jumped up and ran to me. He was so tall the top of his head reached my chin. He put his arm around me, as if he were greeting a man and, for that moment, I regretted having to hide my female identity and play the part of a casual friend.

"Where've you been?"

I longed to tell him I was happily married, had a stepdaughter, and managed a vineyard, but if he inadvertently told my stepmother where I lived, she could report me for a crime I didn't commit to the Republicans who would drag me to the guillotine. "Avoiding the bad men," I whispered.

His arm dropped. "Is that true?"

"Yes, I am still wanted. Is Maman well?"

He dragged his boot toe through the coarse sand. "She stays in her room all day."

Why did she ignore her son? If I had taught Etty to read, she could have taught Auguste and the other children. "Do you like school?"

He crossed his arms and stared purposefully at me. "What happened to Papa?"

My shoulders tensed. I wouldn't lie to him, but the truth would hurt. And I wouldn't be here to help him heal. Etty should have consoled him, played with him, reassured him he was safe. "What did Maman tell you?"

"That he went away. I know that's not true." The pout he'd made as a little boy pulled at his lower lip.

"Let's walk." I headed for a stone bench farther away from the other boys and sat. "What have you heard?"

He pounded his fist on the stone bench. "He was a monster."

Who would be so cruel to tell Papa's own child? I covered Auguste's fist, but he pulled it from me. "What else?" I asked.

"He was guillotined."

I closed my eyes. I had wanted to protect him, but it wasn't possible. "Did the other boys tell you that?"

He shook his head. "They don't know."

That was something to be grateful for. But who would tell him? Etty couldn't have admitted the truth. "Then who told you?"

"Madame Suzanne."

A prickling crossed my shoulders. "Did you ask her?"

He picked up a handful of gravel, chose a pebble and threw it at the pond. "The last time you visited, she wanted to know who you were. When I didn't tell her, she told me she knew my father." He tossed another pebble and the plunking it made as it hit the water was an oddly cheerful sound.

"She didn't know him."

He looked up at me. The innocence he'd possessed had tarnished over the past six years.

"I still didn't tell her your name, and she got angry." He flung all the pebbles, plunking and spraying water droplets. "She told me my father deserved to have his head chopped off."

My hands grabbed the bench like I was strangling the bitch. After sentencing thousands—without trial—my father did deserve exactly that which he'd sentenced thousands to, but I could not admit it to his son. "Papa did *not* deserve that."

"Is it true? Did Papa go to the guillotine?" He clung to my hand.

I put my arm around him and hugged him to my side. "You know Papa worked for the old government?"

"So what?"

A trembling moved through me, and I hoped he couldn't feel it. "Papa was ordered to try people who were accused of crimes, crimes that if proven, were punishable by death."

He looked up, his cheeks quivering. "He sent them to the guillotine?"

"Sometimes prison and sometimes he sentenced them to execution. He was not the only person who made that decision. There was a council and jurors who decided guilt."

"If there were others, why did she call only *him* a monster?"

I longed to say: A woman who is also a monster, a woman who cares not one whit for a child's heart. I didn't want to give her the benefit of the doubt, but I didn't want Auguste to think every woman could be so cruel. "She may have lost a loved one to the guillotine, and she blames Papa."

Tears brimmed. "Do you think Papa was a monster?"

I wanted to scream at the top of my voice, yes, but I could not hurt my brother. He loved Papa. Long ago, I did too. "I think Papa did his job as best as he could. And when the old government faltered, the new Directoire needed to get rid of the old members." I longed to caress Auguste's cheek but didn't want the boys to see. "And that included Papa."

He dragged his sleeve across his eyes. I wanted to cry for my brother's hurt.

He sniffed. "Does it hurt?"

"Does—" I realized he meant the guillotine. "No. It is most humane. That is why Monsieur Guillotine invented it." At least that's what the Revolutionaries touted. I wondered why people didn't die of fright before they arrived at the machine.

"Auguste!" One of the boys held up a fish. "I hooked one."

My brother shouted. "It's huge!"

The boy held the flapping fish on a rock, and another smashed a stone on its head. "We can have it for supper!" shouted the fisherman.

Relieved by the interruption, I hoped he wouldn't ask where Papa was buried, for I suspected he'd landed in a mass grave with no marker. Another secret I couldn't tell him.

"Want to go fishing, Gen?"

"You go ahead. I must leave for Paris." I patted his hand. "Thank you for not telling Suzanne who I am. You'll continue to keep our secret? Everyone here thinks I'm a man."

"Am I not your brother?"

A surge of love brought tears, and I swallowed against them. "I am very glad and proud you are my brother."

He watched the boys, busily clobbering the poor fish. He quickly kissed my cheek and stood. "I hope you visit again, soon, Gen."

"I will." I watched him run, his posture returning to that of an excited eleven-year-old. I stood and scanned the estate. I'd clobber Suzanne the moment I laid eyes on her.

First, we had to rescue Aurélia.

# 12

# Genevière

*Paris, France*
*October* 1797

SIMON SLOWED THE horses along rue de Montpensier and stopped opposite a mansion of five floors. Lanterns blazed on either side of the grand doors to Maison de Brissault. A bluster of wind sent dried leaves swirling along the street as I sat sweating in my male finery inside the carriage, waiting. The hour was late, and the street was empty.

Inching my fingers up under my powdered wig, I scratched my scalp, reminding myself not to commit such an inelegant gesture once inside the bordel. I had pushed my hair into a bun at the top of my head before donning the wig, and its weight along with the gold-embroidered tricorne strained my neck and made my head bob. Dressed in yellow breeches and frock coat and black hat, I resembled a sunflower.

I wiped my sweaty palms along my velvet sleeves and stopped—another gesture that would reveal I was not accustomed to such luxury. I tried running my fingertips along the sleeve, as if brushing away lint. Envisioning Louis's demonstrations, I practiced looking down my nose and flicking my wrist in an I-do-not-care attitude.

We agreed Louis and Henri would arrive first and I was to wait half an hour before I entered the bordel—and to be prepared to see both Henri and Louis in the company of a few scantily clad women. That would require acting, for there was no way to prepare myself for seeing another woman tempting my husband. To keep the inevitable shock from my face, I practiced the arrogant look, again.

A man whistled as he swaggered along the street, stopped, and climbed the steps of the bordel. Another Incroyable? A queasiness moved through me. He removed his hat. The Capitaine knocked at the door. I gripped my pistol hilt. We had thought of everything but this. Henri would rip him apart with his bare hands. I gripped the leather tabs and silently lowered the window. Staying in the shadows, I aimed my pistol. I could save us all if I killed the bastard now. But what of Aurélia? I kept my thumb on the hammer.

A small African boy of about eight years, wearing bright yellow and red striped silk waistcoat, breeches, and turban, opened the door.

I lowered the pistol. I could not risk the child.

He bowed. "Bonsoir, M—."

The Capitaine twisted a gold coin in his fingers, offering it to the boy, and slammed his foot on the threshold.

The child screamed, "Madame!" He attempted to shut the door, but the Capitaine pushed him.

I jumped to help the child but sat back down. Attacking the Capitaine could further jeopardize Aurélia.

The horses whinnied, and the carriage jerked.

Simon calmed the horses with a low whisper.

I lifted the gun, keeping it aimed at the Capitaine. Light flooded the steps as the door opened, revealing a tall, bejeweled woman. Behind her stood two huge, bald men, each holding a curved sword aloft.

The Capitaine had not made friends here. His body bobbed and swayed like a snake. But when the woman stepped back and the two men came forward, their swords vibrating, the Capitaine stumbled down the steps, turned, and fled down the street. The huge men laughed and closed the door.

I wiped sweat from my upper lip. What made me think I could do this? Those men probably guarded Aurélia. How would I get her past them? Simon tapped at the carriage door and opened it. His face was grim. "It's time, Gen."

The muscles around his mouth flinched as he forced a smile. He looked as frightened as I felt. There was no time to think anymore. The men had swords, not guns, as Louis, Henri, and I had. I sucked in a breath and pushed my pistol into my waistcoat. Smoothing the padding Joliette had stitched in my frock coat, I stepped onto the street.

"Good luck, Gen. I'll be waiting." Simon patted the gun hidden beneath his cloak.

"Thank you." I forced my feet to climb but stopped and turned back to him. "Be on—"

He held the barrel of the pistol to his lips and nodded.

Louis had taught Simon to shoot, and the young man was as good a shot as Louis. I forced my shoulders down and climbed the steps, pausing at the knocker—a silver sculpture of a woman's breasts, not at all natural, far too large, and the nipples too pointed. I grabbed them, rapped, and wiped my hand on my breeches.

The door opened and the little African boy grinned. "Bonsoir, Monsieur. You come for pleasure?"

I smiled and nodded. Had the Capitaine sold him to the Madam, also? Was that why the boy feared him? A bejeweled woman approached.

She extended her hand. "Welcome, Monsieur. I am Madam Brissault." She tilted her head, a calculated gesture that sent her diamond earrings swaying.

Although tall, she was a head shorter than I and slim, yet the gown's décolletage revealed her ample bosom. Blue and gold feathers sprouted from her flame-red wig. She looked like an overdressed hen. I acted bored. "Bonsoir." I removed my hat and bowed.

"A gentleman! Welcome, Monsieur—?" She tossed my hat to the African boy.

"Detré." I forced myself not to smile.

She hooked her hand around my elbow and led me toward a salon. "Your first time."

It was not a question. This woman would remember a spider if it paid for one of her ladies. She was a police informant, paid to remember every detail. "At this establishment."

Decorated in red, black, and tarnished golds, the salon pressed down on me, until I locked eyes with Louis, quite comfortable in an overstuffed chair and a cherubic woman dressed in a transparent white gown sitting on his knee. She brushed a cluster of grapes along her bulging breasts, then plucked a grape, and fed it to him. I wanted to laugh at the absurdity. I would try alluring him that way—if we escaped. Before the fireplace, a dark-haired woman draped in a Grecian style gown stood beside Henri, running a large plume across his lap. He looked like a hare, ready to bolt.

"See anything you like?" Madam snapped open her fan.

I lifted a critical eyebrow and gave a slight shake of my head.

"We have more salons." She guided me across the hall and into another room decorated in sky blue with white clouds painted on the ceiling. Three naked men lay back on white chaises lounges while women in gauzy gowns poured oil into their hands and massaged the groaning men. Their state of arousal made heat rush up my face. How did the women remain so—bored? Maybe this salon was the men's version of heaven, but I felt like taking a hot bath with lots of soap. I shook my head.

She tapped her fan against her chin. "You wish something specific?"

I could not appear too eager. I stretched my fingers, aiming to catch the candlelight across my rings, trying to give the impression I might go elsewhere for my entertainment.

"Have you a fondness for specialties?" Her eyes were raptor-like as she beckoned me with her fan. "Boys, perhaps?"

Disgust sat bitter in the back of my throat. I pressed my teeth together to hide my certain shock. "No."

She crossed the hall, opened a door until a sliver of light escaped, and nodded her head for me to look.

Sweat collected beneath my bound breasts as I peeked. The room was draped in white cloth and, at its center, sat a woman on a golden throne. I startled, for I thought the regal African woman to be Aurélia, but this woman was not nearly as beautiful. She was naked except for a cape of gauze clipped at her neck with jewels. An angry scar in the shape of a T puckered the skin above her right breast—the brand Henri had told me the Capitaine made on his *property*. The binding around my chest tightened.

At the woman's feet lay a pale-as-bread-dough man, kissing her toes. I hoped the woman was either enjoying it or making a great deal of money for tolerating the pig. I lifted an eyebrow and nodded toward the African.

Madam tilted her head. "You prefer dark beauties?" Her voice hissed like a snake.

I thought of the previous night in bed with Louis so I could genuinely smile.

"Ah." She bustled back to the hall.

I hurried after her, hoping she would offer Aurélia, but I slowed my pace as I remembered Louis telling me to act, above all, arrogant and uninterested.

In the hall, the African boy held a tray with glasses. "Champagne, Monsieur?"

I accepted a glass and pretended to sip. "Merci."

He hurried into the Heaven salon, and I was relieved to see Louis and Henri were still enjoying the feathers and grapes.

Madam took a deep swallow. "Dark beauties are expensive, Monsieur."

"It matters not." I examined my rings.

"Double, sometimes triple the usual gratuity."

I nearly spit at the word *gratuity* but looked down my nose at her.

"I have a very special dark beauty, which requires payment in advance." She wiggled her fingers, jangling her bracelets.

The wine was tart, raw, unfiltered. I imitated Louis's pouting bottom lip, like it mattered not. I pulled out the bulging leather pouch we had filled, not with the worthless new money, but with gold. Solid gold.

Her eyes glinted like a crow's.

I should have made her wait. Now the price would increase, and negotiations would be more difficult. What if I hadn't brought enough?

She waggled her chicken-feet-like fingers. "Ten."

"Pah!" I didn't have to act. Louis told me normal rates were about one gold coin. "No woman is worth ten times the normal rate, Madam."

"This one is." Her smile was sly.

"What makes her so special?" I stifled a yawn.

She chuckled. "She is pure and unmarked."

I envisioned clawing the bitch's eyes out but remembered the branded T above the other woman's breast. I lowered my voice. "Neither matters."

She adjusted her earring. "Perhaps I can arrange a discount if you do not penetrate her."

I gulped the champagne to stop myself from spitting in her face. She was speaking of Aurélia as if she were livestock.

"Eight." Her crow eyes glinted.

"What makes this woman eight times the worth of the other

dark beauty?" I let my disgust boil, for she would interpret it as arrogance and, I hoped, back down.

"Six is my final offer, Monsieur."

I flicked my fingertips along my jabot. "I require a look, first." I would pay nothing if the woman was not Aurélia.

She licked her lips, like she was anticipating a good meal, picked up her skirts, and mounted the stairs.

I caught Louis's eye and nodded toward the stairway. He blinked and bit a grape.

My breath stuck hard below my ribs. As I climbed, I prayed Aurélia was unharmed. I gripped the balustrade to steady my hand, throbbing in want of my pistol. If Aurélia was hurt, I feared I would not be able to stop myself from killing.

# 13

## *Geneviève*

*Paris, France*
*October* 1797

Madam Brissault led me up three winding flights of steps, past sighs, whispers, and cries of passion. A male voice trumpeted like an elephant I had seen at the King's menagerie. A female giggle followed. These women were excellent actresses.

We arrived at the base of a narrow, spiraling flight of stairs where, at the top, a bald man, the size of a bear stood before the only door, a sword hanging at his side. He had terrified the Capitaine with his presence. How would I get Aurélia past him? Sweat seeped through the padding around my chest. Louis would tell me to joke, but he didn't know the size of the beast, which wasn't funny.

Louis had frightened a similar guard with his pistol when I

helped him escape prison, but I could not count on this beast fearing anything. If I tried pressing the barrel of my pistol into his flesh, he could easily overpower me before I aimed. Would a bullet stop him?

My heartbeat quickened as I realized Madam could be leading me into a trap. She had seen the bulging purse—idiotic of me to have flaunted it. The higher I climbed, the farther I was from Louis and Henri. My palm slid on the balustrade.

I forced myself to exhale slowly. Where was the other guard? I hoped not in the chamber with Aurélia. I squeezed my eyes against the image of a man watching a woman being taken against her will. Nausea roiled in me.

The door looked heavy, escape proof. Madam pulled a ring of keys from the sash tied at her waist, unlocked the bolt, and shoved the door open. A sliver of weak light escaped. She tilted her head, inviting me to look.

If Aurélia was hurt, I would not be able to control my rage. Louis's voice shouted in my mind: *Above all, do not lose control of your passion, no matter how repulsed you may become.* My heartbeat was so loud, I feared she would hear it. I gripped the doorjamb and leaned in.

The room resembled the inside of a ship, with a low sloping ceiling of horizontal wooden boards and a small bay window at the end. Candelabra sat on low tables surrounding a four-posted bed with royal blue silk hangings caught up with golden ropes at each post. Against a mound of lace-trimmed pillows lay Aurélia in a sheer white nightgown. Her eyes were closed, as if in sleep, but her position was awkward—her limbs flung out from her body and taut, like something was pulling them.

My heartbeat thundered as I followed blue velvet ribbons

snaking through the links of tarnished chains shackling her ankles and wrists to the four posters.

Flames of hate rushed through me. I dug my fingernails into the wooden door, envisioning shooting the Madam. I had to remain calm and act like a libertine to get her to cooperate. I pushed myself away from the sight and looked down my nose. "I prefer her dressed in finery and unshackled."

The Madam tilted her head. "Whatever for?"

"That is my concern, Madame, not yours."

She relocked the door. "I will return with an elegant gown, Monsieur Detré."

Keys jangled with her every step. The guard stood immoveable as a bolder.

The words I'd spoken tasted like manure. I longed to spit, but a new fear seized me. She remembered my name. She would not forget my face. Neither would the guard. They could report both me and the name Detré to the gendarmes. Although false, my male identity papers were in the name of Detré. I had not thought of this complication.

I leaned against the door. The guard flicked his eyes at me, and I straightened.

How would I get Aurélia out? She had appeared asleep, but that could be her way of fooling her assailants. I prayed she'd not been drugged. If she had, it would be impossible to get her to cooperate and help in her own rescue. She was too smart to take any food or drink. She would be weakened, but I had to rely on her intelligence.

Madam Brissault would leave me in the room, but the guard would stay at his post.

Rage pulsed my vision. I could threaten the Madam—gag

and shackle the old hen. But the guard could easily overpower both Aurélia and me, even if I held him at gunpoint. Somehow, I had to get rid of the guard.

I shoved my fingers up under the wig and scratched my damp scalp. Louis had warned me to think of more than one option. If I asked the guard to get me some champagne, would he leave his post? How would I get Aurélia to recognize me?

Huffing and carrying a blue silk gown, the Madam climbed the steps. She put out her hand. "Your final gratuity, Monsieur?"

Hand on the hilt of his sword, the guard towered above me.

I reached into my waistcoat and handed over six gold coins.

She slipped the money into her bodice, unlocked the door, and shoved it open, motioning me inside.

Searching the room for an open window, another door, a balcony, I followed.

The guard closed the door with a thud. The stagnant air was thick with dust.

Aurélia's eyes opened to slits.

I brought my hand to my heart and mouthed, *It's me.* Her expression didn't change, and I feared she didn't recognize me.

The Madam dropped the gown on a chair and hurried to the bed.

I withdrew my pistol, keeping it hidden under my frock coat, and watched for the opportunity to overtake her.

She stood near Aurélia's head, pulled out her keys, and turned to me. "I will unlock her for you, Monsieur."

But the shackle wasn't fastened. None of them were!

She turned and leaned over Aurélia. I brought up the pistol.

Aurélia's eyes were wild with hatred. Her hand shot out and

clutched the old hen's cheeks and jaw. The Madam jerked away.

I pressed the pistol against the back of her neck. "Don't make a sound." She stiffened. "Do exactly as I say, and you won't be hurt."

At the corner of my eye a glimmer of metal streaked through the candlelight.

Aurélia slashed a dagger across the Madam's neck.

A scream tore up my throat. I clamped my hand over my mouth.

Blood spurted over Aurélia's sheer white sleeve, her face, her hair.

The Madam gagged and pitched forward, arms flailing.

I tried to stop her from falling atop Aurélia, but my hand would not obey.

A gurgling sound and a metallic scent of blood filled the air.

Aurélia shoved the woman off and bolted onto her knees. She brought the dagger above her head and plunged it into the woman's back.

The old hen collapsed, a soggy breath rattling out of her. Her eyes dulled.

Pressure burst in my chest. No, no, no, no, no. We have no plan for this. We will all be guillotined for murder.

Aurélia jumped from the bed and heaved for a breath. *Where is my son?* she mouthed.

"Safe...with Joliette...Louis's orphanage." I rubbed my chest, forcing my words to come out. "No one will find him."

She yanked the blood-splattered nightdress over her head, poured water on it from a pitcher standing on the bedside table, wiped the blood from her face and hair and hands, and threw the wet mess on the bed.

Now clean, she donned the blue silk gown. She was calm, like she was dressing for breakfast, as if she had rehearsed her actions a hundred times. She probably had. "How?" I grabbed the stained nightdress. "How did you unlock the chains?"

Turning her back to me, she shook the bodice, wanting me to button it. She had stabbed a woman and was calmer than I was.

The stench of blood and stink of perfume nauseated me. Candlelight flickered across the Madam's cold black eyes. Blood covered her chest, necklace, bodice. The room swirled, and I forced myself to inhale. I had to take charge, but my body felt like stone. I forced myself to press my fingers against Madam's neck. Not an inkling of life. Why hadn't we planned for this? How would we get past the guard who knew the Madam was in here? He'd kill us both. I balled up the stained nightdress and shoved it under my waistcoat.

Aurélia waved her arms. I forced myself to move, buttoned the bodice, and whispered, "Henri and Louis are downstairs. Simon has the carriage waiting."

She nodded sharply. Her breathing was that of a wild beast, deep and low and paced, like she was preparing for another attack. She was ready. I was not. I was numb.

I swallowed against the bile building in my throat. What should we do with the body? What did it matter? Blood soaked the bed.

Shouts and pounding came from below. Louis had planned to make a ruckus if I took too long to find Aurélia. Please God, let that be Louis and Henri causing a distraction.

Aurélia withdrew the knife from the body and handed it to me.

Like an idiot, I stood paralyzed, gripping the weapon, watching as she ripped off the Madam's shoes and put them on. They could trace the knife. I wiped the blade, secured it in my boot, and grabbed the keys from Madam's sash. Gold glinted in her cleavage. I grabbed the coins I'd given her and shoved them in my waistcoat.

I urged Aurélia toward the door. "If the guard is here, I'll shoot him."

She stood calmly and nodded, like she was going to church. I wished for her serenity.

Voices and a ruckus from below rose. "A fight in the salon!" The little boy's voice came from the other side of the door. Heavy footsteps thundered down the stairs.

Louis and Henri had promised a diversion to summon the guards, and this had to be it.

Gripping the pistol, I opened the door and peeked about. The hall was empty. Thank you, Louis. I waved Aurélia forward.

With the rightful pride of a queen, she marched toward the door. I grabbed her hand. "If another guard comes, distract him. I will take over from there."

She nodded, taking on her regal posture as easily as Louis donned his courtier arrogance. We slipped out into the empty hall. I locked the door behind us, shoved the keys into my waistcoat, and followed her.

As we rounded the top of the last staircase, I stopped Aurélia. We stood on the staircase watching the hall below. Her hand grew cold in mine. The image of the Madam's shackled body made my mouth go dry. I wished Aurélia had killed the Capitaine also. Despite Madam's death, he'd still be after Aurélia, wanting to sell her again—if we escaped this mess.

Aurélia calmly descended. Had I not known her I would not have noticed the slight tremor running through her body.

The African boy stood to the side of the great door, his eyes large, his mouth open as he followed Aurélia's every move.

We hurried down the last steps. Aurélia strode to the door.

He heaved the door open and smiled up at her, his face awash in admiration. "Where you go, my lady?" He held out my tricorne.

Aurélia tenderly caressed his cheek, tilted her head toward the carriage, and stepped into the night.

I grabbed my hat, clutched her elbow, and together we flew to the waiting carriage. I helped her up the step and turned to see Henri's face, stricken with worry. He clambered in, took Aurélia into his arms, and fell back onto the bench, cradling her.

I looked back. "Where's Louis?"

"He said to leave without him," Henri whispered.

I gripped the carriage door. "I will not."

# 14

## Geneviève

*Paris, France*
*October* 1797

I DARED NOT GO back. The horses stomped. "Why did he say to leave?" I hissed.

"The guard stopped him," Henri said.

Louis could be charming the guards, and I could not interfere. But he didn't know the Madam was dead, and if anyone discovered her body, he'd face the guillotine tomorrow. An ache squeezed my heart. I will not leave you, Louis. I pulled out my pistol.

Light and laughter spilled out of the bordel as the door opened.

My thumb tensed on the pistol's hammer.

Louis ran to the coach, jumped in, and slammed the door. The carriage jolted.

Looking out of the window, relief washed over me as the bordel's lanterns receded.

I closed my eyes against the image of my father, his hands tied behind him, standing in the wagon headed for the guillotine. I was glad he was dead, for he wouldn't be the one sentencing me to execution. We passed a streetlamp that lighted up the carriage.

Henri cradled his wife like a baby. He clung to her as if she were life itself. "I'm so sorry I left you." Henri's muffled sobs tore at my heart. He'd been terrified he would lose Aurélia. He'd been lost without her. As lost as I would be without Louis.

I lowered the window and studied the empty streets. Not even a stray cat. We'd not planned to escape a murder. The carriage jolted, pressing me into Louis. I whispered, "The Madam is dead."

"Shot?" His voice vibrated low, like a cello string.

I shook my head, flicked my eyes toward Aurélia, and made a stabbing motion.

He rolled his fist, indicating the knife. He wanted to know if we left it behind.

I pushed my left boot forward and tipped my head toward it.

He closed his eyes, hunched over, and leaned his elbows on his legs.

Now both of us could work on a scheme for a way out of this. The carriage rattled over cobbles as the horses broke into a gallop.

Aurélia lifted her hand to caress Henri's face and the faint light of a street lantern illuminated the angry red welt circling her wrist.

The guillotine was too merciful a punishment for the Capitaine. He had kidnapped a free woman and sold her into slavery, and the Madam had imprisoned her as a slave for sex. Yet we would be the ones to face the guillotine, for in the eyes of the law, Aurélia was a piece of stolen property. The image of the Madam's blood-covered body wavered, and I shook my head to free myself of it. Aurélia was also a murderess, yet she'd killed in self-defense.

The injustice of it burned like fire. Watching out the window for followers, I silently urged Simon to prod the horses. If gendarmes stopped us, every one of us would be tortured until we confessed to the murder.

# 15

# Geneviève

*Château de LaGarde Orphanage*
*October* 1797

**V**IOLET LIGHT CREPT across the frost covering the meadows as the horses galloped east. Perhaps because of the early hour no gendarmes had been patrolling, and we were not stopped. When I glimpsed the orphanage, a tiredness seized my aching arms and legs.

Although I longed for the safety of the vineyard, Simon needed sleep, and we required another carriage to accommodate Joliette and the children. I leaned close to Louis and whispered, "We should send Henri and Aurélia as far from Paris as possible."

"I will have my groomsman drive them to the château." Louis pounded on the ceiling and urged Simon to the stables.

A tall young man pushed open the stable doors and ran out. Louis jumped out, asking the groom for his carriage.

"My lady! My lady," a child's voice called out from behind.

It was too early for one of the orphans to be awake. Had we been followed? I jumped out.

A scuffling noise and a spray of gravel came from behind the carriage. Louis emerged holding the little African boy who thrashed against his hold. He knelt and held the boy tightly. "Where were you hiding?"

"I rode on the back, like a footman, Monsieur." His face beamed with pride. "Where is my lady?"

"You held on all that way?" A shiver of pain crossed my heart at the thought of what might have happened had he fallen.

He smiled. "I open the great door of the bordel all day, all night. I am strong."

"What is your name?" Louis asked.

"Fortuné."

"You live at the bordel?"

"I did, Monsieur." Louis released him, and the boy climbed into the carriage and flung himself across Aurélia's lap.

Henri jolted. Aurélia welcomed him into her arms and patted the boy's back as he cried. "My lady, I promised I go with you."

The dawn's light reflected off the boy's yellow and red silk frock coat casting a golden aura over Aurélia's face. Suddenly I understood. He'd given her the dagger. He'd unlocked her shackles! The boy had saved her life, and Aurélia promised she would take him with her.

The image of Aurélia caressing his cheek when we left was

more poignant, now. Had I been in his place, I would not have left her either.

Aurélia caressed the boy's cheek and kissed his forehead.

"Charles is safe with Joliette," I whispered. "Do you wish to take Fortuné with you to the château?"

She rubbed the boy's back and mouthed, *I want Charles.* Fear filled her eyes, such a contrast to the fierce hatred that had enabled her to kill. Her hands vibrated. Clearly, she realized she was in even greater danger now. We all were.

"I'll bring Charles down to you, and then you all must leave immediately." I ran and retrieved a sleepy Charles. Aurélia wept as she embraced her son. The two boys seemed delighted to meet one another. The groomsman cracked the whip and their carriage sped off leaving a cloud of dust.

# 16

# *Geneviève*

*Château de LaGarde Orphanage*
*October* 1797

Simon drove us to the front of the château. As I grabbed my tricorne, a sinking sensation pulled in me. I searched beneath the benches. Neither Louis nor Henri had been wearing their hats when they left the bordel. I fingered the ribbon inside my tricorne. Stitched inside every piece of Louis's clothing was a pale-blue ribbon, upon which the initials LG were embroidered. The ribbons could be identified by a milliner or tailor, enabling gendarmes to trace Louis back to his former château. We'd left behind evidence.

We entered the great hall.

"Louis! I've missed you." Suzanne, the bitch who'd told my brother our father was guillotined, descended the stairs. "I'm so glad you've returned!"

"Suzanne, you remember my friend, Jean Detré?"

Stopping at the landing, Suzanne nodded down at me. The first time I met the former whore at the orphanage, she ignored me. The second time, I accidentally or perhaps purposefully, spilled wine on her gown. Both times she attempted to seduce Louis, and she'd try again.

I nodded. "Enchantée, Madame."

Suzanne descended the stairs, inhaling so deeply her breasts bulged over her lace neckline. She ignored me and reached for Louis.

Louis put out his hands to stop her, but she cackled and reached for his manhood.

I lurched between them, pushing her away. She grasped my wig.

Cold air tingled my scalp.

She threw the wig on the floor, stumbled back against the balustrade, and shrieked with laughter.

I swiped the wig. "Louis is married."

"Your promise," Louis snarled.

She cackled. "What does a wife matter to a mistress?"

I stood tall, towering over her, the wig shaking in my grip. "He's married to me."

She burst into laughter.

Louis let out a low growl.

Damn it. Why didn't I think first? Heat flushed through me. I broke my promise. I identified myself as his wife. Louis was furious.

"Suzanne, return to your chamber, please." Louis's voice was low.

"I'll await you there." Although short, Suzanne acted tall with her superior attitude. She ascended the steps like she owned them.

Louis glared at me. My shoulders dropped. The memory of his voice taunted me: *No matter the circumstance.* I should have kept my word, but what wife wouldn't react? "Did you want me to put the wig back on and continue the charade?"

He turned away and climbed the steps.

All the good work I had done to help rescue Aurélia, and I spoiled it by telling a big-bosomed whore I was Louis's wife. His voice blared in my mind: *Your word defines your honor and our trust.* I had broken his trust.

My feet dragged as I climbed the stairs. It was not just me I revealed. I exposed all of us to a spiteful woman who was certain to inform upon us. I had to ensure she would not report us.

17

# *Geneviève*

*Château de LaGarde Orphanage*
*October* 1797

**M**Y HEAD HANGING like a scolded dog, I followed Louis. Heat streamed off him.

A lone candle flickered on a side table and, not wanting to extinguish it, I gently shut the door. As the lock clicked, he rounded on me.

"You promised. You said, 'You have my word. I will not reveal myself—no matter the circumstance.'"

"She saw I was a woman."

"Had you not interfered, she would not have grabbed the wig." He slammed his hand on the table, rattling the brandy decanter. "And, you did not have to tell her you are my wife!"

Guilt pricked my skin. I tossed the wig on a chair. "What would you have done if a man did the same to me?"

Although he stood across the room, the air crackled between us. "Had I known you could not keep your word I would not have trusted you to help rescue Aurélia."

I was wrong to not honor my word, and I should admit it, but I couldn't help defending myself. "You couldn't have done it without me." I hated my waspish, taunting reply.

"You act without thinking."

"You're lucky I didn't think about what might happen to me when I took your name off the guillotine list."

The vein in the side of his neck throbbed. "You have endangered every one of us. Does your word mean nothing to you?"

"I was not born a Noble of the Sword," I snapped.

"The devil!" His fist slammed upon the table. "You do not have to be a Noble of the Sword to be a person of honor."

I was sick of his talk of honor. "Being born to wealth makes keeping one's word easier when you're not starving." I lifted my chin. "You expect me to stand by as another woman lays claim to my husband?"

"I allow no one to lay claim to me."

"Does that include your wife?" I wished for more than the watery dawn light to see the effect of my words.

He grabbed my arms, and I winced. "If I wished to be unfaithful, you could not stop me. My fidelity comes from me. It is who I am. I am a man of my word."

I shrank back.

"Who are you without your word?" His grip tightened as he shook me.

"I don't know!"

His eyebrows lifted.

I'd been dressing like a man for so long, I truly didn't know *who* I was. I was Louis's wife, I was vigneron of Château de Verzat, I was stepmother to Louis's daughter. Who I was, without the roles I took on, I did not know. But I knew *what* I was. "I am a woman who dresses and acts as a man."

"I did not marry a man." His eyes darkened.

"I know I act without thinking. It's stupid of me, but I can't stop myself." I squeezed my eyes, the memory of Pierre's widow's face sending spikes of guilt into my chest. Pierre had not wanted to make a false identity card for Simon, but I'd promised I'd convince my father to excuse him if he were caught. My father had sent Pierre for execution before I could remove his name from the guillotine list. "I promised Pierre, and I didn't keep my word."

The early morning light caught the deepening creases around Louis's eyes. "You had no control over that." His grip loosened. "But you did have control this evening. You did not have to say you are my wife. If anyone reports one of us, Suzanne can now connect us all."

"I am sorry."

"Your apology is as meaningless as your word." He let go of me, pulled off his jabot, and entered his dressing room.

The sudden coolness terrified me more than his grip.

I picked up the candle, caught a flame from the fire's embers, and replaced it. I should admit my wrong and beg forgiveness. Why was I being so stubborn? I struggled to inhale against the binding around my chest. If I had lost Louis's love for me, I would die.

I whispered, "Aurélia killed the Madam—we need to devise a plan."

His hand stilled on his buttons.

"The body is in the room that imprisoned Aurélia. I locked it and took the key, but they probably have discovered it by now."

He let out a puff of air, as he did whenever he was stymied by terrible news. "We will figure out what to do after we rest." Wearing a nightshirt, he got into bed. "Good night."

Words stuck in my throat. He had once told me he admired me, my bravery, my courage, my intelligence. But now, he was not only disappointed in me but also ashamed of me. I had to explain why I had failed, but I wasn't sure I understood it myself. I could not change my behavior if I didn't understand it.

"Louis?"

He mumbled.

"Please help me…" I stared at the person I loved most in the world. The sensation of sliding down a ravine made me grab the bedpost, and the words poured out of their own accord.

"I impersonated my brother to attend Université—both crimes. I carried false papers. I lied to nuns. I stole money from my father. I removed your name and others from the guillotine lists. I got you out of prison. I have dressed as a man, harbored clergy, and even killed." I stood still, arms trembling. "Not keeping my word pales in comparison to all my other crimes. Why is this crime so egregious to you?"

"Not keeping one's word endangers others who are depending upon your promise."

"I promised you I'd rescue Louisa's maman, but I failed. And I have never forgiven myself." My shoulders released, and my arms fell to my sides.

He came to me slowly. Wrapped his arms around me. I wanted to stay in his embrace forever.

"And I have never forgiven myself for asking it of you." He

caressed my cheek. "No one could save Magdeleine. But you saved Louisa."

A shudder moved through me. "Sometimes life doesn't let you keep your word."

"You tried to keep your word to Magdeleine and Pierre. And trying to keep one's word is most honorable."

"I should've tried harder. I reacted instead of thinking. I'm so sorry."

He pulled me to him. We held each other, our breaths deepening, our hearts beating against each other. Tears came with the realization that I had never felt so safe.

He pulled back. "Let us not think anymore and get some sleep now." He released me and returned to bed. "We can discuss this when we return to the estate."

I missed his warmth. I longed to return to our comfortable, caring love, but a cold wedge of unresolved anger still separated us. "Good night."

I poured water into the basin and rinsed my face. Blood stained my fingernails. The spurting blood from the Madam's throat blared in my mind. I splashed water and as the water hit, more tears came. Not wanting Louis to hear me cry, I pressed a serviette to my mouth. He asked nothing of me but the best of who I was. And who was I if I could not honor my word? How could he trust me? He could not depend on me if he could not trust me.

I pulled Aurélia's stained nightgown from my waistcoat and threw it on the embers in the fireplace. Flames burst and devoured the evidence. A bloody stink filled the room, and I wanted to gag. Removing the noble finery, I smoothed every piece and hung them on pegs.

Louis could have had Suzanne, but he married me. A queasiness moved in my belly. I felt threatened. Suzanne wanted me to feel threatened, so she had power over me. My body reacted so quickly my brain did not have time to remember my promise. In the future, how would I stop my body from reacting to give my brain time to think?

I unwound the strip of fabric binding my chest and cupped my breasts. Suzanne's were so much bigger and more beautiful than mine. I told her I was Louis's wife because I lacked self-assurance. I unpinned my hair, letting it fall about my shoulders, and ran my fingers through the waves. At least I had beautiful, thick locks the shiny, blue-black color of a raven's wing. I felt a bit pretty because of my hair, but not when it was pinned up under a tricorne.

Suzanne's laughter echoed along with the heat of my humiliation. I tugged one of Louis's nightshirts from a pile of perfectly folded linen. Feeling threatened by a prostitute was nothing compared to the despair I felt at disappointing my husband and, worse, losing his faith in me.

I shrugged the nightshirt over my head and stood watching him. How could he sleep? My mind was in such a whirl, it would never rest. Yet, his soft breathing was as comforting a sound as I had ever heard.

His words rang in my mind. I had no control over my failures. I had tried my best. But those deaths had shaken my belief in myself. No wonder I dressed as a man—I thought it was male clothing that gave me courage. I had to learn to believe in the woman I was, and when I did, maybe I wouldn't need to wear breeches.

The stink of perfume, the splattering blood, the sound of Madam's rattling breath haunted me. I climbed into bed and pressed myself against Louis's back. If Suzanne learned of the Madam's murder, would she report me? Us? Nausea swam in me. I would never forgive myself if Aurélia was recaptured because of my stupid jealousy.

# 18

# *Geneviève*

*Château de LaGarde Orphanage*
*October* 1797


A FIERCE WAVE OF nausea woke me. I bolted out of bed, ran to the wash basin, and heaved a stream of yellow bile.

Louis was at my side in an instant. His cool hand pressed against my forehead. "Take a deep breath." He held my hair back and leaned me against him.

I shivered and whimpered. My body arched as I heaved again, and I shuddered like I was ridding myself of a week of meals. But nothing came up. I had sipped the champagne and not eaten since the day before. I gripped the table, panting, my legs trembling.

Louis pulled a blanket from the bed and wrapped me in it, then poured a glass of water, and brought it to me. "Sip a little at a time."

The room spun as I tried to straighten. Sunlight, too bold for morning, flooded the chamber. It had to be afternoon. The water hit my empty stomach and chilled me further.

Louis rubbed my back. "Feeling better?"

"A bit." His concern relieved the tension in my stomach. "I did not sleep well. I want to apologize."

"I accepted your apology last night. Would you like to have some bread?"

"Thank you." I took his warm, gentle hand. "I am so sorry, Louis."

"It is forgotten. Do you wish to go to the kitchen, or shall I bring some bread and tea?"

"I'll join you. I would like something before we leave for the vineyard."

My breasts were still tender from wearing the binding the day before, so I did not wrap the cloth around my chest. I selected one of Louis's fine cotton tunics, soft against my skin. After tying my hair back with a leather string, I donned my breeches, waistcoat, frock coat, and boots, and grabbed my tricorne.

"You and Henri left your hats at the bordel. And they all had the little ribbons leading back to you."

"You are right." He ran his hands through his hair. "I will ask Adrien to tell any gendarmes who might arrive that clothing was recently stolen."

He locked the chamber door, and we headed for the kitchen where Cook made a delightful fuss at having Louis seated at her scarred chopping block.

She waved her long knife between slicing leeks. "You are

too thin, Louis. Your father had a big belly," she slapped her own, "like mine." She laughed heartily.

I tore a piece of bread, chomped it, and swallowed. The bread calmed my stomach.

"I'm glad to see you eating, Monsieur Jeanne." She winked.

I stopped chewing. She used the feminine form of Jean, but she had known me as Jean Detré every time I visited the orphanage, at least every other month. Would my stepmother discover my true identity and report me?

Suzanne came in, jabbering to Cook. "Did you see the salope Louis dragged in last night?" She saw us and stopped, her face reddening.

Cook sighed her disgust and continued slicing.

Louis poured coffee.

Suzanne pulled a basket from a hook. "I'm off to the market." She left us.

Louis stood and offered his hand. "Let us walk a bit before we gather Joliette and the children."

In silence, we walked along the garden, around the stables, and up the drive to the front of the château. As we turned the corner, we jolted to a stop.

Six armed gendarmes and a coach stood, waiting.

# 19

# *Geneviève*

*Château de LaGarde Orphanage*
*October* 1797

**M**Y LEGS WEAKENED. Had someone followed our carriage last night? At least we had sent Aurélia and Fortuné to the vineyard.

"Let me do all the talking." Louis patted my back.

Trust Louis. Keep your mouth shut, I repeated as I walked. I was glad to give him control; he was much more convincing a liar than I was. I longed to take his hand, but I was dressed as a man. The same dread filled me when I watched my father being driven to the guillotine. The shouts of the crowd, *Join your victims,* echoed. The same alarm rose in me now, like a stink coming off me, and I prayed the gendarmes would not sense it.

The leader, dressed in a marine-blue frock coat with red collar, lapels, and cuffs rested his hand upon the pommel of his sword and stood glaring at us.

Louis stopped. "Good afternoon."

The other men positioned themselves so neither Louis nor I could flee.

The leader grunted. "Names."

"Louis Corrié and, may I present, Jean Detré."

"We have a report that there is a woman masquerading as a man here."

Suzanne must have reported me. If they were here for murder suspects, they would have asked where we were last light. My heartbeat quickened. They were after me. Only me.

Louis waved his hand, as if this were a trifling matter. "This is an orphanage, Citizen. We gladly accept whatever clothing is donated, and the children are glad for breeches or gowns, for they have nothing."

Louis's quick thinking never ceased to amaze me.

The leader grimaced. "Not a child. An adult woman." He thrust out his hand. "Papers."

My heartbeat drummed. Women who dressed as men were condemned to an insane asylum—a place more dangerous than a prison. Why did I not bring a gown with me from the chateau? Because my stepmother would recognize me. I pressed my lips together. Trust Louis. Keep your mouth shut.

"The women who work here also need clothing and are not particular." Louis smiled. "We are a very poor group, poor and humble."

The leader waggled his fingers. "Papers."

Louis reached inside his waistcoat, pulled out his false

papers, and offered them. I was listed on his papers as his wife, but I could not admit to being her. At least my false papers matched my gender and were in my frock coat. I reached, but Louis put up his hand—a warning that I allow him to handle this. Trust Louis. I pressed my hand against my thumping heart.

Louis stepped forward. "This is Magdeleine Corrié, my wife. A not-so-humble recipient of clothing. We are on our way to Nantes and even you would admit two men are safer traveling that distance than a woman and a man. There are brigands who look for weak targets. My wife dresses as a man for safety on our journey. Besides, we are too poor to buy her a gown. She wears donated clothing."

The leader examined Louis's papers, gripped them to his chest, and glared at me. "But you are known to some as Jean Detré?"

"Yes." Regret seeped through me. They were looking for Jean Detré. The name I'd given to Madam Brissault. I should have kept my mouth shut.

"I will give you one opportunity to reveal your real name."

I would not speak and make the same mistake again. I stood tall and stared at the gendarme's pocked nose.

"You are married to a woman who dresses as a man, Monsieur?" The leader spat, spittle landing just before Louis's boot.

Louis inhaled deeply. "As I said, she is Magdeleine Corrié, my wife, who dresses as a man to protect her virtue."

The gendarmes sniggered.

The vein in Louis's neck pulsed.

The leader motioned to his men. "Put her in the carriage."

"No!" I reached for Louis, my hands clutching air. A gendarme gripped my elbow. I yanked away my arm. "No!"

Louis lunged for me, but two gendarmes pushed him aside, knocking him against the carriage.

Hands seized my arms. "I am not a criminal." Nausea rose. I bent forward and heaved. Vomit splashed. The men let go of me and jumped back.

"Putain!" The gendarme called me a whore. Louis would kill him.

Louis pulled me close and handed me his handkerchief. "Go along with them," he whispered, "otherwise they will harm you."

I wiped my face and glared at the men. "I will get into the carriage without your assistance, thank you." I stepped up and slid onto the carriage bench. Two of the men got in and sat opposite me. Another slammed the door, reminding me of the slamming of the door to Louis's prison cell. I shuddered.

"Where are you taking her?" Louis shouted.

The leader climbed up to the driver's bench. "Hôtel Salpêtrière, where all whores are imprisoned."

The insane asylum. I lurched to the window and pulled the leather strap, releasing the pane of glass. I reached, fingers grasping. "Louis!"

He kissed my hand. "Calm yourself. I promise I will get you out."

"Louis." I hated the cry in my voice. "Louisa's favorite poupette is in our chamber."

The carriage jostled and began to roll. Louis stepped back, but I kept my eyes on him. Trust Louis.

He stood before the château's great doors, arms hanging helplessly at his sides, his face so full of sorrow, I regretted looking back. Through all our dangers and escapes I had never seen fear in Louis's eyes.

How would he get me out of an insane asylum? How would I survive it? I wiped my face and wrapped his handkerchief around my fingers, remembering how Magdeleine treasured every lavender-scented handkerchief I brought her. I closed my eyes against the image of her lifeless body lying in filthy, bloody hay. My heartbeat raced. Louis must be thinking of her, also. He must be terrified. I shook my head and forced my eyes to open.

Nausea rolled in me, and the gendarmes' menacing faces swam before me. Perhaps if I vomited again, they would get out of the carriage, and I could run when we stopped. I could not be weak. I had to be strong.

I could not outrun all these men. I had to stay alive, until Louis got me out. He promised, and he kept his word. No matter where they took me or what they did to me—I had to survive—at all costs. I had to trust Louis. And believe in myself.

20

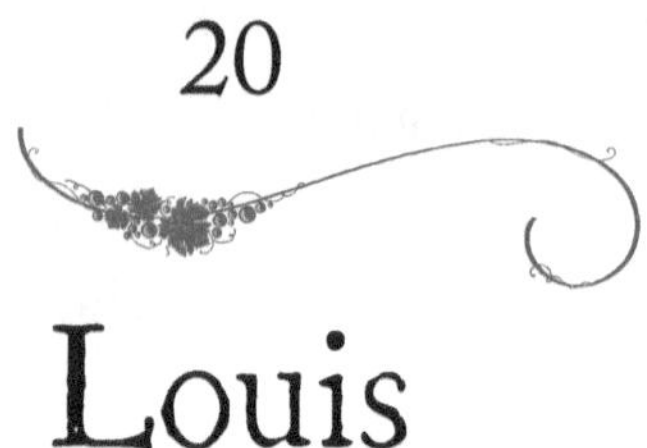

# Louis

*Château de LaGarde Orphanage*
*October* 1797

Louis stared at the rumbling carriage, his fingers scraping air. Not only would Geneviève be locked in a cell, but she would also be warding off insane prisoners—and lascivious guards. The damp stench of the cell he had occupied for two years seeped into him. The rasping of the key in the lock grated in his mind. He raked his hair. She was in terrible danger. And, if they connected her to the Madam's murder, they'd send her to the guillotine.

He rushed to the orphanage. The slam of the great doors echoed in the emptiness. The dazzling light of the chandelier, the lavender scent, the children's laughter rumbling above— none of it a comfort to him. Nothing mattered without Geneviève.

An ache wrapped around his chest as he remembered promising his first love he would get her out of prison, but she had died there. He could not fail Geneviève as he had failed Magdeleine.

He gripped the balustrade and climbed the steps, wincing at the anger he had directed at Geneviève. Although he thought her beautiful, she did not think she was. No wonder she felt compelled to claim him. He should have been kinder. More compassionate. More understanding.

He admired her confidence, her strength. Geneviève often hid her hands in the presence of other ladies because she was embarrassed by her scars and calluses—proof that, although she was vigneron, she was willing to work as hard as anyone else. When she first visited him in prison, telling him he would not go to the guillotine, he had not believed her. And she had pinched him, hard, to wake him up to his good fortune.

His harsh words from the previous night clanged. He rubbed his temples, wishing he had not been so angry. He unlocked his brother's former chamber and locked the door behind him.

Joliette wrung her hands. "Where is Geneviève?"

"You and the children must remain hidden. There is a spy amongst us." He walked to the window and snapped the blue velvet drape closed. "Someone reported her for dressing as a man. Gendarmes arrested her and are taking her to Hôtel Salpêtrière."

Joliette lurched toward him. "You saved the lives of the women and children who live here. Who would do such a thing?"

"Whomever reported her could report you and Guillaume for being noble émigrés."

"We must get her out." Joliette's eyes darkened.

Louis stared at the pattern of stags leaping across the pale-blue carpet. He and his younger brother had pretended to ride the stags when they were children. Geneviève would laugh when he told her.

Joliette brought a taper to the fire, lighting the lit candle. "Who do you know that has the power to release her?"

He rubbed the back of his neck, images of the Court of Versailles ripping through his mind. A thin, sharp-nosed man, wearing a yellow-silk frock coat, entertaining courtiers with his shipwreck stories came to mind. The man had voted to behead the King, yet he had brought down Robespierre and, consequently, become a Director. "There is only one man with the power to release her."

She turned so fast her skirts rustled. "Who?"

"Paul Barras," he whispered.

She jerked. "The same man who decreed all émigrés must leave." She paced. "He will remember you as a courtier and assume you're a Royalist. You would be delivering your head upon a silver platter."

Louis blew out a breath, cringing at the memory of his own arrogance. If he revealed himself, he might be delivering himself and his wife to the guillotine. "I wish I had not treated him like the lowly vicomte he was."

"That was long ago. And your behavior was expected protocol at that time." A far-away look came over her. "Do you know any other members of the Directoire?"

"No."

Holding a rosary, she was as calm and poised as she had

been at Versailles. "If Barras has the power, how can you get to him?"

"I have no idea. He was a corrupt little lapdog." Louis poured brandy. "I despised him."

"I know someone who knows him intimately, in every sense of the word." She sat on the sofa. "You know her, too."

He searched his blurred memory of painted faces, but none was sharp. "Who?"

"Do you remember the creole wife of Marquis de Beauharnais's son?"

"Pah." Disdain flooded him. "He was no Noble of the Sword. He bought his title." Yet he envisioned the lowly creature as if she stood before him. "His wife was the woman who was forever conniving to be presented at Court. The small woman with bad teeth and named after a flower."

"Rose. Rose de Beauharnais." Joliette tapped her fan. "She was widowed and is now Commander Bonaparte's wife, but she was mistress to Barras."

Louis sat next to her, surprised by her candor. He remembered a pamphlet caricature of two naked women dancing for Barras with Bonaparte looking on. One of the women became Bonaparte's wife. He had thought it gossip, but there was some truth to the slander. "You suggest I ask her to persuade Barras on my behalf."

"Bonaparte calls her Joséphine."

"Marriage changes a woman's family name, but what man changes a woman's first name?" Louis huffed a breath, imagining what Geneviève might do in such a circumstance.

"He did not like the common name, Rose, and so used the

feminine form of Marie-Joséphe, another of her given names. It is rumored she is in need of funds."

Louis recalled other caricatures depicting Marie Antoinette as frugal compared to Joséphine.

Joliette rested her hand on Louis's arm. "Have you funds?"

He closed his eyes, seeing his mother's emeralds, rubies, diamonds. He had not touched them, knowing the government could change in an instant, and he might need them to survive another regime. But it was the survival of Geneviève he needed to ensure. "I wanted to give Maman's jewels to Geneviève." He pulled his hair. "But she would never wear them. Trading them for her life is a far better investment."

Joliette smiled. "I am certain Geneviève would agree."

Gratitude moved through him. He stood and shook himself. "I want to get her out of there as soon as possible. She was ill this morning."

"What was wrong?"

"She vomited upon awaking and again when the gendarmes seized her."

Joliette's face glowed. "I believe Geneviève is with child."

The room rocked around him. "With child?" A bubble of happiness buoyed, expanding his chest, yet the image of her in a prison cell sent a shiver through him.

"The same happened to me the first time I was with child, and I thought it sea sickness. It is very early. She might not even know she is expecting."

Louis pressed his fist to his heart and looked up to the ceiling, blinking back tears. Gilded plaster rosettes and cherubs circled the chandelier's medallion. He saw Geneviève with their baby at her breast. The child had Geneviève's dove-gray eyes and black curls.

Joy and sorrow and love and a terrifying helplessness washed through him. "I must get her out of there…Louisa's maman died giving birth to her in a prison cell."

"You will get her out. Félicitations."

He emptied the glass. "I will visit Rose today."

Joliette retrieved the brandy. "Would you like me to write to her and request a meeting for you tomorrow afternoon?"

"Tomorrow?" Louis rubbed his forehead. "Why not this evening?"

"Observing the protocol of requesting a visit puts you in a more powerful position. I can flatter her with a courtier's protocol, which she will lap like nectar. Take clothing and food to Geneviève today and explain you will get her out soon. You will give her hope." She poured another measure of brandy. "You might also tell her of my observation. That will bring her joy."

His legs gave out, and he sat on a chair with a thud. "You do not know Geneviève removed my name from the guillotine list before she rescued me from prison." He shook his head. "Comte Louis de LaGarde is still a wanted man. When I reveal myself, I might be sending us both to the guillotine."

Joliette put her hand on his shoulder. "Is anyone left in the government who knew of your imprisonment?"

He shrugged. "Most of the Prosecutor's papers were used against him. Geneviève and I attended every day of his trial, and neither my name nor any of the papers she altered were provided as evidence."

"Perhaps you are as lucky as Rose."

"I wish I had not been such an arrogant ass at Versailles." He rubbed his eyes, seeing his boastful self, twirling his rapier, taunting a lower courtier. He had no memory of the poor fool's face or name. "The current Directors might seek revenge for my humiliating one or all of them. But I must take that risk."

"Perhaps you can negotiate for Rose's secrecy. If she promises first to get Barras to release Geneviève, you will pay her with a bracelet or necklace. If she promises not to report either of you, you could pay her with earrings or a brooch. You and Geneviève and Louisa may have to emigrate." She looked at something far away. "We all may have to leave France."

Louis pressed the heels of his hands to his eyes. How could he manipulate the greedy Rose? He would have to return to his courtly ways. Flatter. Charm. Lie. "It is rumored that Barras has all the vices of a king and none of the virtues. He could be easily bribed."

"Reminding Barras of the amount of taxes Château de Verzat pays might make him very happy if we promise to increase production—which we could only do if Henri and I are in France and Geneviève is in the vineyard."

She placed her hand at the base of her throat. "I have my maman's emeralds. They should pay for both Henri and my names and your and Geneviève's." She drummed her fingers. "May I go with you?"

"Pah! And endanger yourself?" He could not admit he would welcome her expertise, influence, and her power as a former courtier. He should be able to rescue Geneviève on his own, but Joliette would be thinking clearly when his mind and heart were a jumble.

"My negotiation skills will help save all our lives." She folded her fan. "I will pack some clothing and food you can take to Geneviève."

He lurched to stand. "Please, keep Louisa and Guillaume in their chamber. The person who reported Geneviève could harm the children as well."

"Of course." She hurried away.

He sat rubbing his eyes. He hated asking for help. Worse, he hated owing anything to anyone. Except Geneviève. She had saved him and Louisa, and he owed her their lives. He would reveal his true identity to the scheming Rose de Beauharnais, to save Geneviève. He would beg Rose to use her influence on Barras, the most dangerous man in France. Even if it cost Louis his life.

He pressed the heel of his hand along a burning sensation in his chest. He should have been proud to introduce Geneviève as his wife to Suzanne and the other women, as well as the orphaned children, long ago. It would not have mattered in the least to Suzanne. She was a viper. And the most obvious person to have reported Geneviève. If she did…his hands trembled as he gripped the glass, imagining strangling Suzanne.

He gulped the brandy. He needed it and courage for visiting his wife in a cell—his wife and his child. He would get them out no matter the cost.

21

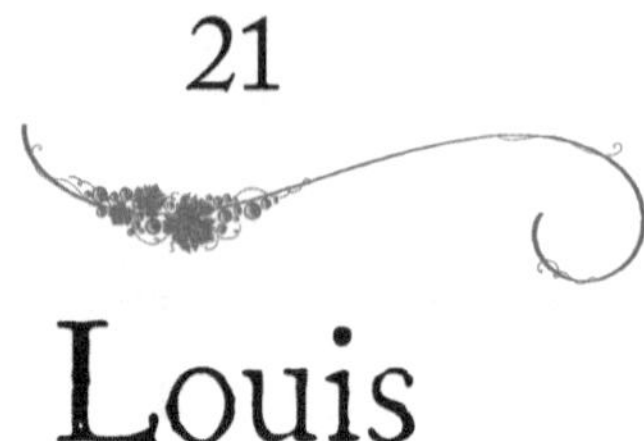

# Louis

*Hôtel Salpêtrière, Paris*
*October 1797*

T HE GENTEEL WORD *hôtel*, indicating a residence, did not make the former prison look any more hospitable. Bars covered the windows, and the asylum's towering stone walls were thicker than the length of Louis's arm. Geneviève had rescued him from prison through the tunnels beneath Paris. But if there were tunnels under this massive building, he had no idea where they might lead. He had to find another way to get her out.

Gripping a basket, he stood before a guard who huffed the foaming breath of a rabid dog.

The guard looked up from his ledger. "A wildcat, that one. Nearly scratched off the moustache of one guard. She's in solitary."

Her fighting did not surprise him—fighting was who she was. But fighting could make things worse for her and hurt the baby. His anger at the guards smoldered, but, dare he express it, they might retaliate and punish her. He offered a bottle of wine as a bribe. The guard seized it and called for another to take Louis to cell fifty-five.

Louis followed a guard whose limp caused his ring of keys to jangle in an oddly gay rhythm. A woman's scream rang out. He prayed Geneviève could not hear the pathetic wails.

As he walked, memories of his imprisonment at the Conciergerie darkened the hallway. When a chalked number, like the ones he passed, appeared on your battered cell door, you faced the guillotine in the morning. A rough voice boomed in his mind, Jean-Luc Ribou, making him stumble. He had known Jean-Luc since childhood, had spent three months in the cell next to his, traded sarcastic jokes. He had bidden his friend, adieu.

The guard stopped, unlocked, and opened the door. "Ten minutes." He lifted his palm.

Louis swallowed against the dryness in his throat. This chalked number did not mean Geneviève was going to the guillotine. He gave the guard a few sous and straightened his shoulders. He had to show confidence in his ability to get her out.

The guard closed the door behind him.

The stench of vomit wafted from a bucket in the corner. Should he tell her why she was sick? She must be thinking of Louisa's maman, dying in such a cell. He did not want to frighten her more.

A narrow open window allowed wind and rain through the

barred opening. In the sliver of light, stood Geneviève, barefoot, wearing a dirt-colored shift of rough fabric, her hands roped together. Did the imbeciles think she could get out of this dungeon if her hands were free? Who were the truly insane in this place? His arms ached to hold her. Mother of God, he prayed, protect her and the baby. "Geneviève."

Her bound hands flew to her shaved head. She must have fought them viciously, for tufts stuck out, like mange on a dog, and a crusted line of blood meandered down the side of her skull. He was relieved the damage was not worse. But he had to convince her not to fight. That would be like persuading the sun not to rise.

He envisioned wrapping the ropes around the gendarmes' necks and choking the life from them. He placed the basket on the straw-strewn floor. "Geneviève."

"I am so very sorry." She shrank into the corner. "It's all my fault. I should have kept my word. You warned me."

Helplessness battled his urge to protect her, making his arms heavy. Afraid a sudden move might shatter her, he inched toward her. "It does not matter. I will get you out."

She brought her arms over her head, wrists straining against the rope. "Don't look at me."

"You are my wife." He pulled her into his arms. "You are beautiful."

"You lie!" Both a laugh and sob escaped her.

He cradled the base of her skull, like he had his infant daughter the day he had met her. Geneviève was as frail and delicate as Louisa had been—like a newborn kitten.

As he kissed the special place on her neck, she collapsed

into him. He rubbed her back as she stifled sobs. "I brought warm clothes for you. Shall I help you dress?"

She kept her face pressed against his chest. "I don't want you to see me."

His tunic grew wet with her tears. "Hush. I give you my word. I will get you out of here."

"I don't deserve your word." Her fingers clutched at her scalp. "Don't you think it ironic they jail me for dressing as a man, strip me of my male clothes, and then they shave my head to make me look more like a man?"

He was glad for her forceful voice; it was a glimmer of her true self. He ran his finger along her strong, square jaw. "Your new coiffure accentuates your soulful eyes."

She frowned.

He gathered her in his arms. "You have never been more beautiful to me."

She raised an eyebrow. "Pah."

He brought out a lace cap from the basket. "Joliette gave this to you." He put the bonnet over Geneviève's head and tied the silvery ribbons under her chin. Dark circles pooled below her eyes, and he wished his kisses could wipe them away. His voice caught, and he cleared his throat. "It is very fetching."

She snorted a laugh, which heartened him. He grabbed a pair of stockings, rolled them over her bare feet, stretched them up her legs, tied ribbons as garters, and kissed her knees. "She gave you these, also. They will keep you warm."

"Thank her for me." She pressed her bound hands to her face. "I am so ashamed."

"There is no reason. You are beautiful." He wanted to comfort her, but how could he take away shame if she did not believe him? "This belonged to my maman. It was her favorite." He unrolled a pale pink woolen shawl, draped it around Geneviève's shoulders, and knotted it at her waist.

She ran her fingertips along the fabric. She never wore the color, yet it reflected a delicate, warm light on her pale skin. She would be a beautiful mother. "I have letters from Joliette," he reached into the basket, "and the children."

"Thank them. Be sure Louisa has her favorite poupette, she won't sleep without it."

"I am not going home without you."

She sat back and let her hands drop to her lap; her fingers tugged at the rope ends. "There is only one way I can live through this. If Aurélia is safe."

He reached for her hands, kissed her fingers, and untied the rope. "I will tie a slip knot so that you can take the rope on and off yourself."

"Thank you. Was it Suzanne or my stepmother who reported me?" The hurt in her eyes stung him.

He straightened. "I don't know."

Her eyes pinched, and then her old spirit flashed. "I bet that bitch, Suzanne."

He rallied at her vehemence. "Perhaps. But someone else may have been spying."

"I suspect my stepmother." She rubbed her chafed wrists. "Suzanne questioned August about who I was, but he refused to tell her. When I revealed myself, she could have told my stepmother. It's my fault no matter who reported me. No one came looking for two Africans?"

He shook his head, pulled out an embroidered handkerchief from the basket, and dabbed it along her cheeks.

She choked back tears. "I brought lavender-scented hand-kerchiefs to Magdeleine every time I visited her." She pressed the cloth to her face. "She was so elegant and proper and feminine; she called a handkerchief a *mouchoir*."

Louis's eyes burned as he tried to shake off the image of Louisa's mother in a cell like this. The image had haunted him every day of the two years he had spent imprisoned.

Something moving along the floor caught his eye. A rat scurried behind the slop bucket. Louis slowly withdrew the dagger concealed in his boot, approached the bucket, knelt, and stabbed. The rat squealed, tail slapping the floor.

"Cut off the tail. I can use it to pretend I ate the rat."

He feared she might already have lost some of her senses. He stood, his heart pounding, the rat writhing at the end of the blade.

She pulled her shoulders back, her normal fight in her eyes. "In less than eight hours here, I've learned you must act crazier than the insane, so they leave you alone."

His heartbeat calmed. He cut off the rat's tail and pitched the body out of the window.

She hid the tail under the pallet.

Wiping the knife on his breeches, he swallowed a foul taste. "Cook packed bread and cheese and sausage and milk…" He could not keep sorrow from his voice. He removed the serviette covering the food and held out a piece of chocolate.

"I'm not hungry but thank Cook." She rubbed her stomach.

Louis hoped the idea of being with child might have occurred to her. "Have you been ill, again?"

She shook her head. "Only once, but I am queasy. I don't know what it is. I wanted to retch when…all that blood…" A tiny, frightened cry, she tried to disguise as a laugh, escaped. "Perhaps fear?"

Perhaps the memory of Magdeleine prevented her from wondering. She needed to know. He rubbed her back. "Joliette thinks you have been ill because you are with child."

Geneviève collapsed against the wall. "How would she know?"

He smiled. "She said it is early, and you may not realize it yourself."

She brought her knees to her chest and covered her head with her hands. "I keep seeing Magdeleine. I can't give birth here."

He pulled her to his aching chest. "I imagine the same. I will get you out of here, soon. But you must promise not to fight the guards. They could hurt you and the baby." He caressed her. "Are you not a little bit happy about the child?"

She would not look at him. "I've longed to grow our family, to give you another child. But if you face execution for trying to save me—"

"Hush." He tilted her chin up. "Let us share this happiness. Allow this child to bring us hope."

"I'm scared." Her voice was so soft, he feared he had imagined it. In all the years he had known her, escaping barbaric mobs, prison, fleeing the guillotine, and killing her attacker, he had never heard her admit fear.

Tears dripped off her chin. "It makes me sadder, being in here, when I need you. I didn't need you before, I mean, I loved you, but now that I love you…I need you so much." Her face contorted as she tried pressing her quivering lips. "And it hurts to be without you."

He choked on the words he wanted to give her, *I need you*, for he had to show her his courage, his strength, his power to get her out, give her a belief she could hold onto. Even though he doubted himself, he would be confident for her, to give her hope.

He wrapped his arms around her. "Joliette arranged a meeting for me tomorrow. I will get you out of here the day after next."

"A meeting with whom?"

He could not bring himself to lie. "A former courtier with connections to Barras."

"That means you will have to reveal your real identity." The fight in her eyes blazed. She jumped up and stood in her man stance, feet wide apart, arms tensed. "I forbid you to risk your life. I am sentenced for eight months. Your life is not worth losing over a short time in prison for me—it is my fault, not yours."

He had not cried since Magdeleine had died, and he feared he might now. Geneviève had returned to her old self, but he could not allow her to see his weakness. "Sit down." Pulling her to the stained pallet, he sat next to her, and kissed her fingers, longing to take her with him. "We will be together in a few days."

"Louis?" Her eyes were bright. "I hope to give you a son."

Warmth flooded him. "I will be happy with a daughter or a son, so long as you remain well." He bent over and kissed her belly.

Footsteps clacked down the corridor. He helped her tie the rope and embraced her. "I know you will do everything, including not fighting, to survive. I believe in you."

"I promise." She grew rigid, like she was preparing herself. "When will you return?"

"Tomorrow. I cannot live a day without seeing your beautiful face."

"Tell Louisa I love her."

As the door opened, he kissed her, his chest heavy with dread.

# 22

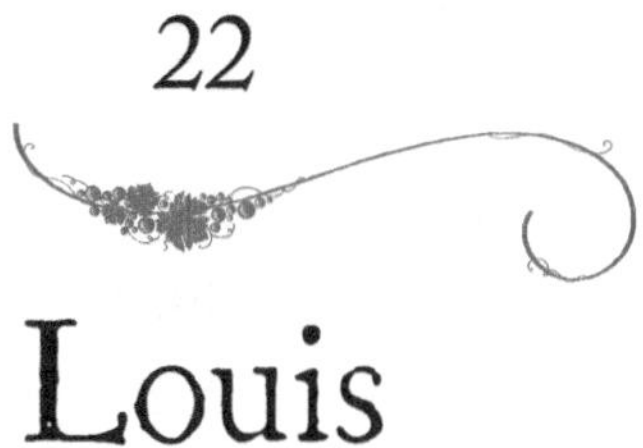

# Louis

*Paris, France*
*October* 1797

Lᴏᴜɪs ᴘᴀᴛᴛᴇᴅ ʜɪs waistcoat, ensuring his maman's emerald bracelet, brooch, and earrings were secure. In the event he was hauled to prison, he would be less noticeable in the drab taupe velvet. Joliette beside him, they stood before a maison not nearly as impressive as the bordel, but certainly built by a noble and seized by the Republic.

Joliette was calm as a statue. Dressed to intimidate, gold embroidery accented the bodice, sleeves, and skirts of her dark green silk gown and matching bonnet. Emeralds glittered at her throat. He would hate to be the one negotiating opposite her. The slight quiver of her earrings was the only thing betraying her self-possession.

A butler, whose frock coat sported more silver buttons than a general's uniform, led them to a salon and announced them.

At the far end of the room, Joséphine lounged on a gray satin chaise, watching the light glitter off her rings. Potted blooming flowers added their fragrance to her abundant rose perfume.

The pale-blue room had been overly decorated to resemble the Queen's salon at Versailles. She was still trying to be presented at a Court that no longer existed. Little wonder Rose, now Joséphine, was in need of funds. The elaborate, silver-embroidered silk drapes trimmed in crystal beads screamed for attention.

The thick carpet made Louis wobble in his red-heeled shoes and long for his sturdy boots. He breathed deeply, taking on his arrogant courtier stance. He would act as if he cared not, a more powerful negotiating position. He dared not think of Geneviève, for Joséphine would detect his soft heart and use it against him, forcing him to offer more.

Joséphine leaned forward, her breasts straining against her décolletage. "Comte de LaGarde!"

She should have greeted Joliette first and had purposefully snubbed her. Joliette smiled demurely, making him think Joliette had won a bargaining chip with this faux pas. He was glad he had her on his side.

Louis bowed his stiffest courtier bow. "Madame. May I present Madame Pricaud, the former Comtesse de Verzat?"

"Comtesse, how delightful to see you again." Joséphine did not rise. If she respected Versailles protocol, she should have curtsied to Joliette's higher rank.

After waiting for that honor which did not arrive, Joliette tilted her head. "And you, Madame Bonaparte."

"Thank you for the cask of Verzat wine. Do you know it is my husband's favorite?"

Joliette looked appropriately flattered, as if it were not well known that Château de Verzat was the finest wine in the country, if not the world. "Then I shall send another."

Joséphine raised her arm, offering her jeweled fingers to Louis. "I haven't seen you, Comte, since our dalliance at the Latona Fountain."

As he brushed his lips against her fingers, he noticed a faint, sweet tang of rot on her breath. He had an excellent memory, but no image of Joséphine in the Versailles Gardens came to him—much less any flirtation. He would have remembered her odor.

She brought her slippered feet to the carpet and patted the chaise. "Do join me."

"Ah, I fear my bulk might break such a delicate piece of furniture." After leading Joliette to a sofa opposite Joséphine, he lowered himself onto a satin pouffe decorated with fringe and crystals. Waiting to start negotiating would put him in a better negotiation position, but he wanted his wife out now. He looked at Joliette, who gave a tiny shake of her head.

Joséphine brought her arm along the length of her body as slowly as a cat's purr. "You too, escaped Madame Guillotine?"

He would use his courtier charm. "You were most lucky. I heard it was by only one day!"

Her laugh was deep. "I have been celebrating ever since. And you, Comtesse?"

"I am Madame Pricaud." Joliette's grace was flawless, except for the fingernail she ran along the silver brocade.

Louis wondered if Joliette wanted to scratch out Joséphine's catty eyes. Geneviève would. He wished she were here.

Joliette's voice was crisp. "I lived in America, arranging the importation of wine and have only just returned."

"An émigrée! Do you not fear the guillotine?"

"I will appeal to Talleyrand…" Joliette pulled a loose thread of the brocade. "And Director Barras."

Louis sat up straighter. Now was his opportunity. Was that not what he and Joliette discussed? His mind was afire.

"Both those men will demand something of great value." Joséphine's smile was smug. "To grant a favor."

Joliette caressed her emeralds. "Château de Verzat already pays many taxes—needed by the Republic. Imagine doubling the amount if my brother and I are permitted to stay and oversee the increased production." Joliette sat back, allowing time for Joséphine to realize that if she made the appointment with Barras, he would be grateful to Joséphine. And Barras would be indebted to her—exactly where Joséphine wanted him.

Impressed by Joliette's élan, Louis quelled a smile.

"And you, Comte, how did you keep your handsome head?"

Louis's heartbeat pounded at this throat. Barras had been a member of the Committee for Public Safety and amongst those who had witnessed his trial. "Like you, I outlived Robespierre." That was true; he had just done it outside prison.

He wondered how her laughter could be so resounding when she kept her lips curled to hide her black teeth.

"Have some champagne?" Joséphine snapped her fingers, and another shiny-buttoned servant entered, carrying a tray with three glasses of bubbly golden wine. Joséphine brought her glass up to toast, and Louis complied. The glasses clinked. She stared into him, as if challenging him to deny her anything. Louis turned and toasted his glass with Joliette's.

Joséphine laughed and swayed her glass, spilling some on her bodice. "Oh. How clumsy of me." She dipped her fingers between her breasts and flicked drops of champagne at Louis.

He forced a polite smile. Geneviève would guffaw at this woman's obviousness. "You know the honorable Barras?" His mouth soured at the word, honorable.

"I've known Paul…" she smiled, "intimately…for many years."

Sourness burned his throat. She had not the least familiarity with honor. He had started too aggressively. He should have acted more reserved. He checked Joliette's eyes, which looked worried. He had rushed the plan they had rehearsed. He had turned the conversation back to Barras too quickly.

Turning his back on Joséphine, he stood and acted like he was examining a painting of a scorning ancestor. "Might you ask him a favor for me, Madame?"

"Can the Comtesse not ask for you?" Joséphine licked her finger, leaving its tip in her mouth and slowly withdrawing it.

Joliette was too much of a lady to correct Joséphine again, and he would follow Joliette's lead. "Alas, I believe you exude much more influence." He was flattering her, and he despised himself. He would crouch at her feet like a footstool if she helped release Geneviève.

More of her full-throated laughter made him feel small. "You are correct, Comte. Tell me, what is it you wish?"

He softened his voice. "My wife…"

All languor dropped from Joséphine like leaves from a tree. "You're married, Comte?"

He nodded and, despite a clawing feeling in his chest, the words rushed out of him like water over a weir. "A very brave woman, not a noble…" Why had he said that? His words tumbled out. "Who saved many innocents. Gendarmes arrested her for dressing as a man." He had lost his attitude. He gripped his glass, lifted his chin. "She is held at Hôtel Salpêtrière, which is extremely dangerous to her health. She is with child. Our child."

A look of pity on her face, Joliette bowed her head over her clutched hands.

Joséphine flicked open a fan of ostrich feathers and waved it at her bosom. "Your devotion is touching."

She mocked him. She would use his devotion against him. His jabot grew damp.

Joséphine stroked the folds of her dress, pulling them from her body and letting them puddle around her curves. "But how can I possibly help?"

He resisted the urge to loosen his collar and stood tall. "I ask you to influence Barras, as he is the only one with the power to release my wife."

Her chuckle was deep, taunting. "Why should I do that? You never petitioned on my behalf at Court, despite my numerous requests to be presented."

This, he had prepared for. Louis looked down his nose. "I do not believe you requested it of me, Madame, for I never would have denied you." The lie singed his throat, but it felt good, as if he were ridding himself of a poison.

She pouted and, as she tapped the fan at her breast, he feared all was lost. She snapped the fan closed. "What do you offer in return?"

He had to play this game, for the better he played it, the more rewarded she would feel with less. He pushed out his lower lip. "What is it you most treasure, Madame?"

She ran her fingers over her rings. "Can you not guess?"

He would draw her out, make her wait. "Château de Verzat wine."

She glanced at the painting of Bonaparte hanging above the fireplace. "For my husband, perhaps."

He walked the perimeter of the salon. Dainty figurines, plates, and bowls crowded the tables. "Sèvres porcelain." He gave her a great grin, pretending pride in his deducing skills.

She giggled. "Try again."

She was enjoying his misery. Should he dig deeper or bait her? He wanted to slap her.

"You are recently married, Madame?" Joliette asked without looking at Joséphine.

He felt a glimmer of relief at her intrusion.

Joséphine sat back. "Nearly two years ago."

"As Louis knows, Versailles protocol indicates that a gift of jewelry would be inappropriate." Joliette flashed him a smile, hidden from Joséphine.

She was brilliant—she made Joséphine crave the forbidden gift of jewelry more. He raised his hand. "Of course, you are correct." She had given him the upper hand. "Alas..." he walked around the room, shaking his head, making Joséphine wait, anticipate, salivate.

He waved his hand at the potted plants. "Flowers?"

Joséphine languidly fanned herself, her pitying look prompting him to speed things up.

A laugh stuck in his throat. "Society's rules or not, jewelry must be Madame's favorite?"

Dragging the feathers of the fan along her décolletage, she nodded.

He paced, speaking to the carpet. "If only the sans-culottes had not rampaged our château, I would have a gift that would complement Madame's unrivaled beauty. A jewel worthy of Madame's stature." His lies tasted like moldy wine.

She snapped her fan shut. "Your mother wore many jewels."

He had to bait her. "I fear all that remains are mere baubles."

"Let me see them. I will decide." Joséphine's voice rose from alto to soprano.

Turning, he asked, "You agree to ask Monsieur Barras my favor?"

She batted her eyelashes.

He had pounced when he should have hooked her first. Yet he could not wait. While Joséphine was lounging in luxury, Geneviève was freezing in a rat-infested asylum. He dug into his waistcoat for the least of the jewels. Twisting the brooch, its center emerald caught the light, and sparks showered Joséphine, making her blink. He stood three paces away, hoping she would move toward him, for then he would know he had hooked her.

She thrust out her hand.

He gazed at the gem and acted like he was reminiscing. "The Queen always complimented my maman when she wore this at Court. I believe she was a bit envious." He sighed. "She tried to win it in a game of whist, but fortunately my maman won the bet."

Joséphine's fingers snapped.

He held the jewel like it was a newborn chick, stopped just shy of her reach, and opened his hands, revealing an oval-shaped emerald surrounded by diamonds.

Joséphine snatched it and held it up to the light, mesmerized.

He returned to his pouffe and leaned back, acting the self-satisfied courtier. She did not own anything a tenth so valuable. He prayed the brooch would buy his wife's freedom.

Joséphine tapped her finger to her lips. "Are there matching earrings?"

He wanted to spit in the woman's face, wring her neck—this courtier attitude he did not have to act. He forced coolness in his voice. "Ah, you remember. Sadly, they, too, were stolen." Damn, now he would have to give up the necklace if the brooch was not enough.

"It is the only thing I have left of my maman." He surprised himself with his lie and humility. "I found it pinned to her gown. The Revolutionaries missed it."

"Hmmm. As this is such a small gift..."

Heat exploded in Louis's chest, and he pushed out a low, hot breath, wishing it were fire to scorch her.

He scooped it out of her fingers. "Since, as you say, it is so small—"

Her extended arm hung in the air. Her mouth dropped open.

He turned toward Joliette. "I should keep it for my wife."

Joséphine jumped up, pushed his shoulder, turning him around, and grabbed the brooch.

He wiped his hand on his breeches, silently urging the greedy bitch to grant his request.

Joséphine pinned the brooch to her bodice and angled her body from side to side in front of the mirror, scattering tiny rainbows of light over her bosom and face. She yanked the bellpull, and a servant appeared.

"Show my guests to the hall where they can await Barras's arrival."

The servant bowed.

Never taking her eyes from the mirror, she said, "I will send a message summoning Barras. But! You must make your own request. That should not be too difficult for a pair of courtiers."

Louis dug his fingers into the satin pouffe, puncturing the delicate fabric, and not caring. This tiny favor cost him his maman's brooch.

Joliette stood. "We are pleased to wait. Merci."

"Show my guests out."

Louis's mouth gaped. She had dismissed him, not even thanked him. She acted like she was entitled to such a treasure. Perhaps she did feel entitled, but no woman was less so. Her name might now be Joséphine, but she was still Rose, the Créole salope with rotting black teeth and stinking breath.

The servant led them to a cold, drafty marble hall.

Joliette sat with the dignity of a comtesse.

Louis's anger flowed into a miasma of indignation, rage, shame, and guilt. He paced. He had to negotiate better with Barras. Dread weighed like a pall. Barras would not be bought with jewels. And Louis had nothing with which to bargain. Except his life. And he would gladly give his life to save Geneviève's. He prayed he would not have to.

# 23

# *Geneviève*

*Hôtel Salpêtrière, Paris*
*November* 1797

THE JANGLE OF keys made me jump up, smooth my cap, retie the rope at my wrists. My heart raced as I imagined Louis's arms around me. God, please let him take me and our child out of here.

The door opened. A narrow figure with a sharp, slanted bonnet entered.

I pressed my hands against my chest. Where was Louis?

The door closed, and she stood with her back pressed against it. A cellmate? No, she would be dressed like me. A breeze blew in from the window, and the woman pressed a lace-trimmed handkerchief to her nose.

At first, I imagined the figure was Magdeleine's ghost, but

a spirit wouldn't need the door. I swallowed against a building nausea.

"Louis couldn't come today, so he asked me to visit."

At the sound of Suzanne's voice, I froze. Louis would never. I had to play her game, or things would worsen for me—and my baby. She could scream for the guards, claim I attacked her, and I'd be thrown in the dungeon—Louis might never find me.

She stepped out of the shadow, her blue gown shimmering like a stream in the gloom.

My hands reached to cover my head and, instead, I forced a smile. "How kind of you."

She offered a package wrapped in a serviette. "He asked me to bring bread and cheese."

No doubt she poisoned the food. She wanted me out of her way for good. I reached out, and she dropped the bundle into my hands.

"Please thank Cook for me." I pressed the food to my chest, like I cherished it. "Won't you join me?"

She shook her head.

"I will save it for later." I placed the bundle onto my straw pallet, slipped out the rat tail I had hidden, and secreted it in my fist. "How is everyone at the orphanage?"

"Fine. We are all missing Louis, though."

My heart lurched. Louis was busy getting me out of here. I drew in a slow breath to calm my rapid heartbeat.

She smoothed her palm over her lustrous silk gown. "He's gone back to his courtier ways," she swung her skirts, "dressing as one, carousing until dawn, and off again this morning." She laughed. "He's enjoying his freedom."

I forced a serene smile while imagining clawing her face.

Getting rid of me wasn't enough for her. She wanted to drive a wedge between me and my husband. "That sounds like Louis." I gave a false laugh. "He must know half the demimonde of Paris."

She dabbed the handkerchief at her nose.

"Does the odor bother you? I'll move the slop bucket." As I picked up the bucket, I dropped the rat tail at her feet and placed the bucket in the opposite corner.

She straightened to her full height, still a head shorter than I. "You don't have to wait eight months to get out of here."

Every whore knew the eight-month term of imprisonment, especially if they had endured it. Had she? I imagined knocking her out, shaving her head, trussing her hands, and stealing her clothes, but that crime would send me to the dungeon or keep me in this asylum forever. I would follow along, but I would win. "Oh?"

She shielded her mouth and whispered, "They want women to populate New France. If you agree to go, they will forgive your crime and put you on a ship tomorrow."

I widened my eyes, hoping I looked thrilled. "To North America?"

"When I leave, I will tell them you volunteer."

My heart thudded. She could do just that. Why hadn't she without visiting me?

"If you don't volunteer..." she rubbed the silk cords of her reticule. "I'll report Louis's escape from prison."

I gripped my rough tunic. "Why would you do that?"

"Are you really that stupid? I have wanted Louis since Magdeleine introduced us. I got rid of her, and now, I'll get rid of you, too." She smiled with self-satisfaction. "If you leave him, he won't pine away, and he'll love *me*."

Rage throbbed in my arms. Shadows darkened. She reported her best friend—she murdered Magdeleine. My baby and Louis were the only things keeping me from breaking Suzanne's neck. I wondered how I could make her death look like she had tripped and fallen. Sweat broke out all over me as I no longer suspected, but knew, the viper had me arrested and thrown in here. And she could send me across an ocean. If they took me, Louis would never find me. I had to scare her so much she would be desperate to flee and forget about volunteering me. I had to give her what she wanted.

"As I wish us both to live, I will volunteer."

Delight flashed in her eyes.

"Oh! Be very still." I pointed. "There's a rat beneath your gown."

She jumped and shoved herself into the corner, her feet pounding the cell floor. She screamed and screamed and screamed.

I bent down, plucked up the tail, and held it up. "There must be two, for one bit the other's tail off!" I pawed at her skirts, searching for vermin. "Where's the other one?"

She screamed louder, higher. Her feet ran in place.

An avalanche of screams from my fellow inmates careened. Hysterical laughter followed. My chest ached for the poor creatures.

"Are you feeling well? You are quite pale. Would you like to sit down?"

She clutched her neck.

"You shouldn't stand there. Rats sometimes drop down through that hole in the ceiling."

She jumped to the door and screamed, "Guard! I wish to leave!"

Like an echo, the inmates mocked her, their voices high and screeching. *I wish to leave, I wish to leave, I wish to leave!* The rattle and scrape of metal cups across metal bars added to the cacophony.

As her back was turned, I tossed the rat tail at her neck.

She screamed and shook her arms while her feet pummeled the floor. "Why does the guard not come?"

"Did he tell you when he would return when he let you in here?"

"No!" Fear elongated her face, making her look like a terrified ferret.

The laughter grew in intensity. "Did you give him a bribe?"

"No." Her forehead creased in disgust.

"Oh, dear."

She grabbed me. "What do you mean?" The feather in her hat trembled.

I shouted over the screams and laughter. "It is customary to tip the guard to ensure he'll return for you."

"I'll give him a whatever he wants." She gripped her reticule to her bosom.

She didn't know they came every ten minutes. And I wanted her to be so frightened she'd forget to volunteer me. I shook my head. "That might be some time."

She pressed herself against the door, like she was willing herself to pass through it.

"Don't worry. The guard will come when he delivers the next meal."

"When's that?"

"Dawn."

Throwing her head back, she screamed like a demented goose.

If I hadn't been so terrified of her volunteering me, I would have enjoyed tormenting her more, but it was about time for the guard to arrive. I would make it look like I had summoned him. I motioned for her to move away from the door. She took a tiny step, allowing me to peek out the screened window. I heard a faint jangle of keys. "Monsieur, I have a visitor who would like to leave." My voice was so rational, my fellow inmates did not repeat it.

I smiled. "He's coming."

As the key ground in the lock and the door opened, she flew, her feet slapping the stone.

I stood in the gloom, the dark cell closing in around me. I hoped she was too terrified to volunteer me. I wiped sweat from my face. If they did come for me, how would I get word to Louis? I stared at the rat tail. I might have to act so crazy they would deny me passage. Louis was at risk, too. But I didn't think Suzanne would report him because she wanted him. She used my love for him to coerce me to volunteer.

I rubbed my stomach, trying to calm the nausea—and my baby. "You're safe little one." Louis, please hurry. Please. Get us out of here soon.

# 24

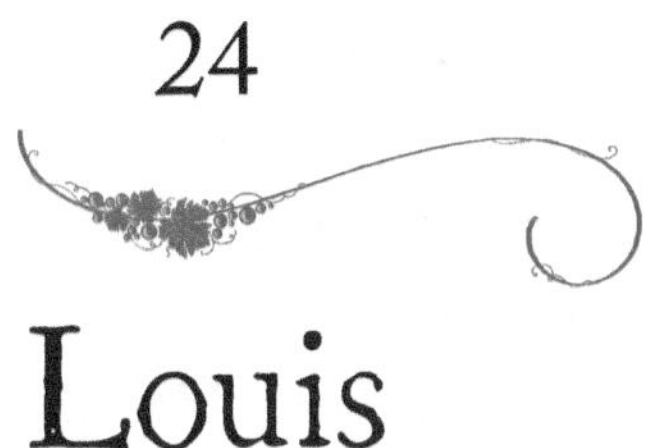

# Louis

*Paris, France*
*November 1797*

Eight hours passed, without the offer of refreshment. Louis squeezed his eyes against the image of Geneviève, her head shaved, her hands tied. He rubbed his arms. The fear of being useless thrummed in him. He would do anything to get her released as soon as possible.

The door opened and a new servant, with just as many uniform buttons, looked down his nose. Louis cocked his head and half-closed his eyes—projecting his former courtier superiority.

The man stepped back.

"We await Director Barras."

He stiffened. "Whom shall I say wishes to be presented?"

Had Joséphine not told Barras they were waiting? He should have given the salope one earring and made her earn the other.

"Louis LaGarde and Madame Pricaud." He prayed Barras, who had served on the Committee for Public Safety, would not remember Louis's trial. He had successfully forgotten the details of that day—everything except the Public Prosecutor, Geneviève's father, sentencing him to death.

The servant led them to another opulent salon.

Barras stood before the roaring fire, hands behind his back. He turned, his eyes shining. "Ha! Sneaking up on me?"

Louis stepped back. "The servant showed us in." He felt the chill in his own voice and hoped it did not work against him. The lowly vicomte was still insecure.

Barras wore a blue velvet frock coat with wide embroidered lapels and cuffs, a striped vest, and white stockings over swollen calves—no less grandly dressed than a royal. Ignoring them, he picked up a paper and scanned it.

Louis's scalp pricked. Was the paper part of Louis's file?

Barras mumbled, "Approach."

Feeling like a marionette with someone else controlling his arms and legs, Louis glanced at Joliette. She advanced, and he followed her. He stopped before Barras, knowing not to sit before Barras did, but not sure whether to bow. Louis's station was far higher than the former vicomte, but Louis was now the lesser. As leader of the Directoire, Barras controlled France.

Barras's thin lips made a straight line. He sat in an oversized armchair of gray velvet and pointed at two spindly chairs, indicating Louis and Joliette should sit. "How did you escape Madame Guillotine, LaGarde and you, Madame Pricaud?"

Joliette smiled, but her eyes held suspicion. "My brother

and I accompanied a wine shipment to America. We lived in Philadelphia and were neighbors of Monsieur Talleyrand." Joliette's elan did not waver when she lied.

A trickle of sweat ran down Louis's neck. Would Barras send him to the guillotine if he discovered he had escaped prison? "Like Madame Bonaparte, I was released."

"The lucky few!" Barras boomed, "I am told you wish a favor."

Words rushed from Louis. "My wife is unjustly imprisoned—"

"What is unjust?" Barras stood and withdrew a rapier from the sheath at his side.

Louis jumped up. Was he going to have to duel with him? He was not wearing a sword. "Her crime was one of safety."

Barras swished the blade, slicing the air, warning Louis. "Speak to be understood, LaGarde. This is not the former Queen's Court."

Louis licked his lips and watched the rapier's blade. "Wishing to avoid being attacked by brigands, she dressed as a man to travel in safety to Nantes."

"Hmm." He stabbed the rapier into the carpet, leaned on it, and crossed one foot before the other.

Louis feared the rapier would crack, as Barras's weight caused it to severely bow. "She was found guilty, which of course she was not." He sensed he was falling into his trap. He had spoken too quickly, giving up a negotiation point. He wished he could wipe the sweat from his brow but acknowledging his own lack of control would give Barras another advantage. "She is sentenced to eight months—"

"She should be sentenced to eight years!"

Louis reached for the hilt of his nonexistent sword. Joliette had warned him to explain as little as possible.

"Dressing as a man makes the woman a spy, a traitor." Barras uncrossed his feet and whipped the rapier in a figure eight before him. "She has committed a crime against the Republic." He swept the blade across the desk, scattering a pile of papers.

Louis forced himself not to back away. Barras's maneuver had no doubt blunted the blade, but Louis was still without a weapon.

Barras threw himself into the chair and flung the sword at the fireplace. The weapon clattered on the hearth.

There would be no bargaining with this power-hungry lunatic. Best to advocate Geneviève's value to the country. "She is no spy. She is a selfless heroine who, as vigneron, also runs the Château de Verzat vineyard, which pays a great deal of taxes to the Republic, the lot of which will perish along with the withering vines should she not be released." He had not even thought of the reality of the vineyard's destruction, but he hoped the truth piqued Barras's mercenary nature.

Barras tapped his knuckles on the chair's arm. "I am told the Verzat émigrés also wish to remain—in order to expand the vineyard." He glared at Joliette.

She sat, regal as a queen. "My brother and I wish to increase production."

"Should the Verzat vineyard increase production, so will the taxes—as long as my wife, the vigneron, is there to ensure its success," Louis added.

Barras collapsed back into his chair and waved at Louis to sit.

Reluctantly, Louis eased into the narrow chair, designed for instability. At Versailles, Barras would never have dared sit in Louis's presence. Louis would wait him out. He had made the buzzard realize Geneviève was of value to the Republic, but only if she was free.

Barras slammed his hand on the desk and grinned.

Louis had been prepared and did not flinch. He held the man's stare.

"What have you been doing since you left Versailles, LaGarde?"

Louis wanted to say, avoiding vipers like you, but he straightened his waistcoat. "I turned my family's château and estate into an orphanage, of which I am the director. We care for forty children and as many homeless mothers. They all work the land and sell fruit, vegetables, eggs, and cheese at the market. We educate the children. The orphanage makes a great contribution to the Republic."

Barras lifted his eyebrow. "How *selfless* of you."

He was directing the conversation away from Geneviève. "My wife is with child. The conditions of Hôtel Salpêtrière endanger both mother and child, a future citizen of France." Louis thought his appeal a bit extreme, but he could not stop himself. He would lose ground. What did Barras want? He ran his finger over the necklace and earrings secreted in his waistcoat. He was prepared to give both to this devil of Satan.

"So the wine business is thriving—due to LaGarde's wife and you and your brother."

Joliette smiled graciously. "We could not produce half the wine if it were not for Madame LaGarde's expert management."

Barras clapped loudly, but Joliette kept her composure. He

leaned forward, looking from Louis to Joliette. "What have you to offer should I grant your requests?"

Dread covered Louis like a soaked woolen cape. "In addition to the increase in taxes?"

Barras slammed his palm on the desk. "Have either you or her brother fulfilled your duty to your country?"

A shiver ran down Louis's spine. Barras had no need of jewels. He needed power. Power over former nobles. Power to humiliate and make a former noble's life miserable. Serving France was a duty. Men were conscripted. This, he had not prepared for.

Louis would face this bastard with the dignity of a Noble of the Sword. He took on his courtier posture. "No, Monsieur Director."

Barras stretched his arms across the desk and drummed his fingers. "Bonaparte is planning a campaign in Egypt. He will need men of your caliber. He sat back, smiling. "I will assign you, LaGarde, the rank of Colonel. And Verzat, since he fled the country, the rank of Lieutenant. Both of you report for training at the École Militaire in two weeks."

"I cannot speak for my brother." Joliette stood, strangling her reticule with both hands.

"Tell him he can join the army or lose his head at the guillotine."

"Merci, Monsieur Director."

He and Henri fight for Bonaparte? That self-serving war monger?

Louis sprang to his feet. "Monsieur. Both Verzat and I are married, with children, and over the age of twenty-five. By the laws of France, we are exempt."

Barras' eyes were as viperous as his smile. "If you prefer, both Verzats can go to the guillotine and your wife can rot in Salpêtrière." He raised his eyebrows, making his cheap wig gap at his temples.

Louis swallowed his contempt. "I would be honored to serve the Republic—provided my wife is released."

"I will release her tomorrow. Give her information to my servant on your way out."

Barras stood and nodded to Joliette. Her eyes were afire. "I will have your names removed from the émigrés list tomorrow. Should your brother not appear in two weeks, he will be hunted down and executed. You will be safe in France, Madame."

Safe? They had all walked into the lion's den and escaped—only for Henri and Louis to go to war. And the women they loved would be managing the estate without protection. Louis followed Joliette out into a cold drizzle.

"How will I tell Henri and Aurélia?" Joliette swiped at her eyes with the anger of a tigress. "How will you tell Geneviève?"

When Geneviève delivered their child, he would be beneath the thumb of a maniacal war monger, in Egypt, a godforsaken desert.

He would not spoil her release with such news. He would take her home to their cottage on the estate and ensure she felt safe before he told her. His foot hit a puddle, splashing water and soaking his breeches. How would he live without her?

# 25

# Geneviève

*Hôtel Salpêtrière, Paris*
*November* 1797

ALL NIGHT, I kept myself awake by talking to my baby. Perhaps I was crazy, but I couldn't let down my guard. If I fell asleep, they could drug me and throw me on a ship. So, I paced and sang the lullaby Maman had sung to me.

At dawn, they came. The key scraped in the lock. I retied the rope around my wrists, jumped up, and grabbed the rat tail. If I pretended to eat the thing, they might not send a truly insane woman to New France.

The door creaked open, and the light from a guard's torch illuminated a matron, thin and brittle as a stalk of wheat. She dropped a pile of clothing at my feet. "Put these on." She yanked the rope binding my wrists and removed it.

Hiding the rat tail in my fist, I rubbed my wrists together, scraped raw from the first day the rough rope had restrained me.

"Where—"

"Quiet." Holding the rope, she clasped her hands before her.

I hated my pathetic whimpering, my helplessness, my fear. They were taking me to the ship. Louis would never find me or our child. Grasping the damp wall, I stood straight and forced my voice to be strong. "Where are you taking me?"

"You do as you are told, and you will not be beaten."

The urge to seize her and knock her to the ground roared through me. But I couldn't risk hurting the baby. Louis would tell me to act compliant, search for a way to escape outside this cell. I picked up the gown. When she let her guard down, when she least expected it, I'd attack. "Merci."

The ice in the woman's eyes cracked, and kindness seeped out like a tear. "Hurry, now."

I turned my back to the matron and the guard, tucked the rat tail under the pallet, and shrugged off the filthy tunic. Picking up a shift of soft linen made me long for a bucket of water to wash myself—for my stink would spoil the clean clothes. Shivering as a cold wind gusted into the cell, I no longer wished to leave. This hellhole was at least safe, and Louis could find me here. I tied a stiff petticoat and skirt of quilted wool around my waist. Both would keep me and the baby warm. Would I deliver our child aboard a ship? My arms jerked as I pulled the bodice over my head. Damn you, Suzanne. I had to escape.

The meager light made the bodice look golden, reminding me of the frock coat I wore to rescue Aurélia. After donning boots and a woolen cloak, I wrapped the shawl of Louis's maman around my shoulders. Please, God, don't let them chain me or hurt my baby. Please let Louis find me before the ship sails.

Ashamed of my shaved head, I tucked the cap Louis had brought under the woolen bonnet, tied the ribbons, and looked at the matron.

She roped my hands together and tightened the knot. "Follow me."

If they knocked me unconscious, I'd have no chance to escape. I placed my hands over my belly. Would the baby feel my fear? I did not want her or him to be afraid, ever. I had been calmed by Maman's songs when I was a child. I hummed to calm my little one and followed the matron.

Carrying a torch, the guard lumbered down the silent corridor. No inmate stirred, screamed, laughed, or witnessed my abduction.

We wound through endless corridors, the torchlight flaring in the drafts. I scanned the walls for any opening I could use to escape or hide, but the rough stone was impenetrable.

Ahead stood a wooden door reinforced with crossed metal pikes. "Open up," the guard barked.

I did not want to move forward and clung to the damp stonewall. How strange to feel safer in this darkness than to risk what lay ahead. I shook myself. I had to envision escaping, had to keep my wits sharp to take advantage of any opportunity. I could not fight, no matter how far they pushed me. I would have to be humble, prey on their compassion. I would plead with them for the sake of my child's life—a future citizen of France. My throat tightened, shutting off my breath, but I forced myself to inhale. I could not faint.

Light flooded in as the door opened. The matron grabbed my arm, and I stumbled after her, squinting in the early light streaming through tall windows of a great hall. As we walked across it, I shrank, like a mouse crossing a newly harvested field.

The glimpse of a blue sky beyond the windows enabled me to take a deep breath. I caressed my belly. I promise you will see the sun and the sky and the clouds, my little one.

The matron headed for a wooden door at the opposite end of the hall. I tripped. She yanked the rope. "You don't keep the superintendent waiting if you know what's good for you."

The heat of my old familiar anger rushed through me, and I struggled to be civil. "I'm sorry. I'm with child and not feeling well."

Her eyes snapped. "You did not tell anyone?"

I pulled my bound hands to my belly. "I…I was not certain until yesterday."

She sighed, and I hoped I had stirred in her some compassion. She slowed her pace. At the end of the hall, a door stood ajar.

"Behave and do exactly as you are told." She gripped my arm and pushed me into a bright room lined with floor to ceiling windows. A balding man sat at an ornate desk that might have been owned by a former noble. He looked up and removed his spectacles. "This is?"

The matron stood at attention. "Madame Detré, Monsieur."

I could throw something through the glass and run. I

searched for something heavy—the fire poker. How would I pick it up with my bound hands?

He looked at me head to toe. "Madame."

"Good morning, Monsieur."

He lifted a paper. "When you arrived, you were carrying false papers of Jean Detré."

A squirming ran up my spine. Evidence. Would my sentence be lengthened for another crime besides dressing as a man? If so, that might keep me here instead of on a ship. "Yes, Monsieur."

He crumpled my false papers and tossed them into the fireplace where flames consumed the identity I had occupied for the past ten years. No matter. As a mother, I would never again be able to impersonate a man. I had to figure out how to be safe as a woman who protected her children as well as herself.

He lifted another paper. "Your married name, Corrié, is also a false identity."

Dread washed in like a wave overwhelming a ship's deck. I gripped my fingers, not knowing whether I should agree or act crazy or fall to my knees and beg.

"Is Corrié a false identity or not?"

Think first. Louis would tell me to comply, even though I wanted to smash the man's skull with the fire poker. I had to save the baby at every cost. "Yes, Monsieur."

"You should be detained for three crimes, not one, Madame LaGarde."

My mouth dried. Had Suzanne reported Louis and revealed his true identity? Had he been arrested? Imprisoned? I gripped my hands before my belly, praying he'd not been guillotined.

"Better yet, you should be shipped to New France!"

The light blared. The room swirled. I grabbed onto a chair-back, lowered my head, bent my knees. I had to keep my wits about me. I could not faint. Darkness encroached.

"Are you unwell?" His hand on my arm, he guided me to sit down.

I held onto the chair arm, shivering. "Please, Monsieur, I am with child."

"Does your husband know?"

"Yes, Monsieur." Tears ran, and I could not stop them. I hated the helplessness that swarmed me like the specks of light circling me.

"Get authentic identity papers at the Hôtel de Ville today."

I jerked my head to face him. "Wh—what?"

His face and posture were stern. "I do not want to see you back here."

I shook my head. Sparks of light flurried. "Today?"

"Today. Remove her, Matron." The beginning of his smile twitched.

The woman was gentle as she untied the rope and led me back out into the grand hall. A rushing sound filled my head. I didn't feel my feet, yet I walked. My legs tensed to run.

She led me to an arched doorway. Beyond, stood a carriage and pacing before it, Louis.

Love charged through me. What had he traded for my life?

"May you deliver a healthy baby." She gave me a gentle push.

Clean, cold air rushed over me. I raced into my husband's arms.

# 26

# Louis

*Hôtel Salpêtrière, Paris*
*November 1797*

LOUIS SCOOPED UP Geneviève, placed her on the bench of the carriage, and slammed the door. He yelled to the driver, "Make speed!" The horses jolted.

Embracing her, he rubbed her back, calming her. His arms would ache for this moment every minute he was away. Where would he find the fortitude to leave her in two weeks? He could not think of that now, could not spoil this reunion. He would tell her when they were home where she felt safe.

When she quieted, he brought a handkerchief to her tears, and placed his hand over her stomach. "How are you feeling?"

"Fine, now that I'm in your arms." She looked up at him, her smile lopsided. "How did you do it?"

He stuck out his lower lip and shrugged. "First you must tell me, my courageous wife, how you rescued Aurélia."

"Aurélia saved herself. But now we must hide and protect her."

Her willingness to fight, so familiar to him, sparked in her eyes. She would never believe him, but even with her shaved head, she was lovely. And it was her spark, her fire, her spirit—glittering in her eyes—that made her the most beautiful of women.

Her smile faded. "Suzanne brought me poisoned food yesterday." Tiny lines creased at the corners of her eyes. They had not been there before her imprisonment. "She admitted reporting Magdeleine, so she could have you, Louis."

His throat, his eyes, his heart burned.

"She also threatened to volunteer me to sail to New France. She said if I didn't, she'd report that you had escaped prison."

A burn flamed up his spine, and he pressed his back into the cushioned bench, trying to calm the fire of hate raging within him.

"I scared her, but then..." she swallowed and inhaled deeply. "A matron and guard came for me at dawn, and I feared Suzanne had volunteered me." Her voice cracked and he pulled her closer. "I thought they would put me aboard a ship, and you'd never find me." She clutched him.

Holding her, Louis squeezed the image from his eyes. "They should have told you I was awaiting you. I am sorry."

She snapped her head up to look at him. Her eyes sparked like flint on steel. "I wanted to strangle Suzanne with my bare hands."

"I will kick her out of the orphanage, despite my promise to Magdeleine."

She frowned.

"Magdeleine begged me to shelter Suzanne and her illegitimate son at the orphanage. I suspected she was a jealous, conniving guttersnipe, but she was Magdeleine's best friend, and I granted her wish." He shut his eyes against the sunlight glinting off the Loire. "I always wondered who betrayed Magdeleine."

"My God." Geneviève placed her hands over her heart and leaned into him.

Birdsong rang out. A pair of swans glided along the river. He had only two weeks with Geneviève, and he did not wish to waste one minute thinking of Suzanne. He would banish the salope before he joined the army.

He patted Geneviève's belly. "Are you hungry?"

"I'm ravenous." She tilted her head. "How did you arrange my release?"

He reached into the basket, tore off a piece of the round loaf, and offered it.

She bit into the crust and closed her eyes, savoring it. "Mmm. Heaven."

He sliced the cheese and took out a jug of milk.

"Aurélia is with child. Is she well?"

He gave her the cup of milk. "She is unharmed and missing you terribly."

"Tell me, how did you get me released?" She drank deeply.

He cleared his throat. "Do you know that Joliette gives you all the credit for the winery's success?"

She caressed his thigh. "You're stalling, Louis."

He relished her touch. He could avoid telling her by making love to her, but the carriage could bounce them, and he might hurt her. And she needed to bathe; she carried the same damp prison odor that had penetrated his clothing in his filthy cell. "She and Henri hold you in high regard."

"I know." She crossed her hands before her bosom. "What I *want* to know is how you got me released."

He grabbed an apple and tossed it from one hand to the other. He would tell her just about the meeting with Joséphine.

"Louis?" she whispered.

"Joliette arranged a meeting for me with a woman who knows Barras rather intimately. I gave her my maman's emerald-and-diamond brooch in exchange for her speaking with Barras. I hope you did not want the jewel?"

"Of course not. Who is this woman?"

Louis bit into the apple, chewing thoroughly and swallowed. "The former Rose de Beauharnais, now Joséphine Bonaparte."

Geneviève grabbed the apple and took a bite. "I knew Rose."

Louis felt like he'd been splashed with cold water. Had he sacrificed his freedom unnecessarily? Would Joséphine have petitioned Barras on behalf of Geneviève without his revealing his identity? It did not matter. Reclaiming his noble identity was long overdue. "How did you come to know Rose?"

"She took refuge at the Abbaye Penthemont where I lived as a child. I helped care for her two children. She liked me. She was grateful I amused her children so she could rest. She was unwell then. She might remember me."

"I did not tell her your real name."

"No matter. She was able to influence Barras." She took another bite of the apple. "I am indebted to her."

Louis sighed deeply. She bought the story. Now he could relax.

"But..."

Sweat broke out the back of his neck. He knew she was too smart to accept half a story.

She tightened his maman's shawl about her. "The superintendent of the asylum burned my false papers and told me to get new papers at the Hôtel de Ville. He called me Madame LaGarde. How did he know?"

He nodded. "Rose de Beauharnais knew me when I was a courtier at Versailles."

"Then you have exposed your noble self." Her voice rose. "Louis, why?"

"To save you and our child." He regretted his quick reply. No doubt Geneviève already felt guilty for having revealed herself. He stared at his boots. "I have not been imprisoned, so it matters not."

"How did you explain escaping the guillotine?"

"All prisoners were released the day after Robespierre's death, including Rose, and I told her I had the same luck."

"Look at me, Louis." She gently squeezed his hand.

He blinked, pushing back the fear and sorrow flooding him. The muscles around his mouth twitched, and he pressed his lips together.

"You had the same look in your eyes the day I told you of Magdeleine's death."

He swallowed against the hard knot in his throat.

"Tell me." She entwined her fingers with his. The tiny lines around her eyes deepened.

The carriage passed a crumbling château probably burned by Revolutionaries. Louis thought of the Ancien Régime. In return for fighting for the King of France, his ancestor had been given land and the title of Comte. Louis and all his ancestors had grown up and lived with a code of honor befitting a Noble of the Sword. He had denied his noble blood to survive prison and escape the guillotine. And now, to reclaim his honor he had committed himself to the army.

He tilted his head back and let his jaw drop. Air rushed in, releasing the tightness in his throat. "I met with Barras, along with Joliette who appealed to him to remove her and Henri's name from the émigrés list. Barras demanded that Henri and I pay our duty to the Republic."

Her grip on his fingers tightened.

Louis stared out the window, past his wife. A brilliant white crane took flight, trailing water droplets shining like diamonds. He could not bear to look at her face. "Both Henri and I have been appointed to Bonaparte's army."

She snatched her hand away. "You are both over twenty-five, married, with children and more on the way. Any one of those facts exempts you both from service."

Louis shook his head. "Henri and I are Nobles—"

"Of the damned Sword. I know. That gives you the privilege of following that warmonger, Bonaparte, into battle? To fight for what?" She flung her hand toward the window. "More land? He hasn't the funds to feed the starving people of France now. Yet he spends more money to conquer more people and lead them to more starvation—all to plunder works of art!" She smacked her hand on the bench. "Is French art not good enough for Bonaparte?"

His wife was far more insightful than most men.

She slammed her boot onto the carriage floor. "Damn your code of honor." She wrapped his maman's shawl tight around her. "I'm going back. Stop the carriage."

He grabbed her.

She yanked away from him. "Eight months in an asylum is nothing compared to you fighting a war! Stop this carriage right now."

He held her arms as she struggled against him. "You are carrying our child. I will not risk both your lives."

"And it is all my fault, not yours. I will take the punishment." Her red-rimmed eyes sparked. "I'm going back." She shrugged off his hands. "You can't stop me."

"Your return will not change Barras's mind."

"You can watch me convince him."

"Henri and I are to join the army in two weeks."

Her red, puffy eyes closed. Her head dropped.

He did not blame her for not wanting to look at him. He embraced her stiff body. "It was a matter of time, my love. I must honor my noble blood."

"Blood. If you come back with any. If it is not spilled all over some other country."

She was right. He might not come back at all. He worked his jaw from side to side as he envisioned holding their newborn babe, whom he would not meet until the child was two years of age—if Louis was lucky. He wanted to hold onto his wife forever.

"Are you to follow him to Italy to steal more paintings and statues?" She kicked at the basket. "Does he think canvases and marble will feed the starving? What does French culture mean if it is built upon plundered works of art?"

Helplessness washed through him. If he were only going to Italy, he would not feel so despairing. He could not tell her about Egypt. She might lose the baby. "Do not worry, my love, If I am captured by the British, I will surrender and help them defeat Bonaparte and bring back the monarchy."

Her fighting posture melted, and she curled up on the bench, her back to him, trembling with silent sobs. He gathered her to him, caressing her. He had no words. He could only give her his strength. While he was with her.

The silence sat between them like a snag in a river, emotions flowing around him, washing his hopes and dreams out to sea, and leaving behind regret and sorrow like flood debris.

She stilled. "I cannot give birth to this baby alone. I'm too scared."

He could not give her his word that he would be there. Nor could he dash her hopes. "Joliette and Aurélia and Tante Nicole will be caring for you."

She shook her head. "They are not you. I am carrying *your* baby."

"You are the bravest person I know. You have the courage of a lion. I know you will bravely bring our child into this world, and you will pass that courage onto him or her. You will be a wonderful mother, and I know you will keep our child safe until I can come home to raise and protect our family with you."

"I don't want you to go, Louis. Please, don't go." Her voice was now a little girl's. "We could board a ship for America." Her plea shattered his heart.

He longed to take her and Louisa away. "I would be arrested for desertion at the border." He cradled her, holding her tighter at every dip and rumble of the carriage.

He would be fighting for a man he did not honor. A man who was no monarch and did not have the divine right to rule France, which was exactly what Bonaparte was after. And worse, Louis had given his word to follow a man he did not respect to the end of the earth.

27

# *Geneviève*

*Loire Valley, France*
*November 1797*

OF ALL THE terrible things I had done in my life, getting my husband conscripted was the thing I regretted most. I'd exchange places in a moment, but he could not do what I faced. Becoming a mother terrified me almost as much as losing Louis.

As we crested the last hill, Château de Verzat towered in the distance, its cream-colored stone walls beckoning me like a warm embrace.

The carriage rattled up the drive and stopped at the château's great doors. Louis hopped out, offering his hand. "We are home."

I leaned back. "Home is our cottage."

He ran his finger along my jaw. "Everyone wants to thank

you for your courage and bravery, especially Aurélia." His voice was as soft as his caress.

"I have no hair. And I stink. People will pity me."

"No one would ever pity you, my darling." He opened his arms. "Come."

I was back at the Abbaye, older girls teasing me in a song about my missing tooth. I pressed my hand atop my bonnet. "I don't want anyone to see me like this."

"My darling, your coiffure is your badge of courage."

"Very funny."

"Are you going to hide in the cottage until it grows back?" He rubbed his chin. "That could take a while. How will you run the estate from there?"

It would take years for my hair to grow back. I was being ridiculous, childish. But seeing the looks of pity in everyone's face? I couldn't do it. "Everyone will know I've been in an insane asylum," I hissed.

"They already know, my darling, and they are proud of you. I imagine Tante Nicole might be a bit jealous." He reached for me. "Be gracious and accept their admiration and thanks." He encircled my waist, scooted me across the bench, and brought me out. I teetered, and a wave of nausea slid through me. His hands squeezed mine. "Let us not keep them waiting."

A stickiness coated my tongue. I was paying a terrible price for not keeping my word. But Louis was paying with his life. I had to be strong for him, for he faced a far more dangerous future. Raindrops plopped onto the gravel, and a gust of wind showered rain upon us. My bonnet would be soaked and reveal my ugly, bald head.

I would have to do this, so I could be alone with Louis. We had only two weeks together. I tied the bonnet ribbons tighter and pulled his maman's shawl over me. "Let us go home soon, please?"

"Certainly, ma chérie."

Forgetting I was wearing skirts, I dragged them through the mud.

## 28

# *Geneviève*

*Château de Verzat*
*November* 1797

THE FIRMNESS OF Louis's hand on my back was reassuring, yet a reminder I couldn't flee. He pushed open the door, and the warmth of the room enveloped me.

Tante Nicole, wearing a long apron over her wine-colored gown, stood next to Thérèse, a mountain of mushrooms on the worktable before them. Tante Nicole handed a metal cylinder, the size of a finger, to Thérèse, who slipped it beneath the fichu covering her neckline.

Did Tante pay for the mushrooms? Odd. We all bartered at the estate.

My hands itched to cover my head. "Bonjour." My voice was weak.

Thérèse grabbed up her basket, clutching it to her bosom, looking from Tante to me. "Welcome home." She hurried out the door, clutching the basket.

"Welcome home!" Tante Nicole, blue eyes bright as stars, hurried to me.

Her gown was shiny with wear, but she was every bit as elegant as the day I'd met her. Her silvery white hair gleamed in the candlelight.

She embraced me. I pressed myself into her warmth, inhaling her lilac scent. "I'm sorry for my stink," I whispered.

She hugged me more fiercely, then pulled back and looked deeply into me. "We were all so worried."

Tears pricked. I squirmed trying to hide my head, but her strong arms stilled me. Her loving gaze reminded me of my maman, making me long for her terribly.

"But knowing your bravery, we need not have worried." Tante Nicole kissed me on each cheek and once again on the forehead. "We have missed you, my dear." Gripping her walking stick, she guided me to the long table at the center of the cavernous stone kitchen. "You must be hungry."

The smell of mushroom soup simmering over the fire made my stomach cramp. I was starving. But another pair of hands clasped mine before I sat. The tender soft touch of Aurélia's fingers stopped me.

I pulled her to me. "I am so glad you are safe."

As she rubbed my back, her tears fell onto my neck. We held each other as the terror of that night in the bordel scored my heart. I squeezed my eyes against the memory. Her fingers brushed my cheek, and I wiped my eyes.

Face wet with tears, she mouthed, *Thank you.* She patted her belly and then mine. She smiled, kissed my hands, and led me to a chair. *I must put Charles to bed.*

"Good night." I hugged her and sat before bowl of steaming mushroom soup. Tante poured wine.

"Papa!" Louisa's screech and laughter shimmered like a bell. She ran from the doorway and leaped into Louis's arms.

I held my breath. She would be angry with me if she learned I played a part in her father's absence. Yet, she would need all the love I could shower upon her. In my heart, I knew all my love would never make up for her missing Louis. I gulped some wine.

He kissed Louisa and tossed her up in the air, catching her with a dramatic swoop. Her giggles rang against the stone walls. "Geneviève and I have a surprise for you." He led her by the hand and sat her upon the table facing me. He joined us.

Louisa leaned toward me, picked up the ruffle of my bonnet, and whispered, "Tante Gen, what happened to your hair?" Her eyebrows scrunched together.

"You don't like my new coiffure?" I patted my head, pretending to adjust luxurious curls.

She giggled. "No."

Louis clamped his hands around Louisa's waist and sat her in his lap. "We shall tell you about her hair this evening. Now, we have a surprise for you."

She held her cheeks. "What?"

Louis looked at me, pride brimming in his eyes. "Geneviève is going to have a baby." He looked at his daughter. "You are going to have a baby brother or sister."

Louisa clapped her hands. "Where is the baby?"

"The baby is in Geneviève's tummy." Louis gently patted my belly.

Louisa's mouth dropped open. "You ate the baby?"

Tante Nicole's peel of laughter yanked a laugh from me.

"No. The baby is growing inside Geneviève," Louis explained.

"How did it get in there if she didn't eat it?"

I tried to put on a serious face, but seeing Tante stifling her laughter, mine escaped.

Louis blushed. "When the baby grows big, it will be born."

"When, Papa?" Louisa's blue-green eyes sparked with wonder.

Louis pushed out his lower lip. "In the summer, sometime."

"Is it summer tomorrow?"

He shook his head. "It is when the grapes are almost ripe."

Louisa's face grew serious. "That is a long time to wait."

"It is." I chewed a bite of mushroom to stop my imagining the vendanges without Louis.

"I can't wait." Louisa snuggled into her father.

The fire snapped, and I relished its warmth and smokey odor. The room smelled like home. I loved this safe feeling. Something hitched in my chest. I would not feel safe again until Louis returned.

The wooden door banged open, and a cold gust rushed into the room. Simon poked his head in and took off his hat, dripping rainwater upon the stone floor. "I have a surprise for you all. Are you ready?"

I took a gulp of wine. I couldn't take another surprise.

Louisa jumped up. "Yes!"

Simon entered, pulling behind him a radiantly smiling young woman. "I would like you all to meet my future wife, Emilie."

He was too young.

"Welcome, my dear. I am Tante Nicole."

"Enchantée." Emilie dipped a curtsey.

Louis rose and shook Simon's hand. "Our félicitations to you both."

Louisa stood before Emilie. "Enchantée, Mademoiselle. You are very pretty."

Emilie thanked Louisa and hurried to the table and stood across from me. "It is an honor to meet you, Madame LaGarde. I have always admired you from afar."

She was younger than Simon. "Merci."

"We need to rest. We've been traveling all night and day." Louis took my hand and led me to the door. "Please excuse us."

I wrapped the shawl around my shoulders and followed him.

"May I ask a favor, Gen?" Simon called out.

I looked back at him. He stood straight and tall with his broad shoulders squared. He'd shown the same dignity and bravery the day I'd met him. The day he'd killed a soldier to save Tante. He'd been only thirteen. He had grown from a gangly colt-like young man to a stallion in the last few days. "Of course."

"May we have a wedding party in the tasting room?

"Certainly, Simon. When?"

"Next week." Joy beamed in his face. "I wish to marry before I join Louis and Henri in Egypt."

Louis's grip on my arm tightened. A sheen of sweat broke over me.

"We look forward to the celebration." Louis led me out into the rain. "I must get Geneviève home."

# 29

# Geneviève



Taking great gulps of air, I yanked away from Louis and stumbled across the vineyard, the vines blurring. He caught me up in his arms.

"Egypt?" I pummeled my fists against his chest. "When were you going to tell me?"

He cupped my head to his shoulder. "Shush, my love."

I let him pet me, soothe me. I was too tired to fight. The heat that had surged through me drained, and I grew cold. "Let me go."

He released me.

I wrapped the shawl over my head. "When were you going to tell me?"

His shoulders hunched. "I could not make things worse for you yesterday. You were so frail; you still are. I am sorry you found out this way."

"Egypt is half a world away."

"I will be back within two years."

"Our child will be two years old before you meet him." I kicked at rocks, sending them tumbling down the muddy hill.

"You will not be alone."

I turned so fast I dizzied and had to spread my feet for balance, like I did when I dressed like a man, but I nearly tripped over my skirts. "How am I to be a leader and manage more than a thousand people without you?" I ripped the ties under my chin and wrenched the bonnet from my head. "And without hair?" I threw the bonnet to the ground. "I look like a newly hatched chicken." The rain pricked my scalp like shards of ice.

The corner of Louis's mouth quivered.

"Go ahead. Laugh. You know it's true!"

He ran his finger along my jaw. "Everyone loves you and is loyal to you."

Sorrow tugged at the corners of his eyes. Rain battered his hat and dripped down his neck. He was the one who had to leave us all. I didn't want to make things worse for him. But I could not bear the thought of my life without him. "Take me with you. Other women accompany their husbands. Bonaparte will be taking Joséphine. She won't let him go without her."

He shook his head. "You and our child must stay here, where it is safe." He wrapped his arms around me and kissed my bald head.

His lips and breath were so warm. "Please," I whispered.

He picked me up and cradled me in his arms. I pressed myself into him, wishing I could meld my body into his, so he *had* to take me with him wherever he went. I had to stop thinking of myself and start thinking of him. He would be facing not only loneliness, but also war. Carrying me in his arms, he started down the hill, sliding in patches of mud.

"Where are you taking me?"

"To bed. I have never made love to a chicken."

My laughter broke the shell protecting my heart, and love surged through me. He had tried to make things easier for me. He had made me laugh and forget for one second that he was leaving. I had to let go of my own fear and do the same for him. "Louis?"

"Yes, my love."

I ran my fingers along his jaw. "I shall make you crow like a rooster."

His laughter rumbled in his chest and reverberated in mine. I'd make him forget for just a little while. He would be traveling half a world away, facing only God knew what.

I prayed I could summon enough strength to show him a brave face and let him go. I knew I would fail miserably.

# 30

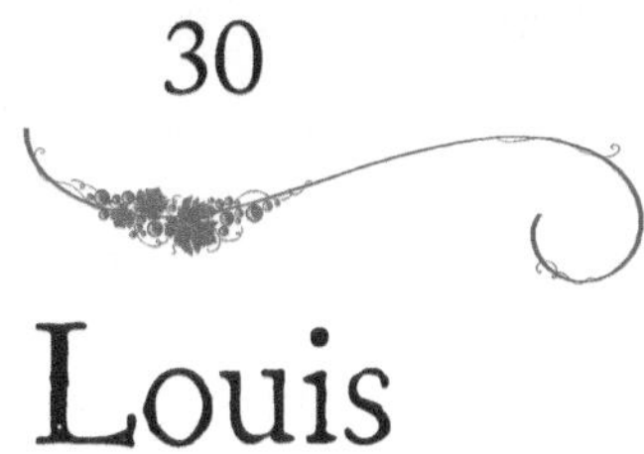

# Louis

*Château de LaGarde Orphanage*
*November 1797*

Riding hard, louis led Simon to the orphanage while he entertained the ways in which he could exact revenge on Suzanne. Before he left the country, he had to ensure she did not harm Geneviève. He prayed he could calm his rage enough to remain a gentleman, no matter how she provoked him, and not kill her.

Dusk fell as he arrived at his former château. Orange light crept beneath a streak of clouds, making the cream-colored stone walls blush like a lady. He tied up his horse and motioned Simon inside.

Adrien opened the door and grinned. "Welcome back, Louis. I am happy to see you, and you, Monsieur Simon."

Louis embraced him and clapped him on the back. "I am here for only a few moments. Would you ask Cook and Maria to join us?"

Adrien, Cook, carrying her stained wooden spoon, and Maria, a nervous, thin woman, whose trembling hands picked at her apron, joined Louis and Simon in the foyer.

"Merci. I am going to ask you all to witness something. Will you?"

They nodded.

"Adrien, please bring Suzanne here. Maria, please pack Suzanne's hat, cloak, and belongings and bring everything here."

Cook bit back a smile and whispered, "I hope you are kicking that viper out."

Louis had no idea Suzanne was so ill-liked. He would have to ask more about the residents in the future.

"Louis! What a lovely surprise." As Suzanne leaned over the balustrade, her bosom spilled over her décolletage. Descending the steps like she was mistress of the château, she spread her arms and hurried across the foyer to Louis, her musky perfume stinking the air.

He removed a length of rope from his pocket, grabbed Suzanne's wrists, and tied them.

"I don't remember you enjoying bondage, Louis." Her laugh was brazen.

He backed away from her, swallowing against the urge to retch. "Did you inform on Magdeleine to the Committee of Public Safety?"

She snorted a laugh. "Where did you hear that rumor?"

Cook moaned and her meaty hand wiped a tear.

Suzanne had not denied it. Pain arced across Louis's chest. Magdeleine had trusted and loved Suzanne. "Did you inform upon my wife?"

She batted her eyelashes. "What wife, Louis? You can't say you are truly married to that man, Jean Detré?"

"Stop the mummery." Louis pressed his fists to his hips to keep from strangling her. "Did you poison the food you gave to Geneviève?"

"Geneviève who?"

Cook's inhale was sharp. Her wooden spoon vibrating, she closed in on Suzanne. "You poisoned my food?"

"I don't know what you're talking about, you old cow." Suzanne was at least a head shorter and half the weight of Cook.

Louis wanted to spit his disgust in her face. "Not even the rats would eat it."

Cook brought up her arm. "Salope." She slapped the spoon across Suzanne's face so hard the wooden handle broke. Suzanne stumbled across the foyer. Cook exhaled like a charging bull.

Louis wanted to thank the woman, but he put his hand on her arm to calm her. Cook nodded, threw the spoon handle at Suzanne, and slapped her hands as if to rid them of filth.

Suzanne leaned against the wall, breathing hard. A trickle of blood ran from her nose. But her dark eyes glinted with defiance.

Maria descended the steps, gingerly placed a portmanteau and cloak at Suzanne's feet, and quickly ran to Cook's side.

Louis withdrew a leather pouch, spilled out a pile of gold coins into his palm, and showed them to everyone. "You all are witnesses. Should Suzanne ever return to this orphanage again, you will report her for stealing this money from me." He spilled the coins back into the pouch. "And have her arrested."

One by one, Louis looked to each person who nodded.

Suzanne cackled. "You're paying me to leave." She licked at her dripping blood.

Louis wrapped the leather strings around the pouch envisioning strangling Suzanne with them. An image of locking her in the family crypt crossed his mind, but he did not wish to contaminate his family's estate. He could hang her in the country: let crows peck her eyes out.

A queasiness moved through him. He did not want to say what had to be said, but he had to save a young boy. "Your son will remain here for his own safety. You are an unfit mother."

She smiled, like she had received a gift.

Any mother would fight for her child, but Suzanne seemed relieved of a burden. Her son would be far better off without her. "Simon, will you put this creature on your horse, please?"

Simon's bootheels clacked as he strode to Suzanne. He grabbed the length of rope, jerked her to her feet, and pulled her after him. Her skirts rustled as she screeched and fought him.

Louis turned to Adrien, Cook, and Maria. "Thank you. I pray she does not return, but should she, make haste to report her. She is dangerous."

Adrien and Maria nodded.

"If I don't kill her first." Cook smiled a wicked smile. "May I give her some food for her journey?"

Louis and she laughed. He embraced each of them and bid them farewell. He longed to tell Adrien where he was going, but it was safer for everyone not to know.

He retrieved the pouch and Suzanne's valise and headed into the dusk.

# 31

# Louis

*Chartres, France*
*November* 1797

With Suzanne screeching, they rode into the night. Simon gagged her with his handkerchief, and Louis was grateful.

Near midnight, they arrived at a village square. The stained-glass windows of a gothic cathedral glowered down at them like angry eyes.

They dismounted. Simon reached to help Suzanne down. She kicked out, hitting him in the chest, knocking the breath from him. He bent over, struggling to inhale.

Infuriated, Louis lunged. Simon grabbed the rope and yanked her off the horse, spilling her across the worn cobblestones. He ripped his handkerchief from her mouth, and she cried out.

She covered her head, fearful the horse might kick her, and Louis wished it would.

Louis threw her valise atop her. She snarled and hugged the bag to her chest. Her henna-colored hair was knotted and matted and stuck out in witchy points around her head.

Louis wished he had brought a razor to give her a coiffure like Geneviève's. He looked down at her. "You have money for lodgings for a few days. As you are too old to resume your former profession, I suggest you start looking for honest work."

Fright pinched her eyes. "There's nothing here but ghosts!"

"If you ever come near my family again, you, too, will be a ghost."

"Untie me!" She struggled against the rope.

Louis mounted his horse.

"I'm glad Magdeleine is dead." Her laugh sliced through Louis.

He jumped down and stormed toward her. She scrabbled to her feet and backed against the stone wall of the cathedral.

Louis's chest burned with a hatred he never suspected he could possess. He grabbed her neck and with one hand, lifted her off the ground.

She gasped, her bound hands clutching his arm.

He pressed his fingers into her neck.

Her eyes bulged.

He pulled her toward him and slammed her against the wall.

Her face paled.

He tightened his grip.

Her arms dropped.

"Magdeleine's kindness is the only thing that is stopping

me from killing you." He shoved her head against the wall and let go.

She dropped to the cobbles, heaving for breath.

He had been a fool. Offering her and her son a home and protection all these years, never guessing she could be so heartless and cruel. He inhaled deeply and spewed his abhorrence out in a slow, steady stream of air.

As he mounted his horse, a breeze crossed the back of his neck, reminding him of Magdeleine's gentle touch. It was good she never knew of Suzanne's betrayal.

"Untie me!" Suzanne screamed.

Across the alleyway, a window shutter banged open. A woman in a white gown stood at the open window and heaved a chamber pot, splashing slops over Suzanne.

Suzanne sat stunned, silent, dripping.

Simon laughed.

Louis urged his horse into a gallop. He did not wish to spend one more moment away from Geneviève.

Only when they were outside the village did Louis allow himself a piteous laugh at the image of the trussed-up, shit-and-piss-covered, conniving bitch. He hoped he would not regret *not* killing her.

Magdeleine's face appeared, her presence wrapping around him like a cocoon of love. He implored her: Watch over our daughter and Geneviève for me.

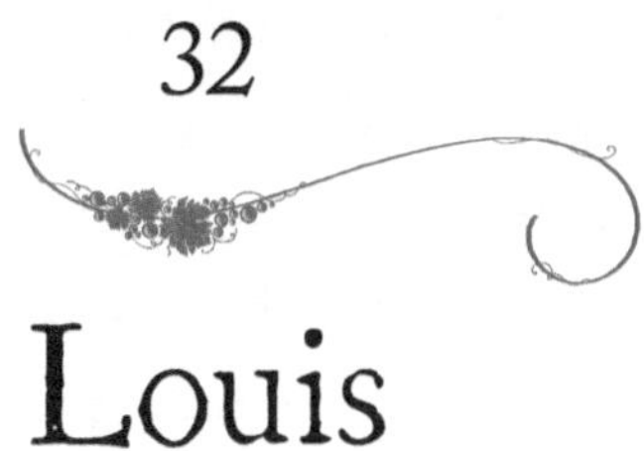

# Louis

*Château de Verzat*
*November* 1797

Louis WANTED TO devour Geneviève. But she was so fragile, he gentled his lovemaking. Exhausted, she lay sleeping, the tufts of her damp hair curling on her scalp. He inhaled the scents of mint and thyme and sage from bundles of plants hanging from the beams supporting their cottage roof. He would forever recall this moment whenever he smelled one of the herbs.

His mind raced. He was honor-bound to defend king and country, but there was no king. He despised the corrupt government and Bonaparte. How could he fight for his country when he did not believe in the battle? There had to be a way of honoring his code without being a traitor. A way of helping the future king of France to return to his throne. And a fellow Noble of the Sword might know a way.

He found Tante Nicole, a woman who once wore diamonds and silks while gracing the elegant salons at Versailles, wearing a stained apron and chopping leeks in the château kitchen.

"How is Geneviève feeling?" Tante's deep purple gown had faded, but her eyes sparkled bright as a blue jay's.

"Tired. She is resting." Louis removed his hat, swept it to the side with a flourish, and bowed deeply. "Madame la Marquise de Bourran, may I have the pleasure of your company on a promenade of the garden?"

Head held high, she lowered herself into a curtsey. "It would be my greatest pleasure, my dear Comte." She removed her apron and tied her frayed bonnet over her silver hair.

Louis took her cloak from a peg, wrapped it around her, and opened the door. He welcomed a chill wind as they walked out into the overcast afternoon.

Tante rested her hand on his forearm as he guided her through the barren garden and up a gentle slope to the viewpoint overlooking the Loire River. Beyond, dark clouds sat over the stubble of a harvested field. After brushing leaves from a stone bench, he laid his cloak upon it and helped her to sit. The damp air smelled musty.

She placed her walking stick before her, resting her swollen hands atop the silver swan-shaped handle. Her serenity shook twenty years from her face.

Sitting next to her, he stared at the swirling Loire. A barge laden with sheep bucked the waves as it struggled upstream. He folded and unfolded his sleeve cuff. "Were you a marquise before you married?"

She tilted her head. "A comtesse."

He wiped his sweaty palms against his breeches as a barge stacked with logs fought the current, yet the bargeman persevered, rotating the tiller until the vessel headed for calmer water.

"Your thoughts have taken you far away." Her voice was gentle.

He scuffed his boot through wet leaves. "It is difficult to know how to begin."

"I am so glad you have lost your arrogant veneer, like the thick maquillage—complete with white paint and rouge—you wore at Versailles." She laughed. "Tell me, everyone knew that wearing a beauty patch on the left meant you were available to your mistress. But you always wore your diamond-shaped beauty patch on your right cheekbone. You must have had a mistress?"

His face warmed despite the chill. He had been so vain and cunning. "A mistress wants a man more if she thinks he is unavailable. Besides, why reveal myself to her husband if he is unaware he is a cuckold?"

"Very wise." Her laughter was deep.

"Wily. I avoided duels."

"As I said, wise." She rotated her stick in the leaves lifting a few into the wind. "I think you will be missing Geneviève and Louisa very much."

His chest tightened, pressing the air from his lungs. "Did your husband fight in Louis the Fifteenth's army?"

"We both did." Eyes sparkling, she looked across the river. "I followed Philipe's troop. He was wounded, and I nursed him. He would have died."

"You followed Philipe into battle? That sounds like something my wife would do."

"I believe she would if she were not expecting your child." She patted his hand. "We Nobles of the Sword have our own way of conversing. Remember all the machinations, witty slights, and double meanings that could charm a snake? Are you not glad we no longer must play that game?"

He huffed a laugh. "Indeed."

"Then ask me what you wish."

He inhaled as if he were about to plunge into icy water. "As a Noble of the Sword, I was loyal to and obeyed the King and promised to defend France." He loosened his neckcloth. "But neither the Directoire nor Bonaparte is king. I cannot find it in me to defend a leader I do not respect, yet I am loyal to France."

The lines about her eyes softened. "What is your *personal* code, Louis?"

"To protect those I love. To be honest, loyal, faithful, and true. To defend the innocent and not kill except in defense."

"Should Bonaparte require you to go against your personal code?"

He jolted. "At risk of facing a firing squad, he could not force me to go against my personal code."

Sorrow filled her eyes. She had seen battle; he had not. Could he kill a man? His wife had. Geneviève was more experienced. He had been trained by the King's own tutor in swordsmanship and marksmanship, had bested every other courtier with his rapier but had the good sense to allow the King to best him. Yet, he had never killed.

Tante's gaze followed a man casting a fishing net from the shore. "After my husband was wounded, he taught me cryptography, and we both served Louis the Fifteenth. When Philipe passed, I continued and then served Louis the Sixteenth."

"With cryptography?"

She sucked in her lower lip, pushed it out, sucked it in, and out again. "Can you not puzzle it out, Louis? Is this not the true subject of your inquiry? The reason for our promenade?"

His thoughts blurred. He could not speak nor accuse her of—espionage.

Her laughter was deep. "Philipe and I spied on and reported those courtiers traitorous to the King. Why do you think I noticed where you wore your beauty patch? The ways courtiers opened snuff boxes, tapped fans, and adjusted ostrich plumes revealed clues in a language Philipe and I monitored."

His mouth grew dry. "Thérèse is your courier. When she sells her mushrooms at the market."

"Neither you nor Geneviève had arrived when everyone on the estate witnessed the first mass drownings of Catholics, whom the Revolutionaries deemed Royalists." She lifted her walking stick toward the river. "They tied Catholics together and forced them onto a barge they had drilled with holes. As the barge listed and began to sink, men yelled to save the children. Women shouted prayers to the Virgin. Children screamed for their mamans. We could do nothing...but watch." Her voice quivered. "The river swallowed them."

The beautiful Loire was a graveyard. "You report these events to the future king?"

She nodded and stared at the dead leaves at her feet. "The silence that followed was worse than their pleas for help."

She pounded her walking stick into the ground. "I despised the Revolutionaries and now the Republicans. Thousands have been put to death by drowning or the guillotine the self-righteous Republicans drag from village to village. She grasped his arm. "None of those horrors ever happened under the monarchy."

A buzzing filled his head. When imprisoned, he had heard rumors of these atrocities but not realized thousands had been slaughtered.

"There are no trials for the hard-working people they murder. Republicans seize their homes, livestock, and land, which I suspect is their true goal." Tante's eyes grew dark. "And the Republicans desire this estate. I will help the rebel Chouans rebels in every way I can. I will help destroy the barbaric bastards who drag the word *Liberté* through the innocent blood they spill."

She was a Royalist…and a spy. His arms grew heavy, as if he had participated in the battles she described. "I always admired you, now even more so." He wiped his brow. "How can I help the future king return to the throne?"

"You are not the only person who is dissatisfied with our current government. Why do you think news of the Egypt Campaign is not published in the pamphlets? Do you think the people of France wish to risk more French blood for a patch of desert? But you can use your position to help restore the monarchy."

"As a traitor," he whispered.

"You swore your allegiance to the King. Not to the Directoire, not to Barras, not to Bonaparte."

"But should France be beaten by the British because of my betrayal?"

"The British do not wish to govern France. They want peaceful trade and the return of the monarchy. King George will deliver Louis the Eighteenth to the throne."

A prickling moved up Louis's spine. How had she kept her espionage a secret for most of her life? "Does anyone else know of your…activities?"

A sly glint lighted her eyes. "Every Royalist wears the sacred heart." Tante reached into her bodice and pulled out a tiny cross stemming from a golden heart. She unpinned it from the inside of her neckline and held it in her palm. "I have been working with the Chouan rebels since I arrived here, six years ago. I send coded intelligence to the spymaster telling him where the Chouans will attack the Republicans." She tucked away the cross. "And should British troops show up to fight alongside the Chouans, so much the better for a restoration of the monarchy. Do you think anyone suspects?"

"No." He rubbed his hands along his thighs. "Have you never feared being caught?"

"When I was younger. When I feared I might lose my husband. But after Philipe passed, I had nothing to lose." She looked back at the château. "I am careful. I do not endanger the estate. But who would suspect an old woman? I do not wear my jewels anymore." She flicked her naked earlobe.

Louis believed she had sold her jewels long ago, to help the winery. Now he realized it was to support the Chouan rebels who protected the Royalists. "I have much to lose—Geneviève, my children. And if I am associated with this estate, everyone on it." He gripped the cold stone bench.

"All the more reason to spy for the monarchy when you are far away."

He circled his fingers at his temples, pressing hard, pushing at an ache running down into his jaw. He had to adjust his sense of nobility.

"I can arrange for the Master to contact you."

A spymaster. He had read about them in books. Louis dragged his fingers down his jaw. "I have kept nothing secret from Geneviève."

"You must keep this a secret to protect her and your children." Her gnarled fingers clasped his hand. "That way she will not fear for you, and she may never know."

"She may never forgive me for taking such a risk."

She laughed. "Have you forgiven her risks?"

He joined her laughter. "I must think about what we have discussed. I will let you know my answer before I depart."

Her fingers were warm. "I am glad you trusted me to speak of this."

"I am relieved you will not report me."

Her joyful laughter rang like a silver bell. "Let us return. Marquise de Bourran must finish cooking. You and your family will join us tonight for Oncle Louis's Lentil Soup?"

He kissed her cheek. "Yes. I admire you and thank you."

Tears glistened in her smiling eyes.

A flock of geese rose from the river and flew across the vineyard. He would miss the peace and calm of this place. He would have to carry it all, along with his love for his family in his heart. And pray to God he would return. Being caught as a spy would destroy all hope of returning.

# 33

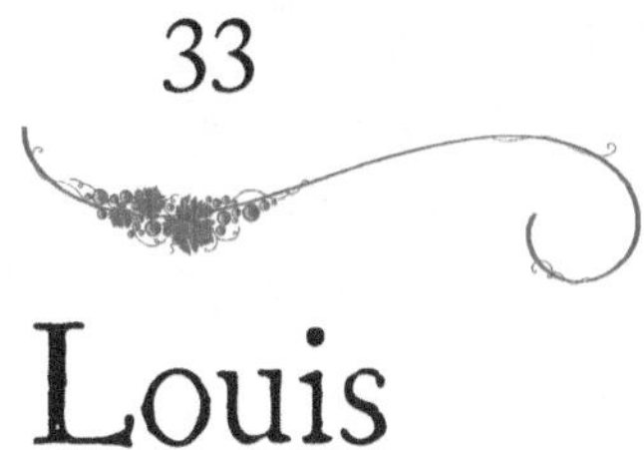

# Louis

*Château de Verzat*
*November* 1797

Wɪᴛʜ ʜɪs ᴀʀᴍ under Geneviève's head and her leg curled over his hip, Louis moved not a muscle and watched her sleep, listening to her soft breaths. The candle guttered. He waited for his eyes to adjust to the watery moonlight, casting a silvery glow over Geneviève's bare skin. He had a terribly short time to cherish her, although he would carry her in his heart no matter where Bonaparte marched him.

A surge of love shuddered him as he caressed her patchy, bald scalp. He loved her fight, her spirit, her strength. Her stubbornness made fights challenging, and he enjoyed their sparring. He most enjoyed the making-up-after their arguments. She brought out the best in him. She had been his partner ever since the day she appeared in his cell, telling him he was going to live. All because of her determination not to let him die for being born a noble.

Geneviève moaned. He caressed her stomach. He longed to be at the birth of their child. Instead, he would be on a battlefield, witnessing the deaths of many men. How would he bring himself to kill a man? He always won duels, but had only wounded the men, never killed one. His wit had been his sharpest weapon. Facing a battalion of men had to be chaos. How would he command his men to kill if he himself could not bring himself to do so?

Louis inhaled Geneviève's sweet smell of grapes, a fragrance that never seemed to leave her, regardless of the season. He had not been able to sleep at all while she had been in the asylum. He would not be able to sleep for the next two years. He should have had a miniature painted of her, to carry with him, but she would not have sat still long enough. No artist could capture her spirit.

A pale violet light seeped into the cottage. He and the others were to leave just after dawn. He did not want to wake Geneviève, but she would never forgive him if he did not. He caressed the curve of her belly. He had to give her confidence that he would return.

Geneviève blinked, and she smiled an alluring smile, nudging herself into him.

He pulled his hips back, not wanting her to feel his arousal, not wanting the memory of their last lovemaking to be hurried and rushed, not wanting her to cry in his arms. He would not be able to leave her. "It is time."

Her lips trembled. "Did you sleep?"

"A bit. Come, I do not want to keep them waiting."

He pulled on his breeches and boots while he watched her slip on her petticoat. Still so unfamiliar with the feminine pieces, she stopped to examine how to put them on. He helped her into the corset and tied the laces in the back and kissed the special spot on her neck. He spied the silver hair ribbon Louisa had wound into Geneviève's hair the night they danced together for the first time. He lifted it. "May I take this with me?"

"I shall not need it until you return." She pretended to run her fingers through her missing long, luxurious hair.

He wound the silky ribbon around his finger, kissed it, and secreted it into his waistcoat pocket. "I hope our child has your hair."

She placed her hands over his and leaned into him. "I hope our child has your eyes."

He took deep breaths, hoping she did not feel his racing heartbeat. He placed his maman's pink wool shawl over her shoulders, praying his mother's spirit would look over his wife and protect her.

"I wish for you and Louisa to live in the château while I am away." He could not bring himself to say the word *gone*. "Living there will be safer for everyone."

"We will move there today." She woke Louisa and wrapped her in a quilt.

Louis picked up his sleepy daughter and rested her on his hip. She wrapped her arms around his neck. "I don't want you to leave, Papa."

He held his breath, but it did not ease the pain stabbing his heart. "I must do my job for France. I have a very important job for you while I am away."

Her fierce spirit lighted up her eyes. "What?"

"Geneviève will need your help to care for the baby. Will you help her?"

She nodded. "I will teach the baby to read."

"That is an excellent idea. I thank you." Carrying her, he followed Geneviève outside. The silence made the loneliness in his chest thud like a hollow bell.

A stableboy waited at the fence, holding the reins to Louis's horse.

"Will you lead him for me?"

The boy nodded and followed.

As Louis turned up the road, he squinted. Men, women, and children lined the gravel path all the way to the château. He swallowed against the tightening knot in his throat. He took deliberate steps, cuddling his daughter, staring at his destination.

Simon's stepfather, Étienne, removed his hat. "God be with you, Louis."

Louis could only nod.

Simon's maman, Madame Françoise, kissed her rosary and pressed it to Louis's forearm. "May God protect you."

Geneviève whispered, "Merci."

"Don't get killed, Oncle Louis," a tiny boy called out from his father's arms.

He could not remember the little one's name. How would he get to the top of the hill? Louis cleared his throat. "I will not." He forced his feet onward.

Madame Ornay, her face wrinkled like a walnut, bent over her walking stick of old vine and reached out.

Louis clasped her hand and kissed it. "Madame Ornay, will

you promise to help my wife in running this estate? I know she cannot do it without you."

Three teeth gleamed as she broke into a smile. "I promise." She gripped his fingers tightly. "And you must promise to come back soon."

"I give you my word of honor, Madame." He bowed.

Louisa stirred. "Everyone loves you, like they love Tante Gen, Papa."

"And I love them and you, too." He pressed her to him, hiding his face against the quilt. She broke from Louis's arms and ran to Charles and Guillaume.

At the hilltop, Tante Nicole stood to the side of the assembled families, her face knowing. Louis took her hands in his and, before he could speak, she pressed a folded paper into his hand and whispered, "Keep the sacred heart hidden on you at all times and burn the letter as soon as you have read it."

He shoved the paper into his waistcoat pocket, next to Geneviève's ribbon, and nodded.

"God protect you, Louis." She resumed her regal posture. "We shall care for and protect your wife and children while you are away."

"Merci, Tante." He kissed her hand.

He crouched before the children, looking from one to the other. "Remember you are Nobles of the Sword."

The children nodded.

"Being a Noble of the Sword gives you great courage and bravery, so that you can help protect the château while Henri and Simon and I are away."

Guillaume stood tall and saluted Louis. Charles nodded, but his eyes filled with tears, and he hid his face behind Aurélia's skirts. Louisa screwed up her face, unsuccessfully fighting tears, and saluted him.

Louis saluted, stood, and turned to the crowd that had followed him. He gazed at faces weathered by picking in sun, wind, rain; some had cheeks scarred by hail. Faces that had laughed at his wedding. Faces masking sorrow and fear with frozen smiles of encouragement and hope.

He feared the knot in his throat might strangle him, but he willed himself to be calm. "Thank you for seeing us off." He put his arm around Geneviève's shoulders. "We know you will help and support both Geneviève and Joliette in running the winery. We thank you for your loyalty and devotion." His words caught. He hurriedly nodded to Henri and Simon.

Geneviève whispered, "I promise not to cry, for I want you to believe and trust that I will be brave and protect Louisa and our baby until you return to us." She blinked furiously.

Her hands clung to his arms. She was so strong. Stronger than he. He exhaled, trying to stop his legs from shaking. He pressed her to him. "I love you for eternity." He could not say goodbye. He let her go and, without looking at her, he bent and picked up Louisa, breathing her in, squeezing her so she wiggled. "I love you, ma princesse."

"I love you, Papa. Come home soon."

"I promise." He gave her to Geneviève, mounted his horse, and nodded to Henri and Simon. He removed his hat and looked at his wife.

Her brave smile dazzled him. She put Louisa down, threw her head back and crowed like a rooster. He was grateful for her humor and the memory of their love making she had stirred with her crowing. She kissed her fingertips and waved to him as he turned and urged his horse into a gallop.

He did not look back. But images of his maman and papa and brother and Magdeleine blurred before him. He never had the chance to say goodbye to any one of them. What if he should die? What if Geneviève should die in childbirth? The pounding of his horse's hooves jarred his heart. Could he live with the anguish of leaving Geneviève without saying good-bye? Without telling her she was the love of his life, his whole world, his reason for living? He had to be brave for her. Show her courage. But he felt fear wrapping the core of his being. Not saying goodbye was one more regret he did not wish to live with.

He stopped his mount, turned the horse, stood in his stirrups, and shouted, "Geneviève!"

She grabbed her skirts and ran like the wind. He dismounted and raced to her.

"I wanted to say…" Tears poured, and he did not care. "Goodbye." He sputtered, tried to tell her she was the love of his life, but he choked on the words.

She held his face in her hands and smiled as tears dripped down her cheeks. "It takes far more courage to cry than not to cry, my love."

"Then we are both terribly brave bastards."

They laughed. And wept.

He reveled in her arms, holding onto a moment that would have to last for two years.

# 34

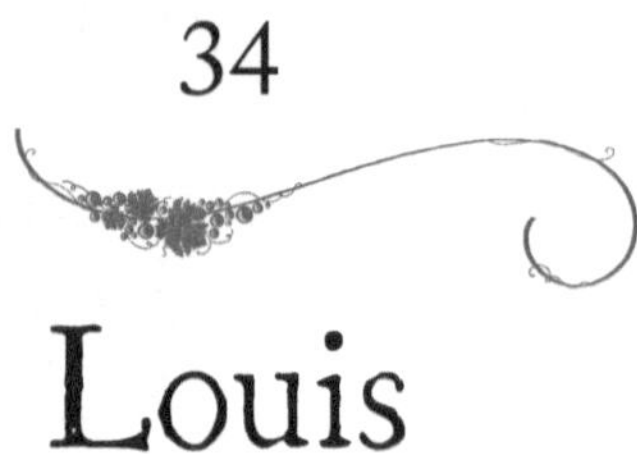

# Louis

*Paris, France*
*November* 1797

EVERY MOMENT TANTE Nicole's letter sat secreted in Louis's waistcoat was a moment sharp with fear. If he ever implicated and thereby endangered her, he would never forgive himself.

He threw his satchel onto the sagging bed of his lodging room, lighted a candle from the smoldering fire, and held her letter before its flame.

His goal was to survive a war he did not believe in. There was only one way he would make it through the next two years: if every one of his efforts undermined Bonaparte's, and at the same time, supported the return of the monarchy. And he would only survive if he were not caught. The sacred heart spilled out of the folded paper, and he tucked it in his waist-coat pocket.

He read:

*We all believe you have the courage and strength to endure if
you remember who you are. Everyone will care for your family
until the glorious day of your return.*

*May God protect you.*

She had not signed the letter. Her writing, delicate as lace, encouraged him, but as the candle burned, writing behind the ink emerged on the paper like a dissipating fog reveals trees. He read:

*I have not seen you since Versailles.
You produce wine, now.
From which port and when will the next vintage be exported?*

He brought the letter closer to the flame, fanning the paper up and down and across the heat to prevent it from burning. Nothing else appeared. He repeated the words until he memorized them, which was not such a great task, but what did the words mean? Surely this was some sort of code.

A soft knock on the door startled him. He wadded the paper and flung it into the fireplace, holding his breath as flames shrank the paper to ash. The knock came again.

He grabbed the poker. "Who is it?"

"Simon."

Louis repeated: *I have not seen you since Versailles. You produce wine now. From which port and when will the next vintage be exported?* He stirred the glowing embers. "Enter."

Simon closed the door behind him and stood rubbing his arms.

"Brandy?" Louis asked.

Simon sat on a ladder-backed chair before the fire. "Please."

"Can you not sleep?" Louis sat on the chest at the foot of the bed and offered his flask.

Simon shook his head and sipped. The flickering firelight made him appear middle-aged.

Louis wished Simon had not followed him and Henri. He was too young to experience war. But was any man old enough?

Simon returned the flask. "Have you ever killed a man?"

This, Louis had hoped to keep secret. He could lie and tell Simon it was a soldier's duty. But lying to him would not be honorable. They were both risking their lives, and Simon deserved to know the truth. "No."

"But you are a marksman, and Tante Nicole said you were renowned for your swordsmanship."

"Both are truths."

Lines gathered on Simon's brow. In the glow of the fire, their bodies cast elongated shadows over the dirty walls, hanging like specters.

Louis took a swallow. "I never wanted to kill a man, and so I used my wit to avoid duels. And when fencing, I always bested my opponent, but I assured them I did not want to kill them. I gave them the opportunity to honorably surrender and prevent my guilt over killing them, which all of them chose." Louis took another swig, hoping his explanation would satisfy Simon. What worked at Versailles would not work on the battlefield. And as much as Louis feared ordering men to kill, he feared killing an enemy even more.

"I've killed a man." Simon's voice was so quiet, Louis was not certain he heard him correctly. He should have brought more brandy.

Simon rested his elbows on his knees and leaned forward, staring at the fire. "A soldier had Tante Nicole pinned against the stone wall of the cave, pressing a dagger to her neck, and threatening to slit her throat. She had dropped her walking stick, and I snatched it up, opened the hidden blade, and thrust it into the soldier's gut." He gripped the flask and took another gulp. "Oncle Albert had trained me how to use the blade but not what it was like to kill a man."

"You defended the life of an innocent. Your act was noble."

"I cried like a baby. And then I vomited" He turned to Louis. "Does killing count as less of a sin if it's a noble act?"

Louis sighed. He wished he knew. "I hope."

"It haunts me so, I'm afraid I won't be able to kill again." He leaned back. "Even if I am commanded to do so."

Louis was terrified of giving that command. He pressed the flask between his palms. "I believe when a man is under attack, his instincts to survive fuel his ability to kill."

Simon burped. "Pardon. Does that mean I will react just as I did for Tante?"

"I suspect we both will behave in the same manner." Louis stared at his muddied boots. He thought being a convincing spy was his biggest challenge. Keeping his men alive in a desert seemed a daunting task.

"I didn't think I'd miss Emilie so soon." He wiped his eyes.

"You fell in love faster than most men fall off horses."

Simon laughed. "There is so much more I want to know of

her, but we didn't have time." He looked up. "Did you fall in love with Geneviève right away?"

Louis squeezed his eyes against the shame washing over him. "Did she not tell you how we met?"

"She never spoke about you to me."

"We first met at Université where she attended, dressed as a man. I did not know she was a woman."

"I didn't know she was a woman either. But Tante Nicole knew right away."

If he told Simon the truth, would he respect him less? Louis dragged his bootheel along the warped floorboards. He had been so ashamed of his actions he had left not only Université but also the country.

"Louis?"

He sat up straight and looked directly at Simon. "I am talented with a rapier, and to embarrass the man I thought she was, I drew it from her neckcloth to her waist, cutting through waistcoat, tunic, and binding," he cleared his throat, "and exposed her breasts." He let his head drop.

Simon guffawed. Stomped his boot, slapped his leg, and guffawed again.

Louis let out a little laugh. He supposed it was funny to someone not involved in the act.

"What did she do?"

"She threatened to report me to her father, the Public Prosecutor."

Simon whistled.

"She did not. But three years later, her father did condemn me to the guillotine, and until she showed up in my cell, I thought she had reported me."

Simon rubbed his hands. "I don't think she could ever do such a thing."

"You are correct, but I did not know that at the time. She replaced my name with one of a man already dead. She could have gone to the guillotine for saving my life." He placed a log on the fire. "She told me my name would not be called for the guillotine. I, being the arrogant bastard I was, did not believe her. But she convinced me. That was the moment I began to fall in love with her, her courage, her strength, her selflessness."

Simon snorted a laugh. "I fell in love with Emilie's passion, her joy…her breasts."

Louis chuckled.

"Are you afraid to die?" Simon's eyes grew glassy.

Louis handed him the flask. He had to act with more bravery than he felt. "Before Louisa was born, while I was waiting to be guillotined, I do not think I was afraid. But since her birth, since falling in love with Geneviève, and especially now, with another child on the way, yes. I am afraid to die. I fear never meeting our baby."

Simon drained the flask. "Tante Nicole told me living requires more courage than dying."

"She is most wise."

"I have a favor to ask." Simon stood. "Should anything happen to me…will you and Gen protect Emilie?"

"Certainly." Louis clapped him on the back. "But nothing shall happen, my friend. You have courage and strength, intelligence and common sense. You need only self-assurance, and that you shall earn while training as a soldier. I shall be proud to have you with me."

Simon turned and clutched him, pressed his face into Louis's chest, and sobbed.

Louis hugged Simon close and, as he held him, Louis let his own tears come. He had worried over being caught as a spy and endangering Tante Nicole. But now his chest burned. He might find the courage to kill an enemy, but where would he find the courage to command Simon in battle?

He rubbed Simon's back. "You are as courageous as a bear, my friend. You and I and Henri will survive this insane war and return to Château de Verzat. I promise you."

Louis prayed he was right.

35

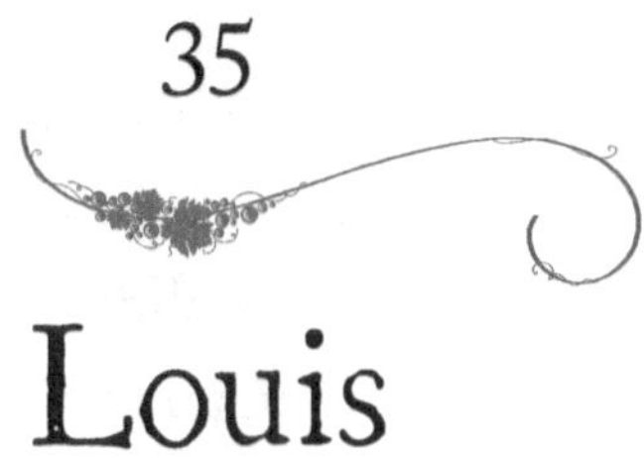

# Louis

*Paris, France*
*December* 1797

DETERMINED TO TRAIN his men for survival, Louis began with the foundation of caring for one's horse. He led his men into the stables, a building as large as the King's Écurie at Versailles. His chest warmed as he inhaled the familiar scent of horses, straw, and leather. Images of the day Geneviève and he had run from a rainstorm into the stables flooded him. Had she conceived that day? He shook himself and faced his troops.

As he turned, a horse whinnied. The animal was lathered, his coat matted. He held his front leg bent with his hoof resting on its tip. Who would be so careless with such a beautiful stallion?

"Who left this horse without brushing him down?" Louis

shouted. He scanned the nearby stalls, but no one appeared or responded.

Louis let the horse sniff him and rubbed the steed's neck, calming the creature. He bent, picked up the horse's hoof, and spotted a wedged piece of gravel, which could cause an infection. Whomever left this horse in pain was a foolish soldier. Louis drew his hoof pick from his pocket and cleaned out the gravel. He released the hoof and the horse gingerly put his weight down. "Brigadier Amoulin!"

Simon stood before him in an instant.

"Please demonstrate how to care for this horse."

Simon retrieved a bucket of water and a brush and set to work.

Louis looked at each of his men. "A soldier's life depends upon his horse. You must take care of your mount as carefully as you would attend a mistress."

"Who dares touch my stallion?" A male voice boomed.

An imposing man dressed as a commandant, his boots shining like mirrors, strode toward Louis. Gold piping ran down the sides of his spotless white breeches and edged the lapels and cuffs of his dark blue frock coat. Although standup collars were the style, his was twice as high as any uniform Louis had seen. He wondered if the man had pillaged Versailles and taken one of the Sun King's wigs, for his hair was so long and curly it did not seem possible for a man or woman to grow such a coiffure. His curls spread over his jaws stopping at his chin to give the impression of an incomplete beard.

Slapping his riding crop against his thigh, he stood before Louis, snorting like a bull. "I am commander of the cavalry, Joachim Murat."

Already standing at attention, Louis stiffened. He had to report to this fop? Louis saluted. "Colonel Louis LaGarde, mon Commandant."

His eyes pinched. "LaGarde, you say?"

His tone indicated that he had met Louis before, but he did not look familiar. "Yes, mon Commandant."

Murat whacked his riding crop along his thigh. "Are you in charge of this imbecile?" Murat pointed at Simon.

Not one of Louis's men fit that description. With purpose, he took on his courtier attitude. "To whom do you refer, mon Commandant?"

Murat tilted his head back. His nose started as a narrow bridge between his eyes, which appeared to be crossed, then sloped and widened at his nostrils so that his nose resembled a duck's bill. "You mock me, Colonel?"

"No, mon Commandant. But none of my men is an imbecile, and therefore I do not know of whom you speak."

The unusually straight fringe of the Commandant's épaulettes quivered. "No one touches my horse," he growled.

"Mon Commandant, the animal had gravel embedded in his foot. As it could become infected, and the horse grow lame—"

"What do I care for a horse? If it goes lame, I shoot it." He stomped to Simon, grabbed the brush from him, and hurled it at the wall. "You will not leave this building until you have cleaned every single stall."

"Yes, mon Commandant." Simon remained at proud attention.

The commandant glared at Louis. "Take care of your own horses, Colonel. Touch mine again, and you'll find yourself demoted to lieutenant."

"Yes, mon Commandant."

Murat stomped away. The back of his blue coat was without lines or creases and the red inset was edged in gold piping. Did his personal valet accompany him in battle? Humiliating Louis before his men gave the Commandant the sorely needed power to inflate his own self-image. Louis would have to anticipate his every expectation, every command. And protect his men from the duckbilled bastard.

The soldiers looked like they had sucked on lemons. Louis shook off his courtier posture and grabbed a pitchfork. "I will never ask my men to do something I, myself, would not do. If we all work together, we can have this building clean in a few hours. Then we will train our horses."

Silently, the men retrieved shovels.

Louis neared Simon and whispered, "I apologize for getting you into trouble."

"His ignorance is not your fault." Simon's eyes sparked like a naughty child's. "Besides, plotting revenge entertains me."

Louis clapped him on the back. "We share a common goal."

Simon stabbed his pitchfork into the filthy hay. "Let's hope his horse does him in and saves us the trouble."

Louis would have to depend upon his old courtier habits—false flattery, insincere concern, innocent undermining of authority—to outwit the bastard, Murat.

# 36

# *Geneviève*

*Château de Verzat*
*January* 1798

A STRONG DESIRE AWAKENED me. Lemon tarte. I rubbed my grumbling belly. Tante Nicole grew lemons in the conservatory, year-round, and had served a tarte that evening. Hopefully, there was a piece left. "I prefer apple, but if it's lemon you want, little one, lemon it shall be."

Not wanting to wake Louisa, I rose and tucked the covers around her.

I wrapped the shawl of Louis's maman around me, feeling his warmth through the soft wool like I did when he'd held me that last day. I lit a candle from the fire embers and gently closed the door behind me.

As I crept down the stairs, another stomach rumble made me smile. "You have Louis's appetite." I walked through the servants' passage toward the kitchen. The muffled sound of a male voice stopped me.

Was it the Capitaine? I pressed my back against the wall. Why hadn't I brought my pistol? Could I reach a knife in the kitchen? What good was a knife if he had a gun? I licked my fingers, snuffed the candle, and inched down the narrow corridor. The voice droned on. If it were the Capitaine, he would not be talking; he'd be taking. I peered around the door.

A candelabra blazed at the end of the long table where Tante Nicole sat with her back to the fire, writing. Opposite her stood a giant of a man, his voice low and stilted. "Third cottage with two chimneys."

Tante dipped the quill and wrote.

A scar ran down the man's cheek, and he held a floppy brown hat at his side. "First night of the new moon. Across the pond. The owl will hoot three times." Despite his proud posture, he leaned heavily on the barrel of his musket, the butt of which he rested on the floor.

The day Thérèse and Anne and the children arrived whirled in my mind. This was the Chouan who had rescued them and brought them to the Verzat caves, seeking shelter, but his face had not been scarred then.

Tante looked up at the giant. "Is that everything?"

He nodded and replaced his hat.

She stood and patted his shoulder. He bowed his head, as if receiving a blessing. She retrieved two loaves of bread and a ham from the cupboard and offered it. "I wish you safety."

"Merci." He accepted the food, opened the wooden trapdoor, descended the steps, and pulled the door closed behind him—quiet as rising smoke.

Tante bent to pull the rug over the trapdoor.

I hurried to her. "Why was that man here?"

Tante dropped the rug and turned so fast she grasped the table to keep from falling.

I steadied her. "The Chouan. What did he want?"

She brought her hand to her heart. "You startled me, my dear. Are you feeling well?"

I held her elbow and guided her to the chair. "I'm fine. What did the Chouan want?"

I thought she was having a spell. She seemed confused, unbalanced. Although seated, she held onto the table. "Why did you come to the kitchen?"

"I had a craving for lemon tarte."

She stood. "We have one piece—"

I pressed her back down. "I watched you both for several minutes. Why was he here?"

She slid the paper off the table and folded it in half. "He cannot write and wanted me to compose a message for his superior."

"Yet, he did not take it with him." Why was she lying to me? A bitterness coated my tongue, like when my father told me he'd followed the laws to the letter by sending thousands to the guillotine.

She creased the paper into another fold.

I sat next to her. "What are you not telling me?"

"I do not wish to endanger you," she whispered.

"We—all—are already in danger. Tell me."

"I wish the future king of France to return…" She twisted her thin wedding band around her finger. "By spying, I turn the tables on the murdering Republicans." Her words spattered like fat hitting flames.

God help us. She was spying against the current government, a crime that could cause the death of every single person on the estate. I forced a slow exhale. I admired her. She was working for change, like I once did. But I had risked only my own life; now I had two children, and I could not risk them.

"Why did you not tell me?"

Cunning flashed in her eyes. "If no one knew, no one could report me."

My face burned as if she had slapped me. "I would never report you. And as vigneron, I have the right to know."

"Years ago, you did not know I instructed the Chouan to bring the women and children to the caves where Simon would discover them. As vigneron, you were the only person who could offer them shelter. If I had brought them to you, you might have made that choice because of me. But I wanted you to make that decision on your own, for it was yours alone to make."

"I trusted you. And you tricked me."

She clapped her hands. "Oh, no. You made that choice independent of me."

My hands grew sweaty. She had betrayed me by omission, just as my father had. She made me think it was my idea when it was hers.

If anyone followed the Chouan, the Republicans will drown every one of us."

"He travels the caves and comes only when I light a candle in the kitchen window." Her lips pressed in a grim line.

The candle flared as I realized we were fighting the same

battle. "I, too, detest the Directoire. And I will do nearly any-thing to hasten Louis's return."

Her eyes brightened.

"How long have you been spying?"

"My husband and I spied for the monarchy before we married. Does this shock you?"

It should have, but ever since the day I met her, when a soldier held a dagger pressed to her throat, she had been incred-ibly strong, dignified, noble. I shook my head.

"I inform the Royalists of Republican activities." She lifted her chin. "I would die in the service of returning the future king to France."

I never thought of her as a Royalist spy, but she had been a courtier—someone the Republicans would delight in murder-ing. I too, hated them, but did I want the monarchy to return? Neither the Directoire nor the monarchy bestowed equal rights to women. A tightness seized my chest.

The fire burned green, blue, orange. A tendril of smoke wound its way up the chimney. I admired her, as I admired my father. But both were human, both flawed, as we all were. Each strived for something beyond their own desires. Was I working for a greater good? I wanted to protect everyone on the estate. Yet, I risked everyone's safety when I harbored the Royalist women and children. I had made that decision with my heart. It had been years since they'd arrived, and no one had reported us. Louis would remind me I was carrying our baby and not to take risks. Yet, he knew I would do what I intended, so he would caution me to think, first, and not endanger our family.

The fire crackled. Would Tante's actions help Louis or put

him in further danger? His voice rang in my mind: *If I am captured by the British, I will surrender and help them defeat Bonaparte and bring back the monarchy.* Could I help him, if I, too, spied against my own country, aid the return of both the future king of France, and our men?

"I wish to hasten Louis's return." I pressed my fingers to my lips not realizing I'd spoken aloud.

Tante stared at the fire, a smile emerging.

"First, I would like some tarte."

She rose, stroked my cheek, and hurried to the counter.

I pulled a log from the pile and added it to the fire. Sparks flurried, and a memory rushed me. I was back at the Châtelet in my father's office where I had burned official documents. The bitter smell of ink swirled. A pressure built in me. My words whooshed out.

"During the Terror, I clerked for my father."

"The Public Prosecutor." She set a plate upon the table.

Louis's name glimmered before the flames. I rubbed my eyes, but his name burned brighter. "I was tasked with copying the list of names of those condemned for execution. Louis's name was on my first list."

She pressed her palm to her heart.

"I replaced his name with the name of one already dead." My words rushed, like a leaf caught in a river's current. "The names of a child and his mother appeared on another." I cleared my throat and folded my hands in prayer. "I left their names off the copies and burned the originals."

She clasped my hands. "How did you avoid being discovered?"

"Who would suspect the Prosecutor's daughter?"

She rested her hand on my shoulder. "You saved lives."

My legs weakened, and I sat at the table. "More than a hundred."

"You are a true counter-revolutionary," she whispered.

Tears slid down my cheeks as the names of those I couldn't save wavered like specters around me. I wished my tears could wash away that memory. My father wasn't the only monster of The Terror. Even now, the Republicans and men like Barras were monsters. Like the innocents I saved from my father, I could save others.

She sat opposite me, her face understanding. Like the day she led me to realize that Louis loved me. Like my wedding day when she wove flowers in my hair. Where were the jewels she'd worn that day?

"Did you sell your jewelry and give the money to the Chouans?"

"Was it not a better use for them?"

"Of course." My wedding day played out before me. Louis's voice echoed as I saw diamonds and emeralds and pearls in my mind. *We will keep my maman's jewels for emergencies—unless you wish to wear them?* We'd both laughed at the absurdity of my wearing such ostentatious necklaces, earrings, brooches. I closed my eyes. This was an emergency.

My lips trembled; I couldn't stop the sorrow. He had used some of the jewelry for my freedom. The remainder should be used to free him. If the King regained his throne, he'd surely recall Bonaparte's army. The fire snapped and the flames flared, casting a golden light across Tante's face, soft with empathy. She reached across the table and intertwined her fingers with mine.

"The Chouans have no home nor food?"

She shook her head. "They live in the Troglodyte caves and move every time they fear being discovered."

"They need supplies and ammunition?"

She nodded.

"I wish to sell the jewelry of Louis's maman. Can you arrange it?"

"Although I have never met the spymaster," she squeezed my hand, "I will arrange for him to meet you at the market."

A spymaster. The guillotine's blade flashed in my mind, dizzying me. "How?"

"I communicate through a former lady-in-waiting. I do not know who the spymaster is."

I laughed. "I hope the spymaster is a woman."

I had the opportunity to change things and help bring Louis home. A frisson of excitement ran through me, just like the day I had entered Louis's prison cell to tell him he wasn't going to the guillotine.

I had no need of men's clothing now. I had the perfect disguise. A tiny laugh bubbled up my throat. "Who would suspect a woman-with-child of traitorous espionage?"

# 37

# *Geneviève*

*Château de Verzat*
*January* 1798

**M**y fingers searched for the leather pouch I had nestled in a drawer among my stockings. Grabbing the silk cords, I pulled the pouch—far lighter, less bulky than I remembered—unwrapped the cords, opened the pouch, and spilled its treasures upon my dressing table.

A strand of pearls slithered out. A gold brooch in the shape of a stag landed with a thud. A small gold signet ring, engraved with the LaGarde crest, rolled across the table. The pouch lay limp, empty.

My gold wedding band was the only thing that had not belonged to Louis's maman, for she had worn her wedding ring to her death. The day Louis had shown me her jewels shimmered in my mind. Where were the diamond-and-emerald necklace with matching earrings, and bracelet? The gold, emerald, and sapphire brooch in the shape of a peacock? The ruby-encrusted hair combs? The butterfly with jade body and wings of aquamarine? The earrings of peridot, topaz, and lapis lazuli?

Putting my hand into the drawer, I clutched at garments and felt only linen fabric and silk ribbons. I searched drawer after drawer, finding only clothing.

The day Louis had rescued me from the asylum played in my mind. I rubbed my forehead. He'd said, *I gave Josephine my maman's emerald-and-diamond brooch…*I'd been so upset then, I might not have heard his exact words, but I remember it was only one piece.

I pressed myself to relive the day I had moved Louisa's and my belongings from the cottage to this chamber. I'd been distracted, missing Louis terribly. I had scooped our clothing into two baskets, draped the chairs and beds with sheets, shut the door and locked it. Could I have dropped pieces of jewelry on my way to the château? No. Someone would have found the gems and brought them to me or Joliette or Tante.

I reached for my cloak and raced to our cottage. As I opened the door, Louis's laughter, his deep voice, his scent of newly mown hay, assaulted me. I pressed the heels of my palms to my eyes. No one would see me here. I let tears drip while images of Louis melted into one another.

My breath shuddered as I opened the drawers, one by one. Empty. All were empty. I sat on the bed, images of Louis and his sparkling eyes filling the room.

Could someone on the estate have taken the other jewels before Louis departed? The warmth of the day everyone climbed the hill to wish Louis goodbye washed over me. Every person who dwelled here was trustworthy. No one had departed, and surely if someone had stolen Louis's trove of jewels they would have fled. That left someone who did not live on the estate. Could a Chouan or Royalist have taken them? Worse, a Republican?

Dust motes flurried in the light streaming through the windows. Like a doe's hoofprints, only my boots marked my presence in the thick layer of dust covering the floor. I had asked Tante to write the spymaster, telling him or her I had a great deal of money for the Chouans to survive and fight the Republicans. With only a gold brooch and string of pearls to offer, might the spymaster think I lied? Think me untrust-worthy?

I shook the dust from my skirts and closed the door on the memories of the life I had lived there with Louis. *I will do all I can to bring you home, my love.*

I hoped it was a Chouan who had taken the jewelry, for the theft wasn't so bad if the jewelry was sold to feed people like Thérèse and Anne. The single brooch and pearls would have to convince the spymaster that I was willing to help the Royalist cause. And to convince him or her to use me as a spy.

38

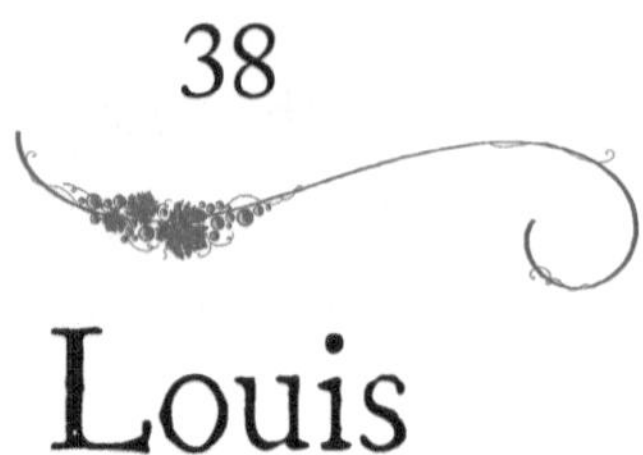

# Louis

*Paris, France*
*January 1798*

Crackling flames devoured logs in the grand fireplace. Louis paced. His men would never survive the frigid night sleeping in the flimsy tents. There was plenty of room for them to bed down in the great hall. Commandant Murat was probably dining with Bonaparte, and if Murat did return, he would be too drunk to demote Louis. If Murat tried to stop him, he would exclaim, *I am ordered to deliver living soldiers to the ships, not frozen corpses.*

Donning his cloak and carrying a torch aloft, he hurried out into swirling snow.

"Colonel LaGarde!" A male voice called out.

The devil! Louis dreaded a confrontation. He turned and peered through the dark, searching the snow-covered courtyard.

A short fellow, his cape ruffling about his boots, approached. He removed his tricorne and bowed his head. "I have not seen you since Versailles," he whispered.

Louis's heart thudded. Tante Nicole's code. Was it a coincidence? She had never told him how to respond. He longed for clarity and thought there would be no harm in repeating the code. "Not since Versailles."

The man's forehead was high and wide, and a thatch of gray hair curled at the top of his receding hairline. Gray eyebrows hooked above his round blue eyes. The man had the appearance of a cupid, but Louis could not remember ever having met him. "You are…"

"Abbé Nodier." His smile caused his nose to rise and twitch, like a rabbit's.

Louis tipped his bicorne. Clergy would not spy. It must be coincidental that he used the code. "Enchanté, Abbé."

"I understand you have been producing wine." He squashed his hat back onto his head and rubbed his gloved hands together. "Before enlisting."

A frisson of alarm shot up Louis's spine. Tante's code was, *You produce wine, now.* How did he know Louis enlisted? Was this man trying to trap him as a traitor?

"The finest wine in France!" Abbé blinked.

Louis stared at him, purposefully making the man uncomfortable. What was this little man after? He would push. "And what wine is that?"

"Château de Verzat, of course."

Everyone knew Verzat was the finest wine, but no one knew Louis helped produce it or lived on the estate. He had to be certain. Tante said spies wore sacred hearts. "Have you any-thing to show me?"

Abbé adjusted his jabot and a flash of gold glittered in the torchlight. A tiny gold heart and cross. This cherubic-look-ing man was the spymaster? Was Louis supposed to show the cross Tante had given him? He dared not. This man-of-god could be laying a trap.

"The finest wine in the world." Abbé clapped. "I understand you export it to America."

Louis nodded. He could not be arrested for admitting either fact.

"Since we are at war with England, it is a pity you can no longer ship through Nantes." He licked his lips.

That was a lie. Joliette arranged shipment on neutral Dutch ships through Nantes. But who, besides Tante, would give him that information? Louis inhaled a shaky breath. He had to take a stand and hoped he was right. "Yes, too dangerous."

Abbé's eyes darted about, appearing to look for anyone who might be near, but the courtyard was empty. "Tell me, from which port do you ship now?"

Louis's mind moved slowly, trying to pinpoint what infor-mation the Royalists needed, for he knew it was not about wine shipments. Ships. Of course. The future king's army wanted to know from which port Bonaparte's ships would depart for Egypt. Louis whispered, "Toulon."

Snowflakes stuck to Abbé's eyelashes. He mouthed, *when?*

Although Louis hated Bonaparte, Henri and Simon and other French soldiers would be on the ships that he would be putting in danger. But he would rather surrender to the British at sea than fight the Mameluke warriors in the desert.

Should anyone overhear, how could Louis camouflage the timing of their departure? He had to continue within the context of the wine. "Since we must arrange for the casks overland, the transport to Toulon can take sixty days or more." He lifted his arm. "But we must wait for these freezing conditions to pass. Otherwise, the wooden casks could split."

Abbé nodded furiously. "Yes, yes. I see."

This man was indeed the spy Tante told him about. Louis looked about then placed his hand on Abbé's elbow and led him to the center of the courtyard, away from any ears hiding in the shadows. Abbé wanted to know when Bonaparte's troops would reach Egypt, but Louis had to conceal that information as well. "Once the ship leaves Toulon, it takes another twenty to thirty days for the wine to reach America." Everyone knew that voyage took sixty to ninety days.

Abbé's smile lifted his eyebrows. "The Americans must wait a long time. But Verzat wine is worth it!" He shook Louis's hand. "I wish you a pleasant evening, Colonel." He turned and hurried into the blizzard.

One would suspect an angel of treason before accusing Abbé. Louis hoped he had been just as believable—had anyone overheard or seen them. He also hoped the information he had delivered would bring the future king closer to the throne of France. And bring Louis and his men back home, hopefully before they reached Egypt's shores.

Louis hurried to get his men out of the cold. They would need all their strength to endure sixty days of marching to Toulon. He hoped the British confiscated the ships before they arrived.

39

# *Geneviève*

*Château de Verzat*
*January* 1798

Tante and I rolled sheets of old pamphlets into paper cones and filled them with raisins. I hid the brooch among the raisins in one cone and folded its tip, so I would remember which held the brooch. The weight of that paper cone was far greater than all the others. I placed it in the back of my basket next to the handle, surrounding it with the other raisin-filled cones.

Dressed like a vendor, I walked through the crowded market, busy with people buying up supplies in preparation for more cold weather. I clutched my basket before my belly, feeling a bit off balance. I could no longer hide my pregnancy. Why had I not thought of this as a disguise before? I couldn't be arrested for dressing like a woman with child.

I called out, "Château de Verzat Raisins. Sweet raisins!" Our Raisins were a delicacy and would draw attention, so at least we would have a bit of extra money for the back taxes we owed due to the hailstorm loss.

A young mother wearing a threadbare cloak, not nearly warm enough to protect her from the freezing cold, clutched her child's bare hand and stopped. "Raisins! My son has never tasted them." She picked up the boy and sat him on her hip. "How much, Madame?"

I wanted to press a cone upon her for the sheer joy of making her happy, but that would not support my selling disguise, and I needed to appear to be a market woman. I thought of the lowest price I dared, leaned close to her, and said, "Do not tell anyone else, but for your son, five sous."

She gripped my hand. "Merci for your kindness, Madame. I know they are worth ten times that." She pulled coins from her hanging pocket and offered them.

"Only because it is time your son tasted raisins." I handed her a cone.

The boy's eyes glowed as he chewed. "More, Maman!"

Her laughter trilled as I walked through the crowd, looking for a spymaster. Tante had no idea what he, or she, looked like. I was happy I'd be able to tell her.

A finger poked my shoulder, and I turned and faced a rabbit-like, short man dressed as an Abbé. Gray hair curled at the top of his high forehead. His cloak was of brown wool lined with fleece. He was no man of the cloth. Although my garments were warm, they were not lined with sheepskin. Wearing a cloak of such obvious wealth drew attention. Surely, he was not the spymaster. If so, he was making an excellent wage.

"Are these the raisins of Château de Verzat?" he whispered. The code words Tante told me the spymaster would speak.

His bright blue eyes traveled over me, lighting up with… desire? I hoped he was hungry for the raisins.

My hands grew moist in my woolen gloves. My thoughts spun. Did I want to give this man, who had much, all that we had? I looked past him, toward the hill, where the château stood in the distance. Tante trusted the spymaster but never met him. Why would a spymaster wear a fleece-lined cloak, which made him more, not less, memorable? I had no choice if I wanted to help the Chouans, the Royalists, my husband.

He cleared his throat. "Are these the raisins of Château de Verzat?"

Think. What were the words I was to say in response? My mouth dried. The names of the grapes. "Muscat…or…Gamay?"

"Muscat. They are the sweeter, no?"

I nodded. My fingers gripped the cone containing the brooch, but I did not offer it. "I wish an assignment." I barely heard my words.

His nose twitched.

A graying, hunched woman, wearing a once resplendently embroidered now faded cloak, grabbed my arm. "Are these the raisins of Château de Verzat?"

I dizzied. They'd both spoken the code words—either of them could be the spymaster. Her cloak was that of a former noble. She could be a Royalist.

"Ah…yes. Château de Verzat."

"How much?"

I blinked. She hadn't asked about the grapes. That was supposed to be the second response. Or was I to have said the names? The ground wavered. I wanted to grasp onto her to steady myself, but she'd not asked about the varietal. I had to get rid of her. "Fifty centimes."

She jutted her chin at Abbé. "By the look of his fur-lined cloak he can afford them." She spat at his feet and stomped away.

I looked back at the Abbé.

His smile faded. "For?" He drummed his fingertips against each other, acting like the woman had never interrupted.

I'd asked him for an assignment. I wanted to start by selling his cloak. I could do more with the brooch than buy him clothing. "An assignment for helping those fighting for our cause."

His eyebrows rose as he stared at my swollen belly.

Did men think pregnant women were invalids? "A disguise. A pillow."

His fingers reached for the cone I grasped. I backed away. Was I endangering myself and my child by not giving him the brooch as I'd promised? No, if he reported me, he'd risk revealing himself. If Tante knew of this man's wealth, she too, would suspect him of skimming. "I've no more Muscat. Gamay are fifty centimes."

Not taking his eyes from my hands, he dug into his waistcoat and withdrew a coin. He licked his lips.

Holding the cone with the brooch firmly against the basket handle, I grasped a cone and held it at arm's length.

He tossed the coin in my basket, grabbed the raisins, and toddled away, tossing raisins to the ground, then stopped. He turned toward me and crushed the empty cones in his gloved fists.

I smiled, waved, and walked into the crowd, looking for the old woman. "Raisins. Sweet Raisins."

Whether or not the Abbé was the spymaster, he needed no further adornment, and Louis's maman's brooch would not be sold to keep the Abbé warm. The Chouans wore goat and deer skins as cloaks and wrapped beaver skins about their feet for boots. I trusted them, believed in them, admired them. I'd sell the brooch to feed the Chouans.

# 40

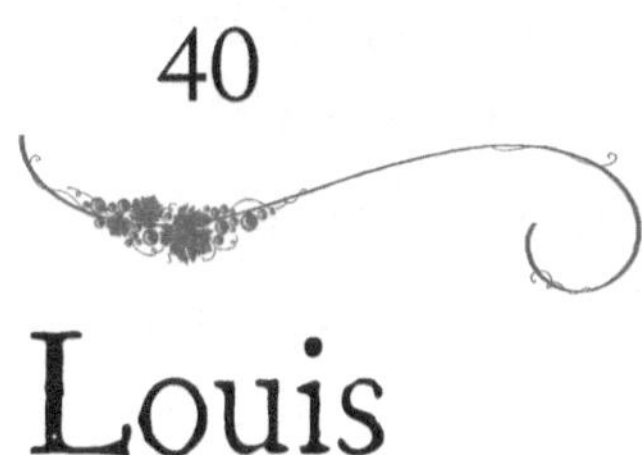

# Louis

*France*
*March* 1798

For TWO MONTHS, Louis marched his men over icy roads that melted into waves of mud. As temperatures warmed, they slept in puddles and ate watery soups. If he had to lead his men into battle, he was determined to give them every advantage to survive. He drilled them in swordsmanship and marksmanship, taught them to handle their horses expertly and, above all, care for the creatures. But how to ride a horse through mountains of sand was anyone's guess. He hoped Toulon's coast was not rocky, so he could give his men a taste of how their horses would behave and move on a sandy beach.

He dismounted at the top of a hill overlooking Toulon and the squat and formidable Tour Royale perched at the tip of land jutting out into the harbor. The British had once held this port, and he wished they still did. His shoulders relaxed as he gazed southwest at the sandy beaches stretching along the Mediterranean Sea gleaming in the distance.

"Fleury!" Louis wanted to instill confidence in the young, stuttering recruit.

"Ye…yes…mon Colonel." He saluted.

"You handle your horse with purpose and grace. You must help me train the other men."

"Yes, mon Colonel." He sat taller in his saddle.

Louis hoped the assignment would give Fleury self-assurance and the other men the skills they would need in the desert.

Tired men trudged past Louis through the mud toward their dinner. Exhausted and sore, Louis hoped to stay awake long enough to eat dinner and write Geneviève. He found Henri hunched over a letter in their tent. The other seven pallets were empty.

Louis stretched his sore back. "News from Aurélia?" The tent was musty from the rains, and the same stink permeated his uniform.

The afternoon light cast a soft yellow glow over the paper as Henri refolded it. "This is her last letter." He raked his hair. "I regret not taking Geneviève's advice. I should have taken Aurélia and Charles to Austria."

"Hopefully, news of your baby will arrive soon."

"If I'm alive to read it."

After plague, despair was the most contagious and dangerous disease for any army. Louis had to destroy this hope-lessness before it destroyed Henri. "If you had emigrated to Austria, you would be serving in the Royalist army."

Henri stood. "If it weren't for you and Joliette, I wouldn't be here."

Glad he had pricked him, Louis pushed further. "And if not for us, you would have faced the guillotine as a noble émigré."

"It was my choice to make." Henri's face reddened.

Louis was glad for Henri's anger—the best antidote to pity. He pulled at his chin. "You would have negotiated better? Joliette saved the estate."

"Damn the estate. Damn her." Henri pushed his shoulder. "Damn you."

Heat raced up Louis's back, but he stood his ground.

"I don't give a damn about wine. I care for my wife and children, whom I have been forced to abandon." Henri's jaw sawed side to side.

"Is it not better to be fighting *in* Bonaparte's army rather than *against* it?"

Henri spat. "That's what I think of Bonaparte. He uses his men up faster than ammunition."

That was probably true. Louis stepped close to him. "Quiet. Someone could report you as a traitor."

Henri lifted his chin. "Better a traitor than to follow a blood-lusting zealot to a country of broiling heat and endless sand." He punched the canvas wall. "We are not defending France. What right have we to bring war to another country?"

"None."

"Then why fight?" Henri growled.

Louis suspected Henri was terrified of dying, as was he. But dare Louis expose it? He did not want to embarrass him. "The only way we can protect our families is to survive this damned war and return home. You owe it to Aurélia and Charles and your unborn baby to survive."

Henri stumbled against the canvas wall and straightened himself. His eyes were flat.

Had Louis pushed too far? Henri's despondence would run through the troops like water flooding the Loire's banks. He had to remind Henri who he was. "After diving into the Seine, fleeing sans-culottes intent on hanging you, did you not rescue Joliette and escape through the tunnels of Paris? Did you not save her and yourself from the tenth of August slaughter? Did you not commandeer a barge and board a slave ship bound for America?" Louis placed his hand on Henri's shoulder. "You have demonstrated the courage of a Noble of the Sword."

Henri shook off his hand, but Louis remained steadfast, staring him down.

"I am no noble. While you sipped champagne and dined on roasted swan at Versailles, my maman and I lived in a room the size of this tent." Henri's voice wavered. "You've no idea what it's like to be cold and hungry."

Louis had known what it was like to freeze in a filthy cell and eat bug-infested bread. But Henri was right. Louis had been born into privilege, taking for granted every extravagance. Both Henri and Geneviève had created their own code of honor to survive. Louis was the only one who had the luxury of parading a code of honor for which he had never had to sacrifice. He had never earned his title as his ancestors had.

"Yes, I took risks back then, for I had only myself to lose. Something happened to me when I fell in love with Aurélia."

Loss. The constant worry of not seeing his wife and children scraped his soul raw. How could he help Henri if he were a prisoner of the same terror? "I think love requires a different kind of courage."

Henri laughed. "Ten times the amount I thought I had."

Louis grabbed at the thread of his laugh. "Facing one's wife can be formidable."

"I've always wanted to ask you why you left Université." Henri rubbed his forehead. "Was it Geneviève's threatening to report you to her father?"

The warmth of embarrassment flushed Louis. Was Henri changing the subject to get him to admit fear? His words tumbled out. "She terrified me, but that was not why I left." He straightened his shoulders and looked directly into Henri's eyes. "I was ashamed of what I had done. The Ancien Regime awarded me the title of comte and the right to humiliate and embarrass anyone below my station. But the moment I exposed Geneviève as a woman, I hated myself. I wanted to change. And I could not change amongst privileged men like myself."

"You have changed," Henri whispered. "For the better."

Simon poked his head around the tent flap. "Mail!" His grin reached his ears.

Henri's eyes grew dark.

Almost as much as a letter from Geneviève, Louis hoped for a letter from Aurélia.

"Two for Henri!" Simon slapped the papers into Henri's hands.

Henri stood blinking.

"Do you not wish to learn if you have a son or daughter?"

Louis held three letters from his own wife, praying Geneviève and Louisa were safe.

Henri nodded. As if in a trance, he broke the seal and unfolded the first letter.

Louis's fingers itched. He broke the seal of the first, praying Aurélia had delivered safely.

Henri clamped his hand over his mouth. He looked up. "I have a daughter…" his voice broke. "Briella."

Louis clapped him on the shoulder. "Félicitations!"

Henri shuddered.

"Aurélia?" Louis's grip on Henri's shoulder tightened.

"She is healthy, as is the baby." Henri sighed and wiped his sleeve along his forehead.

"I will find some wine. I doubt a Verzat vintage graces this port." Louis laughed. "You must be so happy, so proud."

Dazed, Henri nodded.

Tightly grasping his own letters, Louis examined his friend. Surely this news would buoy him, support his will to survive.

Clasping a letter to his chest, Simon's face beamed. "I'm to be a papa! Me! A papa!"

Louis laughed, and it felt so good. He clapped Simon's back. "Félicitations!"

"Thank you." Simon's smile faded as he looked from Henri to Louis. "Are Aurélia and the baby well?"

"Yes." Henri nodded furiously.

Simon grabbed Henri by the arm. "Come. We celebrate!" He dragged him toward town.

"I will catch up with you in a minute," Louis called after them. Holding his breath, he ripped open the letter.

Geneviève's words blurred. She was safe. She was well, wishing the baby would hasten its arrival. Louisa was trying to teach Briella to read.

He read aloud her words to make them real.

*Louisa was next to me when I felt the baby move. I placed her hand on my belly, and the baby greeted us both with a hard kick that took away my breath. We have a little tiger or tigress, my love.*

He pressed the letter to his heart. He prayed she delivered safely. He refolded the letter and tucked it into his waistcoat, next to his heart. He prayed Henri would remain in good spirits. The company needed Henri's superior swordsmanship. Louis would command Henri to train the men every day. Fine-tuning their skills would boost everyone's morale.

One distracted man could risk the entire company. And Louis was bringing every one of his men back home.

# 41

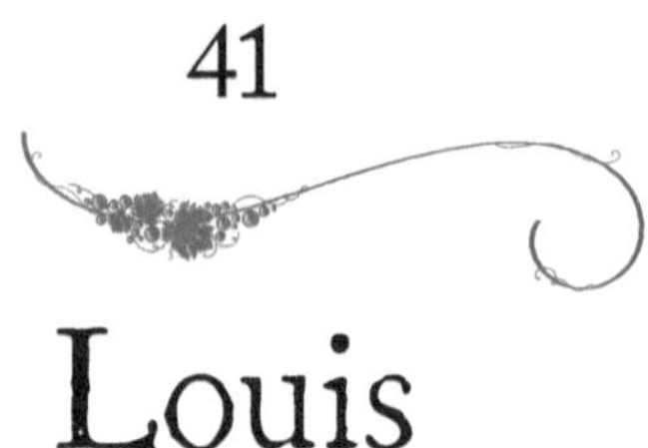

# Louis

*France*
*March* 1798

Despite henri's valiant good humor, Louis feared the deepening melancholy he harbored would infect the other men. Henri was the best swordsman in the company, and Louis encouraged him to tutor the men. Although Henri complied, he lacked enthusiasm. Louis had to find a way to make him want to fight for his life.

During the morning drill, Louis drew his rapier and, making his tone sharp, ordered, "Verzat, advance!"

Confusion sat in Henri's face, reluctance restraining his body.

Louis took first position and saluted. Henri stood frozen, not returning the salute.

En garde, Louis took an advanced lunge. Henri flinched but did not take his position. Although Louis should have recovered to the en garde position, he flicked his épée, touching its tip to Henri's chest.

Henri's nostrils flared. He took his position, whipped his wrist, feinted, deceived, charged—taking Louis by surprise. They parried, rapiers slicing the air. Henri advanced. Louis lost position. Henri blocked every one of Louis's thrusts. Sweat covered Louis; his hilt grew slick. Verzat was better than he had thought.

Henri advanced, lunged, and knocked Louis's rapier from his hand. Henri flicked his épée and, keeping it a breath away from Louis's chest, smiled.

The men applauded. Henri lowered his weapon, and cuffed Louis's shoulder. "I haven't been pushed like that in years, Colonel. Thanks."

"You taught me a few new things, Verzat." Louis laughed and turned to his men. "Who wishes the next match with Lieutenant Verzat?"

# 42

# *Geneviève*

*Château de Verzat & Tours*
*March,* 1798

Tante Nicole arranged a meeting with a another spymaster, whom, she assured me, would be a man.

A knot of gendarmes wandered from stall to stall. A bitter wind whipped my skirts about, and I clapped them against my legs for fear of exposing Louis's breeches I wore under them.

"Raisins!" I called out. "Sweet, plump raisins."

The elderly woman I had met the previous week approached. "Same price as last time?"

"Today, only five centimes."

Her wide smile revealed three teeth. "Thank you." Her claw-like fingers dropped the coins into my basket and grasped the cone.

Sunlight skipped over the icicles hanging from the roofs and window ledges.

"Are these the raisins of Château de Verzat?" a low voice asked.

Placing my finger into the cone containing the brooch and pressing it against the basket, I turned to face a gendarme. Gray streaked his fair hair and mustache, and his brown eyes were alert and expectant. I stepped back. "Yes."

He tilted his head.

I glanced at the group of gendarmes at the market entrance.

He cleared his throat. "These *are* the raisins of Château de Verzat?"

I hadn't said the code back to him. "Muscat…or…Gamay?"

"Muscat." He smiled. "They are sweeter, no?"

He had to be the spy. "Indeed."

He cleared his throat. "How much?"

"Five. Five centimes."

He offered coins, but I stood there sweating. I was no longer risking just my own life. I was carrying a child.

He tilted his head. "Muscat. They are sweeter, no?"

He'd repeated the code. Only the spymaster knew it. I offered the cone containing the brooch.

He accepted it, took a raisin, and popped it into his mouth. "This will be much appreciated." He turned.

I couldn't stop myself. "Please," I whispered.

He paused, glancing about the market.

My heartbeat galloped. "I wish an assignment."

He nodded. "Good day, Madame."

A shaking seized my legs. If he was not the spy, he could have interrogated me. Without thinking, I had endangered my unborn child. I had no right. I stumbled and caught myself on a building, taking deep breaths, willing strength to return to my legs. Something tugged at my skirts. The little boy who had tasted raisins for the first time.

"More raisins, please?" His small hand reached, and I gave him a cone.

He giggled with delight. "Thank you." He ran to his maman, who was absorbed in reading a notice on the news board.

I neared her and stopped. The word Murderess blared in bold letters. A sketch—of a dark-skinned woman, with long limbs and hair curled wildly about her head—stopped my breath.

Aurélia.

A description of the Madam, the stabbing, and the Paris bordel appeared below the sketch. A reward that would ward off poverty for a year, was offered for her capture.

My legs trembled. The market spun around me. I backed up against a wall and slid down onto the cobblestones.

The boy's maman crouched next to me. "Are you well? You're terribly pale."

I nodded and rubbed my belly.

"Ah, you are with child. I fainted often when I was carrying my son."

I wiped perspiration from my face. I had to hide Aurélia. "I'm feeling better."

She gripped my hands and helped me stand and walked me to the wagon. "Rest as soon as you get home. I hope to see you next week."

I snapped the reins. Although I didn't want to worry Aurélia, I had to tell her the truth. And we had to hide Charles and Fortuné as well. The tunnels would be safe but freezing. How would we get them there if a search party surrounded us? Louis once told me to hide the Chouans in plain sight. A dark-skinned woman and two children were rare in the Loire Valley. The only stranger who knew of them was the Capitaine. And the bastard would lead the gendarmes directly to us.

I burst into the kitchen, spilling raisins everywhere. Tante Nicole, Henri's maman, and Aurélia jumped up.

Alarm in her eyes, Joliette scooped up my basket. "What is it?"

There was no way to lessen the news. Worry crept across their faces as I explained.

Joliette headed for the door. "The secret room. The entrance is in Aurélia's chamber."

We huddled in the bedroom as Joliette demonstrated how to open the door by pulling a lever hidden at the side of the bookcase. Aurélia repeated the procedure until she could open the door and close it behind her in one smooth motion and lock it with a final, satisfying click. She reopened the door and smiled.

I held a candle aloft and entered the opening. Cobwebs snapped in the flame. A built-in bench ran the length of the narrow room. Rat droppings littered the wooden floor. The walls closed in around me, as they had when I first traveled the tunnels, but I exhaled the fear tugging at me. I'd lived in the château for five years and never knew this existed, and no one else would suspect either.

I returned to the group and looked each person in the eye, landing on Aurélia. "You'll need to hide at a moment's notice—day or night—and you must take the children and Fortuné."

She mouthed, *I will.*

I looked to Henri's maman, Madame Detré. "And you must help her."

She wrapped her arm around her daughter-in-law.

I stood in the grand hallway, judging how long it would take Aurélia and the children to get from the kitchen to her room and into the secret chamber. Not one of them could be seen in the vineyard. It was just a matter of time before gendarmes came searching.

43

# *Geneviève*

**B**ASKING IN THE glow of the embers in the kitchen fireplace, Aurélia rocked and nursed Briella. The baby had her maman's long elegant hands, Henri's deep blue eyes, and a robust appetite.

Joliette and Tante Nicole sat by the kitchen fire, happily knitting caps and blankets for my baby. Madam Detré's hands guided the yarn through my fingers. No matter how hard I tried, the knitting was more knots than loops. The sound of pounding on the great doors broke our peaceful silence.

I bolted to my feet. "Aurelia, use the servants' stairs and take the children to the secret room. Stay there until we come for you."

I grabbed Joliette's hand and hurried to the entry. Tante Nicole climbed to the top of the grand stairs, looked out, and shouted, "Gendarmes!"

No doubt they were searching for Aurélia. I held my sides and panted.

Joliette rubbed my back. "Take calming breaths. We will send them on their way." She unlocked and opened the door. "Good day, Messieurs. How may I help you?"

Six gendarmes stood at rigid attention, among them, the spy I'd met at the market, whose eyebrows rose when he saw me. My mouth dried. Had he betrayed me and brought them here?

Uninvited, the leader, wearing gold braid looped around his shoulder, stepped into the hall. "We are searching every home for a murderess." He thrust out the pamphlet. "Have you seen this woman?"

Joliette gazed down her nose. "Nearly one thousand people live on this estate, and I can assure you not one of them resembles her."

I longed for Joliette's composure, but the spy's presence unnerved me.

"Anyone could be hiding her." The leader brought up his arm. "Search this house." The gendarmes marched into the entryway.

"You will follow me," I shouted, holding up my ring of keys, "and you will not damage anything."

The leader stepped around me and headed up the stairs. Clutching the balustrade, I hurried to reach the landing first. I pointed to the room farthest from Aurélia's. "We will start at the end of the hall."

"We will start here." He pivoted on his heel and jiggled the doorknob of Aurélia's chamber. "Open it."

The keys jangled in my hand. I shook the ring, brought it close to my eyes, like I was trying to see, selected the wrong key, and tried to insert it. The lock resisted, and I fumbled.

He yanked the ring from me, chose the largest key, unlocked the door, and commanded, "Search it."

Joliette and I followed. God, please don't let the baby cry.

The men crawled over the room like ants on a puddle of honey. The smallest slid under the bed. Another snapped open the drapes. The spy began removing leatherbound books from the bookcase. Not only would they take Aurélia, but he would also expose me as a traitor.

"Idiot." The leader pushed the spy aside. "She's not hiding behind a book." He reached up and ran his hand along the bookcase's vertical edge.

Sweat pooled on my back.

The leader sidestepped his way across the shelves, searching every edge, until he reached the final case. His dancing fingers halted as he gripped the latch. The door popped open. Cool dusty air flowed out. His lip curled into a sneer.

Heat rushed through me as I acted astonished.

Joliette strode to the gaping door. "I was born in this château—lived here all my life—and never knew of this."

His laugh was cruel. "Surprised, Madame?" He kicked the foot of the gendarme who was under the bed. "Light a candle and search this."

The young man scrambled out, grabbed a candle from the dressing table, and spilled the flint and char cloth.

My heartbeat thundered. I had to give Aurélia more time to hide further into the chamber. I took the flint from him and calmly and slowly and ineptly stuck and struck until a tiny spark wavered. I feebly attempted another. This one caught. Damn. The young man cupped his hand about the flame and entered the passage.

Please, God, don't let the children make a sound.

"What do you see?" the leader shouted.

"Noth…Ah!" the younger screamed.

A squeezing gripped my chest.

A rat scurried out the door, right for the leader, who stomped his feet, causing the animal to bolt for the hallway.

The young gendarme, clutching his uniform buttons, ran from the passage, a sheen of sweat covering his pale face. He saluted the leader. "Just spider webs and rats, Commander." He heaved for breath.

Had he not reached them? My head throbbed as my mind raced. Was there a connecting door to another room? If so, I had to keep the gendarmes from searching the surrounding chambers.

The spy stared at me with a hint of a smile. Had he or someone on the estate betrayed us?

The leader urged his men to search, my heartbeat racing as they entered every room from kitchen to attic. They weren't the only ones seeking Aurélia.

Hours later, Joliette and I stood, shivering before the kitchen fireplace. Tante Nicole fixed a tisane. I poured two brandies and handed a glass to Joliette.

Madame Detré stood before the fire, lines of worry scarring her brow. "Are they gone?"

I nodded. "For now. I doubt they will return. There isn't a crack they didn't search."

"Come." She led us to the great hall, ducking under the arching spiral staircase to its back—a rectangle of wall, as tall as Fortuné, surrounded by decorative molding.

She knocked three times on what I thought was the solid support of the stairs. Metal scraping against metal sounded. Slowly, the section, thick as the wall, opened like a door. Madame Detré smiled. "It will only open if it is *not* locked from inside."

Aurélia sat holding her baby and Charles's hand. Behind them, Fortuné grinned. "We hid, Tante Gen!"

A trembling seized my legs, and I leaned against the wall.

Joliette, eyes opened wide, gawped. "I truly did not know *this* existed!" She helped Aurélia stand. "How did you find this place?"

Aurélia stepped out of the space that yawned vertically to the landing of the next floor. *I survived enslavement. I know where to look.*

My hands tingled from the release of tension I'd held since the gendarmes' arrival. "Why did you not tell us?"

Her face serene, Aurélia replied, *They could not arrest you if you did not know.*

"Do you think anyone of us would reveal you?"

*Did they find the secret room?*

The rush of fear I'd felt at that moment hit me. "We were frantic with worry."

*And they believed you did not know where I was.* She stroked Charles's head.

The horror of the night she'd stabbed the Madam ran through me like a shiver. She had planned her own escape that night and today.

Madame Detré pressed the edge of the door, and it closed seamlessly. I ran my fingernail along the left edge and felt a bit of metal. I pressed my nail against it, and the door opened again.

My body sagged like a wet rag. Aurélia had survived horrors I could only imagine. She was far better equipped than I to survive the Republicans.

Aurélia squeezed my hand. *You must trust me.*

Trust. Why was that so hard for me? A dropping sensation plunged me into a memory of my father delivering me to the nuns, leaving me in their care for years. I shook the images from my mind. My father was untrustworthy. I gazed at the beautiful faces surrounding me. Madame Detré, Joliette, Tante Nicole, Fortuné, Aurélia, little Charles. They all loved me.

And I needed to learn to trust them. All our lives depended upon the trust that connected us like the roots of the vineyard.

# 44

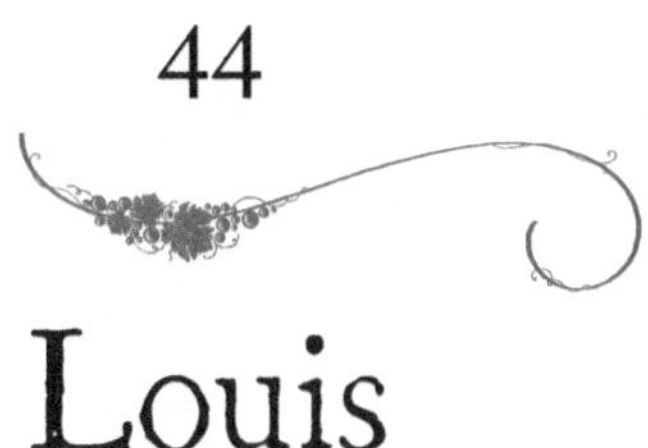

# Louis

*Toulon, France*
*May* 1798

L OUIS STOOD ON the wharf, counting seventy-four cannons positioned along *l'Aquilon's* two decks. A ship of the line, *l'Aquilon* was designed for war and carried not only ammunition and supplies, but also one hundred horses and seven hundred men. Grateful all fifty of his men were on the same ship, Louis prayed Murat would not join them.

Thirty days on the sea would prove difficult. Impossible if Murat boarded the same ship. Louis had stayed awake, planning ways of ensuring Murat would not. He had considered boarding his men on the wrong ship but feared his men would pay for his decision. Hiring a whore would delay Murat, but he could not forgive himself for subjecting any woman to the bastard. He could emphasize the filth, the stink, the lack of comforts and mirrors. Louis snorted a laugh. He would lead with the mirrors.

Sunlight danced over the waves. A stiff wind buffeted countless ships crowding the harbor. Surely the brilliant day was a good omen for their journey. Yet the beauty made it more difficult to leave France.

Louis boarded *l'Aquilon* and stood on the deck. In the distance, the three masts of Bonaparte's ship, *l'Orient*, pierced the sky. The one-hundred-and-twenty-gun warship was so large, Louis doubted its ability to stay afloat. Taking advantage of the wind, smaller ships sailed out to sea, leaving behind a military band playing endlessly. Where was their leader? Joséphine was most likely delaying him.

"Your horse is ready, Colonel," Simon called up from the wharf where Louis's gray mare snorted and whinnied.

Sailors worked with Louis's men to secure Belle in a rope net that acted like a hammock to bring her above and across the ship's railing where they would then lower her down an opening in the deck and into the hold. Half the cavalry horses had been led up a ramp into the hold, the other half were stabled on a higher deck along with his mare.

Louis hoped Belle survived the fright, she could kick out and break a leg. He spoke soothingly, calming her as the sailors hoisted her.

"LaGarde." Murat's voice boomed from the wharf below.

Louis tensed. What damage did the commandant have in store? How would he undermine Louis's authority over his own men? The silver fringe hanging from Murat's épaulettes was thicker, shinier, longer. The breeze dared to tangle the strands. Louis squinted, not from the bright sunshine bouncing off Murat's uniform, but from holding back his contempt for the canard…until he spotted a pile of horse shit, sitting directly in Murat's path.

Louis smiled and saluted. "Good morning, mon Commandant. A fine day for sailing."

"Don't worry about your precious horse." Murat strode toward the gangway. "You can always get a camel!" He let out a mocking laugh as his feet flew out from under him, landing him on his back in the horse shit.

Louis pressed his hand to his mouth and ducked behind his mare, dangling from the rope hammock above the hold. He laughed so hard, he grabbed onto the net to keep himself upright. He dared not look, although he would have loved to have seen Murat's face. How would he get the crap out of his pristine breeches?

Murat's screams of rage could be heard in Paris.

Louis longed to order the ship's capitaine to depart before Murat returned. He smiled at the gull crying overhead, taunting Murat—it would take him at least an hour to clean up. He hoped Abbé had relayed his information. Perhaps the British could take over the ship without killing any of his men if Louis ordered his company to surrender. When he revealed he was a spy, they would enlist his assistance. And he would be glad to give it.

Echoes of Murat's rants bounced along the water. Louis cursed the bastard to the bottom of the sea.

Louis approached the capitaine. "All the horses are loaded, and my men are on deck. We are ready to set sail, mon Capitaine."

The bearded, weathered man pointed a thumb over his shoulder. "The commandant is not sailing with us?"

"No." Louis acted above his rank. He could face execution for his action. "We will lose the advantage of the tide should we wait for the Commandant to clean up, will we not?"

The Capitaine gave him a broad smile. "Excellent. Don't want any shit-covered commandants on my ship." He turned and shouted, "Stand by to set sail!"

Louis hid his grin as his shoulders relaxed, despite knowing that he would pay. He hoped the Capitaine of *l'Aquilon* was not punished for Louis's assumption of power. He shook off the guilt sliding down his back. Hopefully, Murat would drown before they arrived in Egypt. And Louis would keep an eye out for British ships and pray they interrupted their voyage soon. If he promised the Capitaine safe passage back to France, perhaps he could persuade him to surrender.

# 45

# *Geneviève*

*Château de Verzat*
*June* 1798

I PACED BEFORE THE fireplace, massaging a dull ache in my lower back. Moving made me feel like I was doing something since Joliette had warned me my time was near and forbade me to work in the vineyard. I suppose as she'd had a baby, she was wiser than I, but it wasn't time—I wasn't ready. I had to find the courage and strength I knew I'd need but did not possess.

Madame Detré, her gray curls gleaming, hovered like a hummingbird, fussing and cooing, and petting both her daughter-in-law and granddaughter. Henri would be so proud. I prayed he had received Aurélia's letters. I prayed Louis would receive the news of our child.

Aurélia motioned for me to sit in the other rocking chair.

I shook my head. Pacing kept me from feeling the terror that hung over me like a veil, daring me to prick it and surrender to a total lack of control. I had held Aurélia's hand throughout her delivery and knew I would never be so strong or brave. I needed more time to develop a plan for delivering my own baby. There had to be a better way through it all, other than lying there, wracked with pain, squirming, sweating, panting. I was certain I'd scream.

Humming, Tante Nicole sat in the glow of firelight, stitching a small pair of breeches. A large fabric butterfly, its long body protruding past the wings like a handle, rested upon her apron.

"Is your butterfly a fan?" I asked.

Her eyes twinkled. "It is a needle case. Queen Marie had her seamstress sew a papillon for each of her ladies-in-waiting and asked us to embroider them in our own style." She ran her fingers along the butterfly's wing stitched with silver silk thread and edged in seed pearls. "It is the only thing remaining of my life at Versailles."

"Do you miss being a courtier?"

She pressed the butterfly to her lips. "The only person who loved me at that time was my dear husband, Philipe. Now I am loved by everyone around me."

Something squeezed in me, hard. My knees weakened. I grabbed the back of a chair, bent over, and struggled to inhale. "Ahh." My voice was high. A tingling sensation flared through me, like an intense flame. What was happening?

Tante Nicole held my elbow. "I think your time is near."

"Not yet," I panted as the squeezing began to ease. "I'm not ready."

Tante chuckled. "You may not be, but your baby is."

I wiped sweat from my forehead as Tante guided me to the rocking chair. I lowered myself, wondering if I could haul myself up again. Maybe rocking would soothe the baby.

Aurélia mouthed, *You will be fine.*

I tried to smile back, which made her laugh a silent, knowing laugh. She probably knew how frightened I was. I ran my hand over my enormous belly, pushing myself to rock the chair. "The baby never stopped kicking, jabbing, poking me throughout the night. I barely slept."

*You started last night,* she mouthed. *Do not be afraid.*

I hoped my delivery would be as fast and without dangers as Aurélia's had been. Assisting the birth was not as terrifying as Magdeleine's delivery of Louisa. Thérèse, the mushroom woman, was also a midwife, and she had been reassuring to Aurélia. Joliette and Tante Nicole and Madam Detré had all cared for her, as they would care for me. Still…I wasn't ready. Maybe next week.

Tante Nicole offered a bowl of strawberries. Love radiated from her smile. "It will not be long now. You will be nursing your babe."

Panic streaked down my spine and, to calm myself, I took a berry and shoved it in my mouth. Sweet juice exploded. The baby rolled. "You like strawberries, my tiny one?" A cramp stopped my breath, and I gripped the chair arms, pushing against the ache. I did not like this. Not one bit. "Louis, next time, you have the baby." I panted, praying my breath would ease the pain, but that dull ache sat in my back and, as if it had arms, reached around my belly.

A loud knock echoed down the stone hallway. We had received no visitors since the gendarmes' search. I prayed it was not soldiers wanting food or our animals. Joliette was in the winery. Had she arranged a meeting or a shipment? Madame Robert had come once, but if Joliette was expecting her, she would have told us. We all looked at each other as Aurélia rose.

Fortuné ran into the room and yelled, "I am the doorman!"

"No! You must hide with Aurélia and the children." I struggled to stand. Tante Nicole helped me as I pushed myself up from the rocking chair. "Fortuné, do not open the door!"

Holding Briella to her chest, Aurélia hurried to hide.

"Take Fortuné with you," I called after her.

Tante glared at me. "I will go. It is dangerous for you."

"I am going."

She steadied me. As I hauled myself down the corridor, I plunged my hand into my hanging pocket. Guilt poured over me like syrup. The gun's weight had pressed against my belly that morning, and I had left Louis's pistol in my chamber. The devil.

"Wait until Geneviève comes," Tante shouted.

"Is my job." Fortuné's boots skittered across the marble entryway.

Tante Nicole gripped my elbow. "Careful. Do not rush. You could slip."

The screech of the door's lock filled the great hall as I entered.

"Don't open it!" I panted and held onto the balustrade of the grand staircase. If Tante had not been supporting me, I would have collapsed.

Fortuné pulled open the door and bowed. "Welcome to Château de Verzat, Madame."

My heart thudded. God help us.

"What is the doorman of Madame Brissault's bordel doing at Château de Verzat?" Suzanne's smile dazzled in the sunlight streaming through the open door. She reached to touch Fortuné's cheek, but he backed away.

The innocence in Fortuné's eyes faded. Tears brimmed in his eyes as he looked at me.

Heat rushed up my back. Louis had told her never to show herself again. He assured me he had told my brother I was safe at Château de Verzat. Had she tortured Auguste to reveal where I lived? My palms itched for my pistol. I had no time to run upstairs. I couldn't run. Was she armed? I straightened, willing the pain away. Tante Nicole gripped my hand.

Dressed in a low-cut, emerald-green silk gown with matching necklace and earrings, Suzanne brought her hand to her cheek.

The room swirled. Tante wrapped her arm around my waist. I pulled her close and whispered, "Get my pistol from the drawer in my bedside table."

Tante shook her head. "I am not leaving you."

"Where is my Louis?" Suzanne laughed her dirty dark laugh.

I grabbed my skirts, wanting to claw the bitch's eyes out. I inhaled, trying to stretch to my full height, but a cramping bowed me over. "My husband told you never to bother us." As I stepped, my weight shifted, straining my lower back.

Suzanne's eyes snapped, like she had just discovered me. "I thought you were in New France."

If I couldn't kill the bitch, I had to scare her. I wanted to unleash my rage, but I had to protect my baby.

"I wish to see Louis. Not you." Suzanne shook her red locks, reminding me of Medusa.

"He said he'd kill you if you showed yourself again." I hoped my height and my menacing voice would threaten her.

She lifted her chin. "I have a business proposition he'll be very happy to hear about."

Tante Nicole's grip on my waist loosened as I stepped closer to Suzanne. "You have to the count of three to leave. One."

Suzanne's eyes took on the look of a stalking cat.

How could I stop her? I could barely walk. "Two." My voice, arms, legs shook. I panted.

"I'll find Louis myself." She pushed my shoulder and stepped forward.

I lurched sideways, grasping at her. My knees gave way. Despite Tante's grip, I slid to the floor.

Fortuné clasped me. "I have you, Tante Gen."

A pain circled my stomach, as if a giant hand squeezed it. Tante let go of me. I held onto Fortuné's shoulders. Liquid ran down the inside of my thighs. Blood? God, please protect my baby.

Tante Nicole lifted her cane and whacked it across Suzanne's face.

Suzanne shrieked and staggered back. A long red welt rose on her cheek.

"I am warning you." Tante pressed the button on her stick, and the hidden sword blade clicked out of the tip. With both hands, she held the blade at Suzanne's throat. "You are not welcome here. You either leave immediately or I'll run you through—after I scar your hideous face." She pressed the blade into Suzanne's pale skin. A line of blood trickled down her throat and pooled along the emerald necklace.

I bent over my stomach, wincing in pain. I had to terrify Suzanne; make her think Louis was here. "You come here again, and Louis will kill you," I hissed.

Tante kept the blade at Suzanne's throat as she backed out of the door. When Suzanne had stepped over the threshold, Tante retracted the blade and held the stick above her head. "Leave!"

Suzanne fled. Tante slammed the door.

Arms pulled me to my feet, but my legs were useless. I searched for blood. Water pooled on the marble. A cramp seized me again, wringing my belly like a wet rag. I cried out. Darkness encroached. I sank, scratching at the floor. I was so weak. I needed to be strong. "I'm not ready."

# 46

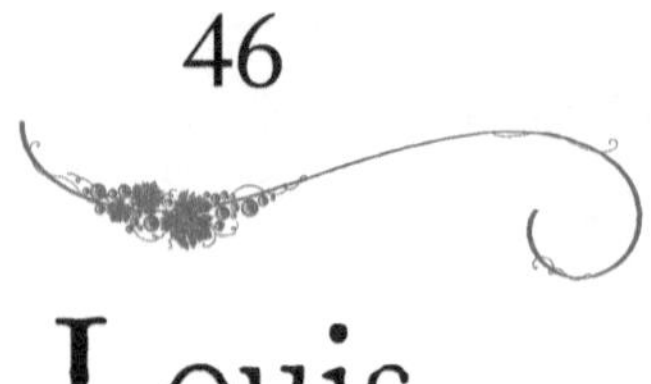

# Louis

*Abu Qir Bay, Egypt*
*July* 1798

Louis STOOD ON deck before his men, all fifty sun-burned, thirsty and hungry, huddled beneath a slice of shade. Each had received a daily ration of a mug of fetid water and a chunk of bug-infested bread for the past three days. He had trained his men how to survive on a battlefield—not how to survive starvation. He paced, fighting doubts. How could he plan an escape route in a country whose reputation was already so inhospitable he feared death might be their only means of desertion?

Eyeing rope nets spread over a railing, he asked a sailor, "Can those nets be used to catch fish?"

The sailor laughed. "Only one so big he'd eat you first."

Louis turned to his men. "Let us find something we can use as hooks and catch our own food."

Fleury jumped up followed by Simon. It took only minutes for them to fasten string and bent nails they cast over the railing. They laughed like boys fishing on the banks of the Loire.

The sand-colored horizon expanded as Bonaparte's fleet of nearly four hundred ships charged toward Egypt. He hoped the sight would revive his men's spirits. Seafoam danced along the waves. If Louisa were beside him, she would want him to capture it for her. He closed his eyes against images of his daughter and Geneviève, his ears against their voices and laughter. But he could not shutter the longing in his heart.

The ships ahead changed course. Their flapping sails sounded like a great flock of geese rising from the water, reminding him of sitting with Tante Nicole at the château viewpoint. If Abbé Nodier had delivered Louis's message, the British should have attacked Bonaparte's navy by now. Where was the much-feared Nelson? The French fleet would lose far fewer men at sea than roasting under the sun in a sandpit.

The wind changed and heat rolled off the land and over the sea like the hot breath of a wild animal.

*L'Aquilon* bucked the tide as she struggled toward a thick yellow haze sitting over endless sand. Not a speck of green anywhere. He scanned the nearby ships. On the deck of the closest stood a familiar figure peering through a spyglass. Louis tensed. Before escaping, he and his men had to survive Murat.

## 47

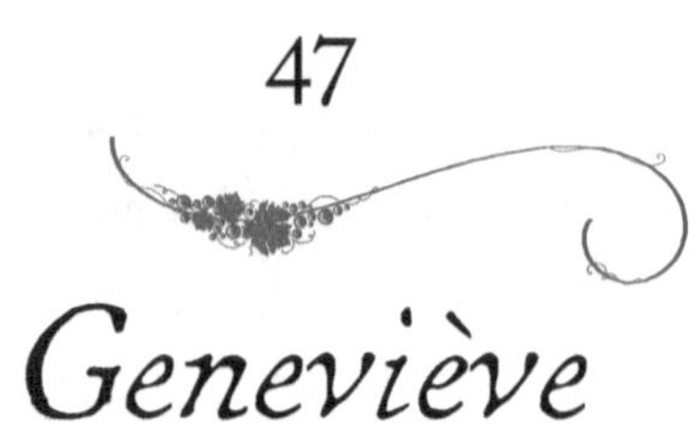

# *Geneviève*

*Château de Verzat*
*June* 1798

I AWOKE IN MY chamber. I rubbed my hard, hot belly. I
jolted. "My baby?"

Thérèse gently pushed me back. "Your child is on its way.
Anne and I have delivered many babies, and I insist you remain
in bed."

Anne dipped a cloth in a bowl of water.

"It's time?" I huffed a breath.

Tante Nicole stood at the foot of the bed; her fingers clutching a rosery. "Yes, my dear. You are in good hands."

Anne placed the cool serviette over my brow and hurried
to the window. She peeked around the heavy damask drape
that shut out much of the light.

Fear jolted me. "Suzanne!"

"She is gone. Rest, my dear." Tante's tone was firm.

A wave of pain rolled through me. I moaned. "Where's Louisa?"

Joliette hurried in. "She is safe."

"I want Aurélia." I cried.

Joliette removed the cloth from my forehead and wiped a cool serviette over my face.

I gripped her hand. My lips trembled so, I had to work at forming words. "Suzanne saw Fortuné."

"Étienne and Monsieur Cambon and more men are armed and surround the château. Aurélia, and the children are in the chamber next door. If gendarmes come, they will hide." She ran her cool fingers across my brow. "Do not worry."

She sat on the edge of the bed. "Aurélia delivered my son. She taught me what to do, so I could help her deliver Charles." She rubbed my fingers. "I will be here. If it is safe, Aurélia will come in for a little while. Louisa, too."

Pain jagged through my body. My heart raced. My legs were so heavy, I couldn't move them. I had always been able to move, to run. I'd never been so frightened. I closed my eyes, feeling like my baby was swimming in my belly. A thrill rushed through me. Sparks of light flickered. I moaned with another wave of pain. "I want Louis."

"He is here in spirit, my dear." Tante tapped her stick on the rug. "And he would be most proud of you."

Joliette rung out the cloth and dabbed it across my brow. "I have been afraid many times in my life, but giving birth requires the most courage I have ever had to summon."

Another pain mounted, making me scream. When it passed,

I panted. "I fear it takes more courage to be a woman than a man."

"I believe that is true." Joliette smiled serenely. "But you have more courage than all of us combined."

I felt like a helpless, quivering child. Anything but courageous. Yet, Louis's baby was making its way into the world, and the thought was magical, like a glimmering full moon reflected in the Loire. The baby jabbed me. "You are a fighter, like your parents." I laughed, then screamed as another pain cut through me.

Pains rolled through me during the night, jolting me awake as I fell into a fitful sleep. When sunlight streaked into the chamber, I feared I was so exhausted I would not have strength to deliver. The baby rolled. *I will take care of you, little one. I promise to protect you all my life.*

Anne opened the drapes, allowing sunlight to cheer me on. Thérèse brought a cup to my lips. "Sip a bit of this."

I was grateful to both sisters for their care of Aurélia during her delivery and now mine. "Thank you." I drank a tisane so bitter I wanted to spit it out. Another pain arced, sharp and deep. A scream tore up my throat.

"Puff out a breath," Anne said as she put her arm around my shoulders. "Puff again."

I panted. Darkness encroached. I scratched at the bedclothes. I had to be brave. I had to stay alive for this baby. I promised. "Louis, help me!"

I breathed into the pain, imagining grabbing it, choking it, slaying it as if it were a wolf. You will not hurt my child. I will fight you with every drop of blood, every breath, every heartbeat. You will not hurt my child.

"Push!" Thérèse commanded.

I screamed. The knife of pain stabbed—ripped me apart. I pushed and roared like an animal.

Tante Nicole held my hand. "You are doing a wonderful job. One more push."

I had no more strength. I gripped her hand and screamed. My body shuddered.

A terrifying silence filled the room. My body vibrated. Please, let my baby live.

A tiny faint sound, like a mewling kitten, shimmered.

"You have a son." Tante Nicole's eyes glittered.

A son. His cries hooked my heart. My chest swelled, bursting with joy and love. I held out my arms. "Louis, we have a son!"

48

# *Geneviève*

*Château de Verzat*
*June* 1798

SUNLIGHT STREAMED THROUGH the window, dazzling my bedchamber. My gown stuck to my sweaty body. My arms and legs were heavy, useless.

Tante Nicole smiled down at me, her face love itself. "Do you wish to hold your son."

"Yes!" I tried to push myself up against the pillows, but I fell back, my arms shaking.

Joliette placed another pillow behind me and helped me to sit up, but pain arced again, forcing me to collapse.

Tante took a bundle from Thérèse and placed it in my arms.

My heartbeat fluttered. His wrinkled red face, his rosy lips gawping, his eyes tiny slits. Love surged through me, tender and ferocious. I placed the tip of my finger in the tiny hollow of his chin—Louis's chin. I uncurled his walnut-sized fist. He had my stubby fingers and wide hands. He grabbed onto my finger and mewled.

My laugh unleashed a stream of tears. "I don't believe this perfect little man came from me. He is so beautiful. So strong." A deep warmth, a sense of protection, a wondering awe flooded me. I held him close to my breast. "I…wish Louis was here." More tears fell. My son cried lustily. I laughed. "He has Louis's voice." I unwrapped the swaddling and held my hand over his chest, so small, the size of a partridge.

"Louis is here in spirit," Tante Nicole whispered. "Do you feel him?"

Louis's scent of newly mown hay washed over me. His laughter echoed.

"Your son is hungry." She untied the ribbon at the neck of my gown and positioned my son close to my breast.

I teased his lips with my knuckle. His tiny tongue reached my nipple, and he suckled. I thought I'd faint with joy at the miracle of it all. I'd never felt so alive.

The tickling sensation brought a contentment I had never known flowing through me. I had never felt such magic. I marveled at this feeling of…motherhood? Why had I dressed as a man if I could feel this as a woman? I laughed. If I'd not dressed as a man, I wouldn't have attended Université or married Louis or experienced this miracle.

Tears dropped, but I didn't brush them away. I had drowned in love for Louis on our wedding night. The love I felt now was different, but it was as intense as the feeling I had for my husband.

Aurélia crept into the room. She kissed my son's forehead and mine.

I entwined my fingers in hers. "Our children will grow up together."

She smiled. She brought her hand to her heart and nodded toward the door. She slipped her hand from mine and left, reminding me she and Charles and Briella and Fortuné were still in danger. I wanted Louisa to meet her brother and tried to sit up. I was so cold, I shivered.

Thérèse rushed to me "You must rest."

"But Louisa—"

"You've delivered a very big boy and lost a great deal of blood. You must not rise." She reached beneath the quilt and pressed a warm, thick roll of bandages between my thighs. Turning away, she removed a bloodied cloth, trying to hide it from me.

Panic jittered up my arms. A memory squeezed my heart. The stink of a dank cell, images of bloodied hay and Magdeleine's slashed wrists swamped me. Seeing in my mind the bloodied dagger stopped my breath. She had felt helpless, but far worse than my body felt now. And I had thought she had been hopeless. I envisioned my friend, finally understanding, and in my mind, spoke to her: *Magdeleine, you knew you would have had no control over what happened to Louisa when they came to take you to the guillotine. Now I understand, leaving your daughter would have shredded your heart. You gave your life, so I would take Louisa out of the prison.* I caressed my son's cheek as my tears dropped. *I had been so sad that you left me, but now I admire your bravery and courage. You trusted me to care for Louisa because you knew you couldn't. You believed in me when I didn't.*

I wept for Magdeleine. And I wept for not having believed in myself. Louisa didn't have to call me maman. I became her maman when Magdeleine entrusted her to me.

I held my son close and kissed his bald head. I had to believe in myself, now; another life depended on me. I shuddered a breath, remembering putting Louisa in Magdeleine's lifeless arms, hoping her spirit was still there at that moment. *Know that Louisa is healthy and strong and safe. Know Louis and I adore her. Know she is happy, and that I protect her with my life, as you would.* A warmth and peacefulness surrounded me, like Magdeleine's presence.

Anne brought me a cup of tisane, this one sweet and minty and wonderful. I was so thirsty. And happy. And sad Louis had missed this. *I will give you more children, my love.* I laughed, remembering my wish that Louis give birth to our next child. I would do it again, many times, I hoped.

My son fell asleep.

"He will be hungry again, soon." Joliette picked him up and handed him to Tante Nicole.

Sitting next to my bed, Tante rested him against her shoulder and rubbed his back. His mewling made us all laugh. "Louis will be so proud of your courage." Tante's face beamed with the pride I imagined Louis would feel. Yet, her eyes looked tired.

I had to tell him. My fingers reached. "I wish to write him."

"There is time. You should rest, get some sleep."

"Please. I want to write of the joy I feel right now."

Her head shook in an oddly trembling way.

"It does not take much strength to draw quill against paper." I used a playful tone.

She leaned over, I thought to open the drawer of the bedside table. But she stopped suddenly, as if she heard a noise.

"Tante?"

A strange film dropped over her bright eyes. Her mouth drooped. Her fingers went limp. My son slid down her bosom.

"Joliette!" I lurched and grabbed him. A sharp pain shot up through me.

Tante collapsed onto the floor.

"Tante!" She had been with me all night. She was exhausted. I should have listened to her. "Tante!"

Joliette knelt next to her. "She has fainted. We must get her to bed."

I couldn't move, couldn't help her. Please, God, don't take her from us.

Joliette, Anne, and Thérèse lifted Tante onto the chaise longue.

I had to be with her as she had been with me. "When you've gotten her to bed, take me to her room, please. I won't leave her alone."

# 49

# *Geneviève*

*Château de Verzat*
*June* 1798

ÉTIENNE, THÉRÈSE, AND Anne carried me and my son to Tante Nicole's chamber on a chaise longue and placed us next to her bed. Tante's pale face appeared to be the size of an infant's so dwarfed was she by the mound of pillows surrounding her.

Holding her hand, I stayed at her side throughout the night. I asked Anne to light all the candles, for I wanted to watch for signs of her recovery.

Anne opened the drapes and, as dawn broke through the mist, a sunray caressed Tante's cheek, like a finger stroking her awake.

Her eyes were clear and bright, and I sighed in relief. She was reviving.

She smiled, but the right side of her mouth did not respond.

I tried to calm a tugging in my heart as I caressed her hand. "I have named my son, Nicolas Philipe, in honor of you and your husband." I gathered all my strength to lean forward and place my sleeping son next to her. I panted with the exertion.

The corner of her mouth lifted in a smile. She gazed at Nicolas with such love the room warmed.

I lifted her left hand and placed her fingers on his chest so she could feel his heartbeat.

"Lou…ou…ou…"

"Louis? You think he looks like Louis?"

She blinked. She eyed the lace ruffle at her neck and lifted her chin.

"Is the lace scratching you?"

She blinked again.

I ran my fingers along the inside of her neckline and felt a metal cross. I tilted my head, and she blinked twice.

My arm trembled. Tante was religious, but wearing the cross was a risk, especially for a spy, even though she wore it inside her gown. I unclipped the pin. A crucifix stemming from a gold heart. My mouth dried. Thérèse and Anne and her children had worn such crosses of carved wood when they came to us. The chill of the caves moved through me. I had insisted they hide them.

Tante made a rasping sound.

Thérèse hurried to Tante's side and brought her ear close to Tante's lips.

"I understand," Thérèse said.

"Is the cross a gift for Nicolas?" I asked.

"Nnnn…"

Thérèse patted Tante's hand. "You rest now." She looked at me. "I will return shortly."

What did Thérèse know that I did not? The cross grew hot in my palm.

"Lou…ou…"

"I will give the cross to Louisa. Is that what you wish?"

She turned her head a bit, and I understood she meant no.

Love poured from her eyes, yanking tears from mine.

I feared there wasn't much time now. I inhaled a shaky breath. "Do you remember the day you insisted I attend Henri's welcoming party?"

One side of her lip curled up, and her left eye sparked.

"You knew I was going to run away. If you had not told me Louis loved me, I might not have figured it out for myself." I laughed. And cried.

She let out a tiny gasp.

My tears came fast. "You are like a maman to me." I pushed through the tightness in my throat. "And I never thanked you. And I've never told you I love you." My voice was a whimper. I shoved myself up, gripped her hands, and kissed them. "I love you, Tante Nicole. I love you." I fell back, exhausted.

Her eyelids fluttered.

"Nicolas and I need you. We need your strength and your courage and your wisdom and your humor and your laughter and your kindness and your boundless love."

Her smile was a ghost of what it had been. All her wrinkles relaxed, releasing the worry and concern she'd held through-out her life. Her face glowed. Her cheek was as soft and pale as my son's.

I couldn't let her leave me, leave us. The château could not exist without her. None of us could live without her.

"Tante?"

She blinked, but her eyes were unfocused, looking at something far, far away.

A soft knock on the door startled me.

Joliette tiptoed into the room, knelt next to the bed, and rested her hand on Tante's arm. Her voice was soft. "Tante Nicole kept vigil over my husband after he was wounded guarding the Queen at Versailles. She told me how she had used maggots to heal the infection in the soldiers' wounds on a battlefield. Had she not placed maggots on Guillaume's wounds, he would have died before we were married."

"Her strength and courage—" my voice cracked.

"She was like a mother to me." Tears ran down Joliette's cheeks. "After my maman died, Tante became my chaperon, and I feared she was a terrible one because she encouraged me to be alone with Guillaume, which was forbidden." A laugh slipped between her tears. "She knew we were in love before I did." She pulled a rosary from her sleeve and wove it between Tante's fingers.

I wiped my face. "She has mothered us all, hasn't she?" I held Joliette's soft hand. Tante Nicole had always been in the kitchen, placing a bowl of soup, a glass of wine, a plate of roast chicken before me. I had always come in search of her wise counsel, her maternal warmth, her humorous insights. "God, please don't take her from us."

A soft scratching sounded on the door. Anne hurried to it.

A willowy man with a thatch of white hair stood behind Magali and three other former nuns who had taught me at the

Abbey when I lived there as a child. Magali rushed to me and kissed my forehead, then knelt next to me. The other women knelt at the foot of the bed. The man carried a tattered bible to Tante's side.

Joliette hurried to the windows and closed the drapes.

Anne picked up Nicolas and gave him to me. His heartbeat thrummed beneath my fingertips. The air thickened, making it difficult to breathe.

Thérèse stood guard with her back against the locked door, her arms crossed, her hand gripping a pistol. Where had she gotten it? I hoped she was a good shot. If Republicans found us, they would truss us all up, throw us on a leaky barge, and drown us in the Loire.

Murmured prayers filled the room. I clung to Tante's hand, rubbing my thumb over her translucent skin. Her worn and scarred wedding ring indented her elegant finger. Rosary beads spilled off her hands and puddled onto her chest.

The man made the sign of the cross upon Tante Nicole's forehead, whispering the same prayers of my childhood at the Pentemont Abbey.

I felt safe then. I longed to feel that again. Don't leave me, Tante. I need you. Please don't leave us.

Prayers rumbled and faded. Tante stilled. Everything stopped. Her breath, the light in her eyes, her heartbeat. A pool of serenity floated over her like sunlight shining on the dew-covered grapevines. She loved the vineyard. Her presence would always be here.

The man crossed himself, walked away, and stood waiting at the door. The former nuns stood and joined him.

Sunlight and a soft breeze made the pale violet drapes shimmer like silver. Tante's lilac scent drifted in the room.

"Say goodbye to your Tante Nicole." I placed Nicolas's tiny hand upon Tante's cheek.

I held her veined, nurturing hands. "I promise Nicolas will know and love you through the stories I tell him of you. I will not forget you, Tante. And I will never stop loving you." I rested my head upon her body. "But I will miss you terribly."

I slid into exhaustion, unable to move. How would I survive without Louis and Tante?

## 50

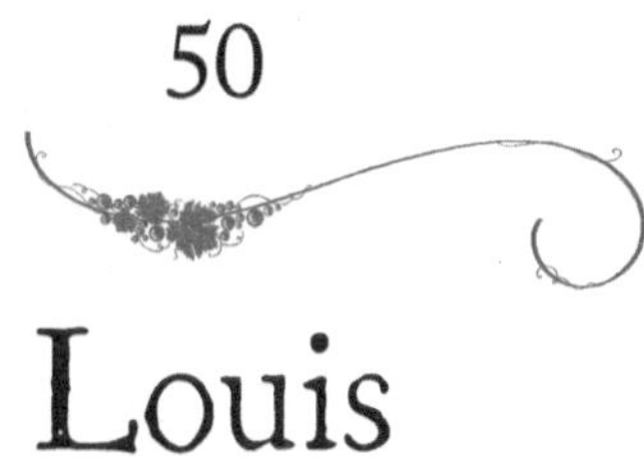

# Louis

*Abu Qir Bay, Egypt*
*July* 1798

**B**ONAPARTE'S SHIP DROPPED sail and released the anchor as the rest of the fleet strung out along a barren shore-line. *L'Aquilon* was bringing up the rear, and Louis was glad. He had no desire to be among the first to face enemy fire. Not a tree nor single hut marred the endless sand dunes. What was there to conquer? This was a bay, not a harbor. How would they disembark?

As the sun set, orders were shouted. Sailors ran up the ratlines to the spars and trimmed the sails. The flapping of the slacked canvas roared loud as artillery fire. *L'Aquilon* slowed as Murat's vessel neared. Sailors dropped a longboat over *le Tonnant*'s side, and Murat climbed down a rope net into it. Sailors readied for the arrival of the commandant.

Louis clamped his teeth together so hard his jaw burned. He commanded his men to prepare for inspection, buttoned his uniform, straightened his bicorne, and hoped Murat would fall into the sea. His men snapped to attention. He was proud of their valiant efforts.

The ship rolled in a swell as Murat came aboard. His uniform wet and wrinkled, he wiped his dirty hands, smearing stains on his pristine white breeches. He shook himself like a wet duck.

Louis suspected his men wanted to laugh, as he did, but they remained focused.

Murat cast his critical eye over him, then turned and examined each of the men, adjusting every one of their hats to an exact fifteen-degree angle. Louis tipped his own before Murat reached him.

Murat arched an eyebrow. "Your men are pathetic soldiers."

At least they stood at attention and were not shaking water from their feathers. Louis's arms tensed, as he imagined plunging a rapier through the commandant. "My men are excellent soldiers. They, and the horses, are weak from hunger and thirst."

"You will prepare your men for battle upon landing."

"They have not had food in days. They will be disadvantaged in battle."

"We all suffer the same." Murat's brows cast a shadow over his rat-like eyes. "Bonaparte will take Egypt by surprise and land under cover of night. I order you to prepare your men."

Surprise? If there were any inhabitants nearby, did they not see the forest of four hundred ships headed for them?

The muscles in Louis's neck tightened, shooting pain up the back of his skull. Bonaparte must have sent a convoy ahead, requesting permission to land and to trade, as he had in Malta. Yet, the army laid siege to that island for six days, slaughtered Knights of Saint John, looted the city, and stripped the monastery bare. The plunder was rumored to be worth six million francs. Bonaparte trained his soldiers as thieves. Although surviving the storm at sea had been terrifying, Louis was grateful their ship had been delayed, and his men had missed that battle. He would not endanger his men no matter the command or booty.

"Colonel! Carry out my order."

Best to act the part of a dutiful soldier. He saluted. "Yes, mon Commandant."

"Do not light any lanterns."

Louis looked back at his men, staring at Murat. One by one, they looked back at Louis, despair quashing their confident posture.

Murat dismissed the longboat. "I will remain aboard should you need assistance in carrying out my order, *Comte*."

There it was. Murat knew he was of noble blood. Had Murat suffered under the Ancien Régime? Why he was antagonistic toward Louis?

"Don't remember *me*, Comte?" Murat's white teeth flashed.

Images of Versailles whirled in Louis's mind, but none included a narcissistic commoner.

Murat's chest expanded as he inhaled. "I've waited for you to recognize me. But there is no reason you should remember your father's groom. He treated me like dirt beneath his boot."

Louis's chest burned. Murat must have been the one to send his father to the guillotine, for every other servant had been as loyal as Adrien.

"And now you are the dirt beneath *my* boot, *Comte*." He grinned and shouted, "Le Capitaine, let us dine."

Louis felt as if he'd fallen to the bottom of the sea. His father's voice boomed in his mind as a scene at the Versailles stables unfolded: his father swinging his riding crop across Murat's shoulder. "You stupid lackey. Brush my horse down immediately!" Little wonder Murat did not care about his horse. Louis's father had valued his stallion more than his groom. Shame for his father's actions burned in Louis. His father had paid for his arrogance with his life. And now Louis would finish paying that debt.

His men, still standing at attention, looked to him for a command. He rubbed his brow, trying to wipe out the memory. He would not let his men suffer for his father's sins. "At ease."

The men removed their hats but watched for any sign of the commandant.

It was nearly dark, making porting more dangerous. They had never practiced landing. It would take all night for the ships ahead of them to anchor and unload.

Did Bonaparte expect the horses to swim ashore? If they forced the horses to jump, the beasts would die of fright before they hit the water for it would be like leaping from the roof of the château. He would leave the horses in the hold. Let Bonaparte figure out how to land them.

How would they transport the cannons and crates of ammunition? Louis eyed the longboat lashed to *l'Aquilon's* railing. It would take endless trips to land his troops on the beach. Should a man fall into the sea, even if he could swim, the weight of his uniform and boots would drown him. Was a shorter route for trade with the Orient worth the lives certain to be lost? Bonaparte was taking senseless risks before the battle began.

If the wind did not change, *l'Aquilon* would not anchor until daybreak. At least the cavalry would arrive long after the infantry brigades. Nonetheless, he had to ensure their safety.

Louis unbuttoned his frock coat and faced his men. "Who knows how to swim?"

# 51

# *Geneviève*

*Château de Verzat*
*June* 1798

W ITH NICOLAS IN my arms, I remained in Tante Nicole's room until the former sisters wrapped her body in the aubergine velvet drapes that had surrounded her bed and men carried her out.

What had she been trying to tell me? The sacred heart cross she gave me sat in my palm, glittering in the morning light. What else had Tante kept hidden?

I laid Nicolas on the bed and opened the drawer in her bedside table. A handkerchief, with a butterfly embroidered in purple, lay atop a bible. She had risked her life owning the leatherbound book. Beside it sat writing paper and quill. An inkpot stood at the back.

The depth of the drawer seemed too shallow for its weight.

With my finger as a guide, I measured the inside depth of the drawer with the outside frame. There had to be a false bottom. I withdrew the drawer, placed the contents on the bed, and examined the corners but found no latch. Not until I ran my fingernail between the bottom and frame, did I hear a click. I found its twin on the opposite side and pressed them both at the same time. The bottom dropped onto my lap. A single sheet of blank paper fluttered. A faint citrus odor piqued my memory: the night I went in search of her lemon tarte and discovered she was a spy. The night I'd become one, too.

Every three days, since that night, I brought a basket to the village market and bought vegetables from the same vendor, whose name I did not know or ask. Sometimes that basket contained a package, which the vendor took. I had delivered the carrots, leeks, and asparagus she sold to me to Tante. Why had I never looked at the produce? Or the packages I delivered to her? Nicolas squirmed, and I comforted him. I smuggled information. And the less I knew, the safer I kept my family and everyone on the estate.

At the soft knock upon the door, I slipped the paper under the false bottom and slid the drawer back. "Enter."

Joliette removed her straw bonnet. "More than twenty men volunteered to help carry Tante Nicole's bier." She wiped perspiration from her forehead. "I asked the stableboys to dig her grave next to my parents' mausoleum in the Verzat family cemetery."

"She would like that."

Joliette's hair hung in damp ringlets. Her apron, gown, and fingers were stained with dirt. She picked up the handkerchief and held it to her heart. Tears dripped down her face, yet she smiled. "My husband gave this to her after she saved his life." She laughed. "I wish you had known him. He was such a thoughtful and kind man."

"I know him through his son."

She pressed the handkerchief to stifle her cry.

"She would want you to keep his gift."

She nodded. "Now Tante is with him." She picked up the bible. "We should bury this with her."

I was relieved I would not have to burn it to keep it from being discovered by the Republicans. "We should honor her with a luncheon."

"Although everyone is working in the vineyard, we could have it outdoors, tomorrow."

My head ached from all the thinking, fearing, crying. "Will the crop suffer?"

She shook her head. "I am certain everyone will work extra hard to finish their tasks later in the day." She wiped the back of her neck. "Besides, it will be cooler then."

"I wish I were strong enough to help." I caressed Nicolas' chubby hand, not wanting to leave him for a second.

"I will arrange for men to carry you on a chaise longue. I know you wish to be with her until we lay her to rest." Tears dropped off her jaw, but she didn't wipe them. She sat next to me.

"I am sorry you are having to do this all alone." I hadn't the strength to help her. But ever since the willowy man had blessed Tante, an unease festered in me like grape pomace at the bottom of the crusher. "Do you know the man—"

"I was as shocked as you were." Creases deepened around her chocolate-brown eyes.

"If he is living on the estate, he is endangering everyone."

She rubbed her temples. "Thérèse told me he lives in the caves beyond the estate."

"How did he know to come?"

"Thérèse fetched him." Joliette reached. "May I hold your son?"

I lifted him to her waiting arms. "Say hello to your Tante Joliette."

Nicolas cooed, his little fists batting the air.

"You are such a big boy." Joliette smiled down at him. "Tante would be very happy to know you honored her and her husband in naming him."

Tante Nicole's loving face hovered before the window, yanking tears from me, but I was too weary to try to stop them. I pushed myself up. The effort sent a pain slashing through me. I hunched back down. "When I am better, I will learn about the priest…and question Anne and Thérèse."

"Thank you. I am worried about their activities." She smiled lovingly at Nicolas. "We need to know more, and you are better at uncovering things than I am."

She had sought my counsel, and I was glad. But my unease grew. Anne and Thérèse were Tante Nicole's couriers. Perhaps, they too, were hiding something more than a priest.

The prayers the nuns had recited at Tante's bed hummed in my mind. "We cannot pray or sing hymns at the grave."

Joliette placed Nicolas in my arms. "We will sing the folk songs Tante loved so much."

"Would you light a candle before you go?"

Joliette tilted her head. The room was bright with sunshine.

"Light it in honor of her spirit, like we would in church."

She nodded and lit the candle atop the bedside table. "I will send Magali to help you."

I'd start my inquiry with Magali. She had not been surprised by the priest. She knew him.

As the door closed, I retrieved the empty sheet of paper and brought it before the candleflame. Faint brown letters appeared as if Tante were writing them.

*My Dearest Geneviève,*

*You are the only one who has the courage to take up where I have left off. I shall watch over you as you continue my work for the return of our King.*

*Your Loving Tante*

I drew in a steadying breath. *Take up where Tante left off.* Why had I not read the messages I smuggled? I'd been so stupid. I replaced the paper in the false bottom of the drawer.

None of the various governments of the Revolution had delivered any of the promises upon which its foundation was built. Republicans used their cause to murder, pillage, and plunder. The imbalance between wealthy and poor was the same. The money had simply changed hands, none of it held by peasants, the very people who died at the Bastille, fighting for liberty. If only I had discussed this with Tante. Now it was too late.

I wished I could search the rest of her room, but I was so weak I couldn't stand. Nicolas made a sucking noise.

A knock at the door sent my heart pounding. "Yes?"

Thérèse entered, carrying clean serviettes and a pitcher of water. Her sleeves were rolled up to her shoulders, baring arms streaked with the white chalky dust of the vineyard. She sat next to me, dampened a cloth, and patted my face. "I'll help you into a clean gown before the men arrive to carry you to Tante's grave."

I nodded. Had she offered to come to me in Magali's place? I closed my eyes against the image of the former nuns and priest. I had rescued Magali and the other nuns years earlier and trusted they kept their former identities and prayers secret. I needed Magali's reassurance. But I also needed to know what Thérèse knew.

"Tante whispered something to you before she passed, and you told her you would tell me. What was it?"

Thérèse's hands stilled, gripping the serviette. "She wanted you to have the sacred heart."

"For Louisa?"

Thérèse blessed herself.

My stomach squirmed like I'd eaten something bad. "You trusted me when you came here, and I gave you shelter. Trust me now." Nicolas squirmed.

"There are priests and nuns, who have not taken the oath of allegiance to France before God, living in the Troglodyte caves throughout the valley."

Tante, why did you not tell me? Nicolas would not quiet, so I untied my gown and brought him to my breast.

Thérèse smiled at him, and her innocent smile stirred my suspicion. Although I thought she was hiding something important, she might not know it. "What has the sacred heart have to do with the priests?"

Tears welled in her reddened eyes. "I took an oath."

"That oath was broken by Tante's death." I caressed Nicolas' cheek. "I trusted you to deliver my son, and I thank you. Now you must trust me."

She wiped her fist across her eyes and took in a jagged breath. "I was her courier."

I closed my eyes at the confirmation. "What did you carry?"

She shook her head. "I never knew."

She was as ignorant as I. Fear made my voice hot. "What *things* did you carry?"

"Usually, messages, other times small packages." Her voice trembled.

"Who did you deliver them to?"

"I gave it to whoever said the code words and, every time, the people and words were different." Her voice was like a frightened little girl's.

"At the market in Tours?"

She nodded. "At our stall." Tears dripped onto her hands gripping the wet cloth.

My heart raced. Nicolas stopped sucking and began to whimper. Had he felt my fear? I brought him to my shoulder and rubbed his back.

"Do you know who Tante's contacts were?"

She lifted her tear-streaked face, looking like a cornered mouse. "The only one I know of is the Chouan who brought us here." She let out a tiny sob and brought the cloth to her mouth.

Why had I not demanded Tante Nicole tell me everything? Nicolas squirmed as I patted his back. Because she would not have revealed anything more than she had to. But she hadn't prepared me for this. I had no idea who she communicated with, nor how to continue her work.

Would my inability to continue her correspondence further jeopardize the estate?

The scent of lilacs floated in the room. A faint image of Tante Nicole, wearing her jewels and aubergine silk gown—pristine as when she'd been a courtier, no longer faded and worn—stood at the window, smiling radiantly. *Oh, Tante, why did you not tell me?* She turned toward the window and looked over her shoulder, back at me. *I would never endanger you, my dear.* She waved goodbye.

## 52

# *Geneviève*



*Château de Verzat*
*July* 1798

Thérèse blamed my son's large size and weight for
my losing so much blood and restricted me to ten days of rest
before she was certain I had stopped bleeding. I treasured
my time with Nicolas, although I worried Suzanne had hurt
Auguste, and I was anxious to learn of Tante Nicole's contacts.

Tante had claimed she couldn't sleep, and I often found her
in the kitchen, sipping a tisane and writing what I thought had
been letters. I often wondered why she received few letters in
return. But it wasn't sleep she awaited. It was the Chouan she
was expecting. I lighted a candle and placed it in the kitchen
window, hoping he'd come—even if he knew she had passed.
I prayed he knew her contacts.

As the clock chimed midnight, I fashioned a sling from the

shawl of Louis's maman and wrapped Nicolas in it and tied him against my chest. He mewled. "You are safe, my little one."

I tiptoed down to the kitchen and flipped back the rug covering the trapdoor of the tunnel that led to the caves. As I opened the trapdoor and rested it against the stone wall, cool air rushed up the wooden steps.

After lighting another candle, I placed paper, quill, and inkpot on the table. Settling my son against my chest, I withdrew Louis's pistol and placed it on my lap. I was a terrible maman to expose Nicolas to such danger. But it would be more dangerous to leave him alone in my chamber, and most dangerous to everyone if I did not uncover Tante Nicole's contacts. I stared at the dying embers in the fireplace. I suspected the Chouans not only fought the Republicans, but also helped keep them from attacking the estate. The Chouans and we needed each other.

Footsteps sprayed gravel in the tunnel below.

A log shifted in the fire, spraying red embers, and sparking light across the shadows. The pistol grew heavy, and my sweating thumb slid on the hammer. Footfalls grew louder. My heartbeat pounded in my head, faster and faster. The barrel of a musket rose above the trap door, followed by a weather-beaten hat. Eyes shadowed by the hat brim stared across at me. My finger tensed on the trigger.

The giant of a man stood before me, his broad shoulders hunched, his eyes peeking out from under the drooping brim of his hat. The candleflame flickered light across his weathered and scarred face. He blessed himself. "I am so very sorry for the loss of a great and noble woman."

I inhaled, willing back tears. I prayed he knew more than I did.

His hands folded in prayer, he looked down at me. He was older, leaner, and stooped, but no less proud. His dark eyes were sadder than when I first met him, when he delivered Thérèse, Anne, and her two children. He had a straight noble nose and thick brows. His hair hung over his shoulders.

"I…" The words stuck. "She did not explain things to me. There was not time."

He nodded and placed his fist over his heart. He wore a white patch on his chest, a red sacred heart and cross. Embroidered below, were the words, *Dieu le Roi.*

I wondered at his courage to wear a badge that claimed God the King. But if he had survived the past seven years of terror, it was because the Revolutionaries nor the Republicans could catch him. I gently released the pistol hammer and shoved the gun into my hanging pocket.

He tapped his musket butt on the stone floor. "I tell…told her our positions and sightings of French ships."

"Ships?" Tante must have had contacts with the British navy.

"Yes. After she wrote all the information I gave, she told me where and when the Royalists would join us."

"Who were her contacts?"

"I do not know." The lines around his mouth deepened. "You do not?"

I had searched Tante's chamber, held every piece of paper to candleflames, unhinged every secret hiding place, read all her letters, and found nothing. She meant not to be discovered. She had protected us. Nicolas let out a little snuffle, and I cupped his head.

The Chouan's eyes widened. "Your child?"

"His name is Nicolas."

The Chouan grinned. "His father is the man who was with you the first time we met."

How did he know? I didn't like Louis at that time. My lips formed the word yes, but I did not speak. Yet, I could not stop smiling. Why did I hesitate? I rocked Nicolas. Loss. I did not wish to lose another person. This man had already cheated death more than ten men combined. I was certain a high price was offered for his head. Yet, I had cared about this man's wellbeing the day he had appeared in the caves with the women and children. I could not allow potential loss to stop me from caring about anyone. "Please sit down." I pointed at the chair. "How can I continue if I do not have her contacts?"

"Wait until they contact you." He sat opposite me. "Tonight, you must write. And then you must put it in code."

What code? Where would I find that if I couldn't find her contacts?

He began, "In October…"

I scribbled and wrote for an hour. Every detail he spoke: a tree at the end of a fence, the number of bird calls, the position of the moon, I recorded.

He stood.

I realized I had offered him no refreshment, no food. Surely, he was hungry. I stood. "Please take some bread with you."

He nodded and headed for the trapdoor.

I held Nicolas to my chest, hurried to the chopping table, and uncovered two rounds of bread. I offered them. "May you be safe."

He reached out his huge hand, pointing at Nicolas.

I uncovered his face, and the Chouan ran his finger along Nicolas's cheek.

The Chouan smiled. "He is well named. God bless you all." He took the bread, descended the steps, and pulled the trapdoor shut behind him.

I rushed to pull the rug back into place.

The fire cracked in the silence. Where would I begin to look for Tante's codebook? A draft guttered the candle. The only sound was my son's soft breathing.

The candleflame snuffed. My eyes adjusted to the dim light cast by the fire's embers. I blinked, remembering Tante stirring soup in the huge iron pot hanging above the fire. She loved making Oncle Louis's lentil soup.

I jerked my head to the shelves behind the chopping block. Her recipes. Not wanting to wake Nicolas, I placed him in the cradle next to the fire, then pulled over a stool, stood atop it, and brought down the tattered leather binder. I leafed through the yellowed and stained pages. Roast chicken, bread, tartes. I stopped. Lists of words with corresponding nonsensical phrases, like: *rabbit beach is orange*. This was no recipe.

A bowl of lemons stood at the corner of the chopping block, reminding me of the invisible letter she had written to me. Tante had tended the lemon trees in the glass-covered terrace like a maman tended a newborn. She said she liked lemon with her tisane, yet I'd never seen her put it in any drink. I cut and squeezed a lemon, took the juice and book to the table.

I stared at my written notes. This was where Tante Nicole's work had left off. If I continued it, and was caught, I would be executed as a traitor. And Republicans could take over and destroy the estate, as they had all the surrounding vineyards.

Was I right to do this? It would be more dangerous for everyone in France if the Republicans were not stopped. And if Bonaparte took control of France, the killing would never end. And Louis might never come home.

Nicolas' tiny chest rose and fell with each precious breath. I wanted him to grow up in a country free of fear. Every one of us was terrified at being caught for the slightest infraction like singing a hymn, wearing a cross, owning a bible. If I were caught it would be because I was trying to make our country better for Nicolas and all the people of France. My heart thundered at the thought of being taken from my children.

The Chouan had told me sightings of French ships. If I could discover Tante's contact with the British navy, perhaps Joliette and I could arrange a shipment of wine to them, a shipment in which we could include valuable information.

I dipped the quill. Lemon juice dropped onto the paper. I stared at it as the paper absorbed it. Who was I now? I was a woman, a wife, a mother. A smuggler. And a spy. Dressing as a man was far easier.

Spying was another secret I would be keeping from my husband. Giving the British navy information about French ships could endanger Louis, but I remembered our conversation before he departed when I asked what he would do should he face the British in battle: *If I am captured by the British, I will surrender and help them defeat Bonaparte and bring back the monarchy.*

A log shifted in the fireplace, showering sparks, igniting a tiny flame. More flames snapped, wavered green-gold, licking the dry log. I dipped the quill and ran my finger along the codewords, searching for the phrase, French ship.

53

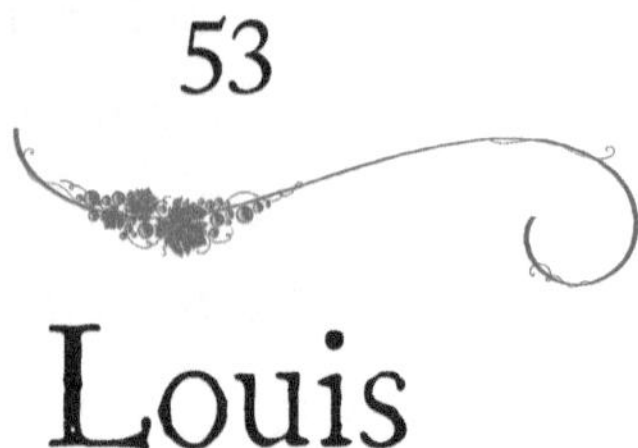

# Louis

*Abu Qir Bay, Egypt*
*July* 1798

Learning half his men could swim, Louis praised his luck. But as the night darkened and the wind increased and the sea convulsed, he wondered if even the strongest swimmers could make it to shore. Two sailors jumped into the longboat and readied the oars. Other sailors let it and a rope ladder down to the waves. One wave swamped the tiny boat. A sailor threw down two buckets and yelled at Louis, "Your men will have to bail all the way to shore. Send two back on the return trip to continue bailing."

Louis rubbed his jaw. That meant five trips to ferry his men. "Remove your boots and uniforms and tie them into a bundle around your hats, muskets, sabers, and daggers."

He stood in his drawers, barefoot and bare chested, and

wrapped his leather belt around his bundle. He held the end of the strap over his shoulder and looked each of his men in the eye, searching for the most frightened nonswimmer. "Each of you carry your bundle with you when you climb down into the longboat. Nonswimmers sit in the center, swimmers on the sides and bail. When the sailor tells you to jump out and head for shore, hold onto the longboat, get out and stand steady— do not grab your bundle if you are not standing. The sailors will row to shallower water if necessary. Once you have your footing, grab your bundle, and hold it above your head until you reach land."

The men nodded.

Louis lowered his voice. "If the swimmers should see a non-swimmer in trouble, leave your bundle in the longboat or on the beach and help the nonswimmer to either the boat or land. Remember, your life is the most important thing and, if you get into trouble, let go of the bundle. Better to lose your uniform than your life." He pointed. "Fleury!"

The young man was bent like a bough against the buffeting wind. "Ye…ye…yessir."

"You wait for me."

The young man nodded furiously, which only increased Louis's unease with the soldier's water abilities. Both his stutter and shyness disappeared when he rode a horse; he was a fine equestrian. Louis smiled encouragingly. "We will descend together."

Fleury's shoulders dropped, and he smiled a frightened smile.

"First group, descend with Lieutenant Verzat," Louis ordered.

A waning gibbous illuminated water and land. The sailors trusted the waves would take them to shore, but if the skiff capsized, would his men know which direction to swim to find land? An experienced and responsible leader would order the first group of men to build a fire on the beach. But Bonaparte was so intent on stealth, he risked every man's life.

Louis shouted down to his men, "Should the boat overturn, stay with the boat!"

Trip after trip, his men descended, bailed, sailed away, disembarked, slogged through the sea, and two returned.

A horse's whinny pierced the roaring seas. Louis squinted, turned, listened. Farther away, a horse screamed. Louis grasped a railing. He could not see the poor beasts.

"Help!" A thrashing, a gurgling, a gasp.

Louis searched the waters. A flag snapped.

"Mother of God, help me!"

Moonlight spilled over whitecapped waves but no men.

"Maman! Maman, help me!" Blackness swallowed the voice.

Louis pounded the railing. Was the man one of his? He could not see the longboat. His breath caught and sat like a rock in his chest. Where was he?

"Maman!"

The crashing of waves and the wind whipping the lines filled the night. He rubbed his palm against his breastbone and shivered in the salt spray.

A wide-eyed Fleury clutched the railing next to him.

"Have no fear, Fleury, I am an excellent swimmer. Let us depart."

54

# *Geneviève*

*Château de Verzat*
*July* 1798

Whoever tante's contact was, I had to let that person know she had passed, and I was taking her place. I rocked Nicolas before the kitchen fireplace. The day the Chouan brought Anne and Thérèse and the children played in my mind. Louis's voice spoke to me: *We will hide them in plain sight, with the former nuns and orphans. They are all Catholics, no?*

The memory brought tears. Had I been in love with Louis then and not realized it?

Logs in the fire shifted, and embers glowed in a bed of ashes. *Hide them in plain sight.* Tante hid the code in her recipe book, which sat on the kitchen shelf. Her contacts had to be similarly hidden in plain sight.

Baskets and pots hung from hooks on the rafters. But writing on either would be evident. Wooden cutting boards and spoons sat on the counter, but etched names would also be obvious. I'd walked this floor thousands of times. If there was a loose cobblestone, I'd have noticed it.

The glow of the fire caressed Nicolas's cheek. Tante's love for us surrounded me like a warm embrace. The memory of her rocking in her chair, hands stitching a small pair of breeches, warmed me.

I placed Nicolas in the cradle, sat in her chair, and scooped up her sewing basket. Atop spools of threads and scraps of fabric lay the butterfly needle case. Her voice was as clear as if she were in the room: *It is the only thing remaining of my life at Versailles.*

All her fellow ladies-in-waiting had similar needle cases. She often sent letters to women; were the former courtiers Royalists?

The butterfly was heavier than I expected a needle case to be. As large as my hand, the butterfly's body was long and stiff, like a handle, and wrapped in white and dark green ribbons. Life-like antennae, wrapped in black silk thread, sprouted from the head. The wings, too, were stiff. Little wonder I thought it was a fan.

Tiny crosses of crimson silk thread were stitched at the top part of the cream linen fabric wings, like a flock of birds in flight. At the bottom, a garden of stitched red and yellow flowers grew. A delicate arc of seed pearls separated the top and bottom of the wings. I squeezed the case and inhaled the scent of lilacs.

Turning the butterfly over, I felt an exposed silkiness. I rolled the wing over the curve of my thumb. The arc of seed pearls gapped, exposing a fine yellow silk. I inserted my finger and, pinching the edge, slowly drew the fabric out. Inked figures covered the silk, like a geometric pattern, but some of the figures appeared darker.

I brought the fabric to the codebook, found the list of figures, and wrote the corresponding letters on the paper. I wrote the first name—Marie-Thérèse. She had to be a former lady-in-waiting. I began writing the family name. The quill dug into my fingers like a knife blade.

I would be corresponding with the daughter of the late Louis XVI and Marie Antoinette.

I crumpled the paper, threw it into the fire, and stirred the embers.

May she never learn that it was my father who sent her maman to the guillotine.

# 55

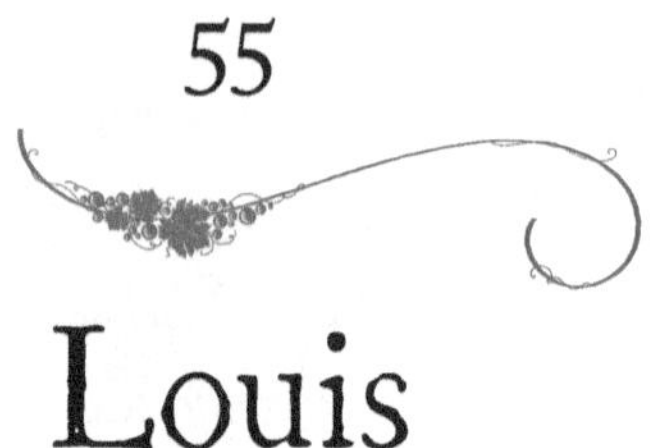

# Louis

*Abu Qir Bay, Egypt*
*July* 1798

**D**AWN BROKE AND the intense sunshine dried Louis's skin, leaving a layer of sparkling, itching salt. His men lay in the sand, exhausted. Who had they taken by surprise? The land beyond the beach was uninhabited. He roused his men and dressed.

"LaGarde!"

Louis gripped his musket hard. He would kill the bastard Murat before the day was over. He stood at attention. "Yes, mon Commandant."

"Where are your horses?"

"In the hold of the ship."

"Are you not Colonel of the cavalry?"

"Yes, mon Commandant."

"Yet you deserted your horses." Murat slapped his crop against his leg.

Sweat dripped through the salt, burning Louis's eyes. He envisioned ramming Murat through with his bayonet, but he would never see his family again. "Had we opened the holes in the hull, the waves would have swamped the ship. And Bonaparte would have lost the ship, supplies, ammunition, and more men, along with all the horses."

"March your men to Alexandria."

"Where is your horse, mon Commandant?" Louis did not add that Murat was commandant of the cavalry.

Murat sawed his jaw side to side. "None of your concern, LaGarde." He pointed away from the rising sun. "The ships will unload in Alexandria."

Alexandria was at least a day's march away. "My men will die of thirst before we reach the port."

Murat smiled. "I can assign your men to a more competent leader if you prefer?"

"No, mon Commandant."

"March out!"

Louis's men watched Murat stride across the beach, belching orders to soldiers who sprawled in the sand, men who did not stir, men who did not rise.

What good was a dead army? Louis motioned his men into a tight circle around him. "Last night twenty men drowned. I want each of you to take an oath. From this moment on, you will obey my and only my command." He looked each man in the eye.

Fleury spoke first. "I pro…promise to obey yo…your command and only your command, mon Colonel."

None of his men hesitated to make his oath.

Louis donned his bicorne and squinted into the heat wavering above sand dunes in the distance. To the Southeast, they shimmered in a circle above the sand. He prayed it was an oasis. It might be hours away.

The ships could wait. The chaos on the beach would make it easy to get away unnoticed. He would be disobeying a direct order. Face the charge of insubordination. But he and his men could die of thirst if he did not find water. He could claim he got lost or attacked by Bedouins.

Henri ripped off his bicorne, bit the threads holding the brim to the crown, and shoved the now floppy brimmed hat back on his head. "I can resew the brim before we see Murat again." He grinned and patted his leather pouch, "My maman gave me needles and thread."

"Do you have enough thread for all of us?"

"Of course."

Louis laughed. "Fashion your hats. We will find water before we reach Alexandria."

# 56

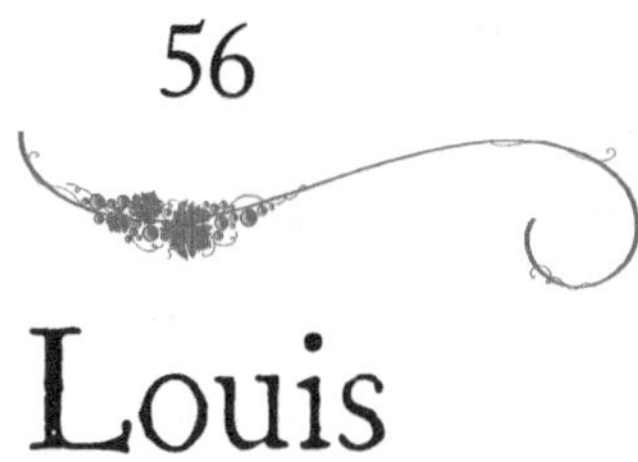

# Louis


*Lake Idku, Egypt*
*July 1798*

Sᴡᴇᴀᴛ ᴀɴᴅ sᴇᴀ water dried on Louis's clothes as he walked in the sun toward the shimmering heat waves. Not a bird, tuft of green, nor drop of water in sight. He had memorized the maps aboard ship and considered paying a Bedouin to lead them across the desert to a different port where they could board a merchant ship on its way to Beirut or Cyprus.

Murat would demote them all if he saw the round-shouldered men, dragging their frock coats and muskets, their hat brims flopping with every step as they trudged through sand dunes, pulling their knees high as if they were plunging through snowdrifts.

Louis feared they would die of thirst before they reached water and hoped the change in heatwaves in the distance *was* an indication of water. The heat waves above the Loire River were always tighter than those rising from the vineyard, and he prayed the same was true in the desert.

Wanting to raise the men's spirits, he began to hum the tune workers sang during harvest. Simon and other men joined in as they traveled until the sun was directly overhead.

The oldest man, Agier, dropped like a wounded bear. Simon stood next to him, casting a shadow before the merciless sun.

Louis knelt next to him, scanning the horizon and focused on a spot of green. Was it a mirage? He shook Agier. "There is water ahead. Come." He tugged at his arm. "I will not leave you for the buzzards."

Agier groaned and pushed himself up. Simon and Fleury helped him.

Louis pointed. "Keep your feet moving and your eyes on that spot of green."

As they neared the greenery, the soldiers' voices lifted, and they stumbled toward a clutch of palm trees shading a vast dark blue lake stretching before them. They dropped their frock coats, hats, and weapons. Simon and Fleury lowered Agier against a tree. Louis untied the man's neckcloth.

"Sip a bit of water at a time, otherwise you will get sick," Louis cautioned his men. He removed his hat and gave it to Simon. "Bring some water back for Agier."

"Keep your eyes open at all times," he shouted. "Warriors could attack at any moment."

His men stumbled to the water and drank.

Louis gripped his pistol, watching the groups of Bedouins camped in the dunes surrounding the lake. Atop a hill, women dressed in black gowns and brightly colored veils tended a cooking fire. Whatever the fuel was, it did not smell of burning wood.

The ring of a blade drawn against a metal sheath forced Louis to turn, his mouth so dry he feared he would be unable to speak.

A bearded man dressed in a black gown, turban, and veil stood, his skirts billowing, his dark eyes as sharp as the blade he held.

Why had Louis's commanders not taught them the ways of this land, like they had warned them of scorpions and snakes? At least he recognized this man as a Bedouin, a nomad, not a Mameluke warrior who terrorized everyone in the desert. His palm sweating, he eased his thumb off the pistol hammer. He bowed his head, with what he hoped would be taken as respect, and looked up at the man.

The Bedouin stood with his feet planted wide, the lines in his face hard as if carved in stone. He raised his scimitar, glinting in the sun. He shouted, waved his weapon toward the lake, and lifted his palm.

Louis understood. The man wanted to be paid for the use of the lake. How preposterous it would be for a fisherman on the Loire to demand payment for a river that was not his. Yet, Louis was a guest in this man's country, and he had to follow the customs or go to battle right now. Murat would shoot the man dead. But Louis's plan was to make friends—he might need them. They knew this land. Knew where the ports were. He dug into his inner pocket and withdrew one of the many silver coins for which he had traded his maman's jewels. He offered it.

The man's eyes brightened; the scimitar lowered. He snatched the coin and secreted it within the folds of his sashed caftan. He brought his hand up, cupped like a bowl, and scooped his other fingers to his mouth. He raised his eyebrows.

Food. Louis nodded furiously and lost his balance. He righted himself and brought up his arm to include his men.

The Bedouin rubbed his fingers against his thumb. Louis would gladly pay for food.

The Bedouin turned toward the women at the cook fire, clapped his hands above his head, and shouted. The women scurried.

Louis reached for another coin, but his fingers were numb. He could not pinch them together. He shook his hands as a shiver washed through him. He began to walk toward the water and stumbled. Darkness encroached. Sparks flurried in his vision. He fell to his knees. Pitched forward into blackness.

Arms grabbed him. Hands tugged his tunic open. A cup of water pressed to his lips. He drank. Water sweeter than any wine. He drank deeply. The sparks faded. The world brightened.

The Bedouin cradled Louis in his arms and continued to help him sip water, all the while speaking, by his tone, a warning. Louis wished to understand. Women waved palm fronds cooling him, their bracelets of bells jangling. His men circled him, concern creasing their faces.

Louis bent forward and exhaled a hot breath. He slowly recovered his bearings and accepted Fleury and Simon's help in walking up the hill. Shouting a welcome, the Bedouin opened his arm toward Louis's men.

He motioned for Louis to follow him to a patch of shade

under a palm tree where women spread intricately patterned rugs of crimson and saffron. They brought melons, jugs of water, platters of dates, dried fish, grapes, cheeses, and roasted small birds. A feast. He and his men would have been thrilled with just one of the delicacies. Louis sat next to the leader and accepted grapes and a piece of roasted fowl. He bit into the grape and the juice reminded him of Geneviève's scent. He savored the memory of her.

A small girl, with eyes as dark and round as ripe Cabernet Franc grapes, smiled at the Bedouin and held out her hand. "Baba!"

The Bedouin smiled, revealing darkly stained teeth, handed her a fig, and tapped his fist to his heart, all the while grinning with pride.

Louis nodded as longing pierced his heart. He pointed to the little girl, thumped his fist against his chest, and smiled.

The man laughed and pointed to him. "Baba?"

Louis nodded. "Baba." Louisa would forever call him Baba after he told her of this. She would teach the baby to call him the same. Louis longed to caress Geneviève's hair ribbon, but if he moved a muscle, he might cry at the thought of her delivering their child without him. He smiled at the little girl until he calmed.

He let his eyes follow long-legged white birds fishing amongst reeds at the lake's edge. Small boats with graceful sails skimmed across soft, rippling waves. He pulled the map from his pocket and spread it on the carpet before the Bedouin. Pointing at their position and, running his finger to the bay they had come from, he lifted his eyebrows at the man.

The Bedouin glanced at the ink lines on the parchment. He flung his arm in the direction of where Louis had come and spoke rapidly.

Louis took this as a warning of danger and nodded.

The man raised his eyes to the sky and back to Louis, his eyes dark. He thumped his chest and shook his head.

Was the territory on the coast ruled by Mamelukes?

Louis drew the outline of a ship in the sand and then pointed at the coastline north of the bay. The man squeezed his eyes and shook his head.

Louis laughed at himself. What use had a nomad for a map? He knew the desert like Henri knew the tunnels beneath Paris. Like Geneviève knew every acre of the vineyard. Yet, the Bedouin clearly dissuaded him from traveling north of the bay. He wished he understood why. It was the most logical way of getting to a British ship.

He rerolled the map and paid for the feast with two silver coins.

When they had eaten and drunk their fill, and all the men bowed their heads in thanks, the Bedouin brought his hands together in prayer and smiled. He then offered up his leather waterskin. Louis gestured to buy more for his men. The Bedouin ordered the women to fill a skin for every man, refusing payment.

Louis wished to tell the man he hoped they would meet again, but he relied on his heart-felt gratitude and smile.

The Bedouin embraced him. "Inshallah."

Louis repeated the phrase. The man grinned, brought his palms together, and nodded.

Refreshed and reluctant to leave this man's hospitality, Louis marched his company southeast to Alexandria.

Simon lifted his waterskin and shouted, "Inshallah." The rest of the men joined him giving their thanks.

Spirits buoyed, the men chattered about the feast, the beauty of the lake, the gracious people. Not a breeze stirred as they neared the coast. The sun was merciless, the desert, silent. The men clutched their waterskins to their chests, afraid to drink, not knowing what lay ahead.

Had Louis quenched his thirst along with his men, he would not have faltered. In the future, no matter how deeply he cared about his men, he had to remember to take care of himself first. Only then could he remain their leader and help them survive.

Bonaparte could achieve much if he respected and befriended these people. They were gracious, hospitable, generous—if you paid them, which was only fair.

How would Louis kill them if ordered to do so? He prayed the British had already defeated Bonaparte and awaited them in Alexandria.

# 57

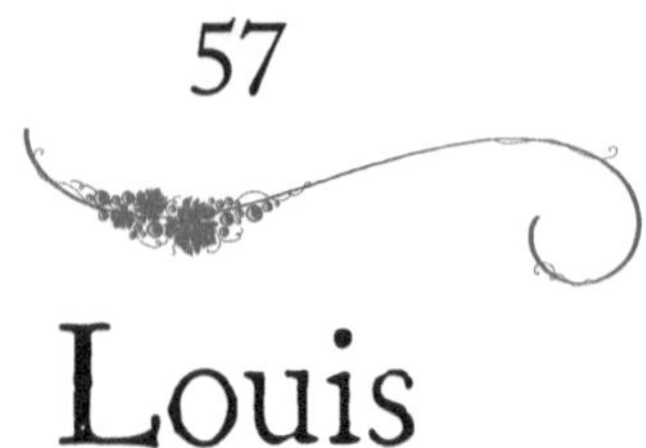

# Louis

*Alexandria, Egypt*
*July* 1798

THEY WALKED FOR eight hours and, late in the afternoon, stopped and gazed at a thick, yellow haze sitting over a walled city in the distance—Alexandria—and no sign of French troops.

Suspicion snaked up Louis's back. He grabbed his pistol and halted his men. Henri pulled out needle and thread and hurriedly tacked the hat brims. The men donned their frock coats and shouldered their muskets. After each had cocked his bicorne at a fifteen-degree angle, Louis marched them forward.

Atop the arched entryway to the city, French soldiers clambered to hang the tricolor flag. Bonaparte had already captured Alexandria. Horses' whinnies and clattering metal and marching feet were the only sounds from behind the walls.

Had the ships arrived, and the soldiers unloaded the horses? Or were the horses owned by the Egyptians?

Where were the British? Louis holstered his pistol and led his men beneath the flag and into a city of blocky, sand-colored buildings with keyhole-shaped doors and windows—many secured with elegant brass locks. Except for French soldiers and their horses, and a few skittish goats, the place was deserted. But at the center of the square, soldiers swarmed a fountain, drinking and showering water upon themselves.

The city overlooked the sea. The French armada sat beyond a T-shaped spit of land that formed two natural harbors. At the end of the T stood a fortress—untouched by cannon fire—appearing deserted.

The sight of nearly four hundred ships must have terrified the Egyptians so that they fled. And Louis hoped they had taken their valuables with them. The thought of pillaging this country sickened him.

Général Bonaparte, sitting astride a white stallion, moved slowly through the crowd of soldiers, who saluted him as he passed. Bonaparte's eyes darted from the windows to rooftops to latticed balconies of the buildings surrounding the square. Soldiers followed him, tacking up proclamations on the doors.

Louis pitied the inhabitants of Alexandria, some of whom he suspected peered out from locked windows.

Bonaparte stopped and put up his arm. Silence fell. He began a speech, telling the unseen natives that he and the people of France were aware of the troubles Egyptians suffered under the Mamelukes' rule. He shouted, "You will be told by our enemies that I am come to destroy your religion. Believe them not."

Sourness filled Louis's mouth. Bonaparte had destroyed the Knights Hospitallers in Malta twenty days earlier.

The Général stood in his stirrups. "Tell them that I am come to restore your rights, punish your usurpers, and raise the true worship of Mahomet. Tell them that I venerate, more than do the Mamelukes, God, his prophet, and the Koran. Tell them that all men are equal in the sight of God…"

Louis wanted to spit. Did Bonaparte think these people understood French? He was here to exploit and pillage these people and their country—just as he had in Malta—the treasures of which sat in the hull of *l'Orient*.

Murat smiled and nodded at Bonaparte's every word, like an empty-headed marionette. Louis struggled to hide his disgust. Bonaparte droned on, but soldiers' faces grew increasingly demoralized with every lie he uttered. Louis imagined even the men who enjoyed pillaging and plundering were thirsty, hungry, and tired.

Bonaparte shouted, "We march to Cairo!"

Cairo had to be days away and Louis feared the soldiers had not had a bit of food or wink of sleep. Louis would not leave without their horses, and until then, he would order his men to rest. He scanned the harbor for *l'Aquilon* and came face to face with Murat's stallion.

"Nice of you and your men to show up, Colonel." Murat's riding crop quivered. "Where have you been?"

Louis squinted at the light reflecting off Murat's shiny brass buttons. "We got lost, mon Commandant. But we found water."

"Lost?" Murat whacked his crop against his horse's flank, making the animal dance and snort. "Did you not follow the coastline—that edge of land against the sea?"

Louis pressed his lips together. His silence would bode better for Murat's poor horse.

Murat leaned down, his face so close, Louis smelled his rancid breath. "Are you certain it wasn't cowardice, Colonel?"

Heat shot up Louis's back. He spread his fingers to keep his hands off his saber hilt.

"Where'd you get that?" Murat's voice cracked.

Louis curled his fingers. He had not thought of a lie for the brightly embroidered waterskin. "A Bedouin, mon Commandant."

Murat grinned. "You stole it?"

Louis kept his voice low, without pride or boast. "I purchased one for each of my men from a group that passed us."

Murat withdrew his saber.

Blood thumped in Louis's temples.

Murat slipped the blade beneath the leather string of the waterskin and, with the flat of the blade, lifted the string from Louis's chest and over his head. Murat tipped the saber up, sliding the string down and onto his wrist. "You'll have to buy another." He sheathed his weapon and took a gulp of water.

Watching the lather drip down the flanks of Murat's horse, Louis wished he had poisoned the water.

"Do you think you will be able to find your company's horses without getting lost, Colonel?" A sheen of perspiration covered Murat's face.

Louis resisted asking if the heat was too much for him. "Certainly, mon Commandant."

Murat leaned over his horse, bringing his duckbilled nose into Louis's face. "And when you do find those horses, I expect you to drive your men to the front of the company—before we reach Cairo."

Longing to punch him in the face, Louis replied, "Yes, mon Commandant."

"If you get lost again, we'll leave you to the buzzards!" Murat's spittle sprayed.

Louis saluted.

Murat whipped his horse and the animal jumped, charging through the crowded square.

Louis chewed the inside of his cheek. He was glad the embellishments on Murat's uniform glittered in the sun—they begged to be fired at. Murat wanted glory, and Louis, having trained at glorifying the kings at Versailles, would give it to him. Maybe flattery would keep the bastard at bay.

In the meantime, he would take his time finding the horses and hope the British arrived before they left for Cairo.

58

# *Geneviève*

$H$EALED AND STRONG, I returned to the market to sell raisins and hopefully receive an assignment. A soft breeze blew off the river and ruffled the leaves of the plane trees surrounding the square. I'd left Nicolas only two hours earlier, and I already missed him desperately. My arms felt useless. I turned to retrieve the wagon.

"Good day, Madame. I wish more of your delicious raisins." The Gendarme greeted me as if he knew me, making me fumble the paper cones.

As I offered one, he whispered, "You are assigned to harbor a spy."

Sounds of vendors' cries, chickens' clucking, the butcher's hatchet whacking—blared. Where would I hide a spy? And should he be discovered would I be executed? I had two children to protect. This was too great a risk.

Nonetheless, I had asked for an assignment and everything I did to undermine Bonaparte brought my husband closer to home. I swallowed against a wave of fear. "For how long?"

He shrugged. "The muscat are delicious, but I am happy to try the gamay."

He was urging me to act like the raisin seller I pretended to be. "Of course." The cone shook in my trembling hand.

"Two, perhaps three weeks." He handed me coins. "If it is safe, light a candle in the north window. The spy will arrive at the château at midnight." He returned to his comrades.

I willed myself to walk calmly, smile, and sell the remaining cones. Where would I hide him? He could not discover Aurélia, Charles, or Fortuné. No one could discover him.

Although Joliette had agreed with our hiding a spy, I paced alone in the hall, reviewing in my mind every room in the château. The only space we agreed on was the attic above the dormitory where the orphans slept. It was terribly hot, but no one would know he was there.

A soft knocking jolted me. Shielding the candleflame, I hurried to the door. A woman, dressed in a fine yellow silk cloak and matching bonnet and reticule, smiled.

I had to get rid of her before the spy arrived. "How may I help you, Madame?"

Her blue eyes sparkled in the candlelight. "The gendarme sent me."

*She* was the spy? I couldn't put such a fine lady in the attic. "Welcome Madame…?"

"Call me Catherine." She was British.

I closed the door behind her. "Do you not speak French?"

"A few words, but it is better I not speak at all."

I longed to ask her how she became a spy, how she worked, how she had escaped capture. She turned, taking in the grandeur. "This will do nicely."

"You're staying in the attic."

"That is not very gracious of you. I've had luxurious chambers at other safe houses."

"Would you prefer a cave?" A tingling ran up my back. "Your presence risks every one of the four hundred families who live on this estate. You will stay in the attic or leave immediately."

She pouted.

I surmised being an aristocrat must still be safe in England. "Follow me." She would not like her new accommodation, but she would stay hidden until I could get rid of her, or I'd report her myself.

59

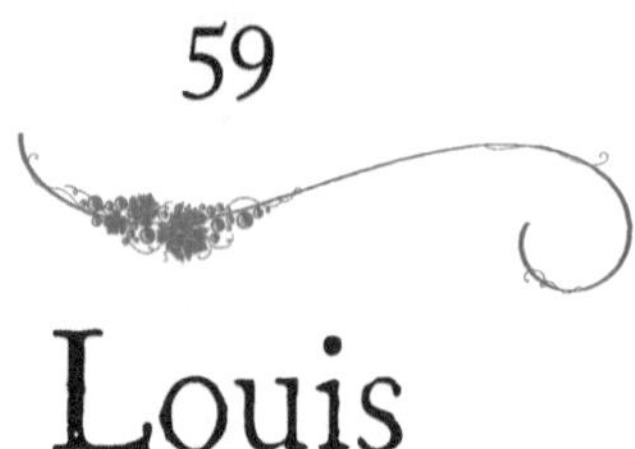

# Louis

WHILE AWAITING *l'Aquilon* to port, Louis and his men slept. The British never arrived, nor did Bonaparte's supply ships before their horses were unloaded. With nothing more than a basket of dates Louis bought from an Egyptian, he led his men out into the desert.

"Stay inline, but at least five horse-lengths apart, and keep watch for Mamelukes."

Fleury offered Louis sips from his waterskin as did every other man. Although reluctant, he forced himself to drink, for if he did not, he would not survive the desert and his men would not survive Murat. He searched the horizon for an oasis. Endless sand dunes stretched in every direction, like crouching lions poised for the kill.

It had been two days since the Bedouin's feast. They had eaten all the dates. The horses dragged their hooves, and Louis feared they suffered more than the men. "Give the horses a rest and dismount."

He dragged a fingernail across the sand crusting his eyelids, hoping a squat structure in the distance was a well or cistern. He stopped his men and dismounted, searching the horizon. "Wait here. Keep watch and your pistols at hand. This might be a trap." He spotted their navigator. "Agiers, ensure we are heading south."

"Yes, Colonel." Agiers pulled out his saber, stabbed it into the sand, and placed a stone at the end of the saber's shadow.

As Louis trudged through the sand, he detected scraps of blue and red fabric. A metallic stink nauseated him. He slowed, placed his hand over his nose and mouth. Black flies swarmed. Vultures sat atop bloodied French corpses littering the area. He swallowed against the urge to gag and clapped to scare away the birds, but they remained, tearing at human flesh, drops of blood disappearing as they hit the sand. He charged them, and a few hopped off, yet stood ready to return to their feast. This had happened recently for there still to be blood. A prickling crept up the back of his neck.

Had there been an attack? He scanned for footprints. Sand had already covered much of them, but there were no sand-covered prints leading away from the bodies. He peered down into the well. A sinking sensation pulled in his stomach.

Sand.

He examined the bodies. One man lay on his stomach, clutching a pistol next to his neck. Why had his weapon not been taken by marauders? With his foot, Louis lifted the man's shoulder and pushed him over onto his back. He had shot himself in the head, for the soldier had no face.

Louis bent over, drew in a ragged breath. Images of his men reaching the same fate seeped into his mind like shifting sand. Imagined cries for water echoed. He could not allow his men to die of thirst or kill themselves. He shuddered as he discovered self-inflicted wounds on the other men. Thirty men had killed themselves rather than endure the agony of dying of thirst.

He straightened and looked back at his men, glad he had told them to remain, glad he had not been able to see the dead soldiers clearly when he had dismounted. He should take the guns so the Mamelukes could not get them, but his men would wonder why the attackers had not taken them. He hated lying to them, but he had to preserve what little morale they had left.

He returned to his company, the men's eyes feasting on the well. "Sabotage. The well is filled with sand. They attacked— French soldiers are dead."

His men removed their hats and placed them over their hearts. A few of their faces told him they suspected he was lying.

"Should we honor the men and bury the bodies?" Simon asked.

"It would be a correct and well-deserved honor." Louis bowed his head. "But I fear this may be another trap."

Agiers pointed south.

With no landmarks on the map, Louis could only guess how close they were to Cairo. He hoped his guess was wrong. According to his map, the Nile was to the east. Cairo would still be there whenever he arrived. "Let us continue on foot to spare the horses. We will reach the Nile soon." Under the broiling sun, Louis led his men east. Damn Cairo. Damn Murat. Damn Bonaparte.

# 60

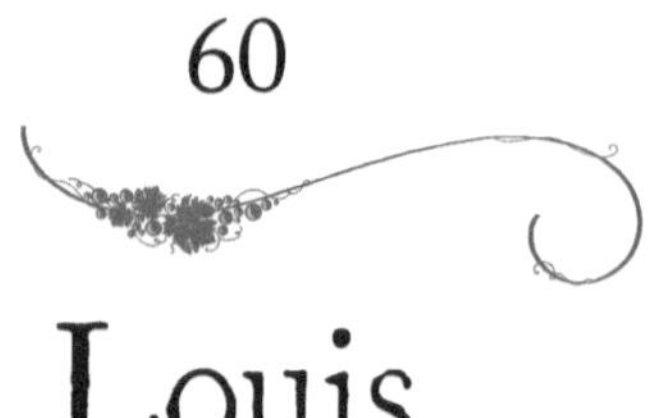

# Louis

*Egyptian Desert*
*July* 1798

AFTER A SLEEPLESS night, Louis stood before his men. "Your stoicism makes me proud of every one of you. We should overtake our battalion and reach the Nile before noon. Let us prove our superior skills to Commandant Murat."

The men shuffled and stumbled alongside their horses. A hot wind whirled the sand, fine as sifted flour, into spirals twisting across the dunes. The horses hung their heads. Their eyes and noses reddened, and they had stopped urinating, as had the men. Bonaparte was a murderer of men and beasts.

"Colonel?" Agiers walked his horse next to Louis and pointed. "That is south."

Louis nodded. "We will travel south after we reach the waters of the Nile."

Agiers grinned. "Excellent plan, Colonel."

They trudged on.

Louis shadowed his eyes. Were the heat waves rising on the horizon a mirage? They walked until the sun reached its zenith, revealing a sparkling blue ribbon surrounded by green—fields and fields of emerald-green.

Agiers hollered, "Water!"

Louis's chest bloomed with joy. They would not die of thirst.

Exhausted, the men stumbled and crawled to the river, and dropped on their bellies to drink. They pulled their mounts downriver and into the water, encouraging them to drink, filling their hats with water and pouring it over their horses. Louis drank, inhaled the fresh scent, filled his hat, and led his mare into the Nile.

Never letting his guard down, he drank his fill, ate of the watermelons his men retrieved from the fields, and relished the shade of palm and date trees. After a few hours, other troops joined them. Relieved he had delivered his men, Louis ordered them to get some sleep and rested himself.

Clanging metal, shouted orders, and hammering of tent stakes shattered the silence. Thousands of newly arrived soldiers set up camp under a waning moon.

Murat, carrying a torch and riding a stallion through the encampment, barked, "Prepare for battle at dawn!"

He was as much a murderer as Bonaparte. The troops desperately needed rest. After mustering his men, Louis and his company rode their horses to the foot of a tall, plateau-like dune. Surrounded by torch bearers, Bonaparte sat upon his white stallion and faced the entire battalion. "Mamelukes will attack at sunrise. Get into position!" he shouted.

Beneath the light of a halfmoon, the band struck up *La Marseillaise*.

"Hold your fire until I give the command!" Bonaparte shouted.

The music dragged back the memory of Louis's prison cell in Paris, where he had awaited execution before Geneviève had rescued him. There were probably many men among him haunted by such nightmares.

The pale moonlight revealed fear etching his men's faces. Louis led his men into the formation of a tight square. Murat corralled six rows of infantry men who knelt in the sand and surrounded Louis's company on all four sides. Another six rows of artillerymen surrounded the infantry, with cannons breaking up the four frontlines.

Bonaparte's squares took shape, spreading over the sand dunes across from the Nile. After they crossed the river, the Mamelukes would have to travel a few kilometers to reach the French. Unless the Mamelukes had cannons, they would not be able to penetrate the highly defended squares. At least the murderer had a brilliant strategy.

"Mameluke warriors are known for their ferocious bravery and equestrian skills." Louis spoke softly, all the while running his hand along his mare's neck. "Watch them carefully. Watch out for each other." His men looked around, nodding. He'd done all he could. They knew their lives depended on each other. Now he had to summon his own courage.

Murat, riding a chestnut stallion, approached their square. "Colonel LaGarde. Do not allow your men to fire until I give the command."

"Yes, mon Commandant." Louis saluted. Despite twelve

rows of soldiers surrounding them on all four sides, he felt no safety. Every man should judge when to defend himself. As Murat rode off, his men turned their eyes to Louis.

"Be prepared to fire regardless of that command." Louis whispered, "I trust you to shoot if you need to." His men nodded, and he sensed their relief.

As the fingers of dawn scratched the sand, sounds of clashing brass bells and muffled pounding hooves advanced like an invisible wall. Searching for the source, soldiers' heads snapped to the east. Thousands of Arabian stallions galloped over the sands before the rising red sun. Astride the magnificent beasts, Mamelukes in their brightly colored, plumed turbans and flurrying robes, resembled a flock of exotic birds clattering against a cobalt-blue sky. Gold and jewels on their harnesses and scabbards flared like flames.

Louis squinted in the brilliant sun, inhaled against the tightness in his chest.

Most Mamelukes held a pistol in each hand—others a javelin, others a scimitar. They commanded their animals with the elegance of ballet masters.

As the brigade crossed the Nile, French soldiers' horses snorted, pawed the sand. Prayers were whispered, cannons readied, muskets aimed.

At the center of the square, Louis's men held their horses. The horses' unease was due not only to the impending battle, but also their confines. They had no room to move, no escape.

Next to him, Simon's trembling hands clutched the reins to his chest. His arms were stiff, moving like a gate on a hinge.

"Exhale," Louis urged him. "Focus."

Simon dragged his fist over his mouth and nodded, never

taking his eyes from the advancing danger. His face was as white as a cloud.

Mamelukes rode like the wind. Clouds of sand billowed like sea foam around their horses. Surely, they were within range of cannon fire. Why was Bonaparte withholding his command?

Having crossed the shallow Nile, Mamelukes rode through the green fields. Thousands of foot soldiers, carrying javelins and wearing short vests and long white breeches caught at their ankles, followed. They hollered a battle cry.

The horses of Louis's company whinnied and stomped, danced in tight circles. Henri sat tall, calm, staring straight ahead, his mouth a grim line. Beside him, Fleury lost control of his horse. With a lunge, Henri grabbed the reins, and spoke to the soldier who was gnawing his finger until blood dripped down his hand. Gripping both sets of reins in one hand, Henri pressed the other onto the soldier's shoulder, and whispered to him. Fleury calmed, dropped his bloody hand, and accepted his reins from Henri. Fleury sat taller in his saddle as he held his horse and focused.

Louis inhaled deeply, grateful for Henri's fortitude.

"Artillery, fire!" Bonaparte shouted.

French cannons blasted. Horses reared and screamed. Louis strained to keep his mare still; the reins cut into his palms. He wiped one hand then the other on his breeches and grabbed the pistol from his belt.

When Mamelukes were close enough for the French to see the gems on the horses' harnesses, the frontline battalion fired their muskets. Two of the closest warriors lost their reins and toppled. Their horses flailed, spraying sand. Foot soldiers ran after the escaping beasts.

Clouds of acrid gunpowder burned Louis's nose. Sand whirled, darkening the sky, stinging his eyes.

More cannons boomed. Hundreds of French infantrymen fired. The roaring blasted, echoing in his body. Louis shook his head, trying to separate himself from the sound, but the blaring pulsed in his veins.

Scores of Mamelukes toppled, some so close they sprayed sand upon the frontline men as their bodies fell. The French soldiers were waiting too long to fire. His men strained to keep their rearing horses from trampling the soldiers surrounding them.

The leading Mameluke, holding his reins in his teeth, fired both his pistols, but he was too far away to reach his target. He flung the pistols at a foot soldier who snapped them up. The Mameluke drew his scimitar, the blade more menacing than the guillotine's. The man bobbed and swayed like a standing cobra, mesmerizing Louis.

A shot exploded. Blood seeped through the man's robes. The warrior held onto his scimitar until he crashed to the ground only meters from the infantry square.

Louis could not let a stray bullet reach his men. Damn Murat's command. He shouted, "Draw your weapons."

His soldiers drew their pistols and aimed at the marauders. Henri squeezed Fleury's shoulder. The artillery and infantry kept up a constant barrage and prevented hundreds of riders from penetrating the squares of soldiers—except for one warrior.

A wizened, white-robed Mameluke rode his black stallion with the grace of a prince. The artillerymen fired their muskets, but not a single shot hit the man as he whooped a battle cry and made his horse dance through the sand. All other Mamelukes rode straight on, but this warrior cut his horse around the side of the square of Louis's regiment, where there were no cannons.

Searching the whirring sand, Louis pressed his feet into his stirrups and stood.

Shoving his reins in his teeth, the Mameluke withdrew his scimitar and raised it above his head. The man's dark eyes locked on Louis's.

Louis's dueling instincts flared. He met the challenge, stared the man down, brought up his pistol.

With fearless precision, the man circled his scimitar and charged. Twenty meters separated them.

Arm shaking, Louis pulled back the hammer. Exhale. Focus.

The scimitar's curved blade glinted as it sliced through the blowing sand. Infantry men fired. The Mameluke did not falter.

Ten meters.

Finger on the trigger, Louis aimed at the man's heart. *You will not take me from my family.*

The Mameluke stood in his stirrups, swinging his scimitar with both hands.

Five meters.

Louis fired.

Crimson blood bloomed across the Mameluke's white robe. His horse veered. Still gripping his scimitar, the warrior soared like an angel of death, arcing head over heels before thudding into the sand, face to the sun.

Louis lowered his weapon. Gulped air. With a shaking

hand, he wiped sweat from his eyes. He drew in a steadying breath and stared at the dead Mameluke. "Inshallah."

His men held their mounts, each one looking back at Louis, then refocusing their aim. As more Mamelukes advanced, Louis's men fired, felling them one after another.

The massacre lasted less than an hour. Defeated Mamelukes rode back across the Nile and into the desert, foot soldiers collecting discarded weapons as they ran after the horses, tinkling bells shimmering in their wake.

Cannons quieted, along with Louis's heartbeat. He had killed. Sand gritted against his teeth. He spat. He had taken the life of a magnificent warrior, a man trained in the grace of equestrian warfare. He wiped his fist across his mouth and looked over his men. Simon squinted, looking over the carnage. What had he asked? *Does killing haunt less if it is a noble act?* Louis shook his hand, numb from clutching the reins. There was not one thing noble about killing. Not one thing.

French soldiers swarmed the booty, cheering at their claims of gold-encrusted and bejeweled turbans, saber sheaths, harnesses.

Louis wiped his eyes and searched for an abandoned waterskin and food for his men.

"We march for Cairo in an hour!" Murat waved his arm. "Get into formation."

Not one French corpse lay in the sand. The artillerymen had fought with great bravery. They deserved praise, rest, food, and water.

Louis doubted Cairo would be as easy to take as Alexandria. Mamelukes ruled this country, and they knew the French wanted Cairo.

He snatched up a waterskin. Dry, but he would fill it in the Nile. Buzzards circled.

"Colonel LaGarde!"

He snapped to attention. "Mon Commandant." He bit down so hard his teeth ached.

"You were the only officer who did not trust the artillery to fell the enemy, and your company followed your lead, wasting ammunition!" Murat yanked his horse's reins, making the animal snort. "You disgraced Bonaparte's army by firing."

Louis kept his salute. "Had the Mameluke released his scimitar, I would have died." He envisioned a scimitar slicing through Murat's neck, his head rolling over the sand.

"You're a coward, LaGarde. I will prepare a challenge for you in Cairo." Murat sneered. "A challenge that will either cure you of your cowardice or kill you."

Louis had enough trouble surviving without whatever additional hell Murat would construct. He stared at Murat's back as he galloped away. "You won't take me from my family, either, you duckbilled bastard."

# 61

# Geneviève

*Château de Verzat*
*July* 1798

I FASHIONED LOUIS'S MAMAN'S shawl into a sling and carried Nicolas against my chest. I needed to feel the earth under my feet, smell the grapes, hear the breeze spin the leaves. The vines that had been damaged by the hail a year earlier were thriving, and I wondered if nature had thrown us that crisis to improve the health of the vineyard. Something to discuss with Joliette.

A shadow crossed before me. I cradled Nicolas closer. A stocky man with rigid shoulders walked toward me. He wore a battered straw hat and a dust-covered tunic. He smiled. "Good day, Madame."

I would have recognized anyone living on the estate. Where had he come from?

"Have you any raisins?" He doffed his hat.

The spymaster. I laughed, releasing my anxiety. "Not today. I hope you are here to accompany our guest to her next lodgings?"

He chewed at his moustache. "Her connection is imprisoned."

Nicolas must have felt my fear, for he squirmed. "Can you not take her?" A sharp turn of his head made me realize that wasn't his job. "She's been here for more than three weeks."

"Her connection is sentenced to death."

I closed my eyes against a memory of Louis in his prison cell.

The spy picked up a few pebbles and jiggled them in his palm. I tasted the chalky scent sparking in the air.

"He is also her husband."

Nicolas began to whimper. I pulled him against my shoulder and rubbed his back. How could I help this woman? Help— without risking myself and my children?

The spy looked out over the Loire. "You export Verzat wine?"

"Nearly all that we produce."

"Some to England?"

"Via neutral ships that depart from Nantes."

His gaze bored into me. "Could she accompany the wine on one of those ships?"

"You mean, hide her in a barrel?" An image of Catherine huddling in a wooden barrel was comical.

"I mean, as a wine vendor."

"If she were caught the Republicans would take this entire estate in an instant."

He shook his head. "If you hired her without the knowledge of her espionage, they could not hold you responsible."

"But I *do* know."

"You are an excellent actress."

Nicolas made smacking noises, letting me know he was hungry. Sending Catherine as a vendor, if she kept her mouth shut, might work. And we'd be out of danger. "I will speak to my partner about it. Can you return tomorrow?"

"With pleasure, Madame." He gave a slight bow and smiled. "He is a beautiful boy."

I jostled Nicolas, my mind whirring with possibilities. We could give Catherine another assignment while she's tasked with delivering wine. I hurried back to find Joliette.

# 62

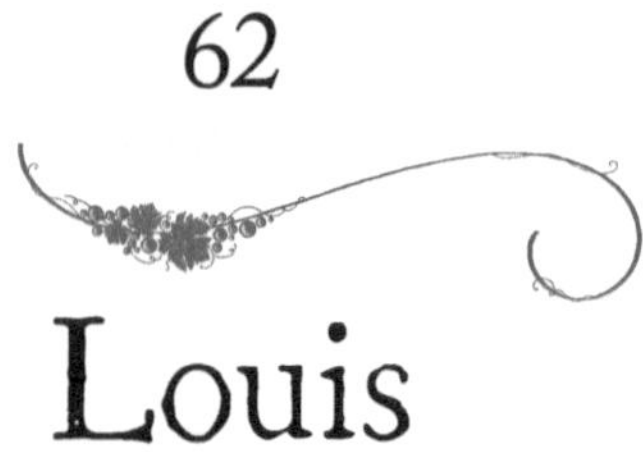

# Louis

*Egyptian Desert*
*July* 1798

THE GANGLY BEAST was two heads taller than Louis and smelled of dry excrement. This was Murat's challenge? His cure for Louis's *cowardice*?

Because he did not wish to be spat upon or bitten, he avoided looking directly at the animal. Its bulging amber-brown eyes were soulful yet harbored distrust. The thick brown lashes were as long as Louisa's fingers. How his daughter would giggle. The camel must be female with such lovely eyes. A quick look confirmed his guess.

Louis pressed his lips against a laugh, blessing the night he and three other courtiers had broken into the King's menagerie at Versailles. Louis had been the only one who not only successfully mounted the beast but also rode him around the enclosure. Despite his past success, he needed a lesson.

A black-robed and turbaned Bedouin held a rope tied around the creature's neck and muzzle.

Louis nodded to him. "Inshallah."

The man's eyebrows rose. Louis could not tell if the man was surprised or impressed or both. "Inshallah." His reply was gritty as sand.

Louis's men stood around the Bedouin and his herd, watching carefully. He stood to the side and stroked the camel's long soft neck, patting her wrinkled curve, and whispering, "I shall call you Sophie. Let us be friends you and I, surprise them all."

Her small ears twitched.

The Bedouin brought a stick behind the camel's front knee and pulled down on her rope bridle. After a bit of growling, Sophie knelt, rested back on her haunches, and sat, calmly chewing, her jaw sawing side-to-side.

Removing his hat, Louis pointed to the Bedouin's turban. Then he pointed to himself. The Bedouin called out to a boy, who unwrapped his own red turban. Louis bent for the child to wrap the fabric around his head and neck. Louis placed his bicorne on the boy's head, brought his hands together, and nodded, for he knew no other gesture for thanks.

The boy grinned. "Shukran."

Louis repeated it to the boy and then to the Bedouin. The Bedouin's lips relaxed their grim line.

Atop Sophie's hump, draped in a colorful rug, sat a leather saddle with a carved wooden post at its front and back. Camel riders kept one leg bent around the front post and used the opposite foot to kick the animal's flank. As there were no stir-rups, Louis held onto both knobs, hoisted himself up onto the saddle, and hooked his leg over the front knob. The Bedouin gave him the rope and stick and slapped the camel's hind quarter.

Sophie jolted forward, lumbering to her knees, and it seemed she was trying with all her feminine wiles to pitch Louis forward and fling him over her head. He leaned back to counter her efforts and gripped the rope. Sophie hissed and spat as she rose. Louis patted her neck. "All will be well, beauty."

Thundering hooves approached.

"Enough romance, LaGarde." Murat's tone was sour. "Ride the beast."

There was no lesson for this, so Louis held onto the rope and tapped the stick against her flank. Sophie leaped and began trotting, swinging him from side to side. He kept his seat as she galloped, leaving Murat in her dust. Louis's men whooped and hollered.

For the first time in the army, Louis felt free. He adjusted his body to move with the camel's swaying gait, loosened the rope, and laughed into the sun. She was, indeed, a ship of the desert. If he could teach his men to ride, perhaps they could successfully escape. Had he enough money to purchase fifty camels?

Hooves pounded behind him, and Louis slowed and turned Sophie. Murat whipped his stallion, an Arabian he had no doubt confiscated from a Mameluke. Louis pulled up the rope and halted Sophie.

Murat circled him. "You'll be acting as decoy for the Mamelukes in our next battle."

Louis's chest contracted. He would be facing those warriors on an unfamiliar mount. He should have let Sophie pitch him on his head and fallen off at the start, making his men laugh, not cheer. He should have let Murat make a fool of him.

But Louis was no fool. He withdrew his saber and locked his gaze on Murat. "Being at this height is an advantage." He lifted the blade above his head and advanced.

Murat backed away. "Better practice. You'll be circling Bonaparte's square." He whipped his mount and galloped toward camp.

Louis would be riding between the fire of the French artillery and the Mamelukes. He gazed across the desert to the Nile. It would be so easy to steal away, follow the river to the sea, await a British ship. But he could not leave his men. He sheathed his saber and stroked Sophie's soft coat. His baby's skin was surely softer. He wished more than anything in the world to be with his family; wishing he could kiss the special place on Geneviève's neck.

He turned Sophie and urged her into a gallop, circling, coming to abrupt stops, making tight turns, earning her trust. Never faltering, she was surprisingly agile. Louis brought her to a stop, lightly tapped the stick behind her front knee. She knelt and sat. Stroking her neck, Louis whispered, "I promise, you and I will survive." He dismounted and walked her back to his men.

Regardless of whether he had enough money for fifty camels, he had to ensure every one of his men could ride one. "Who will be first for a lesson?" he asked.

Fleury jumped and grabbed her rope. "Me."

"She will try to get rid of you."

Pride beamed in Fleury's face. "I'll enjoy the challenge, mon Colonel."

Louis would ensure the young man had confidence in himself for the next battle.

# 63

# *Geneviève*

*Château de Verzat*
*July* 1798

I FOUND JOLIETTE IN the salon, alone, working on the books. Ink stained her fingers.

Still tired from childbirth, I sat down to catch my breath. "We have been asked to arrange Catherine's transport on a neutral ship to England."

Joliette dabbed her apron across her brow. "In a barrel or as an agent selling Verzat wine?"

I grinned, relieved we thought alike. "Do you think her personality would fit in a barrel?"

We both laughed.

"We must take advantage of her disguise. You receive and encode information on French ships?" she asked.

"Along with the wine, information could be delivered directly to the British navy."

"We have a shipment that leaves Nantes next week."

"Catherine and a special barrel of wine for Capitaine Smith will be on it." I promised.

64

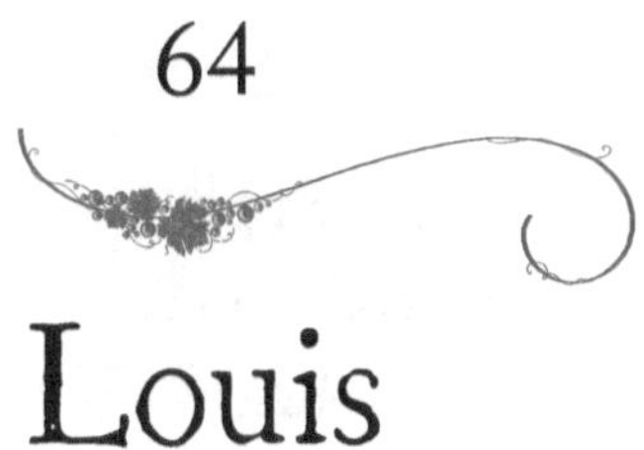

# Louis

*Egyptian Desert*
*July* 1798

A YELLOW HAZE SPREAD across the horizon, veiling the pyramids, which loomed in the distance as the men marched toward their next battlefield.

Bonaparte ordered the same square formations. But this time, Louis would lead a new company of dromedary riders in circling the squares, taunting the Mamelukes, and drawing the fiercest warriors toward the cannons, facing fire from the enemy and the French.

Mamelukes would ride facing into the sun, giving Louis the advantage. He would also keep track of when cannons fired, calculating how much time he had to travel between loading and firing. As his bicorne made him an easier target, he left it and wrapped the Bedouin scarf around his head.

Before reporting to Bonaparte, he hurried to his company's square, hoping to instill confidence in his men. All the horses were skittish, but Fleury kept his mount under control. Louis nodded to him, and Fleury smiled with pride.

Louis addressed his men. "While I am away, Lieutenant Verzat is in charge."

Henri saluted him.

A burning in his stomach put Louis on edge. Murat might interfere with Henri's commands.

"I trust you to defend yourselves and shoot when you feel the need—even if you are ordered to hold your fire—at all costs, protect your life." The men nodded. "After the battle, corral abandoned camels and bring them to camp."

He saluted them and rode Sophie to the edge of Bonaparte's square.

The air vibrated with the thudding of hooves. Waves of Mamelukes, hollering their war cry, rose over the hill. Their horses galloped down dunes, clouds of dust billowing before them. Louis tightened his turban and brought the scarf to cover his mouth and nose.

The clattering of weapons drowned out the band's playing of *La Marseillaise*. French cannons boomed. Louis counted the seconds between cannon fire. Warriors neared. He withdrew his saber and urged Sophie into a gallop, feinting, circling, turning, leading the Mamelukes directly toward the artillery.

Wave after wave advanced—ten times the warriors than the previous battle. As Mamelukes scattered and fell, Louis wiped sweat from his eyes, longing to check on his company. He scanned the gun-smoke-filled battlefield.

Another tribe of Mamelukes changed course and charged

toward his company's square. Louis urged Sophie into their path, leading them toward the cannons before narrowly escaping their fire. Panting for breath, Louis turned Sophie.

The artillery had brought down all but one Mameluke. Holding his horse's reins in his teeth, the Mameluke tossed his spent pistol to the ground and circled the scimitar above his head.

In the center of the square, Fleury stood tall in his stirrups and drew his pistol on the lone warrior. The young man stood straight, his mount calm, his arm strong. Louis silently urged Fleury to shoot. Louis brought up his pistol, but he feared he was too far away to fell the Mameluke.

Murat charged his stallion, screaming, "Hold your fire."

Fleury lost his focus. His arm wavered.

"Don't waste ammunition," Murat commanded.

Louis shouted, "Shoot, Fleury! Shoot!" Louis aimed at the Mameluke and pulled the trigger.

Louis's shot hit the Mameluke in the shoulder, and the warrior lost his seat. But with a battle cry, he rose in his stirrups. With his uninjured arm, he circled his scimitar and released it, sending it whirling.

"Fleury, ride!" Louis yelled.

The blade cut through the air and struck Fleury's neck. Blood sprayed over his uniform. His head fell back. His body tumbled. His horse reared.

Shots erupted, downing the Mameluke.

Louis jumped off Sophie and ran. He dropped to his knees. Fleury's lifeless eyes stared up at his mount, standing over him. Crimson blood seeped into the sand, disappearing, as if it had never been there.

"No." Sorrow choked Louis. His men crowded around him. "LaGarde! Take your position."

Murat had ordered Fleury to hold his fire. He had murdered Fleury. Hate-fueled rage surged in Louis. He sprang up, mounted Fleury's mare, and charged toward Murat.

Louis urged the horse around fallen men and fighting soldiers. He reined in the horse, spraying sand across Murat's chest. The bastard stood as still and arrogant as the Sphinx.

Louis withdrew his saber and sliced it through the air, bringing its tip to rest upon Murat's jaw. The bastard did not flinch. "You killed that man."

"I gave the order to hold fire."

"If you had not, that man would still be alive."

"That man was a coward."

Rage tore through Louis. "That man had more courage than you will ever possess."

Murat lifted his duckbilled nose. His eyes were cold and black. "What is one man's life compared to the glory of France."

Louis wedged the tip of the saber's curved blade below Murat's high collar. "If that life is yours…" he pressed the point just below a thick vein in Murat's neck. "Nothing."

Murat leaned back. Louis leaned forward, mirroring Murat's movement, never letting up on the saber. Murat's blood skittered down the blade. Louis longed to slice the bastard's neck just like Fleury's.

"This is insubordination, LaGarde. Punishable by execution."

"Only if you live," whispered Louis.

Murat's face paled, but he did not pull away.

"Don't do it," whispered Henri.

Louis grew aware of Henri and Simon at his side. He suspected his whole company was behind him. All witnesses.

"We need you." Henri urged. "If you kill him, none of us will survive without you."

Louis blinked away drops of sweat running down his forehead. His arm trembled.

"Think of your men, Louis. No one else will." Henri's voice was calm, reasonable.

The image of Fleury's peaceful, innocent face wavered in Louis's mind. He would tell his parents how brave and valiant their son was. He had to keep his promise to the remaining men. But that meant the viper Murat would live. His chest ached, as if it had been split open.

Murat's eyes crossed as he stared down at the blade piercing his neck. The arrogant bastard wasted Fleury's life—to save ammunition.

Louis knew that when he retracted his saber, he would face a firing squad. Kill now or not, Louis would die. Not one thing noble about it. But he had to try for his men. He withdrew the blade, sheathed the saber, sat tall in the saddle.

Murat turned his mount. "Report immediately to Bonaparte." He galloped away.

Louis shivered in the heat. His arm, chest, head ached. He dismounted and walked to Simon, who held Sophie's reins. Louis's men crowded around, dust staining their worried faces.

Simon's eyes were sad. "Don't let them take you, Louis."

He nodded and rode Sophie across the battleground toward Bonaparte's square. The stink of gunpowder burned his nostrils. Sand scratched his throat. Thousands of Mamelukes, foot soldiers, French soldiers, horses, camels sprawled across the dunes. Gunsmoke drifted. Black flies swarmed. Vultures circled.

Dread smoldered in Louis as he reached the square.

Bonaparte waved him to approach.

The heat reflecting off the sand intensified. Bonaparte would judge him guilty of insubordination and send him before a firing squad. Delicately, Louis led Sophie through rows of men and saluted. "Mon Général."

"Fine riding, Colonel."

His salute wavered. "Merci, mon Général." Behind Bonaparte stood Murat. A pressure built in Louis's chest.

"Murat! Have this man train his company in riding camels," Bonaparte commanded.

Louis braced himself for Murat's accusation, but Bonaparte rode away.

A sinister grin spread across Murat's face. "I shall enjoy prolonging your misery, LaGarde." He whipped the stallion and rode after Bonaparte.

Louis clicked his tongue and walked Sophie away. Murat had spared Louis because he knew Bonaparte had a use for him. He should have killed the bastard.

He would train his men today, right after they buried Fleury. Once he trained every man, he would lead them through the desert to a port and await a British ship.

# 65

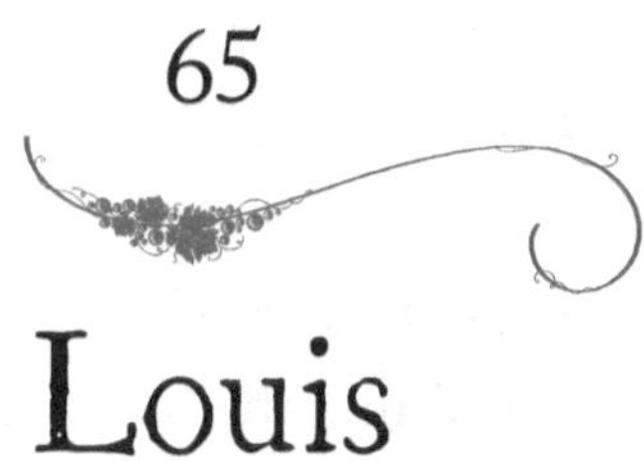

# Louis

*Cairo, Egypt*
*August* 1798

AFTER BURYING FLEURY in the shadow of the pyramids, Louis's men corralled seventeen camels, and he hid Sophie amongst them. He would have his men ride her before training them on the others.

Troops set up a sprawling camp of tents around a well outside the walls of Cairo. Despite Bonaparte's praise of their success at the Battle of the Pyramids, the esprit de corps languished. Rumors of Bonaparte ordering new uniforms of cotton to replace their woolen ones were greeted with derisive comments. Funds for uniforms, but not food, meant well-dressed corpses.

As they endured the heat, they still hungered. Flat breads, dates, and watery vegetable soups were their only food. Where were the supplies carried by the French fleet? Louis fingered the leather pouch. He could not feed the entire army, but he could buy food for his men.

Walking through the camp, he spotted a group of soldiers circling a smoldering fire. They held large chunks of meat skewered by their swords over the weak flames. The aroma was like no meat he had ever smelled roasting. Was it goat or...? He rushed to the fire.

The head and neck of a camel lay at the men's feet, a pool of innards and blood staining the sand. He swallowed against a building nausea. "Where did you get this animal?"

"We butchered it and dragged it back after the battle, Colonel." The young man smiled.

It was not Sophie. Louis sighed. "Good idea." He hoped other men were as clever.

An angry voice erupted, "If the sun don't burn us alive, we'll starve!"

Louis followed other shouts to the camp's center. Enraged men cried out, thrusting their fists above them. One soldier slammed into a tentpole, collapsing the structure. Tearing at his hair, he screamed, "We'll never get back. We'll die in this godforsaken hell."

Tension seized Louis's shoulders. He reached for his pistol to fire a shot that would disperse the men. But in the chaos, he feared they might riot.

Another young soldier ripped off his tunic and shredded it with his dagger, screaming like a wild cat.

Simon shoved through the crowd, panting, sweating, eyes reddening. "The British...destroyed...the French fleet."

He sat Simon down and gave him his waterskin. Simon

gulped. "There's no way home."

Louis shook him. "What do you mean?"

Simon wiped sand from his eyes. "Nelson destroyed all the warships Bonaparte had anchored at Aboukir Bay."

Louis's arms tensed. When he had pointed to the bay on his map, the Bedouin had cautioned him against going there. He swallowed, trying to ease the burning in his throat. "Where did you hear of this?"

"Bonaparte's messenger."

He let go of Simon. "Bonaparte is known for maneuvers and deployments. He would never allow his ships to be vulnerable."

"Well, he did." Tears leaked down Simon's cheeks. "I'll never see my child."

Louis might never see his, either. He clamped down on his teeth so hard, his jaw burned. He *would* see his family.

"Stop it." Louis grabbed a fistful of Simon's uniform and pulled his face close. "We…are…going…home."

Simon dropped his chin, wiped his nose. "We both know that's impossible."

Louis shook him. "If we must ride camels, walk, swim, and crawl the whole way," his voice singed his throat, "we will get home. I promise you."

"Attention!" Sitting atop a camel, Murat rode through the camp.

The back of Louis's neck prickled. He stood and saluted.

Foam dripped from Sophie's mouth and down her neck. Her coat was wet and matted. Murat had ridden her hard, yet she stood in regal arrogance, as if to spite him.

She was still alive. Beaten, but alive. Louis wanted to stroke her neck, but he dared not.

"There are rumors about." Murat jerked Sophie's rope, eyeing his victims. He had fitted Sophie with his horse's saddle and stirrups and two harnesses, one of which was tied around her neck like a noose. No equestrian needed two harnesses. Was it the camel Murat distrusted or himself?

Murat raised his riding crop, circling it about. "Yes." He lifted his chin. "Nelson sank a few ships. But!" He smacked the riding crop on a tent, shivering the canvas. "France will be sending more."

Feet shuffled, raising a cloud of dust. Everyone recognized the lie.

"Until then, it is your great honor to serve your country!" Murat yanked Sophie around, searching until he stood before Louis.

Louis looked Sophie directly in her deep brown eyes, purposefully challenging her. She spat. Louis wanted to thank her.

Murat laughed. "Does this news make you homesick for France, Colonel?"

Sophie's spittle ran down Louis's cheek. He kept his gaze on her and pressed his hands to his sides. She shifted from hoof to hoof and grumbled. Opening her V-shaped mouth, she squawked, as if to say, get this maniac off me.

"Learn to live with it, LaGarde." Murat yanked the rope, but Sophie remained staring at Louis. Murat raised his arm.

As the crop neared Sophie's flank, Louis snatched it, yanking it from Murat. Louis's arm vibrated. "I have made the mistake of using the crop on her myself, mon Commandant. She threw me off. She responds best to gentle tugs on her rope." He widened his stance, bracing himself.

Murat glared and stuck out his hand.

Louis gave up the crop.

Murat brought it down hard across Louis's face.

Louis jerked back. A burning seared his cheek. Flecks of light spun. Blood ran down his neck. He wavered, brought a foot behind him to keep his stance. He splayed his fingers to prevent himself from ripping the bastard's face off. Yet, this was exactly how Louis's father treated Murat, who had endured the same pain and humiliation Louis now felt. He regretted his papa had treated a servant with such disrespect, but Murat had not learned any compassion. He lived to exact vengeance.

"You'll never leave this desert alive, LaGarde." He yanked Sophie's rope, slapped the crop against her flank, and ran her through the camp, forcing men to jump or be trampled.

Curses and moans moved through the men. France would never send more ships to a commander who was foolish enough to lose the ones he had. They were trapped.

The same darkness Louis had endured at the Conciergerie prison descended upon him. The despair he had felt, waiting for his name to be called for the guillotine, seeped through him like the cold dampness of that cell. He envisioned Geneviève's face, when she told him he was not going to the guillotine. She had done the impossible for him. Now he had to do the same for his men and himself.

Simon held out a rag. "You're bleeding."

Louis pressed it against his cheek. Geneviève's face glimmered amongst the sparks of light. He reached into his pocket and caressed her hair ribbon, imagined her grape scent, saw her holding their child in her arms, heard Louisa's giggles. He would not let himself feel hopeless again—ever.

He returned the cloth to Simon. "Tell the company to get ready for a riding lesson."

He would train his men to ride the camels through the desert to the coast. Even if he had to kill Murat, they would escape this hellhole.

# 66

# *Geneviève*



*Château de Verzat Vineyard*
*February* 1799

TEMPERATURES WARMED ENOUGH to begin pruning the vines. By the time I reached the top-most field, my fingers were stiff with cold. I exhaled on my hands as I rubbed them. The muddy earth and budding green scent of the coming spring warmed my heart. I envisioned Louis walking over the crest of the hill, his arms open, his smile dazzling, his laughter booming.

Footsteps made me turn. Thérèse stared at her empty basket, trembling in her grip. Her trembling was not from the cold, for she was dressed warmly.

I slid the secateurs into my hanging pocket. "News?"

She stared at the clipped vines at our feet. "I cannot read English, but I heard the rumor."

A squirming rose in my belly.

She looked about in every direction, reached beneath her cloak, and pulled out a rolled-up newspaper.

"Our contact gave you this for me?"

She pressed her lips in a tight line, her cheek twitching.

I unrolled the paper and stopped at the masthead—it had been published in December, in America. This was contraband. The news would be old, but true. Americans were not pressured to publish the lies of the Directoire. I looked about. We were alone.

The first headline, *Bonaparte Invades Egypt*, stopped me. I searched for names, but none were listed. I pressed my heart and read the second headline. My heartbeat thundered. *Admiral Nelson Destroys French Fleet*.

The paper wavered in my grasp. Nelson had destroyed the French fleet anchored in Aboukir Bay in the first days of August. No wonder we had not received any letters. That meant the men had not received ours. A hollow yawned in my chest. French papers printed lies of Bonaparte's victories. The Directoire would never send even one ship more to a man who lost an entire armada. Would they even send supplies? How will they get home?

Tears streaked Thérèse's ruddy cheeks.

"Have you told anyone?" I whispered.

She shook her head.

I rubbed my hand against the burning in my heart. I would not allow myself—not for one second—to doubt their return. Not for one second.

"Look at me." She raised her tear-filled eyes. "You are not to tell anyone of this." My throat tightened, but I forced my words. "We must keep this news secret from everyone on the estate. Do you understand?"

"Yes…" A sob escaped. "How will they get home?"

Fear roared through my veins. I pressed my feet into the earth and forced myself to inhale strength from the air, the soil, the vines. "I do not know. But I know they will." Remembering her courage in delivering my son, I caressed her cheek. "And you must know it also."

She smiled. "I will try to believe it with all my heart."

I stood alone in the barren vineyard. Had the spy who gave this paper to Thérèse meant for it to come to me? I rolled the paper and placed it in my hanging pocket. If the spy had meant to incite me to take on greater risks, he or she had done the job well. With Bonaparte's fleet lost, there was no risk Louis and his men were on a French ship. The Chouan had given me more information the British navy needed, and I would get it to them.

I wiped my tears. Among the cuttings, a tiny green bud shimmered in the sunlight. I picked it up. Despite the cold, a bud had the courage to show its face. Under the soil, the rootstock kept faith, nurturing the spring buds, supporting the future vintage.

I snapped off a piece of vine and tied it into a circle, a reminder to draw courage from the vineyard. "I believe in you Louis. I hold you to your promise. You will return." I pressed the wreath to my heart. "If you have to walk, swim, and crawl, I know you will return to me."

67

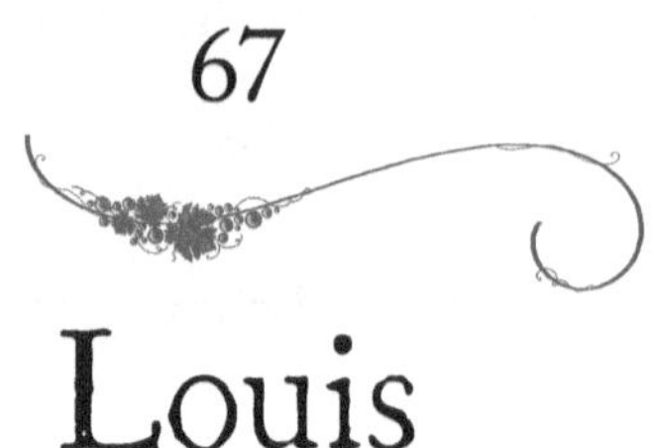

# Louis

LOUIS MUSTERED HIS men before Bonaparte. Expecting to be praised for their fighting, the men were in good spirits, until Bonaparte delivered a speech elaborating on his plot for conquering the Ottoman Empire, starting with Syria. At the end of his declaration, he ordered: "We march north, to Jaffa."

Anger flared up Louis's back. Egypt was not enough? Bonaparte must challenge the Ottoman Empire as well? Bonaparte boasted the Port of Jaffa would shelter his fleet—what fleet? Every soldier knew no more ships would be sent.

Louis unrolled his map. It would take months—marching through the desert, searching for food and water the whole way—because Bonaparte's supply ships were among those captured by Nelson. He hoped they would not be forced to slaughter their horses or camels.

Bonaparte, the *brilliant* strategist, was shoving them into the direct path of the British, who would reinforce the Turks with both supplies and troops.

Louis gazed at his discouraged, sunburned men. The youngest, red-haired and blistered-lipped Ribou, wiped his sleeve across his eyes. Louis had to get the man home to his maman. Louis would ride alongside him, get him to talk, and bolster his confidence. He wouldn't let him be sacrificed like Fleury.

If they could break away from Bonaparte's army, they could then head for a closer port and hope to sight a British ship. He ordered his men to tether their camels alongside their horses. The beasts had a greater chance of surviving when they broke rank. He hoped they would not have to eat them.

After sixty-three days marching through the endless desert, the horses grew jittery and began snorting. The camels squawked and refused to move. A strange rumbling, sounding like thunder, shook them. The air thickened. He looked east and west but saw nothing. The rumbling grew louder, and he turned.

A mountainous wall of dust rose ten meters high, higher than any wave they had endured during the storm at sea. Dragging sand to feed it, the wall bulged, billows of dust spilling before it. An eerie light shone atop the surging mass, which darkened as it devoured more sand, feeding the monstrous wave.

Dust filled his nose. It would bury them alive! He shook himself. "This desert will not be our tomb." He jumped down.

"Dismount! Circle the animals." The men corralled their mounts. Louis whipped out his scarf and waved it above his head. He had bought one for every member of his company. "Wrap your scarves around your mouth and nose."

Wind snapped at the saffron, crimson, and cerulean cloths. The rumbling roared.

Louis grabbed Ribou's horse. "Hold on to your harness and the harness of the horse next to you! Keep them facing the center of our circle!" The men struggled, falling to their knees, clinging to their mounts.

"Pull the scarf up to cover your eyes. Hang onto the horses. Keep your heads down until it blows over!"

Hot sand thrashed them from every direction. Horses whinnied. Louis pressed his face into his horse's neck. The mare shivered with fright and reared. He used all his weight to keep her in position. Dust scraped his hands, stung his eyes, grated his teeth. A whirlpool of sand surged from beneath him, tugging his clothes open and razing his exposed skin.

Darkness entombed them, pressuring them, like it was squeezing the life out of them. Horses stomped. Ribou's legs rose up behind him; his body sailing like a kite. Louis grabbed his belt, yanked him down. Louis's mare rose up on her hind legs. With every bit of his strength, he struggled to control her and keep Ribou anchored. Dust filled his ears, dulling his hearing. He snorted, expelling dust only for more to fill his nose.

Whooshing sand crested over them. He prayed the storm did not bury them. Light penetrated the dark. Louis peeked over his scarf. Sand swirled, but he could see the outlines of his men and their horses.

The wind sucked them apart as the storm passed over them. Louis yanked his scarf. The excoriating sand had ripped the fabric to shreds. Ribou collapsed on the ground. Louis grabbed his dagger and cut through the fabric. Ribou coughed and gasped for breath, clawing at his throat. Louis helped him to sit up and pressed his waterskin to Ribou's lips. He drank and fell back, panting.

Other men struggled with their wrappings, yelling in fright. Louis ran and cut the scarves, helping his choking men to breathe. Sand penetrated their new cotton uniforms. Louis's frock coat weighed him down. His white breeches were brown, like they had been dyed.

He hoped the storm had not carried anyone away. He walked among his coughing men, counting. Forty-eight. He wiped grit from his eyes. "Who is missing?" He searched the small mounds of sand that could be covering a body. A lone horse pawed and snorted. Louis ran to it, recognizing the saddle's owner. "Toupin? Find Toupin!"

Men scurried, kicking at dunes, calling out, widening their circle, searching.

"Toupin did not disappear. We are not leaving without him!" Louis roared.

Simon organized the men into a tight circle and, on hands and knees, they swept their arms through the sand.

Ribou shouted, "Here!" He pawed the sand, and every man ran to help excavate Toupin. They heaved him onto his back. His scarf, twisted around his neck, had strangled him. Sand filled Toupin's once lively brown eyes, his nostrils, his mouth. Simon bowed his head, as did every other man.

A sob threatened to burst from Louis's chest. He had promised to take him home. He would not allow Bonaparte to take one more of his men. Not one more.

"We must bury him with his saddle and the dignity he deserves." Louis had no time to mourn this man's life. He still had forty-eight men to get home.

He scanned the horizon, not spotting another soldier. Now was their opportunity. They would march west, to the coast, where he hoped British ships awaited. And he would surrender to them. Even if he risked a firing squad, he would get them all home.

68

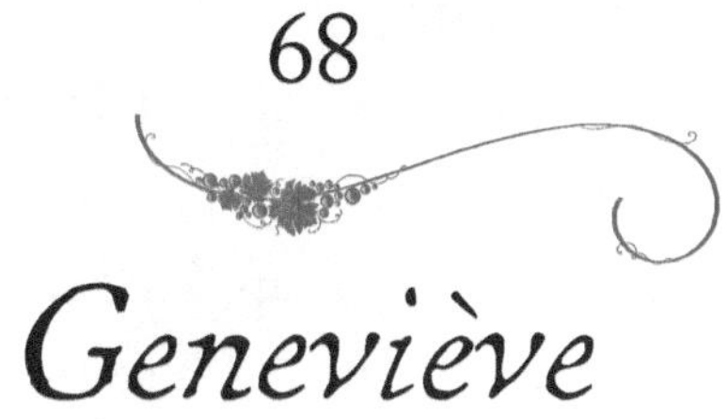

# *Geneviève*

*Château de Verzat*
*March* 1799

**B**RILLIANT WHITE BLANKETS of fog snuggled in the valleys of the vineyard. The sun warmed the air, tinged with a fresh green sweetness. I wish you were here to share this beauty with me, Louis. I know you will be here soon.

Sunshine dazzled the vines, shooting tiny rainbows on the chalky earth. How beautiful. How odd. Tiny drops of sap bulged from the cuttings I'd made the day before. The sap dripped, like tears. My God! I had been pruning the vines every year, and this had never happened. Had I done it wrong?

I ran, screaming for Joliette.

She emerged from the château kitchen, her shawl flying behind her. "What is it?"

I heaved for breath, grabbed her hand and ran with her. "The vines…I pruned…they're dripping."

She knelt and burst into tears.

We had agreed it was the right time to prune but, despite my years of experience, I must have done it wrong. I knelt next to her. "Is the vintage lost?"

Her laughter was joyous, which startled me.

"Grand-mère told me…" She gripped my arms. Her brown eyes sparkled like the drops of sap. "She saw this miracle, but it is so rare, I never have." She fell into me sobbing with joy. "The vines are weeping."

"Is weeping good?"

Her laughter bubbled. "The snow protected the rootstock. Now life flows through the roots into the vines and soon the buds."

She brought her finger to a drop and pressed it to her tongue. "Mmm…living nectar."

I ran my finger over a stream of vine tears. It tasted green, sweet, fresh.

Joliette struggled to stand. "Let us ring the bell. Everyone should share in the joy of this miracle." She helped me to my feet. "It will give us the courage and strength we need until our men return."

My heartbeat fluttered, like the tiny rainbows glittering around us. This miracle was the hope we all needed. I know you will be home soon, Louis.

Hand-in-hand, laughing with glee, we ran toward the bell.

69

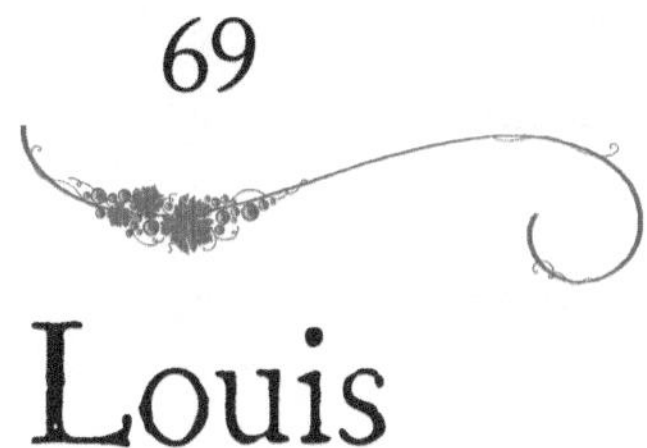

# Louis

*Jaffa*
*March* 1799

Aᴏ FTER A DAY of marching toward the sea, Bonaparte's troops appeared straight ahead. The devil!

Sand-colored stone walls surrounded tall buildings atop a hill overlooking a harbor where twelve ships anchored. Louis's hope floated out to them as he searched for a British flag. But red flags with white crescent moons and eight-pointed stars unfurled and snapped with the wind. The flags of Turkey. Louis's hope plummeted to the sea. Not one French or British ship.

High towers flanked the citadel's' thick walls. From the parapets, cannon barrels glared down like all-seeing eyes. Troops stood at attention in the broiling sun, awaiting the return of Bonaparte's messengers sent to demand immediate surrender from the Turks.

Shouts came from atop the wall. The heads of Bonaparte's two messengers were raised on pikes and brandished.

Louis swallowed back bile. The sight yanked him back to the Place de la Révolution, slick with blood from the guillotine's carnage.

Bonaparte galloped behind the squares. "Attack!" Canons fired, but the explosions did little damage to the four-meters thick walls.

The acrid stink of cannon fire choked Louis and made the horses jittery.

Spotting Turks streaming from the fortress side, Louis yelled, "Capture those men!"

They arrived to find boys dragging fallen French soldiers through a small door. Louis's men charged, but too late. The door banged shut. Minutes later, the heads of the French soldiers appeared atop the wall. Rage cracked like lightning amongst the troops.

French cannons felled one of the towers and breached the wall. Bonaparte sent another messenger. Louis snorted at the waste of another life. Bonaparte was mad.

Again, the messenger's head, atop a pike, rose above the wall. In retaliation for the beheadings, Bonaparte ordered his troops to attack the city surrounding the fortification.

Louis gathered his men. "Bonaparte orders destruction of the city. The soldiers will seek revenge and pillage. I will not. And I will not order you to do so."

"We stay with you, mon Colonel," Agiers growled.

Bonaparte's troops yelled a battle cry and tore through the city. Thousands of Turkish soldiers begged to surrender under the condition they were not killed. Citizens cried for mercy.

When precious food was given to the prisoners, French soldiers erupted in anger.

Bonaparte gave the order to kill all prisoners and civilians—without ammunition.

Louis stood rigid witnessing, until a young woman bent to pick up her baby. A French soldier ran toward her. Louis swung the flat side of his saber, knocking the soldier to his knees. "She is an innocent mother!"

"We're ordered to kill!" The soldier screamed.

Louis's arm vibrated. He closed his eyes and saw Louisa, heard her giggles, felt her arms around his neck. His breath grew hot. Thousands of civilians ran across the beach, hoping to swim for their lives. He hung his head in shame as French soldiers murdered.

"You were given an order, LaGarde!" Murat sat astride a chestnut stallion, his saber aloft. "Move your men out."

Rage cracked across Louis's shoulders. He squinted at the sunlight reflecting off the gold braid of Murat's spotless uniform. Standing at attention, he looked past Murat. He had promised Geneviève he would return—but not at the cost of killing women or children. "I will not disgrace my country by killing innocents. Nor will I order my men to do so."

Louis heard the riding crop cutting the air before it struck his shoulder.

"You will face a firing squad, LaGarde. Order your men!"

Murat had the blood of a cobra. Louis knelt on one knee, pressed his hand over his heart, and stared at the sea blooming crimson. "The glory of France cannot be built upon the killing of innocents."

Murat screamed at Henri. "Lieutenant, arrest this man and order these soldiers!"

Henri dropped to his knee. "I will not disgrace France by killing innocents."

Murat whipped his horse in a tight circle. "I order you all to kill those heathens!"

Man after man dropped to one knee, every one of whom spoke Louis's oath, until his entire company knelt in the blistering sand.

Murat ordered another company to relieve Louis and his men of their weapons. At last, they were allowed to rest—as prisoners. The stench of blood and screams of death surrounded them. Yellow-faced vultures circled.

He and his men sat, defenseless in the broiling sun. The enemy could behead them all.

"I thank you all for your bravery and taking the oath." He looked every man in the eye. "You are men of honor, and I am proud of you."

Ribou smiled. "You are a courageous leader, mon Colonel. I am proud to be in your company."

Regret sat thick in Louis. They might have made it home, but now, they were prisoners until they all faced execution. But Ribou's smile pulled a thread of hope from deep inside Louis. "The only way of getting home is a traitorous act," he whispered.

Agiers leaned forward. "And who among us is loyal to Bonaparte?" He looked around and back at Louis. "Not one of us, mon Colonel."

His men stared at Louis, eyes hopeful, trustful.

"When a British ship sails into port, we will surrender to its capitaine."

# 70

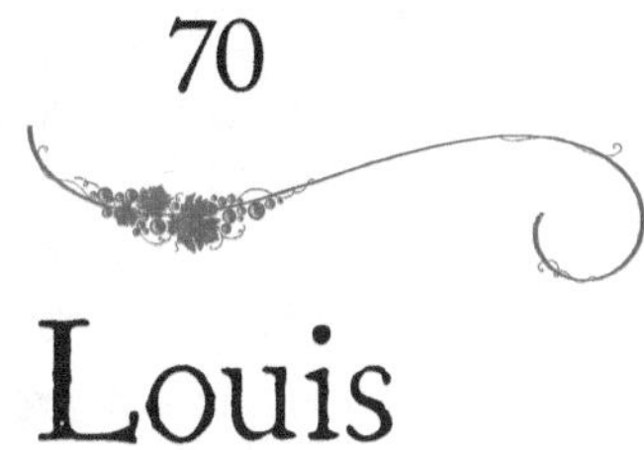

# Louis

*Acre*
*April* 1799

Held in a roped-off gulley, guarded day and night, Louis and his men sat under the blistering sun and clouds of black flies without water or food. His men lay in the sand, often calling out in their sleep. Louis feared they were hallucinating, but perhaps their visions were a better place to be. He encouraged them to sleep during the day so they could escape under the cover of darkness.

Murat trotted his white stallion around the enclosure's perimeter. "You're disposable. You will lead the troops in the next battle. Don't disgrace France with more of your cowardice, LaGarde. The men who fight bravely will not be executed." He smacked his crop against the stallion's flank and galloped away.

Louis ran his tongue against the grit in his teeth.

Weapons were returned but not horses. The horses would have made their escape easier, but the weapons would help them steal fishing boats. Louis marched over endless sand at the front of his company. "We are vulnerable to surprise attacks. Scan the horizon in all directions. Do not let your guard down for a second. Shout if you see movement. Any movement."

The sound of waves crashing on rocks taunted them for three days as they marched south, spotting not one fishing boat. They arrived at a viewpoint over a harbor. Across from them, walls rose from the water and surrounded a fortress and the city of Acre. Built atop a hill on a peninsula jutting out into the sea, the fortress was more formidable than the citadel at Jaffa. There were not enough cannonballs in the entire French army to penetrate those walls.

At the glimpse of a British flag snapping on the mast of a ship in the harbor, Louis felt like he could fly. He would get his men on it no matter what.

His heart plummeted as four Turkish ships entered the harbor and anchored around the two British warships. The Turks and British were allies against Bonaparte. Now Louis and his men would be fighting two enemies and Bonaparte.

Small fishing boats with single masts bobbed close to shore. They could sail the small vessels past the Turkish ships to one of the British warships—but without being killed?

Murat ordered Louis's company to the front line and ready to lay siege to the citadel.

Feeling the heat of guns bearing down from the walls before them and the pressure of their cannon-firing compatriots behind them, Louis and his men awaited the command to fire, all the while searching for ways to flee the battlefield.

Bonaparte sent a messenger to the citadel. Louis thanked God he had not chosen one of his men for the task. Within minutes of entering the fortress, the unfortunate man's head was impaled on a pike above its wall. Disgust coated Louis's tongue.

French cannons boomed. Louis and his men fell to their bellies. Cannon balls sailed over their heads. He raised his arm. "We must wait until the cannons breach the wall. Dig a trench for protection."

After two weeks, a cheer from the French soldiers rose at dawn. Two French ships sailed into the harbor. The men praised God. Until spotting a flotilla of Turkish gunboats in pursuit, firing upon the French ships. The battle was short. The British seized the French ships, and unloaded their supplies and ammunition. Turkish soldiers dropped nets over the walls of the citadel. Sailors loaded the French booty into the nets and Turks hauled guns, food, ammunition up the fortress walls.

With their own ammunition used against them, surely Bonaparte would call a retreat. Yet, he screamed at the infantry to charge. Louis had nothing to lose but his men's lives and his own, so once again, he disobeyed orders.

Crouching before his men, he commanded, "We shall take cover in the trenches and move toward the sea. Use ammunition only for defense."

They scuttled toward the cliff, avoiding the barrage of bullets and cannon balls, wary of an assault from the sea.

Plague ran through the army, killing more men than died in battle. Louis did not allow his men to return to camp, where they were certain to become infected. They rested on a narrow precipice above the beach, the roar of the sea taunting them with dreams of sailing home.

After sixty days of constant bombardment, French soldiers breached the fortress wall. Turks, wearing white turbans, flooded the battlefield.

Louis lifted his saber. "Watch out for one another!" He faced each Turk with his saber poised to kill. The enemy was focused only on brute-force killing, not skill. Louis felled each one with a single feint and thrust.

The clang of steel made Louis turn. Ribou had lost his saber and wielded his dagger, a pathetic weapon against a Turk waving a scimitar. Louis drew his pistol, fired, felled the Turk.

He holstered the pistol and took up his saber as a flash of light blinded him. A weight crashed down onto his shoulder, pitching him to his side. Searing pain charged through his arm. He clamped his jaw against a scream.

A black-turbaned Turk sneered and lifted his scimitar above his head. A shot rang out. Blood exploded across the man's chest.

Louis grabbed his throbbing arm. Sparks of light swarmed his vision. Hooves thundered around him.

Murat shouted, "Don't make me regret saving your life, LaGarde!"

It was not possible. Murat hated him. Louis struggled to his knees.

Murat glared down at him. "Verzat, take charge here. Get Colonel LaGarde to hospital." He galloped across the battlefield.

Louis stabbed his saber into the sand, tried to rise, but he wavered, toppled. Pain shot through his shoulder and down his arm. Had he hallucinated Murat? He dragged in a breath. But if not Murat, who else had saved him?

Henri knelt next to Louis. "This must be stitched, or you'll bleed to death."

Pain dizzied him as Henri prodded the wound. He sucked in gun smoke and the reek of death. "Do not take me to the hospital tent. I will die of plague."

Simon yanked the scarf from his head and wound it around Louis's arm.

Henri pressed his own scarf atop Simon's. "We'll move you someplace safe before I stitch the wound."

Simon grabbed Louis around the waist and pulled him up as his legs gave way. He grasped Simon's shoulder. Ribou supported Louis's other side, and they walked toward the sea. The day darkened to night. Hands guided him to a ledge where waves crashed below.

"Lie down or you'll faint," Henri ordered.

A ripping sound and the stab of a needle made flecks of light flurry in the darkness. "The devil!"

Simon laughed. "For a moment we thought you'd died."

Louis shivered. "Was it truly Murat who saved me?"

Henri knotted a thread. "The bastard is good for something."

Louis wanted to laugh but groaned. Murat hated him, yet he had saved his life. Did the cobra have a heart, or had he rescued Louis for the glory of it? For a moment, guilt for deserting Murat and Bonaparte's army dripped over his vision of boarding a British ship. He shook off the drop of loyalty he felt. "Murat knows Bonaparte values me. He saved my life because Bonaparte will reward Murat with yet another medal and promotion."

"Obvious conclusion," Henri took another stitch.

"Who taught you how to sew?"

"My maman. She also taught me to launder." Henri bit the thread of the last stitch. "Good thing. You need a good cleaning."

A shadow hung over Louis. The sun-burned face of Ribou smiled. "You gave us a scare, Colonel. How would we get out of here without you?"

How would they? A numbness spread down the muscles of his arm. He saw but did not feel the pricking of the needle. He could not move his arm, wield a sword, or shoot a pistol. Nor could he swim, raise a sail, row an oar.

He focused on the surrounding men. He could not let them see his helplessness, his despair, his fear. He had to give them the hope he no longer possessed. How could he save these men when he could not save himself? He had to put a plan in place for his men to get back home—without him.

71

# *Geneviève*

*Château de Verzat*
*April* 1799

AFTER LAYING NICOLAS in his cradle for his afternoon nap, I pulled out Tante's codebook, squeezed a lemon, and sat at the table to encode the Chouan's messages about French ships. If my messages were delivered, the information could endanger French sailors' lives, but my messages could also bring our men home.

The words I wrote wavered, much like when I copied the names of people condemned to the guillotine. Of the thirty to fifty names listed, I could save only one. But I saved more than one hundred lives, and Louis's was the first. These messages cost the same risk: my execution.

The trap door banged open. I jumped up. The Chouan

climbed the steps. He carried a small, limp child. "Help me please. My son's been burned."

"Put him on the table." I grabbed Tante's shawl and made a pillow for the boy's head. "Joliette, Aurélia, help!" I shouted.

He laid the boy down. The child's tiny arm was swollen, raging red, and bloody. His blue tunic sleeve had burned to ash and stuck to his skin. His fine, blond hair was singed, and his right eyebrow and eyelashes were nearly gone. He did not stir.

The Chouan whispered, "I know I should not have come, but there is no one else to help us." He fell to his knees, cradling the boy's head in his huge, calloused hands.

I grabbed a pitcher of wine, splashed some over my hands, and shook them.

Breathless, Joliette ran to us. "My God. I'll get some cool water and vinegar." She screamed, "Aurélia," as she dashed across the kitchen. "She has a salve for burns."

Nicolas began to cry. I shushed him as I gently dabbed the clean cloth on the boy's blood, trying to see if there were wounds below. The cloth caught a sheet of translucent skin, pulling away from his arm. The air tasted of burned flesh, making me want to gag. I swallowed against the urge.

Aurélia's calm hands pulled the cloth away. She mouthed, *lavender oil*. She gently examined the child. I rocked the cradle to calm Nicolas as I looked for the oil.

Joliette placed a bowl on the table. "Vinegar and water."

The child began to thrash. His body arced and slammed down on the table, flopping like a landed fish. His father's strong hands held the child as Aurélia dabbed a wet cloth on his burns.

The faces of Nicolas and Louisa appearing in place of the boy's flashed in my mind. I gripped a chair and searched until I spotted the oil. I retrieved the cruet, and Aurélia dribbled the oil over the wounds. The boy moaned. Blisters rose, straining the poor child's skin.

She pointed and mouthed: *Honey and rosemary, make a salve.*

I pulled down rosemary from the overhead beam, crushed the leaves to a powder, and blended it with honey.

Aurélia commanded me, *Dip cloths in vinegar. Wrap them on his legs, chest, head.*

I worked quickly, sprinkling the dilution on the cloths that I'd wrapped, keeping them moist and cool.

Aurélia took the honey mixture and poured small amounts on his angry blisters.

The boy's breathing slowed. My heartbeat rose to my throat, fearing he was dying.

Still holding his son's uninjured side, the Chouan rested his forehead on the table. His shoulders and chest shook with silent sobs.

An ache squeezed my heart. I forced myself to keep the cloths damp and replaced warm ones with cool ones, averting my eyes from the burns and checking on Nicolas.

The boy's breathing steadied. Aurélia wiped her hands and sat next to the father, placing a cool cloth on his burned arm. She looked at me. *Can we keep them here?*

"Yes."

*Tell him the boy must sleep. And when he wakes, we must give him sips of water.*

I told the man. He raised his head. Tears streaked his

ash-encrusted face. "I am sorry to have come. We are a great risk to you. I will take him away now."

"No!" I wrung my hands. I was risking the lives of all of us and our children. But I could not send him away. His son might die. "You must stay here while your son heals. We will protect you." I glanced at Joliette, who nodded vehemently.

"Merci," he whispered.

I sat down. "Tell us what happened."

He grimaced as he swallowed. I realized he must be parched and poured him some wine.

He drank deeply, then dragged his fist over his mouth. "Republicans arrived on horseback, carrying torches. They set fire to our homes, barns, stables. People fled. Some with their clothes aflame. Everyone now hides in the forest and caves. Republicans still hunt us."

"Your wife?"

He shook his head and crossed himself.

She was dead. Nausea climbed my throat. I ran outside and vomited. My head pounded with images of the burning village, the boy's blistering skin, the sounds of the animals and villagers' screams. Tears burned. What was I doing trying to spy against Bonaparte when I couldn't help these people right here?

A cool hand rested on the back of my neck. "Are you unwell?" Joliette asked.

"No." I pounded my fist against the château's stone wall and screamed, "God damn the Republicans."

Joliette rushed to quiet me, but I backed away. "What gives them the right to burn entire villages, homes, animals?" I threw my arms in the air. "Little boys and their mamans?" I collapsed onto the ground, holding my head and sobbing. "All I could see when I was comforting that boy were the faces of Louisa and Nicolas." I moaned. "I can't do this." I pounded my fist in the dirt. "I can't. Everything I do is so futile."

Joliette rubbed my back. "You saved that boy's life."

"Aurélia saved him."

"Yes, but you took immediate action and screamed for us to help. You did not turn them away. You did everything you knew how to do, and you comforted them." She lifted my chin. "You think with your heart, Gen, no matter the risk. It is who you are."

The tears wouldn't stop, nor would my mind. "I've endangered everyone here." I held my aching head. "I'm being a child, crying, when that man has lost his wife and may lose his son."

She sat next to me in the dirt. "Why don't we allow everyone here to share the responsibility of sheltering them?"

"You mean ask every family if we should hide a village of Royalists?"

"Exactly."

"That might take a great deal of time."

She wiped her handkerchief across my cheeks. "We could sound the alarm and ask them to vote—today."

I accepted her handkerchief and blew my nose. "What if they vote no?"

She sighed. "If my father did anything in his lifetime, he demonstrated compassion, kindness, and generosity. He inspired those qualities in others as well. I think they might be honored by the request. If not, we will find another solution."

That had never occurred to me. But why *wouldn't* they want

to help other people? I gripped her hand. Her eyes and hands were warm and loving.

I stood. "Perhaps I should find out how many people we'll be hiding." I wiped my face and headed back to the kitchen. "I'll ask Fortuné to ring the bell."

# 72

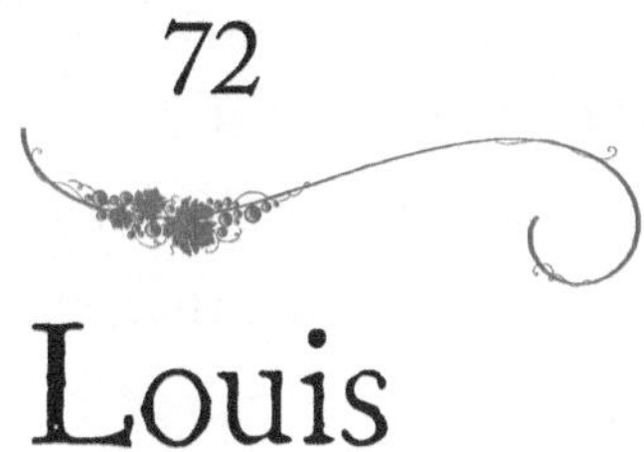

# Louis

*Acre*
*May* 1799

Aᴠᴛᴇʀ ᴀ ᴅᴀʏ of rest, Louis mustered his battle-weary men. They stood on the precipice overlooking the two British warships, taunting them with the possibility of freedom. The sea breeze brought little relief from the blazing sun. His soldiers were tattered, crisp shadows of the men who had first reported to him back in Paris. Yet every one of them was a hero for surviving this hellhole.

"Let us rest while we can." The men sat in a circle around him.

He gripped his biceps, willing the muscle to heal. "I made you a promise, and I will continue to do everything I can to get you home, even in the event I cannot accompany you."

Ribou jumped to his feet. "We will not leave you, Colonel!"

Louis gestured for him to sit. "Calm yourself. Even I cannot live forever."

A grumble moved through the men.

"We go together—" Agier growled, "or not at all, Colonel."

Louis pressed his palm against the pressure building against his ribs. The image of his men kneeling alongside of him, refusing to kill innocents, filled him with a treasured pride.

"You will survive if you follow my plan." He looked every man in the eye. "I caution you that, should you be caught, you will face a firing squad as a traitor."

"Would execution not be quicker than starving to death?" Agiers asked.

Men grunted in agreement.

Relief washed over Louis. "At night, you will return to the precipice and watch for an opportunity to get on one of the British ships." He stared at Henri. "Verzat is the best swimmer. When he swims to one of the British ships, all of you descend to the beach and await the longboat Verzat will request from the British Capitaine. Verzat will surrender, and you all will be taken as prisoners of war. After you board the ship, you are to tell the Capitaine every single detail you know of this army and Bonaparte."

One man whistled a low tone. The men looked to one another. A few mouths repeated *traitor* silently.

"Should we be caught, will they tell my maman I was a traitor?" Ribou asked.

"Would your maman believe it if they did?" asked Henri.

"No." Ribou smiled.

Men nodded. Some grinned. They looked at one another and

stood, removed their hats, and stared at Louis, who remained sitting.

Agiers took a step toward him. "We will do as you command. But—" he looked at each man who nodded in turn. "We are not leaving without you, Colonel."

# 73

# *Geneviève*

*Château de Verzat*
*April* 1799

FORTUNÉ RANG THE bell just before the lunch hour. The smell of grapes and sweat and rich earth filled the cave. Joliette stood next to me, a basket resting on her hip, and we faced the people together.

I held up my arms for silence. "Please do not worry. There is no emergency, only a decision to be made."

Sighs of relief wavered.

"You know that Chouan Royalists are still being hunted by the Republicans and harboring them is punishable by execution." The silence was thick. "You also know that Republicans would like nothing better than to take over this estate for themselves."

Murmurs rumbled along the cave wall. A baby wailed, and

I cocked my head to check on Nicolas, who was snuggled in Madame Detré's arms.

Joliette raised her voice. "You remember when Revolutionaries attempted to burn the château, and you all helped Henri defend this estate."

Fury sat in Madame Ornay's eyes.

"And how Republicans continue to steal our food, our wine, our men." Joliette nodded to me.

"We fight them together, as a community. All of us are committed to making the finest wine in the world, and we work tirelessly to deliver more wine every year." I paused, seeing devotion, determination, reverence in faces. "Republicans burned a nearby village, and fifty-three people escaped with only their lives, some are badly burned. They need work and a home. With the harvest coming, we will need workers. The fifty-three are willing to work tirelessly to help us achieve our goal."

A man removed his hat and scratched his scalp. His wife looked up to him, like she was confused.

"Comte de Verzat wanted this estate to run like the American's democracy, and so he sold every family a piece of this land. Therefore, every adult woman and man has a vote on whether to offer shelter and jobs to the fifty-three Royalists."

The man scratching his scalp spoke up. "Where will we hide them?"

I was grateful the man was already planning. "We can house them in the north wing of the château until cottages can be built for them, *if* you agree to offer them shelter."

The man's wife smiled up at him, pride filling them both.

People's faces seemed open. "Madame Joliette will give you

each a piece of paper. If you wish to vote yes, place that paper in the basket as you leave. If you wish to vote no, tear the piece of paper in half and place both halves in the basket. No one will see your vote as everyone will be putting papers in the basket."

Heads tilted. Whispers flew. Feet shuffled.

Joliette began moving through the crowd, passing out papers.

"The majority will decide. But *all* of us will abide by that decision. Should the majority vote to accept these people into our community, we will keep them safe."

I pressed my palms together. "Are we agreed with taking this vote?"

"Yes!" Their reply thundered. My legs ached. I walked unsteadily to Madame Detré. Nicolas reached for me, and as I pressed him to me, tears streamed. I did not chastise myself for not being able to solve this problem alone. I thanked myself for sharing the responsibility and trusting the people of the Verzat estate.

I inhaled Nicolas's milky scent. Please, God, let them vote yes.

Only three people voted no. And I tried not to worry whether they would remain faithful.

# 74

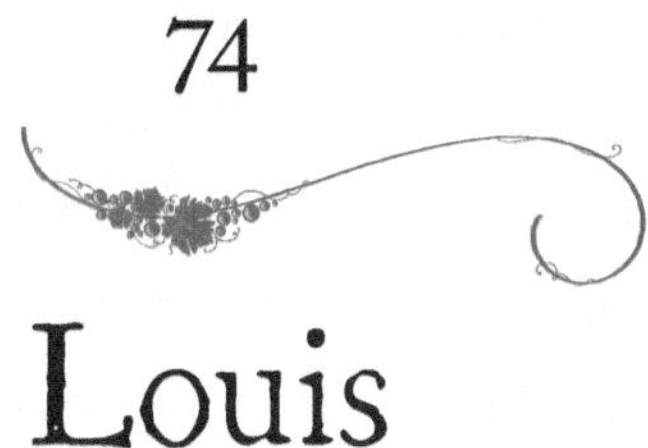

# Louis



Aᴅᴏᴏᴍᴇᴅ ꜱɪʟᴇɴᴄᴇ ʜᴏᴠᴇʀᴇᴅ like a fog.

Murat ordered Henri to return the company to the battlefield and Louis to the hospital. As long as he had breath in him, Louis would not leave his company to the mercy of Murat. He belted his saber.

"You must rest, Louis," Henri urged.

Louis donned his hat.

"If you do not remain, I will shoot you in the foot," Simon threatened.

Louis patted Simon's shoulder and crouched with his men in a trench. Flies buzzed over patches of dried blood, much of which Louis suspected was his.

He held his pistol in his left hand, feeling its weight, moving his fingers over the hammer and trigger, hoping to strengthen his left hand enough to perform as his right. An irritation, like embedded grains of sand, pricked the back of his neck. As was his habit, Bonaparte silenced the cannons before surprising the enemy with a new tactic. Louis wondered what he had in store, for the French were losing…badly.

Murat rode across the smoke-filled battlefield, his tiger-skin saddle blanket flapping in rhythm with the white stallion's canter. A sky-blue sash circled Murat's waist and gold braid curved around the brim of his plumed bicorne. Louis suspected he was right: Murat received a promotion for saving Louis's life. The money spent on Murat's accoutrements could have fed Louis's entire company for a week. Gratitude and hatred tangled in Louis's chest like a nest of river eels.

As Murat headed straight for Louis's company, repugnance swelled in Louis's chest, eclipsing his indebtedness.

"I ordered you to hospital, LaGarde."

Distrust curled up Louis's spine. Holding his arm against his chest, he got to his feet and saluted with his left hand. "I am leading my men, mon Commandant."

"Who is the lowest ranking man?" Murat shouted as he looked down his duckbilled nose.

"I am, mon Commandant." The freckled Ribou saluted.

"The Général has a mission for you. Come with me."

Louis stopped Ribou. "What is the mission?"

"You question Général Bonaparte?" Murat grinned.

Louis's shoulder throbbed with the desire to rip Murat's grin from his face. "I wish to know where he is going and when to expect his return."

"The Général has need of another messenger." Murat's cobra-eyes glinted.

The words pierced Louis's chest like a dagger. He put his hand on Ribou's trembling shoulder. "This man is a valuable soldier. He killed six enemies in the last battle alone."

"I commend his bravery. He will need it."

Louis's grip on Ribou's shoulder tightened. Murat had no soul. But Louis would not send this man to his death. "Surely, the Général values sharpshooters?"

Murat made his stallion dance in a tight circle. "Whom do you wish to send in his stead?"

Louis had fallen directly into Murat's trap. He would make Louis choose the man to die. Sourness filled his mouth. Ribou stared at his boots. Louis would not be able to respect himself if he sent any man to a senseless death. He envisioned Geneviève, standing in his cell, telling him he would not go to the guillotine. She had risked her neck to save his. The image of his men kneeling next to him, refusing to slaughter innocents, flashed. If he could save these brave, true, honorable men, his death would not be in vain. *I am sorry, my love. But I think you would do the same.*

"I will go."

Ribou jerked from Louis's grasp. "No!" He hissed in Louis's ear, "The rest will not get home without you."

Louis would never meet his baby, but he could not feel more love for his children than he did at this moment, looking into Ribou's frightened, trusting eyes. "You all will get home if you trust Lieutenant Verzat."

Louis looked up at Murat, whose lips puckered.

"I will say goodbye to my men and accompany you, mon Commandant."

Murat yanked his reigns. "For some reason, Général Bonaparte finds you useful, LaGarde. Pick another man."

Louis allowed all the contempt he felt to show in his posture, his face, his voice—it was how he had spent his life as a privileged noble, and he was glad he was no longer that man, yet also glad he could choose when to be him. "Should another soldier be chosen, I will accompany him. The Général will appreciate losing only one man when I go alone."

Murat cocked his head. "Are you not grateful I saved your miserable life, LaGarde?"

"Eternally, mon Commandant." Louis bowed his head. "I am grateful I am alive to be of service to France."

Murat's face reddened. He yanked the reins, making the horse rear. "If you wish to commit suicide, it's your choice."

"Better suicide than murder, mon Commandant."

"Idiot." Murat spat.

His men encircled Louis, preventing him from leaving. He extended his left hand to each man. Without exception, every man ignored his reach and clasped him in an embrace. His throat tight, Louis stood before Henri and Simon. "Tell Geneviève I love her for eternity. Be good uncles," his voice skittered, "to my children."

A tear escaped Henri's reddened eyes. He cleared his throat. "I will try…with every breath I take…to honor your promise to these men."

Louis embraced him.

Simon's cheeks were red from holding back tears. Love surged through Louis. Simon and Ribou were both the lowest ranking soldiers. He prayed his life would save theirs. Simon stumbled as he embraced Louis.

Louis held him tightly as he whispered, "I am proud of the man you have become."

Simon shuddered. "I shall love your children as my own… mon Colonel."

He released Simon and whispered to Henri. "Give me your handkerchief. Perhaps I will surrender and not lose my head."

Henri gave him the stained white cloth. As Louis secreted it into his sling, he leaned close to him. "Go to the ship tonight. That is an order."

Henri saluted. "Yes, mon Colonel."

Louis climbed out of the trench and looked upon his men. "I am proud to have served with every one of you. Remember your promise and do not disappoint me." Louis forced a smile. "I shall be watching." With his left hand, he saluted his men. He turned to Murat. "I am ready."

Murat's lip curled. He threw a rolled parchment at him.

Louis caught it midair and tapped it on his leg as he walked.

Murat spurred his horse toward Bonaparte's square.

Louis walked through rills of smoke, drifting over the scarred battlefield. Waves of heat radiated off the fortress's walls, making the two British ships beyond look like a mirage. For him, they were. But for his men, they were hope. The stench of rotting flesh and blood nauseated him. He would not miss this hellhole.

Bonaparte's drummer beat a tattoo, reminding Louis of the march to the guillotine. At least at Place de la Révolution, there were crowds. Now, he marched alone. He spoke in time with the drumbeats: "This desert…will not…be my tomb."

Black flies gnawed at his face. "I will live…to play…with my children."

He would miss the joy of the vendanges, the worker's singing, the yeasty scent of fermenting grapes, teaching his children to swim and fish in the Loire, the patches of mist wafting up from the river and crossing the vineyard, Madame Bourran's cooking Oncle Louis's soup, the orphans' laughing and shouting, the smell of his newborn babe.

A tear dripped. Geneviève's voice echoed: It takes more courage to cry than not.

A funnel of swirling sand danced before him.

He envisioned waltzing with Geneviève the night she had fallen in love with him—the sparkle in her bright gray eyes. His heartbeat pounded with love. I promise, I will survive this. You are right. Life does not always allow you to keep your word. I wish with all my heart this were not true. Help me, dear wife. Show me what to do.

Geneviève's laughter bubbled so brilliantly, he looked about for her but saw only the formidable walls of the fort. Geneviève called out: As you so often told me, my dearest: Surprise them. Surprise them and come home to me. I walk with you, now. Remember: We are both terribly brave bastards.

Her voice buoyed him, making him feel like he was floating on the desert winds. He stood before the fort's towering entry, his body vibrating with love. The carved-timber doors groaned open. Sunlight glinted off hundreds of raised scimitars.

This desert will not be my tomb.

75

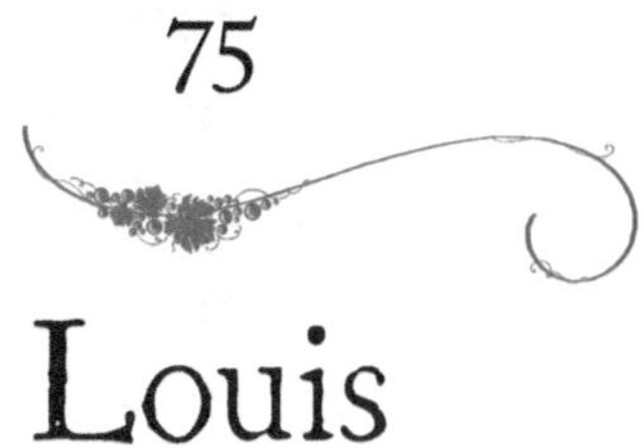

# Louis



Tʜᴇ ᴄɪᴛᴀᴅᴇʟ'ꜱ ᴅᴏᴏʀꜱ thudded closed. Crowds of turbaned soldiers wielded pikes, sabers, muskets. A deafening rally cry rang out and reverberated along the stone walls.

Hand jittering, Louis pulled Henri's handkerchief from his sling, and turning in a circle, waved it above his head, hoping the warriors respected his surrender.

Quiet descended. French drumbeats echoed outside the walls. Before him, in the shade of a short saffron canopy, lounging upon crimson pillows, sat a white-bearded, owl-eyed man wearing a red turban and dark robes. Louis took him to be al-Jazzar, the commander and pasha—who had earned the nickname—The Butcher.

Louis's mouth grew as dry as sand. Not taking his eyes

from the man, he brought his hands together and bowed his head. "Inshallah."

The pasha raised a finger. Two scimitar-wielding soldiers grabbed Louis's arms and thrust him to his knees.

To the pasha's right stood a distinguished man wearing a blue frock coat with brass buttons and épaulettes, white breeches, and the bicorne of a British officer.

Louis sucked in a breath. He could negotiate with this civilized man. "Before you skewer my head upon a pike, I have information I believe you will find valuable."

The British officer raised his hand. "You speak English."

"I do—with a French accent like you. I am injured and unarmed. Would you please ask these men to release me?"

The officer circled his finger, and another man spoke in Arabic to the pasha.

The pasha hissed at the soldiers, and they released him.

A slight flame of hope flared as Louis stood. But if the pasha chose to torture him before beheading him, Louis would regret this path. With his left hand, he saluted the officer, a pointy-nosed, thin-lipped man who wore a small gold hoop in his left ear. "Colonel Louis LaGarde, Cavalry."

The officer returned the salute. "We will speak English for the translator. Why does Bonaparte send a colonel to certain death?"

"I volunteered, to spare my men."

The officer's eyebrows rose.

"And…Bonaparte knows when the French soldiers see the heads of their comrades upon a pike, they fight more fiercely."

The officer spat to the side. "He wastes lives."

"And saves ammunition," Louis added.

"Colonel Antoine de Phélippeaux, formerly of the Armée de Condé and Armée des Émigrés, now of the Royal Navy, serving the future king of France. What information have you?"

The name was familiar but not from Versailles. And then Louis recalled sitting in his tent in Paris, reading an article in which the Royalist traitor Phélippeaux had daringly rescued Captain William Smith from the Temple, where Bonaparte had imprisoned Smith. Was Smith captain of one of the ships in the harbor? Louis's heartbeat galloped, and he forced himself to calm. He needed to negotiate. "We have a common enemy, Colonel."

Phélippeaux reached for the roll of parchment.

Mind spinning as he gave it, Louis searched for a way to convince Phélippeaux to save him and his men. He had to build trust. "I suspect Bonaparte orders surrender."

Phélippeaux shook his head. "Does Bonaparte believe the pasha and the entire world speaks French? Or is he so arrogant he thinks his enemies should hire translators?"

"Indeed, he is that arrogant. You should not surrender."

Phélippeaux tossed the paper to the ground. "And why is that?"

"Every French soldier knows you are winning this battle."

The translator spoke to the pasha, who leaned back and laughed heartily. Soldiers erupted in laughter as word spread. They raised their weapons and jeered.

Phélippeaux smiled widely. "True. But how do we know Bonaparte did not send you to spread falsehoods?"

The sun burned the back of Louis's neck. He would be hanged as a traitor if he was returned to Murat, but he withdrew the sacred heart and held it out in his palm.

Phélippeaux folded back the lapel of his frock coat, revealing his own sacred heart.

Louis blessed Tante Nicole. "All the world knows Bonaparte wants to claim a shorter trade route to the East. He sent scientists, engineers, architects to Suez. He will appear to be sending troops south, to protect them—as a decoy."

Phélippeaux tugged at his earring. "His true intent?"

Louis's news would endanger French soldiers' lives but save his men. "Bonaparte sends his troops south tonight, but they will soon turn west for the coast and Abukir."

"Thanks to Nelson, Bonaparte has no more French ships. Why head for a port?"

"Please, Colonel, if I give you his strategy, which I suspect he has not revealed even to his generals, will you take me prisoner and get me back to France?"

"Agreed."

"And I have a favor to request, Colonel."

Phélippeaux raised an eyebrow. "You are not in a bargaining position."

"That is why it is a favor. I appeal to your sense of honor and loyalty to the monarchy."

Phélippeaux's expression was one of cool elegance.

Louis's arm throbbed, but he resisted easing the pain. "I have ordered my company of forty-eight men to scale the precipice to the beach tonight and wait for one of your ships to send longboats for them." His throat tightened as he rushed, "They are all loyal to the future king of France and wish to serve him *in* France, where they can help him return to the throne."

Phélippeaux crowed a laugh. "If they are as loyal and audacious as you, they just might be worth saving."

The translator spoke to the pasha, who chuckled.

"Why does Bonaparte head for a port?" Phélippeaux demanded.

There was no retreat from Louis's traitorous words. "Bonaparte cannot become King of France from Egypt. He needs only one ship."

Phélippeaux's lips pressed into a grim line.

The pasha spoke and the translator said, "Send the scorpion home."

Phélippeaux shook Louis's left hand. "Captain Smith will be eager to learn of Bonaparte's strategy." He led Louis along the parapet toward the sea. Louis stopped next to a cannon and peeked through the embrasure at the battlefield. His men stood, their hands over their hearts, watching the citadel. Behind them, atop his white stallion, Bonaparte brought his saber to Murat's waist and flicked the blade, slicing the sky-blue sash. Caught by the wind, the fabric floated out to sea. Bonaparte whacked the flat of his saber against Murat, sending him face-first into the sand.

Louis whispered, "Adieu, you duckbilled bastard."

# 76

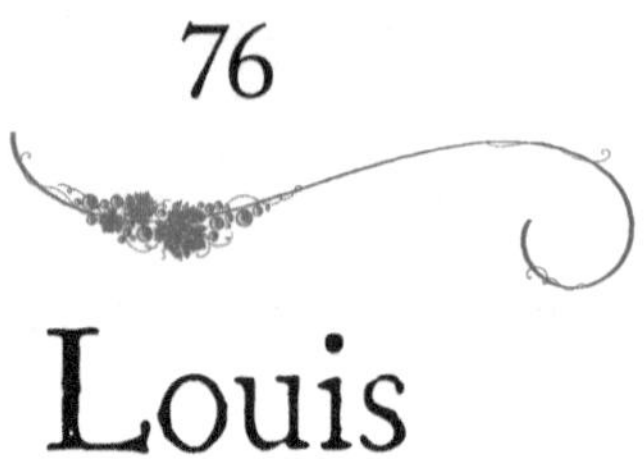

# Louis



*Mediterranean Sea*
*May* 1799

Louis stood on the deck of *HMS Tigre*, grateful the former seventy-four-gun French ship of the line had been captured by the British. In the distance, torches wavered at the top of the precipice where Bonaparte's troops camped.

"Captain wishes to see you in his cabin." A sailor led Louis below deck.

Captain William Sidney Smith had a broad forehead and narrow chin, giving his face the shape of an egg standing on its tip. Yet he was a handsome man, with curly brown hair and bright eyes. Terribly young for a Captain, he was small in stature but noble in his bearing. Shelves of books in French, English, and Russian lined the walls of his quarters, which smelled faintly of cloves. He reached for a bottle of wine that stood upon a map-covered table and poured himself a glass.

Louis stood at attention, his mouth dry, yet the ruby-colored liquid brought the tantalizing memory of the pressings at Château de Verzat. He inhaled the faint scent of currants. He supported his injured arm with his left hand, but the throbbing mounted. "I ordered my lieutenant to swim to the ship tonight and assured him you would send longboats for the other men."

"I am astounded by your courage…and stupidity, Colonel. Your head could be atop a pike right now."

Louis huffed a laugh. "I gave my men my word of honor—I would get them home."

Smith drained his glass. "I proposed to evacuate the wounded French. Bonaparte refused my offer. Why?"

"He told his troops you were offering plague ships for transport, making his soldiers pathetically grateful *not* to accept your offer." Louis longed to wipe the perspiration trickling down his neck. "Bonaparte builds his glory upon the lives he squanders." Thirst burned his throat. "Please, Captain, will you take my men to France?"

"What have they to offer in return?" Smith's eyes glinted in the lanternlight.

"Every one of my men will provide information: about Bonaparte, his army, and this desert." He forced a smile. "They can even teach your men how to ride camels."

Smith poured himself another glass of wine.

The room rocked, and Louis worried the tide was turning. "I suspect Bonaparte is headed for Abukir so he can return to France."

Smith paced. "All his ships have been captured."

"He needs only one…he will abandon his troops." Time

was wasting. Louis wanted Smith's word to transport his men. He opened his fist and held out the sacred heart, glowing in the soft light.

Smith's eyebrow lifted. "You will tell me everything you know?"

At the risk of execution, Louis would tell Smith every detail to stop Bonaparte. He pressed the sacred heart against his heart. "In exchange for transporting my men to France."

Smith's smile grew as wide as his forehead. He poured another glass of wine and offered it. "Welcome aboard, Colonel."

Louis lifted his glass to Smith's and sipped the wine. The burst of lavender and currants dizzied him. Joliette and Geneviève had sent wine to the enemy. Formidable. "Château de Verzat."

Surprise sat in Smith's eyes. "You can identify this wine?"

"It is the 1794 vintage. My wife is the vigneron of Château de Verzat."

"Let us greet your men, Colonel."

Louis followed him above deck. The night was dark and soft as velvet. Gentle waves hushed against the hull.

"Are your men on shore?" Smith asked.

Louis focused a spyglass on the rock face. "Not yet."

"The tide changes within the hour. We leave then. With or without your men."

"They have always obeyed my orders, Captain. They will be there."

"My dinner awaits." Smith left him.

The hollow in Louis' chest gouged his ribs. He would not abandon his men, even if it meant he would not get home. He envisioned the faces of his men, Henri's, Simon's—the most vivid—Ribou's. Louis supported his useless arm. Should they not arrive in time, he would demand to be rowed ashore before the ship sailed.

Waves grew taller. The slapping against the hull increased. The ship bucked. Louis focused on the precipice while urging his men to hurry. Something dropped onto the rocky beach, shadows crossed the rocks to the water…nothing but a moving creature could cause them.

He stopped one of the sailors. "Please tell the Captain my men are on shore."

A speck of white appeared atop one wave, reappeared, and bobbed between the shadows of the two British ships. Rhythmic splashing brought sailors running. They dropped rope nets over the side and fastened them. Two sailors reached down.

"Do you have our Colonel LaGarde?" a voice hissed in heavily accented English.

"Henri!" Louis's laugh burst. They were going home.

77

# *Geneviève*

*Château de Verzat*
*September 1799*

Memories of the vendanges, when our men were with us, weighed upon every grape cluster I picked. I imagined them walking across the vineyard, their arms open, faces smiling, voices cheering. The harvest was late, and everyone was picking, for the danger of frost did not allow us a moment of rest.

"Tante Gen!" Fortuné raced down the hill. "The Capitaine!"

I dropped the secateurs and grabbed his shoulders. "Where's Aurélia?"

He heaved for breath. "Kitchen. That nasty lady—"

"Suzanne?"

He nodded. "They come on horses."

"Take Aurélia and the children to the secret tunnel. You stay with them. Do not open the trapdoor until I come for you. Understand?"

"Yes. Hurry, Tante Gen!" He ran.

Workers called out as I ran by them, but I refused their help. I wanted no witnesses to the crimes I was about to commit. "Keep picking!" My legs burned as I pushed myself uphill. I prayed Joliette was in the château.

Their horses weren't at the great doors. I headed toward the far side of the château and spotted three horses in the garden, outside the salon where Joliette worked on the accounting books. They'd brought an extra horse for Aurélia or brought a third man. I needed another pistol.

I raced to the kitchen and slowly opened the door, listening. Hearing nothing, I prayed Aurélia and the children were in the tunnel below. I took Tante Nicole's pistol from behind the vinegar cask and took Louis's gun from my hanging pocket and loaded them both. Holding a gun in each hand, I hid them behind my skirts and crept outside along the garden toward the open glass doors of the salon. Inside, voices cracked like roaring flames. I inched my way along the wall, stood to the side of the entrance, and peered around the edge of the door.

At the center of the room stood the Capitaine. He gripped Auguste's arm and held a pistol to my brother's head. Auguste stood defiant, his hands fisted, but his reddened eyes told me he was enraged and hurting. My heartbeat thundered.

Opposite the Capitaine, Joliette held Guillaume's hand tightly, her face creased with terror as she watched, not the Capitaine's pistol—but Suzanne.

Dressed in an elegant white gown, plumed bonnet, and emerald necklace, Suzanne stood smiling down at the squirming, crying babe in her arms.

She held my son.

Heat exploded in me. I gripped the door's edge. My vision narrowed until I saw only her dagger-sharp fingers gripping my son. I forced myself to take deep breaths. Louis's voice rang in my head: Be calm. Surprise her.

Pressure built in my chest. God damn you, Suzanne.

The Capitaine pulled Auguste in front of himself and, using my brother as a shield, he aimed the pistol at Joliette. "Where is she?"

Coward. My arms and legs shook as I fought my instinct to seize my son. I could not get a clear shot at the Capitaine without risking Auguste's life.

Joliette stood erect and shoved her right hand in her hanging pocket. I knew she was gripping her tiny pistolet. Guillaume clung to his mother's skirts.

Nicolas wailed and pummeled Suzanne with his fists.

"I already purchased Aurélia for quite a large sum, upon your ship, if you recall." Joliette's tone was sharp as ice.

"I recaptured the dark beauty, and she is worth double now that she has a son. I own them both." The Capitaine's words dripped like oil. Auguste strained to pull away, but the Capitaine yanked him back. Auguste cried, "You're a bully," and rubbed his shoulder. I trained my pistol on the Capitaine's head.

Guillaume stomped his foot. "I am a Noble of the Sword. You leave my maman alone!"

"She is free. As is her son." Joliette walked with Guillaume to the fireplace where an ancient sword hung from the mantel. Her eyes flicked to the chair. I suspected she was calculating how she could shove Guillaume behind it. She was stalling, distracting the Capitaine, waiting for me.

"Maman!" Nicolas wailed and kicked Suzanne's chest.

I wiped my sweating hand on my skirt and regripped the pistol.

"You want to come along?" Suzanne grabbed Nicolas's fist and laughed. "And Madame's doorman, that charming little boy. Fortuné? We own him, too."

How could I kill before these children? Louis would kill the Capitaine and Suzanne in an instant. I had to calm myself, for there was only one chance to save them.

Louis's voice drummed: Agree to their terms to get the children away. Flatter Suzanne. Take her by surprise.

I gulped a steadying breath, put one pistol in my hanging pocket, and hid the other amongst the folds of my skirts. Exhaling slowly, I stepped into the salon, and smiled. "Suzanne, how lovely to see you." I hurried to her. "Oh, the baby soiled your gown. I'll help you."

She gasped, pushed Nicolas at me, and searched her skirts for the nonexistent stains.

I scooped up Nicolas and thrust him on the chair, reached into my hanging pocket, and gripped the other pistol. Nicolas cried and pulled himself up. My heart ached to comfort him.

"Gen!" Auguste cried.

"Everything will be fine, dear brother." I watched for an opening, any opening to kill either of them. The Capitaine ducked, peering around Auguste like a striking snake.

Suzanne hands fluttered like bat wings. "Where is Louis?"

"Right behind you," I whispered as I cocked the pistol.

She turned. I shot her in the center of her back.

Nicolas wailed.

Suzanne staggered, dipped into a circle. Had I killed her? She grasped her chest and dropped in a heap.

As I pulled out the other pistol, I faced the Capitaine. His eyes bulged as he stared open-mouthed at me and then Joliette.

Clutching Auguste to his chest, he aimed his pistol at me and then Joliette and back at me, like he was deciding who was the greater danger.

Auguste bit the Capitaine's arm and stomped on his foot. The Capitaine cried out. His gun wavered at me.

Nicolas wailed. I aimed, trying not to kill my brother.

A shot rang out. Blood exploded from the Capitaine's face; his head snapped back. Auguste jumped away and dove behind a chair. The Capitaine crashed forward.

Joliette stood with her pistolet aimed but unfired.

At the hallway entrance, Aurélia stood with her arms extended, holding Henri's smoking pistol. Regal as a queen, she lowered the gun and walked to the Capitaine. Shoving his shoulder with her foot, she rolled him over. And spat in his face.

A cheer filled the room.

I lifted Nicolas and turned. A group of stable boys holding pitchforks, and Étienne and Monsieur Cambon holding muskets surrounded a smiling Fortuné. "I bring help."

I pulled Nicolas to my bosom and kissed him, kissed him, kissed him all over. Fortuné had intervened, saving us all. "Thank you."

Auguste ran to me, and I embraced him while pressing my crying son to my breast. The room swirled. I bent over my legs, trembling, words rushing out. "With all these witnesses—Aurélia and I will face the guillotine for murder!" Sobs shuddered through my body.

Auguste and Aurélia locked their arms around me.

I kissed Aurélia's hand. "You saved our lives, dear sister."

Aurélia eased Nicolas from my arms. She mouthed, *As you saved mine, dear sister.*

I clung to her, feeling her strength pulsing in her arms, remembering the night we escaped the bordel together. She caressed my hair. *I am free now. Truly free.*

I kissed her cheek. "Yes. Free."

Auguste patted my back. Joliette helped me to straighten. I clung to her hand, the heat of hers pressing into my palm. She gripped Aurélia's hand and stood tall. "These men and I admire you and Aurélia." Her voice was strong. "Do we not, gentlemen?"

"Brava, Tante Gen!" Étienne shouted. Monsieur Cambon shouted, "Brava, Madame Aurélia!" The boys cheered and whooped.

Joliette pulled me close. Her strength unleashed my fears. "We are all your family, Tante Gen. Not one person on this entire estate is disloyal to you or Aurélia." Her strong arms encircled me. I let myself weep.

Suzanne and the Capitaine were dead. Aurélia and her children and Fortuné were safe and would remain free. The boys and men risked their lives to protect us. I and my children and brother were safe among these people. All of them were my family. They would help me bury the bodies in the cave next to the men Simon and I had killed. And they would keep our secret.

Auguste wiped my face. "They told me they were taking me to visit you. I didn't know they would try to kill you. I'm sorry. I shouldn't have let them take me."

I kissed his hand. "I know. You were very brave. I'm so glad you're here."

He pointed to Nicolas. "Is he your baby?"

"You are his oncle. Would you like to hold your nephew?"

Auguste's eyes shone with wonder as he let Nicolas grip his fingers. "You're strong." He laughed. "I'll fold boats for you, and we'll sail them on the pond. What's your name?"

Love blossomed in my heart and surged through me, but the coursing warmth tore a hole in my chest. Despite the love of my huge family, I was so lonely.

Come home soon, Louis. I can't do this anymore without you. I will do anything to get you home. Anything.

# 78

# *Geneviève*

*Château de Verzat*
*November* 1799

I STOOD SHIVERING IN a fine mist on the ridge overlooking the vineyard. A thick fog sat over the Loire, obscuring the distant fields. Joliette was overjoyed by the plentiful vendanges. We paid the back taxes and bought a small vineyard to add to the estate. Why was I not relieved? It had become a ritual to me, turning in the direction of the ocean, envisioning Louis sailing home.

I wrapped the shawl of Louis's maman tighter, imagining my husband's eyes, his smile. Our son has your chin and fine nose, and my wide hands and stubby fingers. He possesses your calm spirit. Should Louisa fall and cry, he pats her back and, when her tears stop, he kisses her. Nicolas runs without fear, never stopping. He is such a rascal. I laughed a little sob. I suppose he gets that from me. My chest shuddered.

My love, where are you? We are not a complete family without you. I allowed myself to cry to the count of fifty.

The day we had killed the Capitaine and Suzanne, when I cried myself out, sheltered in Joliette's arms, a new strength infused me, and I hoped shedding tears would continue to replenish my dwindling supply of strength and courage.

As I reached fifty, I wiped my face and headed for the cave. I had to relieve the men who were pouring the juice into barrels. It was dangerous to inhale the fumes for very long.

Thérèse hurried toward me. Please let it be good news. A newspaper trembled in her hand. Tears filled her eyes.

A chill crossed the back of my neck. Numbness seized my hands and crawled up my arms. I did not want to know. Please, God let them be alive. I shook my hands until they tingled and took the paper. I scanned the page. *Général Napoleon Bonaparte returns triumphant. All of Paris celebrates.* I searched the other pages. One ship had returned. Not one word about the thirty-five thousand troops or hundreds of ships that had accompanied him.

I felt like I would snort flames. I ripped the paper to shreds and stomped on them. Thérèse stepped back. I glared at her. "I will not let you nor anyone else lose hope. At this very moment Louis is walking across the desert or riding over the alps or swimming the sea. He and Henri and Simon are returning to us. Do not think otherwise for even one second!"

She held her hands in prayer against her bosom and nodded furiously.

I knelt. She crouched next to me, and we filled her apron with the papers.

"I will burn these." She rose. "I won't tell anyone."

I whispered my thanks as she left me. Like trying to slam a door against a fierce wind, I pressed my hands over my ears, blocking the words, but the thought charged at me. I had never allowed myself to think: What if Louis never returns?

The mist swaddled the estate, nurturing its vines, cloaking the cottages and château with loving protection. God, let this same mist comfort and protect our men.

We, all, everyone at château de Verzat, were a family. But Louis's absence left an emptiness in me that only he could fill. I inhaled the scent of fermenting grapes that hung over the vineyard. I bowed my head. God, give me strength, for I have none. I pushed my hands into the tufa soil. The chalky dust, like a damp powder, clung to my fingers. I know you are on your way home to me, my darling. I swiped at tears. Please, hurry.

I stood and headed for the caves. There was wine to be made.

79

# Geneviève

*Château de Verzat*
*November* 1799

THE VENDANGES HAD been so plentiful, we were still bar-
reling the juice. The thick syrupy odor permeated my clothes,
and the air in the caves was sticky. Fruit flies swarmed the
pomace as the stableboys dragged the grape residue out to the
stables where they distributed it to families who raised hogs.
The men and boys rotated their duty every half hour. Although
I was overseeing and not exerting myself, I was beginning to
feel a bit light-headed from the fumes.

A clanging stopped everyone in their tracks. The men
looked at one another and ran to the doors. They had reacted
so quickly, I stood alone in the huge room, blinking. What
was that noise? A stinging sensation rushed through me.

The bell—rung only for emergencies. Had gendarmes come for Aurélia? My hands trembled as I reached into my hanging pocket. Republicans stealing food and horses? I pulled out my pistols, readied them, and peeked out of the cave.

A group of men stood at the crest of the hill, yelling and shouting. A wiry young man pulled the bell with all his might. How dare he?

If they threatened us, I'd kill the leader and negotiate with whoever was left. With my hands plunged between the folds of my skirts, I strode toward them. Aurélia and Joliette would have their pistols and the men their hunting muskets. I wasn't alone. My family was with me.

Étienne stopped in my path, stretching out his arms. "You don't need your pistols, Tante Gen." He lifted his chin toward the hilltop.

I slowed. The strange, bearded men waved, smiling, shouting. They wore ragged frock coats, stained breeches, and were without hats, some without boots. I didn't recognize these men. Were they Chouans, needing our help? Who—?

My heart thumped wildly. The tallest man, with a golden scarf looped about his neck and holding an arm to his chest—

"Louis!" I shoved the guns at Étienne. I pounded up the hill, my heart bursting. "Louis!"

He ran to me. His arm encircled my waist. I clung to him, weeping, kissing, laughing. He stumbled, kissing, and embracing me.

His right arm, held by the saffron scarf, pressed between us. "Louis, you're hurt?" I lightly caressed his arm.

"Only a scratch. The only arms I care about are yours, my darling." Deep lines sprang from the corners of his eyes.

"You have a beard."

"And you have hair." He untied my bonnet and ran his fingers through my curls.

I broke away. "We have a son!"

His smile burst. "Where is he?"

"I've named him Nicolas, after Tante Nicole."

"Where is the Marquise de Bourran? I must thank her for saving all our lives."

I could not speak. The golden flecks in his eyes dulled and disappeared, mirroring the sorrow I could not contain. A grimace yanked his mouth. He could not stop his tears. Nor could I stop mine.

"Hon…! Hon…!" A shout rose above all others.

We turned toward the château. Aurélia stood, her arms stretched to the sky. "Hon…Hon…reeeeee!"

Henri raced and embraced her. Weeping, laughing, tumbling to the ground wrapped in Henri's arms, Aurélia shouted his name, again and again.

Tears coursed down Louis's face and mine. I pulled him to me, breathing in his scent, not the odor of freshly mown hay, but the smell of salt air and mud and sweat. "I never doubted you would come home to me, my love. Not for one second."

# 80

# Geneviève

*Château de Verzat*
*November* 1799

CELEBRATIONS CONTINUED, UNTIL every drop of Château de Verzat 1799 was drained into casks. Joliette predicted the vintage would be blessed by the men's return.

Determined to deliver every comfort to the men, I sought out Joliette. "I would like to invite all the soldiers to stay here and recover their strength before they begin their journeys home. What do you think?"

"It is an excellent idea."

"Could we offer the North wing as a barracks?" I asked.

She held my hand, worry lines crossing her forehead. She whispered, "We will have to relocate the Chouans."

"I forgot."

Her smile radiated. "I'm certain they will welcome them."

Her laughter loosened mine. We embraced each other. Joliette treated me as her sister. It had taken Louis's absence for me to realize how lucky I was to have such a huge family.

"Now we must feed the army." I hoped we'd manage without draining our winter supplies. Now that I didn't have to rescue Louis, perhaps we Royalists could band together with the Chouans and undermine Bonaparte. I would discuss the idea with Louis as soon as he was rested, and his arm healed.

Women brought steaming platters of food to the tasting room where long tables were filled with people all hours of the day and night.

Simon was as happy and uncontrollable as a puppy, playing with his sixteen-month-old son, Bertrand, named after Simon's father. Even Emilie could not lure Simon away from the baby. When I suggested they move into the cottage Louis and I had vacated, she yelped with glee and hurried Simon and Bertrand down the hill toward their new home.

Henri had changed, often staring into the distance, removed from everyone. Aurélia and Charles were the only ones who could reach him. Aurélia's soft voice, calm presence, and patience helped Henri welcome his daughter, Briella, who clung to her papa like a barnacle. Charles engaged Henri in games, and Aurélia constantly whispered to her husband.

I longed to hear Aurélia speak, but there was plenty of time.

Louisa did not leave Louis's side and coached him. "You must support Nicolas's head, or it will fall off, Baba." Louis took her instructions with great seriousness.

"Baba?" I asked.

Louis grinned. "I will tell you later."

While I held Nicolas, Louis lifted his daughter to the heavens, Louisa screeching her joy.

Madame Ornay climbed the hill and steadied herself with her walking stick. She sought out Louis and kissed his cheek. "Your wife saved my life, in an ice storm, Louis. And my goats!"

His calm, deep chuckle opened my heart.

"I have no doubt. But my wife tells me she could not run the estate without you."

Madame Ornay stomped her stick. "That's true." She laughed so hard I feared she'd fall.

There would be plenty of time to ask Louis about what had happened. But I was too selfish to think of anything beyond his presence. Whatever we did to undermine Bonaparte, we would both remain home, caring for our children and creating more.

81

*Geneviève*

*Château de Verzat*
*November* 1799

By THE END of the week of merry-making and settling the soldiers into their makeshift barracks, exhaustion seeped into my bones as I lay with Louis in our bedchamber. Our love-making had been explosive at first, but now we were rediscovering each other, taking our time pleasuring the other.

Louis's wound was not a scratch. A vivid red scar swirled over his shoulder and down the length of his right arm, and he had lost control of the muscles that raised his arm above his chest. Although he tried to strengthen them, his arm responded in jerks. I hoped time, rest, and nurturing food would bring back his strength. Although I would have expected him to be angry at this weakness and limitation, he was grateful to be alive. He trained himself to eat and write with his left hand as a challenge, all the while reassuring me his right arm would recover. I knew he would tell me all about his experiences when the time was right. Then the golden sparks in his eyes would return and remain.

I had a meeting with the Chouan at midnight and waited for Louis to fall asleep. I slipped out of bed, dressed quickly, and tiptoed to the door. Nicolas cooed. He was teething and should the pain flare he would cry and wake Louis. I wrapped him in the shawl of Louis's maman and carried him with me to the kitchen.

I sensed the Chouan's presence before I spotted him in the shadows. "Bonsoir."

After lighting the candles, I collected paper, ink, and quill and placed them on the table. I pulled a plate of roast chicken and fresh bread and cheese from the larder, placed them opposite me on the table, and poured a cup of wine.

He lifted the cup in a toast and then sipped. I suspected he toasted the men's return for he gave me a hint of a smile.

"Your son is well?" I asked.

"And very happy. He enjoys playing with the orphans. And your daughter is teaching him to read."

"I'm glad." Nicolas gurgled in my lap. I began writing.

"What are you doing?"

My hand jerked at Louis's voice. Ink spattered.

The Chouan gripped his musket and turned.

Louis stood barefooted in his nightshirt, a scarf looping his right arm, his left hand gripping his pistol.

I placed the quill on the table and stood, holding Nicolas to my chest. "You have met this gentleman before. Do you remember?"

The Chouan removed his hat.

"Ah, you are the Chouan who saved the women and children."

The man nodded. "And you are the babe's papa."

Louis smiled.

Nicolas began to cry. "You've frightened him." I took the pistol and pressed Nicolas into Louis's arm. "Calm him." I pointed at the chair before the fire. "He likes to be rocked."

He clutched Nicolas to him, sat and hummed until Nicolas quieted.

The Chouan finished his recitation, tucked the food into his sack, lifted the trapdoor, and descended.

I wiped my hands on my skirts and fetched lemon juice and Tante Nicole's codebook. When I sat back down, Louis's bearpaw hand covered mine. Nicolas lay sleeping in the cradle next to the fire.

"What are you doing?" His eyes were confused, and my heart ached.

I unpinned the sacred heart from the inside of my bodice and placed it on the table. "Tante Nicole gave me this before she died."

His focus sharpened.

"She said, 'Louis,' and I thought she was trying to tell me to give it to Louisa. She asked me to take over where she had left off."

"Left off what?"

I pushed out a tightness in my chest with a sigh. "Tante had been a Royalist spy most of her life."

Louis sat opposite, capturing my hand. "Have you become a spy?" he whispered.

I nodded.

"You did not tell me?"

"Well, I couldn't have written, could I?"

"But I have been home a week."

"We've been busy. I forgot about it, until I remembered the Chouan would arrive this evening. I should not have told you this, for knowing my activities could endanger your life."

He released my hand.

My hand grew cold. "I am sorry I kept this from you."

He reached into the scarf looped around his neck and placed something before me.

A sacred heart. Identical to the one Tante had given me.

The tightness around his eyes softened. "Tante gave this to me before I departed. If not for her encouraging me to become a Royalist spy, I and my men would all be dead."

I pressed my hand against my heart and looked at my beautiful, battered, proud husband. "You kept this a secret from me."

"I could not have very well written, could I?" A grin slowly spread. "It takes great courage to spy for the future king of France."

I wanted to embrace him. But I sat still, blinked back tears. "Only if we are caught."

He rose and pulled me to him. I wrapped my arms around him, breathing in the scent of newly mown hay. His chest rumbled with his booming laugh, which spread through me. We held each other, laughing, weeping.

He lifted my chin. The golden flecks in his eyes sparkled. His eyes overflowed with sorrow and love and joy. "We, both, are terribly brave bastards."

## THE END

# THÉRÈSE & ANNE'S MUSHROOM SOUP

## SERVES 6–8

## INGREDIENTS

2 pounds of cremini mushrooms

2 pounds white button mushrooms

2 cups diced sweet onion

2 shallots finely chopped

extra virgin olive oil

12 sprigs fresh thyme

1 ½–2 quarts chicken or vegetable broth

2 tablespoons soy sauce or umami (optional)*

1 teaspoon smoked sweet paprika

1–2 cups 2% milk

2 cups nonfat Greek yogurt

sea salt and pepper

chopped fresh parsley or additional thyme

fresh lemon wedges

# PROCESS

1. Thoroughly wash the mushrooms and allow them to dry on a towel. (Tip: I use new shower mitts, originally made for exfoliating, but I wear them to rub the mushrooms clean under running water. They remove all the clinging grit from the mushrooms quickly and easily.)

2. Separate the stems from the caps and chop both into ½ inch cubes.

3. Heat a heavy-bottomed pot on low to medium. Add enough olive oil to coat the bottom and lightly sauté the mushrooms in batches with a sprinkling of fresh thyme in each. (As Julia Child is known for saying: "Don't crowd the mushrooms!") You may need to add a splash or two of oil as you continue to cook the mushrooms.

4. Remove and reserve the cooked mushrooms and their juices.

5. Add more olive oil to the pan and sauté the diced onion and shallots.

6. When onions and shallots are soft and translucent, add the cooked mushrooms, their juices, and the broth.

7. Allow to cook on low, occasionally stirring, for 20 minutes. Add soy sauce or umami if using.

8. Add paprika.

9. Add milk, stir continuously until fully incorporated.

10. Ensure the heat is at the lowest setting. Add the yogurt by tablespoonful, stirring continuously.

11. Add salt and pepper to taste.

12. Add a squeeze of lemon and chopped fresh parsley or thyme before serving.

# NOTES

1. Cooks at Château de Verzat would not have had soy sauce. They would have used powdered dried mushrooms (umami) and wine to boost the flavors of the mushrooms. If you use red wine be aware that the soup may turn a lovely shade of purple.

2. This soup can be kept warm in a slow cooker—but keep the heat on low as the dairy in the soup will curdle and separate when the heat is high.

3. This soup freezes well. Be sure when reheating to simmer.

4. If you like a creamier soup, use an immersion blender and blitz ingredients to the thickness you desire.

## MY HEARTFELT THANKS TO TASTE TESTERS OF RECIPES IN
*Soups of Château de Verzat: A Literary Cookbook*
*& Culinary Tribute to the French Revolution*

I wrote the cookbook, *Soups of Château de Verzat* for adventuresome cooks, who like me, aren't afraid to experiment and for cooks who have little to no experience. I thank them all for their comments and suggestions, all of which are deeply appreciated!

## GENEVIÈVE'S EASY LEMON CHICKEN ORZO SOUP

"I served it at book club last night and everyone raved. It was super easy too! — Biblioberg

## ETTY'S ASPARAGUS SOUP

"This soup was also easy to make though the next time I make it I would double the recipe. Each recipe has the ingredients, process and special notes." — Carol Dosher (carol_dosher_reader)

"Dreamy and delicious—easy enough for beginner chefs to conquer, but impressive enough to serve to your guests with pride."
— Chrissy Consolã, *Parisian Niche*

## ETTY'S CARROT, ORANGE & GINGER

"I could not believe how easy this recipe was. How could something so easy be do delectable?!" — Stephanie Rabell

## MADAME BOURRAN'S APPLE AND PARSNIP SOUP

"Debra Borchert has an amazing history with making soups! I love Madame Bourran's Apple and Parsnip Soup, the parsnips add an earthiness to the sweet apples, and the two are very much in keeping with the time period. Thanks for this wonderful recipe, *Chef du Potage*, Debra!" — Dorette Snover

## MADAME DETRÉ'S CHICKEN VEGETABLE SOUP

"We substituted turkey since we'd cooked a turkey and had the carcass with plenty of meat to use. We also substituted leeks for broccoli and my Italian husband tossed in some pasta! It was amazing! We noted that by the next day, the pasta had soaked up the broth and wasn't as visually appealing but still tasty."
— Norma Fourchalk (theliterateleprechaun)

## MADAME FRANÇOISE'S FRENCH ONION SOUP

"We had it several times on our recent cruise and even bought 'proper' French onion soup bowls with long handles while on holiday. When we came home and the days got shorter and colder, we were excited to try this one. We had a bottle of Oak Hill Farms Vidalia onion vinaigrette in the cupboard and added a couple of tablespoons at the end of step 6. My husband had made his own baguettes, so we sliced them and used them. I loved how stringy the cheese was and noted that the broth wasn't as salty as the one on the cruise ship. I also noted that the thyme (fresh from our neighbor's garden) was an integral part of the dish." — Norma Fourchalk (theliterateleprechaun)

"Madame Francoise French Onion Soup was absolutely delicious! I have been looking for a great French Onion Soup recipe for a long time since it is my favorite soup." — Robyn Konopka

## SISTER MAGALI'S VELVETY BUTTERNUT SQUASH & PEAR SOUP

"Although Jeffrey used a different squash, Magali thought the pear was a delicious twist." — Magali & Jeffrey Belt

"I roasted the butternut squash (I've never done that before) and garlic and was amazed at how it intensified their natural flavours. On a whim, I added our 'leftover' Moscato wine and noticed it really elevated the flavours. My husband suggested I sprinkle blue cheese to garnish next time." — Norma Fourchalk (theliterateleprechaun)

"I'd been eagerly awaiting this book—and it definitely lived up to my hopes! I had a glut of apples, so I pounced on Madame Bourran's Apple Parsnip soup and it was delicious. I'd not actually thought of using the apples in soup before but their sweet-tartness mixed with the sweet-earthiness of the parsnips wonderfully." — Rosalind Stirzaker

## THÉRÈSE & ANNE'S MUSHROOM SOUP

"I love making mushroom soup but never thought of using Greek yogurt as a substitution for cream, and I loved it. It gave a more rounded flavor and, as an add on, gives more protein to the soup." — Vivian Gelber

Holy yum! It was warming and delightfully umami. I typically love a nice cream of chicken and rice or something really substantial, but sometimes I just crave that mushroom flavor and this recipe hit the spot in a healthy way. Instead of cream, it uses milk and Greek yogurt, so you're adding some protein in while still getting that creamy texture. I was feeling like something crunchy but didn't want to add crackers so I sautéed some shallots and a couple of leftover mushrooms until I got that crunch and it was the perfect addition. — Chelsie Stanford (seasonedreader)

# THE VERZAT COOK'S POTATO-LEEK SOUP

I'm not normally a fan of potato-based soups so I wasn't expecting to absolutely fall in love this soup! What a nice surprise! This soup has the best of both worlds—an earthy flavor juxtaposed with a fresh aliveness. This soup titillates your taste buds. Très magnifique! I am especially impressed with the simple ingredients and how easy it is to make. A wonderful soup for fall and winter and, along with a piece of French bread or naan, a filling meal. This soup is now on my favorites list and I'll be making it again soon.
— Carol Despeaux Fawcett

"This recipe is definitely going to be a keeper for my family! Easy to follow, and the taste is superb! Rich and creamy with just the right amount of potato chunks ... served with foccacio bread - superb!!!!"
— Susan Patten

"I love the Verzat Potato Leek soup, using vegetable broth. You don't need to put potato blossoms in your hair or wig like Queen Marie Antoinette. It won't make a difference in flavor, but it might add to your enjoyment!" — Shelly Westholm

## COMMENTS FOR
### *Soups of Château de Verzat*

"What a terrific little cookbook! If you're a soup lover, you need this one. We tried three soups. All of the soups were tasty, but the clear winner was the Butternut Squash soup." — bookmarked.by.becky

"This is my first cookbook share and I think it's a great one to start with." — booksy.tx.ana

"So easy to make and so delicious. I crumbled bacon and scallions on top to make it like a loaded baked potato." — Carol Dosher (carol_dosher_reader)

"I collect cookbooks and am happy to add this special book to my collection. All of the recipes sound delicious, are easy to follow, and are made with locally found ingredients. I also loved reading the stories that accompanied each of the recipes and who they

are named after, such as: Joliet's white grape gazpacho, Madame Detre's white bean soup. As a bona fide Francophile, I love reading anything to do with France and its food. This is such an enjoyable, interesting, and informative book! I'm so glad to have it!"
— Catherine Poe (catherine.poe.reads)

"I love cookbooks that go along with books! The cookbook is easy to use, and the recipes are varied. Freezing instructions and slow cooker instructions are also included making the soups easy to fit into busy schedules." — Chris (marbooks88)

"I am a person who loves to try out different kinds of dishes and trust me this book is a whole new level of recipes. My personal favorite is The Creamy Zucchini Soup, a delicious French dish that my mother cooked for me. I was enchanted by its rich and smooth flavor. Zucchini is a healthy fruit that provides both Vitamin B and C. You can enjoy this soup either hot or cold. I highly recommend this literary cookbook for anyone who loves food and literature."
— darkfantasyreviews

"This book is perfect for this week's cold weather. Plenty of yummy and hearty soup recipes to indulge and prepare." — enthuse_reader

"Make sure to grab a copy." — Jena M Massey

"Easy to follow directions. I was even able to deliver a delicious dinner that was family approved…and a big hit with my family."
— Joy F Free (joyffree)

"I enjoyed reading the French methods for making the soups in this book, and all of them are very doable!" — Karen (infinite.readlist)

"I absolutely loved reading this book and I learned so many new things and I have made some of the tastiest soups I have ever had!"
— Katie Wascisin Hathaway (simplefairy_book_magic)

"These recipes are like a hug in a bowl!" — Lori Collins (chapterswithcollins)

"Borchert's recipes are concise and mouth-watering with easy-to-find, simple ingredients. She has a manageable amount of recipes complied, all written and tested herself, and they range from thick, creamy, chilled, and vegetable-based, to a poultry-based chili. Furthermore, she's placed them in cultural and historical context. I thought it was a nice touch to include the excerpt from the book that inspired the recipe." — Norma Fourchalk (theliterateleprechaun)

If you are a soup lover, this soup cookbook is pure gold!" — procaffeinate_withbooks

"I love this little soup cookbook! It was so fun to make an actual recipe from the novel *Her Own Revolution*. If you love soups and are always looking for new recipes, I would highly recommend this cookbook. The recipes are so simple to make, nothing too in depth and most of the items I have in my cupboards and the produce and fruit were not expensive at all." — Reading_is_my_remedy

"I absolutely loved this cookbook. My favorite recipe is Debra's Zucchini Soup. This creamy zucchini soup is the best way to use up garden zucchini with no need for a roux to make it nice and thick! You can serve this healthy (zucchini is rich in Vitamins B and C) soup cold or hot. It's simply delicious and full of flavor." — Tatyana Tweedie

I loved this cookbook - there are so many different recipes that would be perfect all year long. I chose to make the Chicken Vegetable Soup Recipe which was a huge hit in my house. The recipes were easy to follow and were so flavorful. — Connie Hill

## SOUP PARTY ATTENDEES

Thank you for your courage and honesty in tasting many, many soups over the years.

Paulette Adams, Pattie Allen, Cynthia Baxter, Alice K. Boatwright, Tiffanny Brooks, Luanne Brown, Andy Chang, Berry Edwards, Bill & Jan Edwards, Conner Edwards, Lauren Edwards, Elaine Gibbs, Gyda Harris, Wendy Kendall, Joanne Kuhns, Jill MacGregor, Ib Odderson, Erik Odderson, Eva Odderson, Donna Reynolds, Ingrid Salmon, Albert Sbragia, Jane Sutherland, Jennifer White, Holly & Larry Williams.

# DISCUSSION QUESTIONS

1.  Why do you think Aurélia is mute?

2.  Were you surprised by the events of Aurélia's rescue?

3.  Do you think Aurélia's actions in the bordel were justified? Why or why not?

4.  Can you relate to Geneviève's not keeping her word? Have there been times when you've not been able to keep your word?

5.  Did Louis do the right thing when he traded his freedom for Geneviève's and joined Bonaparte's army? Can you see any other choice he could or should have made?

6.  Were you surprised by Tante Nicole's confession of having been a spy most of her life?

7.  Although hiding Aurélia was a crime, did Geneviève and Joliette do the right thing? If you had been in their position, what would you have done?

8.  Geneviève risked her and her children's lives as well as all the people on the estate when she spied against the Republic. Was she right to do so? Have you ever done the wrong thing for the right reason?

9.  Joliette suggests to Geneviève to share the risk of sheltering Royalists with all the families on the estate, which was a risk. Were they right in involving the other families in the decision?

10.  Do you think Joliette also spied?

11.  Louis could have saved himself if he abandoned his men. Why do you think he didn't leave them?

12.  Murat was humiliated and treated with disrespect by Louis's father. Did this experience justify Murat's actions toward Louis LaGarde?

13. Why do you think Murat saved Louis's life?

14. Was Murat's comeuppance deserved? Sufficient?

15. Was Geneviève's action toward Suzanne justified?

16. Was Aurélia right in her action against the Capitain?

17. Do you think Geneviève and Louis will continue to spy for the return of the future king of France?

# ACKNOWLEDGEMENTS & RESOURCES

## UN GRAND MERCI À

Dr. Berry Edwards who often resorted to speaking French to drag me back from the eighteenth century. Thank you for making me laugh. You are my chevalier.

Aunt Di for your love, support, laughter, and craziness.

Mireille Belt without whose generous gift of two weeks in her Paris apartment this book would not have been conceived.

Paulette Adams for being an eternal inspiration.

My web designer, Elena Saygo for her brilliance and humor.

My editor extraordinaire, Lorin Oberweger. Thank you for helping me become a better writer.

David Blixt, author, actor, playwright, and fight director, for his expertise in swordplay and book, *Fighting Words.*

Teachers and coaches: Susan Penberthy-Nowak for instilling in me a love for the French language and culture, Priscilla Long, Don Maass, and Lorin Oberweger and Brenda Windberg of Free Expressions.

Attorney Matthew Dresden, Dresden Law PLLC, for his generous time and counsel. And Washington Lawyers for the Arts https://www.thewla.org/.

Librarians everywhere. In particular, the Bibliothèque Nationale de France, and Art at the Lionel Pincus and Princess Firyal Map Division of the New York Public Library.

My fellow supportive writers of the Historical Fiction Affinity Group of Women Fiction Writers Association: You all ROCK!

Critique partners, first readers, and editors who asked the right questions and demonstrated great insight, patience, humor, and honesty: Lesley Ackerberg, Cynthia Anderson, Allison Basile, Dr. Marty Blalock, Cynthia Blair (Cynthia Baxter), Tiffanny Brooks, Kate Dane, Bill Dickett, Ejner Fulsang, Joanne Khuns, Jill MacGregor, Jane Sutherland, Terri Thayer, Jennifer White.

Cultural events and websites helpful to my research and cultural understanding:

- *Emilie* and *The Revolutionists*, plays by Lauren Gunderson https://www.laurengunderson.com/
- Bonjour Paris https://bonjourparis.com/
- Courtney Traub's Paris Unlocked https://www.parisunlocked.com/
- France Magazine https://francetoday.com/
- France Today https://francetoday.com/
- Gallica, the digital library of the National Library of France and its partners. https://gallica.bnf.fr/
- Janine Marsh's The Good Life France https://the-goodlifefrance.com/
- Kristin Espinasse's French Word-A-Day https://www.french-word-a-day.com/
- Paris American Club https://parisamericanclub.org/
- Parisian Niche https://www.parisianniche.com/post/top-5-paris-based-books-we-can-t-wait-to-read-in-2024
- Seattle-Nantes Sister City Association (SNSCA) https://www.seattle-nantes.org/

Communities in which I have participated with many generous writers: Community of Writers at Squaw Valley, Free Expression's Inner Circle, Historical Novel Society, Hugo House, Sisters in Crime, The History Quill, Women fiction Writers Association.

If you're looking for a book club that reads and discusses books that take place in France, check out Christina Consolé's Parisian Page Turners: www.parisianniche.com/parisian-page-turners

PHOTO BY BERRY EDWARDS

# ABOUT THE AUTHOR

Debra borchert has had many careers. She debuted, at the age of five, as a model at a local country club where her crinoline petticoat dropped to her ankles in the middle of the runway.

Since then, she's been a clothing designer, actress (starring in her first television commercial with Jeff Daniels for S.O.S. Soap Pads), TV show host, spokesperson for high-tech companies, marketing and public relations professional, and technical writer for Fortune 100 companies.

Her work has appeared in *The New York Times*, *San Francisco Chronicle*, *The Christian Science Monitor*, and *The Writer*, among others. Her short stories have been published in anthologies and independently.

A graduate of the Fashion Institute of Technology, she weaves her knowledge of textiles and clothing design throughout her historical French fiction. She brings her passions for France, wine, and cooking to all her work. The proud owner of ten crockpots, she is renowned for her annual Soup Parties at which she serves soups from different cultures.

Debra's Château de Verzat series follows headstrong and independent women and the four-hundred loyal families who protect a Loire Valley château and vineyard and its legacy of producing the finest wines in France during the French Revolution. She's also written a companion cookbook to her series, *Soups of Château de Verzat: A Literary Cookbook & Culinary Tribute to the French Revolution.*

She lives in the Pacific Northwest with her family and standard poodle, Clicquot, who is named after a fine French Champagne.

## SPREADING THE WORD

Word of mouth is the best way to discover books, so if you'd like to help spread the word, please share your review. Your feedback is greatly appreciated.

AMAZON.COM/AUTHOR/DEBRABORCHERT

GOODREADS.COM/DEBRA_BORCHERT

If you'd like a complimentary e-story or a recipe, visit:

DEBRABORCHERT.COM

# PRAISE FOR CHÂTEAU DE VERZAT SERIES

"An amazing heroine…" *Historical Novel Society Editor's Choice*

"Borchert's historical work is a marvel." *The Independent Review of Books*

"Breathtakingly complex and intriguing, the novel delivers in spades." *The Prairies Book Review*

"…a suspenseful page-turner…unexpected love story…" A captivating tale of female triumph in the late 18th century." *Kirkus Reviews*

"This accomplished historical novel finds a young woman making her own choices as revolution sweeps France." *BookLife Editor's Pick*

"…passionate…multifaceted…sustained intrigue…effervescent… A compelling wine tale…" *Kirkus Reviews*

"…a deftly crafted and inspiring portrait of the past." *The Independent Review of Books*

"One of the Top 5 Paris-Based Books We Can't Wait to Read in 2024." *Parisian Niche*

"Borchert is a writer to watch." *5-star, Gold Badge BookView Review*

"An empowering and dramatic story of romance in deeply troubled times…" *Self-Publishing Review*

Filled with absorbing turns, this is a captivating story led by a courageous and likable heroine." *Readers' Favorite 5 Star Review*

"…fearless female lead. …crafted by a master of relationships and emotional tension, making this revolutionary novel a tight, heart-pounding twister of a tale." *The Independent Review of Books*

"Perfect for those who love history, romance and well written stories. I can't wait for the next one." *The Good Life France*

"An engrossing depiction of feminine courage—a renegade heroine whose compassion for innocent people leads to both loss and love." *Foreword's Book of The Day*

"Borchert's extensive research shines through a narrative that is enhanced by her mastery of character development. Borchert quickly immerses readers into the dangers of late 18th-century France and highlights the struggles of women seeking independence and equality." *BookLife Editor's Pick*

WWW.AMAZON.COM/DP/B0B9KN1536

# SEND YOUR OPINIONS AS A TASTE TESTER

I greatly appreciate hearing about how you tried my recipes and any suggestions you may have. Send your thoughts and I'll thank you in my next book.

Contact me:

DEBRABORCHERT.COM/CONTACT/

# THE VINEYARD AND CHÂTEAU THAT INSPIRED CHÂTEAU DE VERZAT

WHILE RESEARCHING IN France's Loire Valley, I discovered Château Brézé, an historical monument surrounded by a vineyard not far from Saumur. The BBC filmed a wonderful video, "The Medieval 'Doomsday Bunker' Hidden Beneath a Castle," walking viewers through the deep network of tunnels under the château that forms one of Europe's largest underground fortresses. Video by Mathieu Orcel and Augustin Muniz.

View it here:

DEBRABORCHERT.COM